PRAISE FOR
THE BATTLE DRUM

"The ending has a few twists that will surprise even the most dedicated fantasy readers. Fans of Tomi Adeyemi and Sabaa Tahir will enjoy this action-packed fantasy powered by its characters and their relationships." —*Booklist*

"[El-Arifi] weaves hypnotic African and Arabian myths into the tumultuous tale of a blood-caste-segregated empire mired in conspiracies. . . . By toggling between key points of view, El-Arifi grants readers a dramatic bird's-eye view of both an unraveling world and the indomitable spirits of the women embroiled in its maelstrom. This is a knockout." —*Publishers Weekly*

"It's darker, faster and twistier than its predecessor and expands nicely on everything that came before." —*Geek Girl Authority*

PRAISE FOR
THE FINAL STRIFE

"Saara El-Arifi deftly facets every layer of her debut. Epic in scope, its world building as intricate as filigree, *The Final Strife* sings of rebellion, love, and the courage it takes to stand up to tyranny, following three women whose journeys will keep you gripped to the last."
—Samantha Shannon, *Sunday Times* bestselling author of *The Priory of the Orange Tree*

"Epic, gripping, and searing, *The Final Strife* weaves a fascinating tale of destiny, magic, and love set in a richly imagined yet brutally divided world. Its unexpected, gritty heroine is one you cannot help but root for, and the story will stay with you long after the last page."

—Sue Lynn Tan, author of *Daughter of the Moon Goddess*

"El-Arifi is a game-changing new voice in epic fantasy, and *The Final Strife* is a triumph of a book, full of rage, charm, and a cast of misfits you can't help but root for. There are no Chosen Ones here—only bad choices and blood."

—Tasha Suri, author of *The Jasmine Throne*

"With a heroine with bite, a supporting cast of flawed but deeply human characters, and world building that is raw, unforgiving, and richly textured, *The Final Strife* is the real deal: epic fantasy turned on its head in the most compelling way imaginable. El-Arifi is a bold new voice in epic fantasy, and I cannot wait to read more of her work."

—Kalynn Bayron, bestselling author of
Cinderella Is Dead and *This Poison Heart*

"El-Arifi tells a tale as fierce as its characters, plunging you into a sandy, stratified world until you can feel the grit between your teeth. Heart-wrenching and heart-pounding, *The Final Strife* is an unmissable debut."

—Andrea Stewart, author of *The Bone Shard Daughter*

"*The Final Strife* has a rich world with a complicated story about what happens when the hero—or their heroic actions—may not be who or what you thought they would be. The interweaving of the three women's stories kept me turning the pages."

—C. L. Clark, author of *The Unbroken*

"An expertly layered world that is equal parts beautifully rendered and brutal in its depiction; a protagonist who is as likely to save the day as she is to ruin it; delicious tension—I loved every page."

—Ciannon Smart, author of *Witches Steeped in Gold*

"*The Final Strife* is everything you could ever hope to experience in fantasy—magnificent worldbuilding, unpredictable plotting, entertaining twists and turns, gorgeous slow-burn romance, and characters you're rooting for from the start."

—LONDON SHAH, author of the Light the Abyss series

"A compelling, charming, sexy fantasy debut whose controlled fury sets it apart." —*The Daily Mail*

"Timely themes and a gripping narrative draw the reader in and keep them there." —*Kirkus Reviews* (starred review)

"The undercurrents of friendship, betrayal, and sapphic love, and the twists and turns of the competitive trials and political intrigue, come together to kick off a magnetic and appealing new series."

—*Booklist*

"El-Arifi debuts and launches the Ending Fire series with a fast-paced epic fantasy inspired by Ghanian and Arabian folklore. . . . El-Arifi keeps the pages flying even while building an intricate secondary world, allowing readers to learn its rules through action rather than exposition. This sets a high bar for the series to come."

—*Publishers Weekly*

"An epic adult fantasy full of rebellion, a sapphic friends-to-lovers storyline, rideable desert lizards, blood magic, a tournament, and lots more epic fantasy type things . . . Seriously, the world El-Arifi has built is so thoroughly fleshed out and brought to life. The characters are intriguing (like a 'chosen one' protagonist who misses her calling), and the issues it addresses current."

—*BookRiot*

"*The Final Strife* is a book designed to be savoured. . . . This was such a stunning book. . . . El-Arifi has set the standard for what promises to be an excellent fantasy series. . . . *The Final Strife* is a thunderstorm of a book . . . a fully fleshed-out, epic fantasy that will capture your mind." —*A Short Book Lover*

BY SAARA EL-ARIFI

THE ENDING FIRE TRILOGY

The Final Strife

The Battle Drum

THE FAEBOUND TRILOGY

Faebound

THE BATTLE DRUM

THE BATTLE DRUM

A NOVEL

SAARA EL-ARIFI

NEW YORK

The Battle Drum is a work of fiction. Names, characters, places, and incidents either are the product of the author's imagination or are used fictitiously. Any resemblance to actual persons, living or dead, events, or locales is entirely coincidental.

2024 Del Rey Trade Paperback Edition

Published in the United States by Del Rey, an imprint of Random House, a division of Penguin Random House LLC, New York.

DEL REY and the CIRCLE colophon are registered trademarks of Penguin Random House LLC.

Originally published in hardcover in the United States by Del Rey, an imprint of Random House, a division of Penguin Random House LLC, in 2023.

LIBRARY OF CONGRESS CATALOGING-IN-PUBLICATION DATA
Names: El-Arifi, Saara, author.
Title: The battle drum: a novel / Saara El-Arifi.
Description: New York: Del Rey, [2023] | Series: The Ending Fire trilogy; book 2
Identifiers: LCCN 2023007731 (print) | LCCN 2023007732 (ebook) | ISBN 9780593356999 (trade paperback) | ISBN 9780593356982 (Ebook)
Subjects: LCGFT: Fantasy fiction. | Novels.
Classification: LCC PR6105.L429 B38 2023 (print) | LCC PR6105.L429 (ebook) | DDC 823/.92—dc23/eng/20230301
LC record available at https://lccn.loc.gov/2023007731
LC ebook record available at https://lccn.loc.gov/2023007732

Printed in the United States of America on acid-free paper

randomhousebooks.com

9 8 7 6 5 4 3 2 1

Book design by Alexis Capitini

For my mother, whose battle drum has never stopped beating.
My fighter, my friend, my champion.

A Child of Fire whose blood will blaze,
Will cleanse the world in eight nights, eight days,
Eight bloods lend strength to lead the charge
And eradicate the infidel, only Gods emerge,
Ready we will be, when the Ending Fire comes,
When the Child of Fire brings the Battle Drum,
The Battle Drum,
The Battle Drum,
Ready we will be, for war will come.

—The foretelling of the Ending Fire, preserved
in oral history by the Zalaam

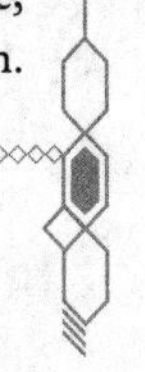

Recalling the events of *The Final Strife* as told by Griot Sheth.

The spoken word has been transcribed onto the page;
the symbol of ◊ represents the beating of the griot's drum.

It all started with a babe, stolen, on the run. A rebellion beginning, a rebellion begun.

And the tidewind, of course, with its nightly hurricane, stronger and stronger, as the days fade.

Ember children taken.
The Sandstorm born.
The Wardens' Keep breached.
Families torn.

◊

Sylah Alyana was one of those stolen for her red blood, the only caste that can rule. For over a decade she was schooled by blue-blooded Dusters to one day compete in the Aktibar trials. The winners of which determine the next four rulers, our wardens, who preside over the guilds of duty, strength, truth, and knowledge.

◊ ◊ ◊

Aho, I see you raise your eyebrows, you think I've missed off a fifth? Why yes, indeed the Warden of Crime does exist, but not in the Keep up there on the hill. He lives underground . . . well, he did . . . there's more to tell.

◊

Sylah's destiny was to win the Aktibar for strength. But destinies can be thwarted, especially when confronted with Uka Elsari's vengeance. Warden Uka's hatred of the Sandstorm ran deep, as deep as a mother's love, for it was her child the rebels had taken, leaving Anoor Elsari masquerading as an Ember in the Keep.

◊

Children lost.
The Sandstorm dead.
The Wardens' Keep sealed.
Uka's bloodlust fed.

◊

Only three survived the massacre Uka reaped: Lio, Sylah, and her training partner Jond. Take a bound, or a leap, skipping the years. I take us to six mooncycles ago, the tidewind stronger than ever, when Jond reappears.

◊

Twenty years old, with more lives behind the eyes, Sylah made a name for herself fighting in the Ring run by the Warden of Crime. She barely noticed the beginning of the Aktibar, once the culmination of her dreams, now out of reach. She traded for joba seed drugs with anything she found: a frame, a picture, or perhaps a map?

◊

No, the map she kept because it looked out of sorts, with a swirl in the corner where there shouldn't be. There's no land beyond the sea, so the wardens preach. The Ending Fire killed every life-form, now there's just you and them and me.

◊

Now back to Jond we go, with the Aktibar starting, he came to the capital to have his reckoning.

◊

The Sandstorm resurrected
A new master to lead
Sylah's purpose rekindled
A secret revealed.

◊

Lio told Sylah that she's the true daughter of Uka Elsari, the Warden of Strength, and encouraged her to sign up for the Aktibar. With Sylah's curiosity set aflame, she infiltrated the Wardens' Keep to take a look at the imposter; the girl who stole her life. But Anoor's mind was sharper than anybody knew, and she trapped Sylah. They made a trade: Sylah was to train Anoor in order to win the Aktibar, and in return Anoor would teach Sylah how to bloodwerk, a privilege of power, only given to Embers.

There was a third deal made unbeknownst to Anoor: Sylah would teach Jond her bloodwerk skills and spy for the new Sandstorm leader. But who was this leader?

Perhaps Sylah should have known.

An interlude. Let us not forget the tidewind with its nightly hurricane, stronger and stronger as the days fade.

◊

Five trials completed
Love overcomes hate

Now Sylah must choose
What is Anoor's fate?

◊

The Warden of Crime, Loot, reveals himself to be the new Sandstorm leader; Master Inansi is his true name. Inansi commanded Sylah to kill Anoor before the final trial against Jond.

◊

Now a predicament presented itself: the Sandstorm or Anoor? Loyalty or love?

◊ ◊ ◊

Aho, it wasn't even a question in Sylah's mind—it was always going to be Anoor. So she locked her away to stop her competing.

◊

Now, there's someone who's been lurking in the silence of my words. But without the silence, how does a sentence form? That is Hassa's integral effect on this tale. As a Ghosting her reach is far, but her knowledge all the deeper. She knows more than Sylah of the Sandstorm's plans, and even more than that besides. Hassa guides Sylah toward the truth. Remember the map that had Anoor and Sylah searching? A mere quarter of the whole.

◊

An empire of lies
There's a world beyond
No Ending Fire at all
The Ghostings' land gone.

◊

Dusters and Embers had invaded the Ghostings' home, taking their knowledge of bloodwerk and silencing them by severing their hands and tongues forever more. Sylah returned to Anoor, equipped with this knowledge, but the woman had burst free from her jail, blue blood marring her exit.

◊

Eyoh, yes. Anoor had known she could bloodwerk with her blue blood, ever since she escaped her mother's clutches. For Anoor's childhood had been marred by the shade of "what could have been" if the Sandstorm hadn't stolen Uka's true child.

◊

Anoor's sword is leveled
Her armor bound
The empire on its knees
A winner crowned.

◊

But it wasn't Anoor, was it? Dressed like her love, Sylah fought Jond for the win. Anoor was drugged and hidden, safe for a time, ready to claim her prize as the new Disciple of Strength.

And the tidewind with its nightly hurricane, stronger and stronger as the days fade.

◊

But what of Sylah? Anoor's trust broken and hunted by the Sandstorm, there's only one place she can go. A voyage, across the sea, to the lands beyond. A quest instigated by the Ghostings, to seek aid to combat the growing strength of the tidewind.

◊

On her journey to the Ghosting settlement Sylah is intercepted by Loot and Jond. Did they not learn? Sylah is not so easily killed. Instead, she captures Jond, and murders Loot. But Loot's blood isn't red or blue or clear.

It is yellow.

◊

A Duster disciple
The Sandstorm gone
A new beginning
A journey to come.

The Winterlands
Souriland
Garif
The Forests of Midori
Glacies Ocean
The Shard Palace
Hadir Mountains
Bushica
Souk
The Entwined Harbor
Oarigha Plains
Tenio
Ica Sea
The Volcane Islands
City of Rain
Nsuo
Mist Forest
The Grasslands
Truna Hills
Chrysalis
Marion Sea
The Wardens' Empire
Zwina Academy
Nar-Ruta
N
The Wetlands

THE BATTLE DRUM

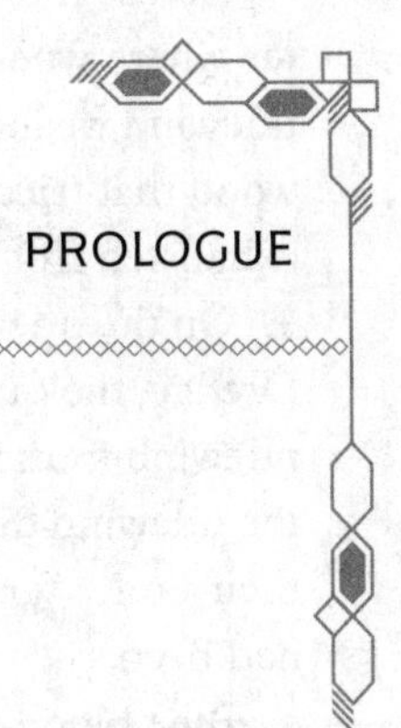

PROLOGUE

The tidewind came every night.

It billowed in from the Marion Sea between the clock strikes of ten and six, clawing up sand from the Farsai Desert with invisible talons. Six mooncycles ago the tidewind only unleashed havoc for two strikes of the clock. Now, the hurricane's chaos reigned for longer each night. It swirled through the thirteen cities of the Wardens' Empire wreaking destruction and scattering debris.

In the capital city of Nar-Ruta, the tidewind pummeled at the iron gates of the Wardens' Keep, but the four wardens didn't wake from their slumber. The wardens' seconds-in-command slept less soundly. As newly assigned disciples, the weight of the empire struck them with each gust of the wind.

To the north, the tidewind slipped through the expansive villas of the Ember Quarter, but money bought protection, and the wind found no access behind their metal doors.

Across the Ruta River the tidewind went, to the Duster Quarter where wooden shutters were easier to break. Each gale of the tidewind weaponized the sand of the Farsai Desert, splintering the wood that tried to protect the Dusters within, the sleeping bodies, exhausted from a day in the plantations.

On the tidewind blew, toward the final district of Nar-Ruta, the Dredge, the quarter that traded in sex, drugs, and drink. Here the tidewind found three bodies. Death had claimed them long before the tidewind did, but still the wind ripped their skin and flesh from their bones, grinding them to mere fragments of what they once had been.

Blue blood scattered like sand.

"Sixth strike," the clockmaster called out from his protected podium in the Dredge. Few heard his words. Even the tidewind didn't heed him. The gusts remained, bloated with particles and cadavers as the sun rose.

Those in the Maroon tavern didn't know the pink sun had begun to shine. The tavern was set deep inside the tunnels of the city.

The patrons were drowsy with firerum, the drumbeat from the lone player on stage was without melody, but the crowd shifted slowly to it.

Most of the dancers were Dusters, field workers at that. It was clear from the oozing welts on their backs dripping blue blood to the floor. On the edges of the crowd was a handful of Ghostings, satchels held between their limbs, ready to trade.

The Ghostings' gray-brown skin was a feature of their translucent blood. But it wasn't the only thing that marked them. Their hands and tongues had been severed from birth, taken by Embers to silence their truth.

There were no red-blooded Embers in the Maroon.

But there was someone else there that night who was neither Ember, Duster, nor Ghosting.

She wore a cowl that draped her face in darkness. The sleeves of her dress were long, the skirt pooling around her ankles. But as she surveyed the Maroon, flashes of her features revealed themselves from the shadows. Her dark skin was glossed with a slight sheen of sweat from too many bodies pressed into too small a space. The smell too, but her nose didn't wrinkle. She'd grown up in worse-smelling places.

She was searching for something, for someone, among the crowd. Her eyes darted left and right, assessing each face as it passed. Her hands twisted beneath the table as she fondled a silver spider brooch studded with black diamonds.

She grew careless and the pin of the brooch pricked her.

"Divine's web." She muttered the curse with a growl and then instantly chastised herself. Doubly careless, letting slip a phrase that would mark her out in this empire. But no one had noticed. The Maroon was the Nowerks' small slice of freedom, and freedom was more intoxicating than anything.

She looked down at her hand with a scowl. A bead of blood grew like a drop of liquid sunshine on the tip of her finger.

Yellow.

A droplet of truth that could shatter the empire.

She wiped it on her dress and stood. The doors to the Maroon had been opened. The tidewind no longer raged.

It was time to go home.

She would keep searching. For years, if she had to. The Child of Fire would let themselves be known when they were ready.

And then war would come.

She smiled under her hood.

Let it come.

PART ONE

EXPLORE

A stone archway with the words "Zwina Academy" greeted me. As I stepped under it my eyes widened with the endless vibrancy of color. It was as if my world had been black-and-white until that very moment. I thought the Academy would have been a studious, quiet place, but the citadel that has built up around it is a dynamic center of activity. I saw someone with the same pallid skin as me, and my friends, you won't believe, that there are colorless bloods here too. They hark from a land known as the Grasslands though they grow their beards longer than I like.

—Journal of Elder Petra, year 237 B.W.
(Before the Wardens' Empire)

CHAPTER ONE

SYLAH

The Marion Sea is so named by the natives of the Drylands after the Eastern Star, "Marion." Those who follow the star will find themselves at the shores of the mainland in three weeks. Celestial navigation appears to be the main form of wayfaring for the clear-bloods in the west who have made it to the continent. It is why we have struggled to map their land as precisely as I would have liked.

—Head Cartographer of the Zwina Academy, year 238 B.W.

The world bled blue. Sylah wasn't sure why she hadn't realized that before—the earth was a Duster.

Her toes clung to the sand, clenching and releasing the particles of dirt. Something swirled among the waves. She recognized the movement of it, the dips and twirls of the current. The laugh of a splash that she knew, she knew. Her feet left the ground, leading her toward the laughter.

Has she found me? Here at the edge of the world?

The Marion Sea curved across the horizon like an endless smile as it beckoned her closer. She waded in until her pantaloons were sodden to the waist and looked for the woman she loved between the eddies of the water.

Something sparkled beneath her, and as she bent to grab it the current became more urgent. The waves that had once been frothy as lace dissipated into a foam like fresh spittle. The sea picked and pulled at her clothes, and the smile on the horizon became a gaping wound bleeding into the oncoming sunset.

"Sylah, what the fuck are you doing?" Jond was shrieking like an eru in heat. She could hear the worried pitter-patter of his sandals at the edge of the shore twenty handspans away.

Her mouth twisted into a scowl at the sound of her friend's voice. *Former* friend. Friends don't try to kill each other.

Sylah didn't indicate she'd heard him. She lifted up the shell she had found and watched the water trickle away. The water was not blue after all but colorless. Transparent.

"Of course, you're a Ghosting," she mused to the ocean. It seemed to tug back at her in confirmation.

The land she stood on belonged to the Ghostings: every grain of sand, every droplet of water. It was *their* world that the founding wardens had invaded. To silence the truth the Embers had taken the Ghostings' tongues and hands. For more than four hundred years the wardens told the lie that the Ghostings were serving a penance for a rebellion. A rebellion that never happened. All they were trying to do was defend their own home.

Stolen.

Sylah had also had her life stolen. She had thought it was Anoor who had taken it, living the life Sylah should have had. But no, that was a lie too. Anoor was exactly where she should be.

A Duster as a disciple and they don't even know it. The bitterness of her thoughts faded as the sweetness of Anoor's face filled her mind.

Oh, how she missed her.

She looked at the piece of shell in her hand. The conch was pearlescent green, vibrant, happy-looking like the opulent dresses Anoor wore. Each shade of dress had a name, like "emerald" or "aquamarine." Fancier names than "puke" and "mold" like Sylah had suggested.

A swift wave struck Sylah hard, and she found herself struggling to regain balance. The shell in her hand came loose, and for a panicked moment she lost it. Lost *her*, all over again.

"No, no, no."

Her inkwell flashed silver under the water as she tried in vain to part the waves. It was embossed with a sprawling cascade of poison ivy. A reminder of the Warden of Crime who had procured it for her. Though Sylah couldn't help but wonder if it wasn't a true reflection of her nature; she had poisoned every relationship she'd ever had.

A glimmer of turquoise.

Sylah lunged for the shell, pulling it from the clutches of the ocean. She clasped it against her chest.

"Maiden's tits," she hissed.

In her eagerness she had squeezed the shell too tightly and the edge had sliced a fine line through her palm. The salt water prickled as it sated itself on her red blood.

Just like Anoor, the shell has bite.

Smiling wryly, Sylah reached for the sword that hung from her waist. It was sheathed in a scabbard that still smelled of Anoor. Sandalwood. As she withdrew it, the sunset illuminated the embossed gold of the hilt.

—Yellow arterial blood sprayed like warm honey.—

She winced at the memory. Not because of Loot's severed head that she held in her mind's eye, but because of the impossibility of it. Loot had been the leader of the Sandstorm, but no one Sylah had ever met had *yellow* blood.

Sylah looked up to the sky.

"Lies upon lies upon lies," she whispered in anguish to the God the Abosom priests said lived behind the clouds. Sylah wasn't so sure.

Crunch.

She thrust the tip of the blade through the outer shell, chipping away some of the color. The Anoor-shell would be braided in later. Another piece of Sylah found.

"Sylah?" Splash, splash. Jond really was worried if he'd got his feet wet. The sandals he'd been wearing were threadbare enough without sea salt getting into the leather.

"What are you doing?" His voice careened into another octave.

"Waiting," Sylah called back without turning her head. She

stole another look at the horizon, wondering if the truth lay somewhere beyond it.

"What for?"

I don't know.

She sighed and began to wade back toward the shore where Jond was standing. "Just waiting for you to start the dance."

Jond's eyes narrowed in anticipation of the insult that he hadn't yet grasped. "What?"

"I heard male erus shake their balls during the mating dance. If you're expecting to attract Boey, you've got to try a little harder. The shrill was pretty good, though, right, Boey? Maybe on the high side?"

The giant lizard settled herself deeper into the blue sand, her third eyelid closed as if blocking out the sight of them could drown out their incessant bickering. Jond's face screwed up in disgust, and he turned toward the carriage hooked onto Boey's haunches. His own pantaloons were wet and clinging to his muscular legs. Sylah tilted her head and surveyed him.

Jond hadn't weathered the four weeks of travel well. Although they never spoke of the injury he had sustained in the rune bomb, he held his left shoulder closer to his chest. Sylah had seen him wince more than once. His tight curls, usually kept tall on the top of his head, had matted together with sweat and grime.

Sylah's own black curls had grown just long enough to braid again. The plaits hung limp over her large brow. Every time they had found a source of fresh water Sylah had diligently washed her hair and rebraided in the piece of bone from the Sanctuary and the spider brooch she had taken from Loot's corpse. Now she had another token to add to the collection.

A gale laced with salt brought tears to her eyes.

"We need to find shelter." Jond's words cut through her thoughts.

He was right, the tidewind was coming.

"Ood-Rahabe isn't far from here. The Ghosting settlement is meant to be in the caves just beyond it." Sylah reached past Jond to retrieve the map that was never far from her sight. She unraveled it on the ground and carefully avoided looking at the bottom corner, though the shape of the word "Nar-Ruta" seared into her peripheral vision. She didn't want to see how far they had come, how far away they were from the capital. From Anoor. All she wanted to do was go back to her. But Anoor had tasked her with bringing back aid to help stop the tidewind, and Sylah wouldn't let her down.

"How long?" Jond asked.

"Half a strike, maybe less." Ood-Rahabe was a dot of ink on the map, smaller than a coin among the towns and cities of the Wardens' Empire, but it was a mere grain of sand in the wider world. Sylah's hand splayed across the new world where they were headed. It could have swallowed the Wardens' Empire ten times over.

"The tidewind will be here before then. We need to go," Jond said.

Sylah nodded and rolled away the map, slapping Boey's rump with the tube.

"Stop sleeping, you've got to get us to Ood-Rahabe in under half a strike and according to Hassa, there will be someone to greet us and lead us to the Ghosting Settlement."

Boey huffed through her nostrils but didn't move. Sylah ground her teeth.

"Want me to drive?" Jond asked.

"Get in the carriage." Truly, Sylah was sick of driving, but she couldn't trust him not to turn Boey around at the first opportunity.

"Can I get some help?" The words were cruelly twisted, as if Jond's mouth spat them out without his mind wanting them to.

Sylah rolled her eyes and grasped hold of his left shoulder. He hissed through his teeth and she lessened her grip a bit. She guided him up the steps to the metal carriage, giving him a boost on his ass when he needed it. It wasn't graceful, but she wasn't about to remove the restraints on his hands or feet.

Sylah locked the carriage door and withdrew her stylus from her neck. She hastily drew a series of bloodwerk runes to keep

Jond trapped. A necessary precaution she had learned the hard way. Three times he'd managed to escape his bindings, though he'd never got far enough to outrun Boey.

The small platform at the front of the carriage was the driver's seat. It was slightly arched to allow for Boey's tail to tuck beneath the rolling carriage. Sylah jumped on and flicked the reins connected to the harness around the eru's waist.

"Right, Boey, final stretch. Come on, girl."

Boey rose up on her hindquarters and farted before settling back down. Sylah could hear Jond laughing in the carriage behind her.

"Come on. Go." Sylah flicked the reins harder. "I bet you weren't this stubborn with Anoor—" It was as if Anoor's name set a fire alight under the eru's belly as Boey sprang forward in the sand, the carriage and all its contents lurching with her. There was a moment, a mere breath, where it looked like she was going to settle down again, but something in the distance caught the creature's attention. Then they were off, Boey's shrill sounding suspiciously like a laugh.

THE TIDEWIND HAD started a quarter of a strike into their journey. It raged and swirled around Sylah with the ferocity of a hurricane made deadlier with the force of debris and dirt. The blue sand of the Farsai Desert was whipped into a frenzy and began to draw blood, so she had to resort to joining Jond in the carriage. It was tidewind-protected and had been their shelter for the entirety of their journey.

"Do you think Boey will keep going?" Jond had to shout to be heard.

"I pointed her straight, so I hope so." Erus' thick scales had evolved to withstand the worst of the tidewind, but still Sylah worried. Anoor loved Boey almost as much as Sylah loved Anoor, and she didn't want any harm to come to the beast.

The tidewind paused for a breath and there was an unsettling silence.

"How are we going to cross the Marion Sea in this?" Jond spoke the question they had both been wondering about every night. The sea was known to be dangerous in the day, let alone in the evening when the tidewind raged. It was also said monsters roamed the deep. But Sylah gave little credence to children's tales.

Sylah shivered. "The Ghosting elders will know . . . wait. Is Boey slowing down?"

She was; the rhythm of her claws in the sand had dropped in tempo. Sylah used one of the peepholes to look outside.

Village was an exaggeration. There were two houses, maybe three that Sylah could make out beyond the swirling sand. A gust blew dirt into her mouth. She hawked and spat by Jond's feet, slamming the peephole shut.

"We're here."

"Oh."

"The houses are small, shutters down already. We should sleep here tonight."

"You promised me a bed," Jond said.

"You promised you'd always have my back," Sylah snapped back. "Instead, you tried to kill me, and the woman I love. Seems like neither of us are good at promises."

Jond flinched. Sylah wasn't sure whether it was from her words or from the weather, as a vicious gale slammed into Boey's side. The lizard settled deeper in the sand, eventually burrowing so deep only her nostrils and the carriage strapped to her haunches were visible.

Sylah reached behind Jond to retrieve her waterskin. She unscrewed the lid and pulled out the small leather pouch that looped around her belt. Even in the darkness she could see the warm red of the powder within. The ground-up joba seeds were so fine her fingers could barely feel the powder as she reached into the pouch. She withdrew her hand and frowned. Only a few grains left. She tipped what remained of the powder into the waterskin.

Six mooncycles ago she had been addicted to the drug so completely that she'd been unaware that the seeds were taking an irrevocable toll on her body. Now she had come to rely on the drug and needed to take a small amount each day just to survive. She downed the waterskin. Jond's eyes glittered as he watched her. His mouth opened. Closed. Opened again.

She waited.

"You are not blameless," were the words he finally settled on.

Sylah snorted, rolling the phlegm in the back of her throat.

"Blame?" she whispered with an exhale. Her fingers traced the lettering in the dirt of the carriage. "You see the letters? B L A M E." She showed off her handiwork to Jond, but his face held no expression. "Anoor taught me to write, but that word always came easy to me." She held his gaze. "Because it has been seared into my mind with a scythe ever since that day over six years ago now, when I caused the death of everyone in *our* family. I am the one who scores it across the walls of my mind every morning. Don't for one moment assume that I think I am blameless. I am the cause and the catalyst, the kindling and the spark."

She turned away from Jond and pulled her knees up to her chest, feigning sleep for strikes until she fell into an uneasy slumber.

CHAPTER TWO
SYLAH

The people of the Academy are as lively as the minds that occupy it. Every house is painted a different color; there are greens, blues, purples, and reds. Even the cobbles beneath my feet are varying hues of pink marble.

—Journal of Elder Petra, year 237 B.W.

Sylah was awoken by a gentle tap on the side of the metal carriage. She slurped in the drool that had pooled between the back of her hand and her mouth.

"Jond, wake up."

His eyes slid open with the readiness of one of the Stolen. Only this time Azim wasn't standing above them with an unsheathed blade, ready to pounce. Sylah shook the training exercise from her mind.

"What is it?" Jond asked.

"Someone's at the door." Sylah stretched her sword hand, the fingers popping. "And of course, Boey didn't move a handspan." She thumped her fist on the wall of the carriage. But there was no response from the slumbering beast.

"Untie me," Jond demanded.

Sylah laughed. "Nice try."

"They might be trying to attack us."

"Sure, because that's what we'd do—knock politely first."

Jond shrugged but his eyes were brimming with mistrust. Sylah's hand reached for the pommel of her sword just in case. She unbound the blade; it was just a slice of shadow in the dark carriage. She held it behind her as the knock came again and opened the peephole.

A Ghosting looked up at her. She had seen less than seventy years but surely more than forty. Her face was a conundrum that had Sylah exploring her lines and dashes like a word she struggled to write.

"Hello, would you be able to lead us to the Ghosting settlement? To the elders?" Sylah asked.

"What's going on? Who is it?" Jond was urgent behind her. Was that hope in his voice?

But there was no savior today, not for him anyway.

The Ghosting looked at Sylah and released her muscles in a smile. Sylah settled on sixty years of age.

Welcome, the older woman signed, *I am Memur, sister of Elder Dew.* Her limbs circled wide as she signed the greeting. Born into servitude, Ghostings were always named by their Ember masters after animals or objects. A memur was a type of marsupial that lived in the green hills of Jin-Gernomi. *The elders are waiting for you*, Memur continued.

Sylah had learned the Ghosting language a long time ago. Mute with grief after causing the death of all the Sandstorm, Sylah had met Hassa, a young Ghosting with a dry sense of humor that matched Sylah's own. Hassa taught her to read the signs, the subtle twists of their arms and the small movements in their wrists and jaw. It was a complex language based on more than two thousand gestures, and Sylah was as fluent in reading them as a non-native could be.

"The elders haven't left yet? That's good." Sylah wasn't sure if it *was* good. Part of her wished they had started on their journey without her. With Loot out of the picture Sylah was free to return to Nar-Ruta.

Sylah saw Anoor's face in her mind. The wide rounded eyes, perpetually startled by the joy of life. A force of energy as fierce as the tidewind. And like the tidewind, Anoor's power had grown, and the safety of the citizens of the Wardens' Empire was now her responsibility.

No, I won't return without aid, Sylah told herself fiercely.

She opened the carriage door and stepped out into the cool morning air. A dozen Ghosting faces looked back at her. Musawa, women, men; of all shapes and sizes, but connected by the mutilated arms by their sides and the severed tongues in their mouths. But there was something different about these Ghostings. They wore their hair longer than the required shaven style of a servant. Few dressed in the beige uniform that singled them out as hired help, and instead they wore faded woven patterns that Sylah was more accustomed to seeing on Dusters. Beyond the aesthetic there was something less tangible that set them apart from other Ghostings she had known. It was in the way they held themselves.

They were free.

Memur gave her a knowing smile as she gestured for Sylah to follow her toward the village.

Sylah looked around. The hamlet was even smaller than she had thought last night. The three houses were actually one, connected through enclosed corridors that protected them from the tidewind. Drying fish hung from every structure, but Sylah couldn't smell them on the breeze so she knew they were from this morning's catch. The shore was less than twenty handspans away, and she found herself being drawn back into the depths of the sea.

This was it: the last step before leaping across the abyss.

"How is it you are all here, out in the open? Won't the Embers grow suspicious?" Sylah looked beyond the crowd of Ghostings searching for any signs of Embers.

Someone snickered and Sylah looked for the culprit, but whoever it was had pushed their face smooth.

You need not worry about Embers, Memur signed.

"What about the imir? Is their representative here? An overseer perhaps? I'd like to see them." Sylah fingered the ambassador token in her pocket. Her last gift from Anoor, it allowed her to use the wardens' credit for supplies and services she might need, including mail. Anoor knew she'd be here; maybe, just maybe she'd sent a letter.

Something like mistrust slipped into the curves of Memur's face. *Why?*

"I have the wardens' seal in order to restock, it could help us on our journey." In small villages such as these, the imirs, who were the leaders of the twelve cities outside of Nar-Ruta, sent overseers to maintain the running of the smaller towns that orbited their main strongholds.

Memur cleared her throat and signed, *The elders have all they need. They have already postponed their journey enough. We must go now.*

The detour to the Sanctuary must have delayed Sylah more than she'd thought. But her family's ghosts had long yearned for rest. She pulled on the braid at her neck where the bone she had found there was braided.

"I must still see them," Sylah said firmly.

A girl pushed through the crowd. Her skin had the ashen tinge of a Ghosting, though her eyes were darker than the usual grays and blues. Her pale brown hair had been pulled into four tight plaits. She reached out to pull on Memur's robe with her hand.

"Memur, is she come, is she here?" And she spoke. With a tongue.

Sylah watched her with unconcealed fascination.

Yes, she is here. Go to the elders, warn them we'll be coming, Memur signed back to the girl, who nodded and slipped away.

"How? How is it that she lives without the Embers' knowledge?" Sylah asked.

A movement behind them drew her gaze away from the disappearing back of the girl. Something, no, someone fell out of the carriage beside Sylah. He was clutching a spoon between his two baby fingers that were bucking against his hand restraints like worms.

Sylah pinched the bridge of her nose. "Jond, did you try and attack me with a spoon?"

"No." He spat sand from his mouth as he wriggled to sit up from his sprawled position.

"Ah, I see, you were just hungry and thought, *hmm, now is the time to try a spoonful of sand.*" She took a step toward him, and he brandished his weapon toward her. "How long have you been hiding that spoon for?"

"It is *not* a spoon." He began crawling away on his elbows toward Memur. "Will you help me? Free me from this woman? She's keeping me prisoner."

The Ghostings stepped back with a look of disgust as if they knew him, knew his sins.

"Not a spoon? Oh, I'm sorry, I see now, you've been carefully shaving the sides to a point. You have a nice sharp spoon. Well done." Sylah clapped her hands. "Oh, how rude of me. Everyone, this is Jond. My ex-lover."

"Don't call me that," he growled under his breath as he crawled ever farther away.

"And yes, I know you're all wondering, he was an adequate lover—"

There was the sound of sliding steel and the slapping of leather straps. It took less than a breath for all the Ghostings to brandish their weapons. They leveled them at Jond, their lips pulled back in snarls. Sylah jumped in front of their blades.

"Skies above! If I wanted him dead, I would have done it before now."

Move aside, let us kill the traitor. Even Memur had produced a dagger from the folds of her cloak. It was tied to her forearm and she held it steady, pointing at Jond's eyes. Sylah had never seen anything quite as menacing as a Ghosting signing with a dagger strapped to their wrist. It was as if generations of anger and oppression had only made their signing more lethal.

We understand he was one of the Sandstorm, as important to you as family. You would not be able to kill him. But allow us, a young musawa countered. They were the gender of those neither man nor woman—neither, but never less. Ghostings believed that musawa were blessed by Anyme to be born with both spirits of man and woman within them. It was in this musawa's eyes that Sylah saw the echoes of those souls, each with the same bloodthirsty look in their eyes.

"No, no, I was keeping him alive to get some truth out of him." The sound of Loot's spinal cord crunching invaded Sylah's mind again. She stumbled, righted herself and looked back at Jond. "Well, I suppose he hasn't been very helpful there so . . ."

"Sylah," Jond groaned, noting the mirth in her voice.

The thing was, she was enjoying it, dangling death before him. He had after all tried to kill *her* first.

"No, you can put your weapons down. I mean to bring him with us on this journey." Sylah smiled. "And leave him there."

Memur barked out a laugh. *Maybe crueler than death, no?*

"That's the plan." Jond growled behind her, but Sylah felt no remorse. She continued, "Will you be able to take me to the overseer?"

No.

"No?"

The overseer is not in town. I will take you to the elders. Maybe you will be able to see the overseer before you go.

"But—" There could be a letter from Anoor . . .

Come, bring your prisoner, let us see what the elders think of their new captive. They were not anticipating another. Memur spun on her heel, her dagger disappearing up her sleeve.

"Come on, Jond, time to drop your spoon." Sylah pulled him up by his shoulders and pushed him ahead of her as she followed the Ghostings through the village.

THEY HAD BEEN walking for half a strike when Sylah noticed the footsteps in the sand. Hundreds of them, of varying sizes, pressed into the shoreline, yet to be washed away by the rising tide. But the beach was empty, with no sign of a settlement or caves.

"How much farther?" Sylah called out ahead. Jond had been

dragging his feet, so Sylah was forced to cattle prod him to speed up. She ignored his grumbling as they came level with Memur.

"How much farther?" Sylah tried again.

Memur turned to her. *We're here.*

Sylah wasn't sure if Memur had lost her wits.

Jond laughed. "All this traveling, all your threats . . . and there's nothing here. There's nothing here," he chortled. Sylah wanted to punch him in the throat. And she would have done it, too, if they weren't with company. Anoor had taught her that wasn't polite.

Sylah scanned the horizon. There was nothing. The sea to her left, the sand dunes of the Farsai Desert to her right. No cliff face, no caves, no settlement sprawling across the shoreline. It was like someone had punched *her* in the throat. No words could encompass her disappointment.

This way, Memur signed, leading them toward the sand dunes. A smile lifted the corners of her lips, as she enjoyed Sylah's desolate expression.

"Jond's right, there's nothing—" Sylah stopped speaking, but her mouth remained open. There was something strange about the sand dune in front of them. Though this dune curved upward like the rest, the sun shone a little differently on its surface. Still glittering like sand, but shinier, more reflective than it ought to be. And when the wind blew, not one speck, not one grain shifted from the structure, as if each granule of sand was glued in place.

No, not glued. *Forged.*

The sand dune was pure glass, frozen like crystal.

"How?" The word formed on her lips, but Sylah wasn't sure any sound followed.

Memur smiled sadly. *Our ancestors' bloodwerk, knowledge lost to us long ago.*

She led them toward an archway leading into the center of the glass dune, and Sylah's awe intensified. Above them the glass swirled through the air like a river of sapphire. Shades of blue shifted in the sunlight, casting a network of refracted rays across the ground. Sylah reached up as if to catch one of the beams of light. It rippled across her fingers like water. She breathed in, trying to still her heart from the wonder, and noted how the air was even sweeter here than by the sea.

Because it was touched with the smell of home cooking.

The aroma of fried flatbread, the edges charred for flavor, flooded Sylah's mouth with saliva. The honeyed scent of kelewele, made from overripe plantain, transported Sylah back to the streets of Nar-Ruta. But it was the smell of groundnut stew that truly made her feel like she was home. Spicy, just like Mama used to make it.

Sylah was so busy yearning for the Duster Quarter that she hadn't realized the procession had stopped. She slammed into the person in front of her.

"Sorry," Sylah said until she saw it was Jond and scowled. She looked past him to see why they'd faltered. There they were: the four elders of the Ghostings.

Sylah had last seen them in the Nest, the cavern deep under the ground of the city of Nar-Ruta. It was where the elders had held their court for centuries without the prying eyes of Embers or Dusters.

You never know what is under your feet until you look deeper, Sylah thought. *And it seems like you never know what's in front of you, until you look within.*

She stepped forward and greeted the elders. The four of them cut a fierce image in the twinkling light. They all wore the soft beige fabric of the Ghosting servant uniform, though they styled it without the woven kente belt that indicated where they worked. Rather than signposting who their masters were, the elders' long dress-like garments were each knotted with an intricate band of silver rope in finely spun metal. Elder Dew held Sylah's attention first. The eddies of skin around their gray eyes crinkled upward as they gave her a welcoming grin. Their thin arms leaned heavily on their crutch. It was much more worn than the last time Sylah had seen it. Dew had come a long way.

"Elders." Sylah returned Elder Dew's smile.

You are late. Elder Reed's piercing blue eyes conveyed her anger. *You were meant to meet us at twelve noon on the final day of the Aktibar. Then we received word you would be joining us here. But still we have waited three days longer than we intended.*

"Ah, sorry about that . . . I had some things to attend to." Namely, dressing up as Anoor and winning the trial of combat for her.

Elder Dew raised their eyebrows. Somehow they knew. *Who is this you have brought?*

"Jond, say hello." Sylah nudged him with her elbow, but no word escaped him. Oddly enough, he looked scared. Sylah wasn't sure she'd seen that expression on his face before, even when she'd held the sword against his neck.

"Not so chatty all of a sudden?" Sylah turned back to the elders. "He tried to kill me."

He is the Warden of Crime's lackey, what did you expect? Reed signed, snorting.

"Former Warden of Crime."

Elder Dew tilted their head.

"I killed him."

The silence in the glass cavern was absolute.

Elder Zero had never spoken to Sylah; even in that candlelit room beneath the city, Zero's arms had stayed fast. Until now.

He tilted his head back and roared, the laugh echoing around the chamber and shivering his jowls with delight.

She killed him? This waif of a girl killed the leader of the Sandstorm? Tears streamed down his face, his silvered locs quivering around his smile.

Reed threw him an annoyed look and turned to Sylah. *Why didn't you kill that one?* She pointed an arm at Jond.

She was raised with him. They were lovers once. Dew stepped in before Sylah could respond. She smarted; she would have killed Jond, *should* have killed Jond, but she wanted more information.

"Loot's blood ran yellow."

Elder Zero stopped laughing.

"I thought Jond might know something about that," Sylah continued.

And has he told you anything? Reed asked, her emotions carefully blank for the first time.

"Not yet."

"Ha," Reed replied and signed. *So, kill him now.*

Sylah shifted her feet. “I want to exile him. Leave him on the mainland. It’s not his fault . . . Loot brainwashed him.”

Sylah heard Jond turn to look at her. She didn’t meet his gaze but said out of the corner of her mouth: “But it is still all your fault.”

This isn’t an eru bus that anybody can just jump aboard, Reed said.

Nor do we harbor traitors and thieves. Elder Ravenwing entered the conversation, his eyes swimming with malicious intent. His shadow of dark hair hadn’t grown since Sylah had last seen him, and she wondered if it was a type of bloodink tattoo—dark hair was rare on a Ghosting.

“It’s only one more person. I can’t leave him on this island. I can’t risk—” Anoor’s name stuck in her throat. She coughed and continued, “If supplies are an issue, I have an ambassador token. When the overseer comes back, I can use it to stock up.”

The overseer? Dew asked.

In the village, they’re away at the moment, Memur interrupted.

Why do you need to see the overseer? Dew asked, expressionless.

“I thought . . .” Sylah couldn’t bear to lie. “I thought there might be some letters sent from the capital for me.”

Dew shook their head firmly. *No, the Ghostings in the village have received no mail on behalf of you, nor has the overseer.*

Sylah swallowed her disappointment.

Elder Reed rounded on Dew, blocking off the elders signing to each other. Memur averted her gaze politely, but Sylah had no time for that. She shimmied around and tried to spy in.

We do have the extra prisoner, we had counted on the warden’s daughter being here, Elder Zero signed, a laugh still hanging off his lips.

Taking on this girl is bad enough, Ravenwing responded.

Sylah couldn’t see Reed’s reply, but there was a nod in it.

Hassa asked us to bring her. Plus, if she killed the Warden of Crime, she might be helpful, Zero signed.

Hassa is a child, Ravenwing countered. Sylah frowned. Eighteen was not a child.

She has never been a child. We took that away from her when we severed her hands and tongue beneath the city. Elder Zero’s face was solemn.

Sylah winced. She had only recently learned that Hassa had been born without the wardens' knowledge. In order to keep her safe, the elders had maimed her just like the others. She became a spy, an undocumented Ghosting who could infiltrate any household in the guise of a servant.

"Do you think the walls could cave in during the tidewind?" Jond whispered to her right.

Sylah batted him away. "Shut up, I'm trying to read their conversation."

"But seriously, it's glass, right? It must be so . . . fragile."

"They're discussing your fate and you're scared of the ceiling?" Sylah shot him an annoyed look. Jond's eyes were glued to the roof. His harsh jawline had been softened by the thick beard he had grown during their journey.

"They can kill me if they want." He shrugged. "As long as I don't die under the weight of this place."

"You want to die?"

Jond leveled his gaze at Sylah, all trace of fear gone from his features.

"No, Sylah, I want to live, I want to fight for the Sandstorm, I want to see the Embers suffer—"

"Oh, shut up, would you? Your righteousness is boring me to death. I wish I'd never taken off your gag." Sylah turned her gaze back to the elders, but she caught the start of Jond's smile.

The elders broke apart from their semicircle and turned to Sylah.

Come, we have decided. Elder Dew beckoned to her, though their expression gave nothing away. The four elders turned on their heels and walked deeper into the depths of the glass dune.

Reed and Ravenwing were signing darkly to each other up front, though Sylah caught only their fevered looks in her direction.

"What have you decided?"

No one answered her.

She jogged to keep up with them. *Maiden's tits, Dew can walk fast*, she thought.

Sylah was about to ask again when the sand beneath her began to slope and harden into man-made cement. They had reached a cliff edge of some kind. Sylah peered past the figures of the elders to the scene below.

"By the fucking blood," Sylah whispered. None of her usual curses seemed strong enough, so she used one of Anoor's. With a flourish of course.

As Sylah looked down on the scene below she was plunged into a state of stupefaction. "Settlement" was too small a word: it couldn't encompass the splendor of what she saw. Sprawling homes were built into the hollow glass dune. And the streets, constructed of whitestone bricks but clean of any grime, resembled the Ember Quarter in scale and aesthetic. Domed roofs covered the many villas, with wide courtyards lacking the signature joba tree.

Everywhere else in the empire joba trees signified wealth and prosperity—the larger the tree the more you had. But here, in this glittering cavern, everyone had wealth. It may not have been the material wealth the citizens of the empire valued. But freedom brought a wealth with which no treasure could compare.

As light shimmered in hues of blue across the whitestone structures her eyes were drawn to an open space where children played. Children with hands and tongues. Children the empire hadn't cut down.

Her breath caught in the back of her throat and her eyes burned with the beauty of it.

Hungry for more, Sylah's gaze followed the narrow streets as she took in all the surrounding buildings. Schools, market stalls, even what looked to be a library. Her eyes roamed to the shadowed edge of the cavern, a league away at least, and saw a squat collection of villas that were set apart from the town. She thought she saw the silhouette of a group of people, but she couldn't be sure.

"Those look like barracks," Jond breathed next to Sylah, his eyes as wild as his unkempt beard.

Elder Ravenwing gave Jond an appraising look, a sly grin spreading across his features. *Yes, we're building an army.*

CHAPTER THREE
SYLAH

The dhow is the most common boat used by emissaries from the Drylands. Though they rarely visit our shores I have hopes that we may learn their ways and traditions of seafaring.

—Journal extract from the First Sea Lord of the Queen's armada, year 280 B.W.

The steps that led to the town below had been chipped into the glass and clinked as they walked. As they got deeper into the town, the sunlight receded, and the soft glow of runelamps began to light their way. She noted that, rather than red, the lamps glowed a clear white, and wondered who had written the runes on the glass orbs.

"What is the army for?" Sylah asked the elders. None of them turned to answer her. They lent their concentration to the steep staircase as they carefully lowered themselves. Sylah estimated Reed was the youngest at forty years of age and Elder Dew nearing eighty, with Zero and Ravenwing claiming the years in between.

Though there was no breeze, the air hummed with activity and life and the smell of fires and stews. This was what the Dredge was meant to be like, maybe even what it had been before the founding wardens invaded.

"Elders, why do you need an army?" Sylah asked again when they reached the glass dune floor.

Ravenwing's sharp mouth curled, and he signed, *Once the tide-wind is tamed, we intend to fight for our land.*

Come. Elder Dew interrupted their conversation. *We will leave at dawn on the first morning waves with the fishermen. For now, you will stay with me. I am sure you have many questions.*

Panic struck Sylah.

"We left Boey in the village."

You brought another traitor? Ravenwing rounded on her.

"No, no, the eru."

Elder Zero laughed, though he hadn't really stopped laughing. It was like he'd been cracked open and now he couldn't scoop the chuckles back into his shell.

The eru will be fine, though we cannot take them with us on this journey. They will be safe in the village. Elder Dew put their wrist on Sylah's arm. Sylah was sad she didn't get a chance to say goodbye to the blue beast. To hug her scales and whisper stories about Anoor one more time.

"They'll look after her?"

Dew inclined their head.

"What of our belongings, our packs?" All Sylah had was the pouch of joba seed powder—now empty—and the sword that hung by her waist, the familiar weight of it pressing against her hip.

I sent my sister to organize bringing them over.

Sylah must have missed another subtle discussion. She hadn't even noticed Memur leave.

Sylah nodded. "Thank Memur for me."

Come, this way.

Sylah and Jond followed the elders through the streets of the city. Ghostings stopped in their work and watched with open mouths as Sylah and Jond, so clearly not Ghostings, walked through their home.

They don't like invaders, Elder Reed signed.

"Invaders." Sylah flinched as the word hit her in the chest. She realized for the first time that it was true. She was an invader; every red-blooded and blue-blooded citizen was. Even if it was her ancestors who had done the crime, her very existence took up a space a Ghosting should have had—if disease and servitude hadn't killed them. Centuries-old guilt hung heavy in her heart.

But that guilt was light as a feather compared to the oppression the Ghostings felt every day.

"I can understand that," Sylah replied quietly.

As they got closer to the buildings, she began to see the difference between this hidden world and the rest of the empire. The domed roofs had a small opening in the center where smoke from a central hearth seeped through. Though there were no plants—there was no sunlight to sustain them—the Ghostings still decorated their homes with fine carvings of flowers and petals. The carvings hung off the doorframes and dangled in windows, as small expressions of joy. There were no metal tidewind shutters on any of the doors or windowpanes.

This wasn't just a world free of oppression. It was a world free of the tidewind.

"How long have you lived down here?" Sylah asked.

Our ancestors found the glass dune fifty years ago. Though we didn't have the means to turn it into a settlement until the last decade. Elder Dew looked at the glass joba flower that Sylah was gazing at which swung off the roof of the closest home. *Slowly, day by day, our settlement blooms.*

Sylah mashed together her quivering lips. Hassa would have loved it here. Instead, she'd stayed behind, giving up her space on the journey to help Anoor and to save the other Ghostings in Nar-Ruta.

They weaved through narrow alleyways until they came to a stop at one of the larger homes on the lane. Dew pushed open the door with their crutch.

Go in, the elder indicated to Sylah and Jond. They entered the dark home while the others signed to each other outside.

"Can you see the runelight switch?" Sylah asked.

"No."

"Help me find it."

"I don't think I'm much help with my hands bound together," Jond said.

"I'm not releasing you until we're on the boat, leagues away from the shore—ah. Got it." The switch had been modified with a leather strap large enough for a Ghosting's arm to hook under their wrist.

The room was lit in a white glow. Furniture lined the walls neatly. A simple rubber-wood desk, a bed, a few stacks of books. Sylah looked for a privy but couldn't find one.

"Maybe they don't shit?" Jond suggested, lying back on the elder's bed.

"Get up, you can't just lie on Dew's bed. Stop being an eru turd and show some respect."

"I hardly slept last night." Jond threw in a yawn to prove his point.

"So?"

Jond gave her a sullen look and rolled onto the floor where he proceeded to tuck his bound hands behind his head and close his eyes.

Dew entered a moment later.

They will meet up in the town hall for dinner later. For now, I have sent for a couple of pallets for you two. Dew sniffed at Jond's prostrate form. *And we shall await your belongings. I will answer any questions you have in the meantime.*

"Where is your privy?"

Dew smiled. *We have not managed to fine-tune our sewage system, so you will have to go outside. Follow the path around the back. It will lead to the outhouse.*

"Thank you." Sylah slipped outside, hoping that leaving Jond with the Ghosting elder wasn't a bad idea.

Sylah heard a small sound beside her and saw the big eyes of a child watching her with an expression of fear.

"Oh, hello." Sylah tried for a smile, but she knew she wasn't entirely kindly looking.

"Eeep." The child screeched and stumbled over their feet as

they tried to get away from Sylah. They fell to their knees, their hands breaking their fall. Just like the other children Sylah had seen in the town, this one hadn't been maimed at birth either.

"Are you okay?" Sylah asked, reaching out to help the child up.

"Mama says not to talk to you," the child whispered.

"Oh no, is your hand bleeding? Show me, I won't hurt you." Sylah reached for the child's hand, but they clutched it to their chest and slipped away before she could help. But she saw the cut before they ran away. She saw the color of their blood.

It was red.

"What have you done?" Sylah burst back into Elder Dew's home and stood a hair's breadth from Dew's face.

Sylah felt the telltale signs of her muscle spasms. The dose she had taken the night before hadn't been enough to sate her body's need for joba seeds and her withdrawal symptoms were returning.

What is the meaning of your anger? Dew asked, their face blank and submissive.

"The child, I saw them, their blood ran red. You stole them." Sylah began to pace, her mind full of memories of the Stolen. Fareen's smile flashed beneath her blinking eyes.

"How could you? They're just children, they belong with their family." Sylah's muscles were visibly shaking now. Jond watched her from the floor with slitted eyes.

I know of what you speak, child. Sit, take some water. I will tell you what you have seen.

Jond didn't know Ghosting speak, but he knew what was happening to Sylah. He had watched her drink the dose every day on their travels. "It's the joba seeds. She needs a small dose of joba seed powder to alleviate the symptoms of withdrawal." He shifted on the ground and closed his eyes again, his duty done.

Sylah couldn't even muster a scowl in his direction. She collapsed in a chair opposite Elder Dew and placed her head in her hands, waiting for the worst of the tremors to pass.

What felt like many strikes later, a warm mug of tea was thrust under Sylah's nose. She knew it wasn't Elder Dew giving it to her, because the person's hands brushed Sylah's own as she took the cup gratefully. She closed her eyes as she drank. The tea was laced with joba seed powder, and it only took a few minutes before Sylah felt her muscles relaxing. She leaned back in the chair and surveyed the room. Jond still lay on the floor, seemingly asleep. Elder Dew watched her passively, perching on the edge of their bed.

In front of her, cross-legged, was the young girl who had met them in Ood-Rahabe.

"Hello, again," she chirruped. She was small in stature, but up close, Sylah realized she was older than she had first thought. Nearer to Hassa's eighteen years of age. The four plaits on her head were sectioned so precisely you could see the pale shade of her scalp underneath.

"Hello," Sylah said.

"Was the tea okay? I don't know how old the joba seeds were, we don't get a lot of supplies. Only what we can steal on the trade routes."

Elder Dew sighed behind the girl, and she stiffened. "Sorry, wasn't supposed to tell you that, I guess. I'm not used to strangers in the Chrysalis."

Elder Dew snorted.

"Chrysalis?" Sylah repeated.

"This, our home, we call it the Chrysalis."

"Oh," Sylah said. "Thank you for the tea. It helped a lot."

"I'm called Ads," she said.

"I'm Sylah."

Ads nodded in confirmation. She knew who Sylah was.

"Here's the rest of the powder I made. I thought you would need it for the journey."

The bag of joba seed powder was weighty. Relief flooded Sylah.

"Thank you." She placed the bag into her pouch at her waist. It was as comforting as the sword by her hip.

Elder Dew shifted, and Ads turned to look at them. *Thank you for getting the tea and the powder. Please return at sunset. You can escort our guests to the town hall for dinner.*

Ads nodded enthusiastically. "Yes, Elder." The girl slipped out of the door as fast as a mouse.

"Is she always that happy?"

Yes, every day she lives is a blessing.

"What do you mean?" Sylah asked.

Her blood runs red.

Sylah made to stand, though she didn't know where she was going.

Rest. Be still. I do not have the strength to get up and down like you. Elder Dew waved to their crutch resting on gnarled knees. *She is not stolen like you were. We do not harvest children's lives. We simply preserve them.*

"How?"

Her mother is a Ghosting. Her father is a rapist.

Sylah sank deeper in her chair. "Her father is an Ember?" She puckered her mouth to spit.

Please do not soil my floor.

"I wasn't going to." Sylah swallowed. "So, she's half Ember, half Ghosting?" It made sense why the girl had such dark eyes, unlike the grays and blues Sylah was used to seeing in a Ghosting. Except—

"Hassa . . ."

Elder Dew nodded. *Her father is also an Ember, though her blood runs clear. She was able to live in Nar-Ruta without the father knowing any better.*

"So, there's a fifty-fifty chance their blood will run red or clear?"

Or blue. Not all couplings are with Embers.

"How many rapists *are* there in Nar-Ruta?"

Not all are violent. Some are love. Some are paid for in maiden houses.

Sylah had never heard of a child from a mixed coupling surviving the empire's clutches—lying with another color was illegal and penalized with a ripping if you were a Duster or Ghosting. A sentence in jail if you were an Ember.

Ads was one of the first children we smuggled out of the city. She has been here since the beginning.

Sylah nodded slowly. "I understand why you call this place the Chrysalis."

Dew smiled. *Change is coming.*

CHAPTER FOUR

SYLAH

I am losing supplies. Every trade caravan over the last three mooncycles has disappeared. There is something not right in this village. It is overrun with Ghostings and every day I am sure there are more. I request a platoon of officers to help investigate what is happening on the trade route.

—Letter hidden in Elder Dew's desk, written by
the overseer of Ood-Rahabe

Sunset was beautiful in the Chrysalis. Though they were deep underground, the blue glass from the dune above them rippled and reflected the sky outside. The blue merged with the pink rays to create violet shadows.

". . . and this is my cousin's house. She thinks she's taller than me, but actually she just wears bigger shoes." Ads was giving Sylah and Jond the extended tour while Dew trailed behind them, their crutch clicking on the ground.

"And this over here is the town hall." Ads flourished her hands backward, waving toward the circular house that looked exactly the same as all the others. It wasn't even much bigger.

"This is it?" Jond raised an eyebrow.

"Seems like it," Sylah said.

They entered to the familiar silence of Ghostings signing to one another. The vibrancy in the air and small sounds of movement were a comfort to Sylah. The elders stopped and looked at their guests as they walked in. They sat cross-legged by a wooden table that arched around the hearth in the center. Elder Dew lowered themself slowly to the ground, folding like paper, thin with lots of sharp edges, as they sat on a bright pink cushion beside Reed.

Welcome. Zero waved toward the empty seats at the table.

Sylah and Jond sat side by side at the far end, farthest from the door.

Eat, Reed commanded.

There were steaming bowls of simple fare. Rice spiced with 'shito, spinach stew, and mountains of flatbread to act as cutlery and sustenance. Sylah reached for the food hungrily.

"Sylah . . ." Jond waved his hand restraints in her face.

"No chance."

"How am I meant to eat?"

"Slowly. If the Ghostings can do it, so can you."

Ravenwing put down his flatbread from between his residual limbs and leveled his eyes at Sylah. *There is nothing a Ghosting can't do.*

Sylah nodded; she knew the statement to be true.

You can untie him. Our guards will apprehend him if he attempts to escape. Ravenwing nodded to the far room adjoining the main hearth. Out of the shadows crept two Ghostings armed with knives attached to their wrists. A silver emblem was pinned to each brown uniform.

I told you, there's nothing we can't do. The smile Ravenwing gave Sylah sent shivers up her spine. He shifted the scarf by his neck revealing his own silver emblem pinned to his brown uniform. *Our motif, the gazelle, fleet of foot and sharp of wit. It outmaneuvers even the fastest predators.*

The horns on the pin looked like weapons in themselves.

"You see them?" Sylah said to Jond. She waved at the soldiers. "They're trained to kill you if you move a handspan from this table."

Jond smirked as if to say "two guards are no match for a Stolen"—and he was right. Sylah went to her waist and pulled out the sword from the hook on her belt. She laid it flat on the table farthest away from Jond, but within reaching distance for her.

"They're not the only ones who are armed."

Zero laughed.

ONCE DINNER WAS eaten the elders turned to talk of the journey. Elder Reed rolled out a map and began tracking the course for Sylah's benefit.

We start northeast of the Empire and pick up the current that the fishermen call the scorpion's tail. That will lead us east until we hit the mainland.

"How long will it take?"

Reed shrugged. *Half a mooncycle, maybe more.*

"You haven't done it before, have you?"

That does not mean we do not know the journey. Long ago our ancestors traveled between the lands as easily as the tide moves the sea.

Sylah leaned over the map again. It was more detailed than the one Hassa had given her, with notes of their nautical crossing jotted in blue ink.

We expect to meet the Tannin within the first week at sea.

Sylah choked on her wine. "The Tannin? That's a children's tale." She thought of the half-forgotten stories she had exchanged under the cover of darkness with her foster sister. She remembered Fareen's shriek as Sylah had whispered "Tannin" over and over until the words ran together like a drumbeat. Then the shadows across the bedroom wall stretching as Sylah lurched around like the monster that prowled the depths of the Marion Sea.

"The Tannin is real." Ads said the words softly. Sylah looked at her sidelong. She'd forgotten she was even there.

"As real as Anyme's wyverns that fly in the sky and spit fire." Sylah couldn't help the mocking smile that split across her face.

The girl lifted her shoulders. "Can't say about the wyverns, haven't seen them with my own eyes."

"Did someone give this girl joba seeds?" Sylah laughed.

The elders shifted and looked to one another.

"I've seen the Tannin. Just once and I lived," Ads said. "My mama wasn't so lucky."

Sylah took a big gulp of wine to steady herself.

Ads has worked the seas since she was a babe. All of the fishermen know of the Tannin. It is as ruthless and restless as the tidewind. Prepare yourselves, Dew signed.

"If it's real, how do you get past it?" Jond asked, his eyes wide, plucking the threads of conversation from Ads's words.

We have our ways, Dew said, and Sylah relayed the words to Jond.

Reed continued, scowling at Sylah as she signed. *We will arrive at this port.* The elder tapped the west side of the mainland continent.

Sylah leaned in and read the archaic wording scrolled across the dot she pointed to. "Port Nsuo."

Yes, according to our ancestors' notes, this was the old trading post with the Drylands.

"The Drylands" was scrawled above a small island farthest west. The island fitted inside of Sylah's fist while the land mass of the main continent splayed outward on the table, ten handspans across.

"The Drylands. That's the empire, isn't it?" Sylah asked, recognizing the oblong shape of the island from her own map.

Reed nodded. *From the port we will make our way on foot to the Academy.*

"What of the tidewind, how will we protect ourselves there?"

There is no tidewind on the mainland, Dew signed.

The mainland. Sylah's eyes skittered across the name of the largest landmass that housed the Zwina Academy: the queendom of Tenio. A world with no tidewind. A lump formed in her throat.

"Why do you think the city will have the answer to stopping the tidewind?" Jond asked suddenly, fear fracturing his voice.

Reed looked at the other elders. Sylah tried to see the communication that subtly happened between them but missed it completely.

Ravenwing slipped away from the group for a moment. He returned a few breaths later holding a book within his long limbs.

It was old, Sylah could see that. The cover was wrapped in protective latex, but she could still see the fraying cotton underneath the shiny outer layer. The pages were browning and faded. Ravenwing placed it carefully on top of the map.

We know because we have this, he signed. *This is a diary from before the wardens invaded. Before they stole our home. It claims that the Zwina Academy is a beacon for all the brightest minds in the world.*

Sylah reached for the book, but the air shifted as every Elder signed, *NO*.

How dare you reach for our ancestors' words uninvited? Reed turned on Sylah.

"Sylah, they look mad . . . what did you do? Why are they all staring at a rotten old book?" Jond shifted in his chair.

"I'm sorry." Sylah held out a placating hand to the elders. "I will not touch it."

"What is it?" Jond whispered to her.

"It's a diary from one of their ancestors, before the wardens colonized their land," Sylah said. "Now shut up." She turned back to the elders. "Thank you for showing me the diary. I understand that the words are sacred to you. If you believe that the Academy will have the answers, I believe you."

Jond snorted. Sylah kicked him—hard.

The tension was released in the room.

Sylah continued. "There's one thing I'm not clear on, though. What about the tidewind? How will we survive *that* out *there*?" She waved toward the sea.

Ravenwing gave a smile for the first time, and it was as dark as his hair.

Wait until you see our ship.

THE EVENING HAD ended abruptly with the elders spending the last few waking strikes with their families and loved ones. Even Elder

Dew slipped away into the night leaving Sylah and Jond alone in their home, guarded by four soldiers.

Sylah slept with the sword flat against her chest, her back propped on pillows so she could survey Jond beside her. He was staring up at the ceiling watching the curls of smoke from the hearth dissipate out of the chimney.

"What do you think is out there?" he said, feeling her eyes on him.

She thought for a moment before she spoke.

"Aid."

"Aid?" He turned onto his side, and his lips spread into a smile. "I meant more like erus with two heads or trees that can talk."

Sylah was surprised by her own laugh.

"Trees that can talk?"

"Could be. You never know."

"Our ancestors might have had something to say about trees that can talk. Remember we came from the mainland."

"But we were made in the empire," Jond countered. "We have no idea what's out there, or what the wardens have hidden from us."

It was true. Each one of the Stolen had been crafted to cut down the empire, not knowing the web of lies the wardens had spun. Once it had been her life's mission to kill all Embers. Now, her goal was to save them all from the tidewind.

"Aid," Sylah repeated firmly. "That's all we need."

Before the tidewind killed them, including the woman she loved.

Jond grunted. Sylah's solemn words had sucked all humor out of the room. He rolled away but she kept her gaze on him until eventually she fell into a restless sleep.

She dreamed of a land far away overrun with erus with two heads, ridden by talking trees. She woke with a start.

Disoriented, she looked around the room, expecting Anoor's body next to hers. Instead, the cold sword was her only companion. Reality hurt harder in the dark, and she brought her knees to her chest and rested her brow on them. Sweat cooled in her collarbone and beneath her breasts.

The silence was a thunderous absence in the room. It took her a while to realize why the quiet set her on edge.

I can't hear the tidewind down here.

It was the first time in her life when the churning hurricane hadn't accompanied her sleep. It was unnerving. She wondered if the silence had woken Jond up too. She unfurled from her cocoon and looked to where he lay.

He wasn't there.

"Fuck, I knew I should have tied him back up," Sylah swore, stumbling out of the house. The guards stood drowsily to attention as she rounded on them. "He's gone, when did he go?"

One of the guards signed with a knife strapped to their wrists, a sight Sylah was getting used to seeing. *Who's gone?*

"Jond. The idiot you're meant to be guarding."

Two of the guards looked to each other dubiously. Sylah grabbed the nearest one by the collar, their gazelle emblem stabbing the skin on her hand.

"Where did he go?" Her mind reeled with all the awful things he could do to Anoor. He could out her as a Duster, he could assassinate her in her sleep, he could tell the wardens about Sylah, about the Sandstorm, he could—

There was a chuckle behind her, and Sylah turned, ready to rip out the culprit's throat.

"Hello." Jond waved, a satisfied grin stretching across his lips. "I went to the privy. You can put them down now."

Sylah dropped the guard, who fell in a heap on the floor. "Sorry," she said, though she didn't mean it. They were as surprised as her to see Jond standing there. There was no use wondering how he'd slipped out; he was one of the Stolen.

She followed Jond back into Elder Dew's house and didn't relax for the rest of the night. Though Jond's breathing slowed as he went back to sleep, Sylah couldn't risk letting him out of her sight again.

CHAPTER FIVE

SYLAH

I have taken tea with the five councillors of the Zwina Academy. They have housed me in the Blooming Towers in the center of the citadel as an honored guest. My mind cannot comprehend the power that they speak of. I cannot compose my thoughts enough to write them tonight, nor can I sleep for the sound of the towers' petals in the breeze. It sounds like the wings of a giant bird, filling my nightmares with talons.

—Journal of Elder Petra, year 237 B.W.

Exhaustion hung heavy on Sylah's shoulders as she slipped out of Dew's homestead and into the glittering light of the Chrysalis. Dawn twinkled through the glass above and she stood there mesmerized by refracted beams of sunlight.

There was a movement beside her, and Sylah's head snapped toward it.

It was the guard she had assaulted in the night for missing Jond's evening visit to the outhouse. Their signing was a little sheepish. *Morning, guest of the elders, how can I help you this day?*

Sylah's eyes took in their uniform in the morning light. The outfit was sturdier than she had thought, with leather under the beige dresses. The blades of their daggers strapped to their wrists glinted with danger. This wasn't the attire of someone who merely sacked trade routes. This was the uniform of a soldier ready for war.

Sylah felt a pang of worry for Anoor. No matter how much she trusted the elders, the problem was they would never trust *her.* And so, she would never know what they were truly planning.

"Where can I find the kitchens?"

The guard signed over Sylah's shoulder to their comrade.

She will guide you. The guard jutted their chin to their lean-looking partner. She was young, perhaps nineteen or twenty, with tufts of golden curls that grew wildly upward. Unlike her comrade she wore her uniform short around her thighs, revealing a patterned skirt of patchwork fabric that was dizzying to look at.

She saw Sylah staring.

I like fashion, she signed.

Sylah suppressed her laugh and nodded. "It's lovely."

The guard smiled, exposing a silver replacement tooth.

My name is Petal. You can follow me.

"Thank you, Petal." Despite the Ghostings' niceties Sylah knew she was being escorted like a prisoner. She followed Petal in silence.

The Chrysalis was slowly awakening. Though she didn't have the clockmaster's call to know the time, the lack of tidewind swirling through the glass above suggested it was at least after sixth strike. The air smelled of the acrid fumes of new fires, and smoke puffed out of the central chimneys of their whitestone villas. Children emerged, bleary-eyed and grumpy, their feet dragging them forward toward their schools. Sylah watched their eyes brighten as they caught sight of a friend in the playground, their unhappy scowls lifted with the spirit of fun.

"Mama, why is there an Ember here?" a child whimpered as they passed Sylah, clutching their mother's skirts.

Be quiet, the child's mother responded. She gave Sylah a tight-lipped smile that was more like a grimace.

I'm the trespasser in their home, Sylah thought. *I sully the peace they've built here, away from their oppressors.*

Sylah wanted to curl up, feel smaller, but she recognized this was born of self-pity. She rolled her shoulders back and held her head high, following behind Petal.

Furs of desert lions and foxes hung from the walls of the villa to Sylah's left, the leather drying out to make clothing.

Or armor, she thought.

Petal stopped and gestured to a larger building ahead of her. The smells emanating from it once again reminded Sylah of Lio's cooking. Not groundnut stew this time, but okra soup, slow-cooked with tomatoes and onions.

The thought of Lio tinged the moment with a bitter sadness. Sylah would never see Lio again, nor did she wish to. Her adoptive mother didn't deserve a place in her heart any longer.

You'll find food in there, Petal signed. *I will be waiting here.*

"You don't have to. I think I can find my way back."

Petal smiled once more, her silver front tooth glinting. *I will be waiting here.*

"Got it, I'm not to be trusted," Sylah growled and stalked into the kitchens.

There was a collective intake of breath as she walked in. It was clear that the kitchens were mainly to service the Ghostings' army, as a hundred pair of officers looked back at her.

Their pale eyes were unblinking, and Sylah shivered as tension filled her muscles. Their haunting disdain was over in a second and they returned to the steaming plates of food in front of them.

But Sylah wasn't here for food.

She scanned the faces of the crowd until she saw who she was looking for.

"Are you the cook?" Sylah asked the young woman whose arm was strapped to a wooden spoon.

The woman gave her a salty look before removing the spoon and signing, *No, I just enjoy stirring soup.*

Sylah liked her immediately.

"Would you be willing to sell me some of your herbs?"

Herbs?

"Yes, I need just a few, I'll trade you for them."

You think we have herbs? The cook laughed.

Sylah smarted.

"Anything then, it doesn't have to be herbs, but maybe look like herbs?"

The cook cocked her head at Sylah.

What are you up to, Ember?

Sylah exhaled through her nose.

"Look, I've got this." She withdrew the last of her salted goat from her satchel. "You can have it all, all I want is a few things that look like herbs and something to keep them in."

The cook narrowed her eyes at the salted goat. It wasn't much, but Sylah hoped it would be enough.

I have some dried molokhia that could be crushed into a powder. And maybe some old lemon rind that I dried in the sun . . . The cook began to pull open cupboards, withdrawing items for Sylah to peruse.

Sylah smiled. "Perfect."

JOND WAS STILL asleep by the time Petal escorted her back. When he opened his eyes, Sylah was waiting.

"Drink this," she demanded, holding out a small vial of liquid.

He rubbed his eyes and sat up. "What is it?"

"Poison."

"Oh, sure. Pour me a gallon." He smiled crookedly but Sylah wasn't amused.

"I mean it, you have to drink this, Jond."

His smile dropped and he ran a hand through his matted beard. "Sylah, why would I willingly drink poison?"

"If you want to stay alive you will." Sylah unsheathed her sword and Jond rolled his eyes.

"You're not making sense."

"Every morning I will give you a vial of an antidote that will keep this poison at bay. Without it, you'll succumb to the potion's effects. And die." Sylah couldn't help the smugness from invading her words. She'd thought it up while Jond had been asleep. It was a technique used by Loot whenever he took an audience. It had prevented anyone from killing him. Well, until Sylah did.

Jond's face lost all mirth. "Where did you get poison from?"

Of course, it wasn't poison, just the dregs of ingredients the cook could scrounge together. The molokhia leaves turned the drink pleasantly green and the lemon rind made it bitter. She'd distilled cabbage leaf and rice water in firerum for the "antidote."

"The Ghostings were very willing to part with the poison herbs I needed, especially when they learned what their uses were."

"Sylah, you don't need to poison me. I'll come quietly, I promise."

"Your promises mean nothing to me, Jond." Sylah unstopped the vial and thrust it toward his mouth. "And don't think about trying to steal the antidote either. I've used bloodwerk to lock the vials away in a metal container."

Jond took the vial. "You really don't need to do this."

"I do. I won't risk you trying to harm me or anyone on this journey. I've promised the elders you wouldn't be an issue. And this, this makes sure you're not." Sylah grinned, and it was a nasty, twisted thing.

Jond's eyes didn't leave hers as he drank. He retched and coughed as it went down.

"Perfect, now you have ten strikes before you *really* need the antidote. I am finding myself a little absentminded at the moment, so I'll try and not forget," she said, and Jond's gaze quivered with loathing.

"Oh, I think I can hear that girl coming, Ads. Must be time to go. Your pack's over there." Sylah picked up the vial and returned it to its metal container with the rest of the herbs.

"WE'VE BEEN BUILDING the ship for almost ten years." Ads chittered away. "It's called the *Baqarah*. The elders let me name it because I spent so long helping them. And," she dropped her voice to a whisper, "I'm their favorite." She grinned widely, revealing a slight gap between her two front teeth.

Sylah wished she'd shut up. Her head throbbed, and all she

wanted to do was curl up in bed with Anoor and maybe one of those zines she liked to read. *The Tales of Inquisitor Abena*, they were called. The stories were centered around a brilliant detective unraveling different crimes, often brought on by lusty romances that were interrupted with one or both of the lovers being killed. They were ridiculous nonsense, but Anoor loved them. And eventually so did Sylah. She had come to enjoy the twists and turns as Inquisitor Abena uncovered the culprit.

". . . there's a hull large enough for twenty as well as all the supplies. There's food to last you a few mooncycles. Took a lot of raids on the town, that did . . ." The steps to the entrance of the Chrysalis didn't seem to tire the young girl, and Sylah drowned her out with her thoughts once more.

The rays of sunrise grew brighter the higher they climbed. When they reached the top, Sylah turned to look back on the sprawling city below one last time.

The Chrysalis was still stretching awake. Bakers were dropping off loaves at doorsteps and fresh goat's milk in jars of various sizes. The town was coming alive, and Sylah let the energy of it run through her veins.

Anoor would love it here. It was a reflection of the world Anoor saw in her mind's eye: a world of no color classes, a world of freedom and choice.

Someone coughed behind her, and Sylah whirled around. Dew stood in the entrance of the Chrysalis, their clothing newly pressed, the beige like a second skin that covered them to their sandaled feet.

You feel Anyme's presence. It's strong here, they signed.

"What do you mean?" Sylah asked.

Anyme is the energy you feel. The vibrancy of life. When we die, we become Anyme and in turn Anyme guides us.

Sylah knew that the Ghostings believed in Anyme differently than the way the Abosom priests sermonized about their deity. Hassa had told her more than once, but now Sylah saw their beliefs in a new light.

"You believe Anyme is a spiritual force all around us?"

Dew shook their head in a "so-so" manner but didn't expand.

"Is it in the air? The sky?"

A smile played on Dew's lips. *You Embers and your skies. You took our beliefs and twisted them to your purposes.*

Sylah flinched at Dew's words. Another thing the invaders had violated.

"Anyme isn't a God, then?"

What is a God but a leader you cannot see? And if that is the case, should we not pray to the wardens on high? No, Anyme is not a God. Anyme is a guiding force, an energy. A feeling. It is the voice that tells you not to steal the bread and the voice that grants forgiveness for those who do.

"So Anyme is a positive force."

Their smile became a laugh. *No. For our ancestors are angry, and there will be a reckoning.*

Dew's eyes drifted to the barracks at the back. Sylah wondered how many soldiers they had.

Come, the others wait.

They made their way out of the cavern entrance onto the beach beyond. Ads had thankfully gone ahead with Jond, though her babbling could still be heard on the breeze. The wind was still a little frenzied from the nightly tidewind and carried with it sea spray and sand. It woke Sylah up a little.

She tugged her pack closer to her chest. There wasn't much in it. The sword and scabbard were by her waist, the map and joba seed powder in the bag. Along with a change of clothes, the vials of herbs for Jond, and her inkwell on her wrist, that was all she needed.

Dew led Sylah away from Ood-Rahabe, following the footsteps of Ads and Jond in the sand. The sun rose as they walked, warming Sylah's brow and peppering it with beads of sweat. She savored the rays, knowing it was going to be a long time until she got to see the blue sand of the Wardens' Empire shimmer again.

As they walked Sylah noticed small glass greenhouses to her right. A Ghosting waved from the doorway of one of them to Elder Dew, who nodded in response.

"You're growing your own plants? Takes a lot to feed the entire city. You must have over a thousand Ghostings there."

Yes, we grow seedlings out here, and plant as many as we can in the field near the village. Dew nodded. *The light in the Chrysalis doesn't lend itself to growing vegetables.*

Sylah noted that Dew didn't confirm or deny the number of Ghostings. Her mind went back to the barracks.

"Eyoh! Can you see it?" Ads's scream of excitement was so loud that Sylah could hear it fifty handspans away. Sylah watched her skip ahead of Jond and point toward a mast in the distance.

With every step Sylah took, a sour hole of disappointment grew larger in the pit of her stomach. As she approached the ship Sylah turned to see if Ads's gaze matched the direction she was looking in. Sure enough, the skipping of her excited feet led them straight to the ramshackle harbor that Sylah had been scrutinizing.

The remaining three elders were waiting on the shore, along with a crew of five others who all wore the silver gazelle pinned to their breasts. Sylah recognized Petal among them. The woman nodded in Sylah's direction with a smile. Though Sylah barely knew her, it was a comfort knowing she was going to be part of the crew. Perhaps it was because her whimsical clothing choice reminded her of Anoor. The patchwork dress she wore under her uniform lifted in the breeze.

"Sylah, Jond, meet the *Baqarah*." Ads swept her hand toward the sticks poking out of the sea. Sylah surveyed the *Baqarah* once more.

The boat was hideous. It was made of mismatched wood and what looked like bits of furniture. Six masts—old gutter pipes?—held up a main sail with two smaller triangular ones on either side. The main sail itself was sewed together with different pieces of leather and hide. A patchwork of skin that limped in the breeze.

Over a hundred handspans long, it was still smaller than Sylah had expected. Its pointed nose looked to be carved out of a bedpost. She could only hope it could cut through the raging waves of the Marion Sea.

"I'm not getting on that," Jond whispered as she came to stand beside him.

For once Sylah agreed with him. "They can't be talking about the same thing, right? Do you see other ships in the harbor?"

It was a fruitless search. All the other boats were small fishing vessels with nets piled high like tangled locs.

Elder Ravenwing's grin was cruel. *Are you ready?*

"How precisely is this going to survive the tidewind? In fact, how is it going to survive a wave?"

Ravenwing just barked a laugh, turned on his heel, and climbed the ladder to the ship. Elder Dew winked at Sylah then followed the others.

"Are you seriously getting on that?" Jond said, wide-eyed.

"When Ads said she helped make the ship, I didn't think she meant the whole thing . . . it's like a children's toy made large." She looked for the girl to ask her about the vessel, but it was just Sylah and Jond left on the beach. Ads had probably gone back to the Chrysalis.

Sylah rubbed her brow, and the braid with the green shell knocked against her knuckles. She rubbed her fingers lightly over its surface. Anoor was counting on her.

"Let's go," she said to Jond.

Jond hesitated and Sylah called down from the ladder. "Don't make me tie you up again." A breath later she felt the weight of his body on the rung beneath her.

The boat smelled of coconut wax and roasted nuts. The deck was sturdy enough, but Sylah still wasn't convinced of its durability. The crew got to work, and had Sylah known anything about sailing, she would have questioned why no one was working the sails.

Instead, Ghostings were moving in and out of a hatch in the center of the ship, making small adjustments that Sylah couldn't see.

One of the crew members shrilled a high whistle through their teeth. It was a signal for the others.

Ravenwing's dark head appeared out of the hatch. *We're ready. Time to get in position.*

"Position? Where are we going?" Sylah noticed all the other elders had already disappeared.

This way. Ravenwing waved them over to the opening in the deck.

Sylah looked down the hatch, glimpsing the familiar glow of a runelamp, but nothing else. She looked to Jond, expecting him to complain, but his eyes were drawn to the shore. The last glimpse of the only home he'd known.

Sylah went down the ladder first. The air shifted. No longer could she smell coconut wax, but something harsher, like blood. Iron.

Her heels touched the ground of what should have been the hull. Runelight illuminated her surroundings, and what Sylah saw made her gasp, the sound of which echoed through the expansive space in front of her.

She was standing on an underground deck. Crew members shifted in and out of the white haze of the runelamps. Jond dropped down beside her, his breathing fast.

The floor beneath them moved, and they lurched to hold onto the railing. It was cool metal, and it stilled Sylah's beating heart. She looked up and the roof seemed to be moving backward. No—not backward: they were moving forward, leaving the shell of the ship behind.

Sunlight began to pour onto the deck ahead of them as the *real Baqarah* moved away from the shore. The sun revealed the breadth of the ship, double the length of its wooden shell. Shaped like a runebullet with wings, the entire body of the vessel was made of steel. The deck—the only flattened part of the cylindrical ship—was surrounded by a thick metal railing with a gate at the nose of the vessel where it carved through the waves. Sylah peered over the railing and was surprised to see the depths of the Marion Sea less than ten handspans away. Like a whale coming up for air, the *Baqarah* hid its bulk under the ocean. It moved through the water by an unknown force.

Bloodwerk.

"How?" Sylah whispered to Elder Dew, whose crutch chimed on the metal floor as they came to stand by her.

We caught a few Embers of our own. Dew smiled, and though they had a kindly face, Sylah knew it was vengeance that drove them. *Let me show you to your chambers.*

THE WOODEN OUTER shell allowed us to work on the ship beneath just in case agents of the empire raided the harbor. It's a subaquatic ship.

"What?" Sylah had never seen a sign like it. Dew repeated the phrase over and over until she understood. "It can be fully submerged beneath the ocean?"

Yes, allowing us to avoid the tidewind.

"This must have taken . . . ten years . . ." Ads had said it, just that morning. Sylah hadn't believed her.

Dew led them into the belly of the vessel via another ladder that dropped down into a narrow corridor. It was sturdily built, despite Sylah looking worriedly for a flaw. After all it could be *fully submerged underwater.* It didn't seem possible.

For years we claimed back our lands' natural resources. We forged the Baqarah *from steel and iron. We lost many Ghostings during its construction. Though you don't see their blood, you must feel it in every join.*

Dew stroked the metal panels of the corridor with the seams of their scars.

For the second time that day Sylah tried not to cry.

Down there, to the right, is the mess hall. We have a lean crew, so you will take turns to cook for the others. The larders are stocked, Dew signed.

Sylah relayed this to Jond, who hadn't said a word since entering the hatch.

This is your cabin. Dew led them to a small door to their right. *There are two hammocks as we had initially expected the warden's daughter to be accompanying you. You will have to make do with sharing. This may seem like a large ship, but when we go underwater there are very few places to stretch your legs.*

Sylah nodded. She preferred to keep Jond close anyway, just in case he got any funny ideas.

They entered the cabin. It was small, with two hammocks

swinging with the movement of the ship. At one end a cabinet stood bolted to the ground. The porthole was the size of Sylah's head and fully submerged in the ocean. She watched a fish swim past and shuddered. *What if they sank?*

Jond put down his pack with a clunk. The bag was filled with spare clothes and essentials the Ghostings had graciously offered. Sylah wondered why it sounded so heavy. She pushed the thought from her mind as Dew began to move down the corridor.

"Thank you," Sylah said to them. "I don't think I've said it before now. But thank you."

Dew smiled and inclined their head. *Let me show you the mess hall.*

Sylah followed and Jond trailed silently behind them. White runelight shone above them.

Sylah heard a bang coming from the cabin at the bow of the boat.

"What was that? Are we sinking? Is the ship broken?"

It is nothing.

Petal slipped out of the room in question. Anger marred her brow, but she shook the expression away as she saw Sylah and Jond. She bowed to Elder Dew.

All is well? Dew asked her.

Yes, just a slight disturbance in the storage chamber. One of the panels had come loose. Nothing to worry about, she replied.

"What do you mean, a panel came loose?" Sylah piped up.

Go on your way, Dew said to Petal, then turned to Sylah. *Do not go in there, it is not safe.*

Sylah nodded reluctantly.

If you want to make it to the mainland alive, don't go in there, Dew repeated.

Sylah swallowed uneasily. "Okay, I get it. Jond, we can't go in there. Something to do with the paneling. Nod that you've heard." He did as he was bidden.

"Not so chatty all of a sudden?" Sylah said. "You didn't think we would get this far, did you? You didn't believe me when I said I was going to the mainland."

"I don't feel well," Jond said, and he did look a little queasy. "I think it's the poison, it's making me feel sick."

Sylah muffled her snort. "I'm sure you'll be fine."

Dew looked at Sylah sidelong with a knowing gaze.

This way. Dew led them farther down the corridor where natural light began to filter through.

"Skies above," she breathed.

The mess hall was at the tail end of the *Baqarah*. Double the height of the corridor, it encompassed the back of the top deck as well. Dew led her up a few short steps to a seating area.

This is the viewing platform, they signed.

Sylah took a sharp breath in.

The back wall was entirely made of glass panels that had been painstakingly aligned to allow the occupants a view of the world they'd left behind. Half of the landscape was submerged in water, but the topside showed the shore of the empire disappearing behind them.

The other elders stood at the glass wall, taking in the curves of the sand dunes. Sylah and Jond joined them.

All of them wondered if it was the last time they would see the Wardens' Empire. But Sylah knew she'd be back. Even if she had to swim across the Marion Sea herself.

I'll come back to you, Anoor.

CHAPTER SIX

ANOOR

The Warden of Crime has not been seen for over a mooncycle. Now is the time to strike for his throne.

—Note found in the Dredge

"Wait, what was that? Sign that again. I didn't catch it." Anoor watched Hassa's arms move slowly one more time.

The Ghosting settlement is in a giant glass dune, Hassa signed.

Anoor's nose wrinkled as she concentrated. She'd been learning the Ghosting sign language every day for the last mooncycle, but with her time filled with bureaucratic nonsense for most of the day, it was taking her longer than she would have liked. "Glass? Did you say glass?"

Hassa nodded patiently. The skin that stretched over her high cheekbones looked wan and clammy. She let out a tired sigh as she helped Anoor get into her dress. The floor-length gown was a deep purple, almost black. The bodice was structured and formal, and the shoulder pads wide and fierce, like two blades within easy reach.

"There's a sand dune made out of *glass*?"

It's why no one's ever found it. A network of sand dunes fossilized into the coast.

"Huh?"

Preserved.

"Slower, please."

Preserved. Like jam in a jar?

"Tasty?"

Hassa snorted. *No,* preserved, *like it won't go bad.*

"Oh, *preserved.* I can't believe how subtle the arm movements are. This language really is a marvel."

If only more people thought to learn it.

Anoor nodded, her shoulders drooping, the blades of fabric turning down to the ground. She looked out of the window at the blush of dawn.

Anoor was glad she'd kept her chambers instead of moving nearer to the wardens' courtroom. The west side of the Keep was plagued with the haughty families of the other disciples and wardens who all resided there. Though the view of the gardens was enviable, and the trip to her office shorter, she liked the sight of the whole city ahead of her in the morning.

The plantations crested the horizon, the tops of the rubber trees a mere pencil stroke in her vision. In front of them was the Dredge—the old Ghosting Quarter—now a derelict husk of its former vibrance. The Duster Quarter showed more life, with clusters of residents chatting next to cramped villas before they were moved on by officers.

Her gaze trailed over the Tongue, the bridge that separated the rich districts from poor. She wanted to knock it down. See how the Ember Quarter survived without the goods carted over on the trotro every day, rattling over on tracks as bloodwerk pushed the train back and forth.

Demolish it all, she thought. Though Anoor knew it wasn't as simple as all that.

Then her eyes swept over the courtyard in the Keep. Clumps of blue sand brought on by the gales of the tidewind clustered in dunes across the ground. The tidewind had roared until the early strikes of the morning. The Ghosting servants were busy sweeping the wreckage and sand away. A blank slate, to rage again the next day.

Anoor's eyes lingered on the joba tree that cracked through the cobblestones of the courtyard and into the sky. Its white branches had bloomed late this year, the red flowers only just bursting from their buds. Anoor wished Sylah could see them.

She clasped her hands together and turned to Hassa. "Thank you for helping me dress, Hassa. You know you don't have to come every day."

Hassa stood patiently while Anoor let her thoughts lead her out of the window, lead her back to Sylah, as they always did.

I miss her too, Hassa signed.

Anoor gave her a watery smile, then with resolve pushed her thoughts away from the beautiful wraith vying for attention in her mind.

"You look tired, Hassa, and thin, thinner than normal."

I'm fine, Anoor, stop worrying about me. I want to be here. I like to see you every morning.

Because of the promise she'd made Sylah, to look after Anoor.

Three seconds.

Anoor had gone three seconds without thinking of Sylah. She sighed and ran her fingers across the baby hairs on her brow.

"Will you help me?"

Hassa knew what she meant. She brought out her leather straps and attached the thin comb to her limbs. Anoor sat at her dressing table while Hassa carefully brushed the baby hairs into curls with styling jam.

"Thank you, Hassa." Anoor's hazel eyes met Hassa's dark ones in the mirror. "I mean it, you don't need to help me like this . . . you are not my servant, I want you to know that."

Hassa put down the comb. *I know, not servant, no. But friend.* And she smiled, lifting her hollow cheeks out of their concave.

Are you ready? Do you know what you have to do?

Anoor looked at the pile of papers on her desk. She had been poring over them long before the sun rose.

"Yes, I'm ready." Anoor nodded, just to confirm it.

"You're up early, Granddaughter."

Yona Elsari was standing outside Anoor's chambers next to the guards that Anoor had stationed there.

"Grandmother?" Anoor was dumbstruck. She was sure Yona hadn't been to this side of the Keep before, so close as it was to the servants' quarters.

"Close your mouth." The words were said harshly, but a hint of a smile lifted the corners of her thin lips.

That day her grandmother had chosen a burnt copper wig. The henna-dyed curls fell to her waist and made her seem younger than her sixty-eight years. Wigs had been fashionable during Yona's early years as warden, but the trend had faded over time.

Yona didn't care for fashion like Anoor did and had worn the exact same style of dress for as long as Anoor could remember: high-necked, long-sleeved, with full-length trousers. Not a slip of skin showed except her face.

"Are those your papers?" Yona gestured to the folder in Anoor's hand, and she nodded. "Today is the day. I would pay good money to watch the wardens as you present your work. Did you get the statistics of deaths in the Ghosting Quarter?"

Anoor frowned. "No, Bisma, the librarian, couldn't track those down. It seems that deaths in the Dredge were only recently monitored. There were no records before the year 350."

Yona's face twitched, with disapproval? Anoor wasn't sure.

"Have you not yet been granted access to the warden library? You may find some statistics in one of the former warden's journals."

Anoor shifted her feet.

"No. Uka . . . she says I need to be a disciple for three mooncycles before she'll approve it."

Something like mirth flashed across Yona's face. "Did you ask the other disciples? If they'd been granted access?"

"No." Anoor hung her head. Except for Tanu, who was an old school friend, the other disciples ignored her completely.

"No matter, you still have enough data to prove that changes are needed."

Yona had been helping Anoor with her transition to disciple over the last four weeks. Uka had kept Anoor away from her grandmother for most of her life, so it was nice to finally have a semblance of family.

Not that I understand her motivation at all.

Some days Yona was caring, almost motherly toward Anoor. Other times Anoor caught a look in Yona's eye that terrified her. It was there now.

"I'm proud of you," Yona said.

Anoor felt her legs tremble with shock. No one had said those words to her before. She wasn't sure what to do. Her instinct was to hug Yona, but Anoor was worried that she would crumple beneath her grandmother's grip. Instead, Anoor offered a sincere smile.

"Thank you, Grandmother."

"Now go and let me know later how it goes." Yona waved her away with a brittle laugh.

ANOOR'S HEELS CLICKED on the marble floor as she walked down the corridor toward the upper courtroom. The clockmaster called out eighth strike and Anoor quickened her pace. She wanted to get there before her mother.

She clutched her folder of reports to her chest. The notes laid out the new policy she was hoping to instate. It had taken her weeks just to understand the process required to make a bill a law, but with the help of her chief of staff and her advisers she was ready to present her findings to the other wardens and disciples.

"Anoor." The call held a smile in it.

Anoor turned to the sound of the voice. "Kwame, how are you?"

He skidded to a halt beside her. He wore a cream-colored blazer and blue pantaloons. It was still a shock to see him out of his servant attire.

When creating her Shadow Court, Anoor had elevated Kwame from servant to adviser. Though he had no military training, as was expected in an adviser for the Disciple of Strength, he was someone she trusted, and that was rare. He knew her secret and would die before letting it be known.

Anoor had only instated two people into her Shadow Court so far, three if you included Sylah as an ambassador, which she had yet to announce to the wardens. Her decision would raise some eyebrows. Each of the four disciples was able to have up to ten advisers in their Shadow Court. And a shadow it was, because even though Anoor was part of the legislature of the Upper Court, she wouldn't have the ability to decree a bill as law until she ascended to warden—a ten-year apprenticeship.

Not that the Wardens' Empire would be standing in ten years if the tidewind wasn't stopped.

"I'm good, Anoor, I spent the morning inspecting the army barracks with the general. He doesn't like me much."

"How could he not like you?"

Kwame shrugged, his grin dimpling his pockmarked face. "Probably because I used to bake bread for a living, and now I'm nearly his equal."

Anoor sighed through her nose.

Kwame touched her shoulder. "Are you *sure* you want me to be a part of your Shadow Court? Gorn, I understand, she's fierce. In fact, you wouldn't even need an army to quell a skirmish, just Gorn and one of her disapproving glares."

Anoor laughed and it eased some of the tension in her shoulders. "Do we have to go through this every day?"

"No, boss."

He knew she hated it when he called her that, but the mischievous glint in his eyes prevented her from chastising him.

Kwame was one of five people in the empire who knew Anoor's true blood color. Her mother, Gorn, Hassa, and Sylah were the other four. Though Sylah probably wasn't still *in* the empire.

Was she even alive?

Anoor swallowed down her panic. Kwame didn't seem to notice.

"You do realize you're a strike early for court," Kwame said.

"Yes, I know."

"Then why . . ."

"I just want to make sure I'm prepared."

"Oh." He cleared his throat. "You're ready? To present the work?"

"Yes, I need to get the wardens to agree to send it to the Noble Court for amendments." The Noble Court had no real power; it was all a bureaucratic farce to make the empire's twelve imirs feel a part of the governing of the empire. They would review and amend the bills sent down from the Upper Court—if correcting spelling and grammar really counted as "amending." Half the imirs didn't bother attending; rather, a representative was sent in their stead while they remained in the comfort of the cities they governed.

They had reached the doors of the wardens' courtroom. The first time Anoor had seen it, she'd been surprised how unadorned the room was. There were no opulent oil paintings, or gold-framed windows popular with the elite. The bare whitestone walls weren't even painted.

"Disciple Anoor." The officer guarding the door nodded to her. She greeted him in turn.

"Officer Hora, how is your sister?"

"Doing better. Thank you for the medicine."

"It is no trouble. Is my mother in there?"

"Not yet, Disciple."

Anoor's smile grew. It was a small win. "Let me know if you need anything else for your sister, won't you? You know my chief of staff? Gorn? Bring it to her attention and she'll let me know."

"Thank you, Disciple."

"Just Anoor."

"Thank you . . . Anoor." The officer sounded uncomfortable using Anoor's name, but he stood up a little straighter.

He pushed open the door for Anoor and she entered the courtroom, Kwame on her heels. In the center was a lacquered white joba-tree table. The wood of the joba tree was sacred, and it was illegal to cut one down due to its connection to the God

Anyme. It was believed Anyme had climbed a joba tree into the sky and it was now a conduit for the prayers of those who lived on earth.

Of course, the wardens were the closest to Anyme, possessing the attributes the God deemed the most important: Strength, Truth, Duty, and Knowledge. And so, if they wanted a joba-tree table, they got one.

Anoor took her seat beside her mother's designated chair while Kwame sat in one of the plain wooden seats that lined the walls, reserved for the advisers who chose to attend.

There was one window in the courtroom. No matter the time of day, a square patch of sun beamed through it, illuminating the joba-tree table fully. Anoor watched the small patch of sun and waited.

Around twenty minutes later her mother appeared, flanked by four of her advisers including the general of the wardens' army—*her* army. Uka was dressed in a slitted pair of gray pantaloons, tied at the waist with a gunmetal belt. She faltered as she saw Anoor there before her, half a strike early.

"Good morning, Disciple," Uka said, brushing her fingers through her slicked-back afro. The roots were grayer than they had been half a year ago, when Anoor had first entered the Aktibar.

"Good morning, Warden." Anoor shuffled her notes to hide the quivering of her fingers. Kwame coughed behind her, and she knew it was his way of reminding her he had her back.

They all sat in uncomfortable silence until more of the court began to drift in. The other disciples entered together, without paying Anoor much heed, though Tanu threw a wink her way. Like Anoor, Tanu had been raised in the Wardens' Keep, and once upon a time they'd been close friends. Whereas Tanu's ambition for the title of Disciple of Knowledge had led her toward more studious pursuits, Anoor's love of the make-believe had led her to *The Tales of Inquisitor Abena*. Their differing interests became a gulf between them, and they drifted further and further apart. Now, as equals, Anoor hoped they'd return to the friendship they'd once had.

The last court member to arrive was Warden Pura, dressed in the white cowl of the Abosom, though as the head of the priests his robe was fringed with gold. He sat at the head of the table.

"Court is in session," he croaked. The Guild of Truth didn't just encompass the Abosom, but also the legal system. Pura chaired both the Noble Court and the Upper Court.

One by one the wardens discussed the issues plaguing their guilds. It was a long and arduous morning. The guild of knowledge was struggling to recruit more students into their ranks, and there were fewer and fewer masters-in-training. Warden Pura droned on about the newest regulation that Disciple Qwa had drafted to penalize Dusters who missed their taxes. Qwa smiled at being mentioned, hiding his teeth behind pouting lips. The circle of hair that surrounded his perfect bald spot had been stretched out with hot tongs. He was yet to speak to Anoor, or even acknowledge her existence as a disciple.

". . . the bylaws' detail is exquisite. The Nowerks, even the ones with brains, won't be able to wriggle out of this one . . ." Pura was still speaking.

Anoor relaxed her features every time the phrase "Nowerk" was used. The insult weighed heavy on her, and so did the truth.

Not one Ghosting in the room. Not one Ghosting ruling the land that is rightfully theirs.

She felt anger throb behind her eyes.

No, now is not the time to confront them, Anoor reasoned with herself. *First, we must deal with the tidewind.*

Then . . . retribution.

On and on Pura droned. With the sound of each "t" in the word *taxes*, Anoor slumped further down in her chair. Then the floor was passed to Warden Aveed, who was concerned by the dwindling number of Ghostings, and at that Anoor perked up.

"We're running low on Ghosting serving staff. I sent my team to recruit some of the younger Ghostings and found very few left in the squalor across the river."

"It's the sleeping sickness, it's killing them off," Pura grumbled, dismissing the topic with a wave of his hand.

Aveed's face flickered with an emotion Anoor couldn't read. Was it doubt? She sat forward, her heart beating in alarm.

"Yes, you're right," Aveed said. They tilted their head to their disciple, Faro, who was also musawa. They read from a list with a voice as thin and frail as their body:

"Over two hundred and fifty Ghostings died this year alone. An increase of nearly sixty percent from the year before." Faro's top lip was lined by the thinnest mustache Anoor had ever seen.

"Interesting," Uka said, making Anoor jump. Uka glanced at her and flared her nostrils before continuing. "And the birth rate is still down?"

"Yes, I took the liberty of looking into the abattoirs. There hasn't been a Ghosting cut for over a mooncycle," Aveed said.

"Hopefully they're dying off," Pura mumbled.

"You may say that, but who will be our servants then? The Dusters? Remember the night of the Stolen? Our children taken, right under our noses," Aveed said. They wore their hair in two plaits that ran to their waist. They were small, smaller than Anoor, but great was Aveed's power. The guild of duty was the largest of the four guilds. It encompassed all the plantations, skilled labor, and maintenance of the empire. If there were ever a war between the wardens, the guild of duty would crush the others in sheer numbers alone.

"Employ more of the lowly Embers. I hear the Al-Binras have been slandering the word of our God, claiming that the tidewind has been sent to punish the wardens." Pura laughed, but Anoor thought the smile didn't light up his face.

"Why don't we just force them into service?" Uka shrugged.

"You're suggesting introducing servitude as a form of punishment?" Aveed drummed their fingers on the table. Faro leaned forward and whispered in Aveed's ear. "We will consider it and put forward a bill."

Pura nodded. "That concludes our agenda for the day—"

Anoor cleared her throat, then choked on her spit.

"Disciple?" Pura raised a white eyebrow in her direction.

"I have a bill I would like to put forward," Anoor wheezed, as she stood to address the room.

Uka grabbed her arm with nails like eru claws. "Sit. Down. Now."

Anoor shrugged her off; though it hurt, she knew her mother wouldn't rupture her skin. Too risky.

"Proceed." Pura yawned, but the rest of the room watched her with beady eyes. Anoor looked down at her notes, though the ink swam before her like slippery eels she couldn't grasp.

"I-I would like to present a set of new laws, titled the Tidewind Relief Scheme. We all know the severity of the issue I am raising. The tidewind shows no signs of slowing—"

"Heresy. It is just one bad season," Qwa piped up, and Anoor was surprised at how loud his voice was. Like Pura he too wore the holy robes of the Abosom.

Because truth is religion and religion is truth. The thought rang with sarcasm in her mind.

"Disciple, hold your tongue until the end," Pura chastised Qwa.

Anoor tilted her head in recognition that she had been given permission to continue.

"No, it is not just one bad season," Anoor said with more confidence. She caught the look exchanged by Pura and Aveed. Anoor had once overheard them discussing the "siege from the sky." They knew it was growing deadlier by the day: they didn't want to admit the truth. The tidewind would one day kill them all.

"My suggestions are as follows:

"One, introduce a curfew to ensure no more needless death. All establishments must close between midnight and sixth strike. Those that lose significant livelihood owing to the curfew will be compensated."

There were some snorts, but a soft nod from Tanu emboldened her to go on.

"Two: set up a research laboratory to document and explore the tidewind's wrath."

"That's my jurisdiction," Wern, Warden of Knowledge, screeched. Anoor was prepared.

"Under bylaw two hundred and eighty-two, any member of the Upper Court seated at the table may introduce a bill that impacts any guild, if passed by the wardens."

"If," Wern spat back but then remained silent.

Anoor continued, "Three, set up tidewind relief shelters in all quarters including one in the Wardens' Keep—" The grumbles rose in crescendo as the wardens and their disciples openly guffawed at the suggestion. Anoor went on, shouting to be heard. "More villas are being destroyed than ever before and it is our responsibility to take care of every citizen of the empire, no matter their blood."

"Order. Order!" Pura was quivering with indignation, or the effort of having to stand from his chair, Anoor wasn't sure. Either way, the room went quiet and looked to him. "Disciple Anoor, how many points are on this 'Tidewind Relief Scheme'?"

"Twenty-five, Warden."

"And do you have these points written out?"

"Yes, Warden."

"Can I suggest, to prevent further calamity within these sacred walls, every member of the court read them on their own and the contents are debated at a later date?"

"But—"

Uka stood. "I agree, that sounds pertinent, Pura." Uka had remained as silent and stoic as a block of ice.

"No, it is my right to present my findings, under by—"

"Anoor, hold your tongue." Uka's words weren't loud, though everyone heard them and went silent. "You remain silent every day for a whole mooncycle within these chambers, and today you decide to speak?" It was the most out of control Anoor had ever seen her mother in public. Uka's eyes blazed, her jaw shook.

"I—"

"Sit down," Uka spat, then turned to the room. "I can only *apologize* for my disciple's impertinence."

Disciple, not daughter.

"It is no trouble, we were all young and impetuous once," Pura said, savoring Uka's apology like fine wine. "Now the day has gone away from us. We will reconvene tomorrow."

And that was that. Anoor sat humiliated in her seat. She busied herself with shuffling her papers, the sentences blurring from unshed tears. She let everyone file out first because she didn't want to hear the jaded whispers about her terrible presentation.

She had failed. Her first time trying to change things and she'd failed.

"Well, that was fun."

Anoor looked up into the crooked smile of Tanu. "Oh, yes, great fun."

Tanu's eyes and hair were the same shade of black. She kept the sides of her head shaved, with a thatch of curls spiking up to the sky on top. Her long, thin nose and her high cheekbones all added to the fine bird-like quality of her figure.

"You know you should have come to me first."

"Huh?" Anoor sniffed and dabbed at her nose with a handkerchief.

"You need to get allies to get these bills through the court."

"But the bylaws say I need to present them in session first."

"Fuck the bylaws, kid. This isn't school." Tanu rolled her eyes and picked up one of Anoor's reams of notes. Anoor ignored the use of "kid" even though she was older than Tanu's nineteen years of age. "Some of this is really clever. I like the lab idea. We need to start discovering ways to tackle the issue."

"You would have helped me? If I'd come to you first?"

"I wouldn't have agreed with all of it, but some of it, for sure. Didn't know you had the guts to suggest opening the Keep's doors to *all* blood colors, though," Tanu snorted.

Anoor smiled weakly. "I want to make a difference."

"You will. Just next time don't spook them. Meet with them. Put ideas in their head. You know, diplomacy and all that."

Anoor groaned.

Kwame moved out of the shadows and stood by Anoor's chair.

"Look, I've got to go, but I look forward to reading all twenty-five points." Tanu smirked and ducked out.

"I don't get her," Kwame commented. "She seems . . . secretive . . ."

"She's odd, yes. But I like her. She's very smart."

Kwame helped Anoor pack up her notes. "Your mother wants to see you for dinner."

A headache began to pound behind Anoor's right eye. "Here comes the scolding . . ."

"I've never seen her so mad. She was almost scarier than Gorn," Kwame laughed.

Anoor tried to join in.

As they left the courtroom she looked behind her and noticed that the patch of light streaming in from the window had shifted ever so slightly.

It cast her chair in shadow.

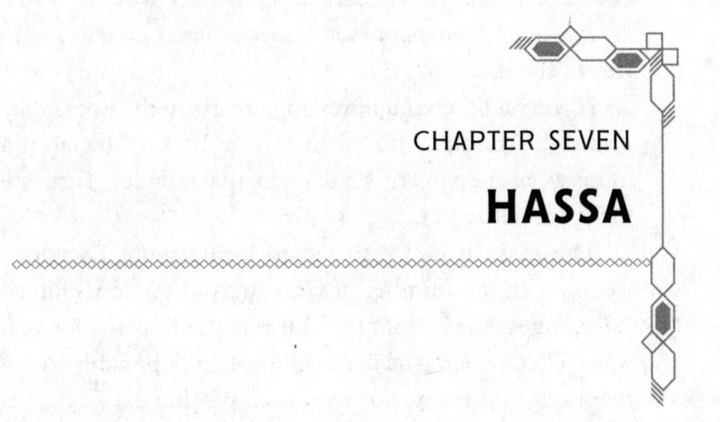

CHAPTER SEVEN

HASSA

As each day passes I become more and more intrigued by my granddaughter. There is a fire in her I never saw in Uka. She is the leader we have been waiting for.

—Extract from the journal of Yona Elsari,
former Warden of Strength, year 421

Hassa moved through the Dredge. She pressed the heels of her feet into the ground, then curled each of her toes down in succession. The movement was slow, but silent. She felt exposed above ground; she rarely moved through the city streets anymore. The tunnels underground were her domain—the Ghostings' domain. One day they would reclaim their land and move out of the darkness.

Hassa still rented a room at Maiden Turin's. Though she didn't work in the maiden house, her mother had been a nightworker and the guilt of her death kept Turin soft on Hassa. As soft as stone can be.

The maiden house had always provided more information than

anywhere else in the city. When Embers sought pleasure they said all sorts of things. Especially when they believed that Ghostings couldn't speak. But Embers thought voice was just a sound.

It is much more than that. It is with my voice that I share all their secrets, she thought.

Hassa had grown up pressing her ear to the doors. She'd memorized the triumphant murmurs from Ember officials that slipped in between the violent sexual acts that Maiden Turin's establishment specialized in.

The maiden had resorted to hiring more Dusters in recent weeks, with the number of Ghostings in the city falling from the "sleeping sickness" that the elders had fabricated for years. Hassa was still convincing as many Ghostings as possible to let her help them out of the city, but with each passing day, it became harder to uphold the ruse.

If a house was found to have had the sleeping sickness, a black cross was painted on the door to prevent anyone else coming in. Only kin could enter and extract the body, which was then immediately burned. These small elements of deception had allowed the Ghostings to covertly disappear over the course of ten years.

Hassa had never been to the Chrysalis herself. Though she yearned to make the journey, she knew Anoor needed her.

Thud. Thud. Thud.

She heard the trudge of boots and slipped off the main road to hide behind a tidewind-damaged wall. A group of officers on patrol was heading toward her. She listened to their chatter as they walked past her hiding spot.

"Found another body in the north of the Dredge."

"Another one?"

"Yes, Warden Uka has ordered us to bury any we find. But I ain't touching a dead Duster."

"Why are we burying them?"

"No idea, but I tell you this, I'm just going to drag them out in the street and wait for nightfall. Tidewind can take them."

Their laughing echoed around the empty street as they disappeared from Hassa's view.

More patrols in the Dredge than I have ever seen before. What is Uka up to?

Hassa dragged her thoughts back to the task at hand.

The villa in front of her was quiet, but not silent. Hassa could see the flicker of movement behind the tidewind shutters.

She rubbed her arms together, the cotton of her brown servant's garb chafing her skin. The uniform was Hassa's true power: it allowed her to get into the Keep and meet up with Anoor whenever she wanted, despite never having worked anywhere officially. Hassa had been cut from her mother's dead body after her father, a client at Turin's, had murdered her for getting pregnant. Mixed blood couplings were illegal and would have put both parents in jeopardy. The man who had fathered her had been the son of an imir but Hassa wasn't sure about the details. She didn't care to know who he was.

The tidewind shutters opened in front of her, the screech of the rickety wood coincided with the pulling of a lever on the other side. Anoor's tidewind shutters were bloodwerk operated. One yank on the switch and they pirouetted up, tucking under the architrave of the window. Hassa loved yanking on that switch every morning.

Hassa pushed herself into the crumbling ruins of the villa opposite the one she was watching. The Dredge was in a bad state, worse than she'd ever seen it. The tidewind was pummeling the foundations of every limestone villa. Limestone, of course, because it was cheap. The Embers hadn't wanted to waste money on mere Ghostings when they built this quarter, four hundred years ago.

The villa she was spying on was a shop. Above the door hung a broken blade, the edge shattered and tarnished. As it was illegal for anyone but Embers to write, shopkeepers had to use tokens in order to distinguish their stores. The tokens tended to be unique, personal things specific to each store that could help to direct customers to the right place. It was pointless if every apothecary used the same symbol; you'd never know which one to go to. And Hassa always went to this one, as she liked the owner the most.

The door to the apothecary opened and a woman appeared. She had a wide nose that spread flat against her face and large eyes that dipped down at the corners. Her hair hung in short twists by her ears. She clutched a shawl against her shoulders, but Hassa saw the maroon fabric underneath before she closed it. The maroon fabric of a member of the wardens' army.

The woman marched out into the street and disappeared around a corner. Hassa stayed watching the store, waiting for the second occupant to make their appearance. And they did, not long after.

Hassa recognized her limping gait and the sound her cane made as she moved across the Dredge. Like Hassa, she had affirmed her gender as that of a woman. Hassa only knew this because the woman was the storekeeper who sold her the hormone herbs that supported Hassa's growth. Ren was her name. And Hassa knew, without having to see the branding burned into her wrist—the only real difference between Embers and Dusters without slicing them open—that the woman heading out into the street was a Duster.

An Ember and a Duster awakening under the same roof, that *was knowledge worth having.*

Hassa savored the words with her phantom tongue.

"The joba tree . . . is a fish?"

Hassa's face creased with mirth.

No, "the joba tree moves in the wind." Watch my arm now. She signed the two words. *This is fish. This is wind.* Both had a ripple-like movement, but fish included the downward flick of her elbow.

Kwame nodded deeply, his face the perfect picture of sincerity.

You have no idea what I just said, do you?

His face crumpled in distress. "I know what you said *then*. I'm sorry, I'm trying so hard. Thank you for the extra lessons."

After giving her report about the officer to Gorn, Hassa went to Kwame's chambers for lunch and their daily lesson.

It is a hard language to understand. Even Sylah took years to truly be fluent in reading my signs. You will get there with lots of practice. We'll have to spend more time together, you and I. I hope that won't be a problem.

"Sylah took years?"

Of course, that was the only thing he'd picked up from her words. Hassa sniffed and reached for her tea. She surveyed Kwame over the rim of her cup.

He had just returned from court and wore his formal clothes that gave definition to his narrow form. He sat hunched on the sofa in front of her waiting patiently for the next thing to learn.

Hassa had been coming to Kwame's rooms every day for the last mooncycle. Sometimes they met at night, sometimes in the day. He had struggled to pick up the Ghosting language, more so than either Gorn or Anoor. So, when he had shyly asked for further help, Hassa couldn't turn him down.

Since becoming Anoor's adviser he'd let his hair grow longer. Each curl was slick with rose-scented oil. Though the aroma was a little overbearing, Hassa found she liked it.

"Did you hear what happened in the courtroom earlier?"

Hassa nodded; she'd spoken to Gorn on her way to meet him.

"Uka was so mad. She's asked Anoor to dinner." His grin dipped downward. "I hope she'll be all right."

Hassa was surprised by the flicker of jealousy she felt as she saw the unabashed concern for Anoor. She followed the contours of his face until his frown turned into a tentative smile.

"What are you looking at?"

I'm thinking about how attractive you are. Hassa signed quickly, knowing there was no way he understood what she meant.

His eyes narrowed. "What?"

I have to go, there are a few things I need to do today, she signed more slowly, and he nodded.

"Gorn having you work hard?"

Hassa scowled. Gorn was not her master. Neither was Anoor for that matter. She helped them because their alliance would one day help the Ghostings. And because she liked them. With Sylah and the majority of the Ghostings gone, Hassa found she was lonely in the city that was her home.

No, what I have to do is Ghosting business.

Kwame nodded slowly. He respected her privacy.

"Same time tomorrow?"

Same. Time. Tomorrow. She turned his last words into a final lesson.

"Oh interesting, 'tomorrow' includes a backward push with your forearm."

Hassa laughed and got up to leave.

"Anyme bless," he said at her retreating back.

Hassa gave him a sly smile and slipped out of his chambers.

HASSA PLANNED TO spend the night in the tunnels beneath the city. She caught a few strikes of sleep in the afternoon in preparation for her investigation. Tonight, she was sneaking into Loot's chambers.

Her limbs brushed against the damp wall of the tunnel, her other arm holding a runelamp in the crook of her elbow. It illuminated the dark passage with a familiar red glow.

Hassa sighed and shoved the lamp into her open satchel. The darkness was absolute. She couldn't risk one of Loot's Gummers finding her so deep in his lair.

Not that anyone has seen him in weeks. She scowled, hating the void of information that surrounded Loot's disappearance.

Hassa was used to knowing everything. She'd been a spy from the moment she could sign. Now, with the elders gone, her purpose had diminished. To fill her time with purpose, she'd been working with Gorn to secure information to support Anoor's rule.

Hassa liked the work. It kept her busy, and she liked Gorn, too; the woman reminded her of Marigold, the person who had raised her.

Grief squeezed her lungs and Hassa exhaled loudly through her teeth. It had only been a few mooncycles since the tidewind had killed the only real parent she'd ever had, and the anguish of their passing haunted Hassa still. What would Marigold say if they could see Hassa now?

You're walking into the spider's web. You foolish girl, they'd say.

Hassa smiled at the words she'd conjured in her mind. Distracted, it took her a moment to realize the sounds ahead of her weren't her imagination.

". . . well, if you didn't kill them, and I didn't kill them . . ."

Hassa pushed herself flat against the wall. She was glad that she had turned off the runelamp early as a precaution. The light from the talking Gummers appeared from behind a corner.

"No, I didn't kill them."

"Well, if neither of us issued the order, then who?" The Gummer had a nasal voice that made Hassa wince.

"It has to be the Warden of Crime."

"But no one's seen the warden since he went off to fight the betrayer."

The betrayer? Sylah?

The two Gummers moved ahead of Hassa, crossing over to another tunnel. She followed them twenty handspans behind.

"Could it be that another crimelord has moved into the city?"

"No, they know Loot wouldn't allow it."

"But where is he? If I were a crimelord I'd take advantage of the situation, move in on his territory."

"I suppose . . ."

Another crimelord? Hassa rubbed her limb over her eye as a wave of exhaustion struck her. She couldn't deal with yet another enemy.

"It's the only solution. Why else would there be so many bodies turning up? They think that the tidewind is covering their tracks, but we know the signs . . ."

"What did you do with the body?"

"Sent the cleanup crew, but they're spread thin already. A lot of Gummers have been stepping out of line with the warden gone. I've had to issue more deaths than usual."

"Are you *sure* the bodies aren't yours?"

The woman ground her teeth.

"Yes, they are not mine. I wouldn't be so callous as to dump them in the street before sunset."

This was more information than Hassa had hoped for. She paused, letting the two Gummers disappear off into the Belly, also known as Loot's headquarters.

Once their voices disappeared, she slipped a limb into her satchel and tugged on the strip of yellow fabric there. She tied it around her waist quickly. It distinguished her as one of Loot's Ghosting servants. Hassa had a whole box of sashes of different kente patterns. The simple deception allowed her to drift between jobs without being detected.

The runelamps in Loot's chambers were a clear bright red, made from refined glass so the globes were almost translucent, unmarred by the blue sand from the Farsai Desert. The two Gummers relaxed in chairs in the main room. They twitched as Hassa entered.

"What are you doing here? I dismissed all the servants." It was the Gummer with the nasally voice. He was larger than Hassa expected, with crooked eyes and a scar along his jaw.

I'm a spy here to learn all I can about your idiot leader so I can ensure he's not plotting to kill my friend, Hassa signed.

"Eyoh, don't flap your arms at me, no one knows what you're saying." The Gummer spat on the floor by Hassa's feet.

Exactly, you disgusting lout.

"Just let her clean, no one's been in here for ages." The other Gummer sighed. Hassa recognized her. Dredge-dwellers called her the Purger; she was Loot's personal assassin. The first tendril of fear unfurled in Hassa's stomach.

"Fine, clean. But be quick."

Gladly.

Hassa pulled out her duster from her satchel and strapped it to her arm. She headed to the books first. Loot had a lot of books, so many he lined the walls with them.

There must be a clue there, Hassa thought.

After fifteen minutes, Hassa's arm cramped. She'd found nothing among the tomes except dust and spiders. She padded to his desk, her eyes darting around the room to check the status of the Gummers. They both paid her no mind.

Idiots.

The three-legged stool that Loot used to sit on was upturned and she could see the letters Y.E. engraved on the underside. Word on the tidewind was that Loot had stolen it from Yona Elsari's privy room when she was warden.

Hassa dismissed the stool and turned to the letters on the desk. Letters that would have got Loot killed if an officer had seen them. Dusters were not allowed to write.

She used the feather brush to separate the pages silently, her eyes reading as quickly as she could. Elder Zero had taught Hassa to read, as Ghostings weren't permitted to go to school, but Hassa rarely got a chance to exercise the skill.

There was nothing of note on the table. One letter detailing the smuggling capacity of an eru wagon, the other a list of contenders for the Ring, the fighting tournament Loot fronted. The final paper was a scribble and Hassa was about to rifle past it until she recognized the shape of it.

Two curved blades crossing over a shield, the symbol for the guild of strength. Beneath it there was just one word.

Mine.

HASSA FOUND NOTHING else in Loot's chambers that shed light on his disappearance. It was as if the man had vanished like the tidewind in the morning, and as with the tidewind, she dreaded his return.

Dawn creased the sky as she left the darkness of the tunnels beneath her. It was time to wake Anoor. But when she arrived at Anoor's chambers, her bed hadn't been slept in. Hassa knocked on Gorn's door. It was early, even for Anoor's chief of staff, but Hassa always spent the first few strikes of the morning with Anoor.

"Hassa?" Gorn cracked open her bedroom door, her eyes

blurred with sleep. "What time is it?" she asked, quickly followed by, "What's happened?"

Gorn had also been learning the Ghosting language, although she was picking it up less quickly than Anoor, given the lack of time the two of them had together.

Anoor is gone. Hassa had to sign painstakingly slowly.

"Gone?" Gorn confirmed the translation and Hassa nodded. Gorn disappeared from the crack in her door, and it swung open to reveal a messy desk and an already-made bed. Papers fluttered in the breeze Gorn made as she pulled on her robe over her night-clothes. She bustled out and walked with purpose toward Anoor's bedroom.

As Hassa confirmed, Anoor was not there. Gorn checked the privy twice. Once her search was complete, she stood in the center of the room. Though Gorn's large cuboid face didn't twitch, Hassa knew from the stiffness of her shoulders she was worried.

"I'll wake Kwame. You look in the kitchens. She might have gone for a snack," Gorn said.

They separated at the front door to the chambers, Hassa going down the stairs and Gorn going next door to wake Kwame.

It was easy for Hassa to slip into the goings-on in the kitchen. She'd pretended to work there enough times that when a cook turned to her and asked her to pass a ladle, Hassa knew exactly where it was.

As she clutched it between her wrists and passed it to the cook, someone touched her on the shoulder. Hassa knew it wasn't Anoor, but still she hoped as she turned to meet the Ghosting.

Hassa. The Ghosting that greeted her was one of the few who had refused to move out of the city. Hassa had been trying to convince them for mooncycles, but the man was too stubborn. He liked his life of servitude.

Sami, Hassa greeted him back.

Did you hear about the murder last night?

What?

I haven't heard much, only that someone died in Uka Elsari's chambers, Sami signed.

Anoor. Anoor was supposed to have had dinner with her mother last night. Kwame had told Hassa during their teaching session yesterday.

Hassa didn't wait to hear more. She elbowed her way past Sami and leaped back up the stairs as fast as her small body would carry her.

CHAPTER EIGHT

ANOOR

Aol uld slhkly vm aol Zhukzavyt dpss thrl aoltzlsclz ruvdu. Mvy uvd, jvuapubl hz dl ohcl wshuulk. Code 7.

Decoded translation: The new leader of the Sandstorm will make themselves known. For now, continue as we have planned.

—Letter found in the bin of the schoolroom at the Keep

After the farce in the courtroom that morning, Anoor made her way to the kitchens. Despite the chaotic energy of cooks at work, the kitchens always soothed her frayed nerves. The noise helped to distract her from her thoughts. She took a shortcut diagonally through the courtyard. As she neared the kitchens, she felt something on her face. She touched her cheek, and it came away wet.

Am I crying? she thought numbly. Then she looked to the sky and felt the light caress of rain.

Rain was so rare in the empire. Summer showers were even rarer.

The tempo of the falling rain grew faster, flattening Anoor's curls to her head.

She saw servants dashing for the cover of the cloisters and laughed. Did they not realize how good standing in the rain felt? How cleansing?

The rain shower only lasted a few minutes, but it flooded the courtyard, turning the cobblestones blue with mud. The clouds were already departing, and the afternoon sun would evaporate all evidence of the rain in a strike, maybe less.

Once the sun's rays struck her forehead, Anoor continued on her way.

Her mother had thought to embarrass her daughter by providing her with chambers above the servants' quarters, but Anoor loved it. She stood under the kitchen doorway and watched the workers toil.

There were few Ghostings left working within the halls of the Keep, but here in the kitchens a group of eight was cleaning crockery and stirring stews. Anoor watched them and wondered why they hadn't left the city with their brethren. Hassa had said a few of the servants had refused, preferring the stability of their life here rather than leaving with the elders. Others had decided to stay behind to keep the Embers from getting too suspicious.

Not that it had worked, if today's court meeting was anything to go on. Aveed was investigating the disease, and if they looked too closely, they'd find nothing at all. Anoor made a note to tell Hassa later.

An elderly cook spotted Anoor leaning against the archway. "Disciple Anoor, is there anything we can get you?"

The servants in the kitchen paused at the cook's words. They turned to look at Anoor as if they were rabbits and Anoor was pointing a bow and arrow at them.

"Disciple?" The cook gently prodded again, then gulped at the fear of being too presumptuous.

Cook Eren had known Anoor for years. He'd made her hundreds of dishes and watched her grow up under the foot of every servant in the kitchen. Now he stood in front of her *gulping*.

"No, I'm fine, thank you, Eren. Please, everyone, continue your work, don't let me intrude."

Eren gave a sheepish nod and ambled off. He was known to bark orders at the other cooks. But now Anoor watched him politely asking for some chopped greens.

She tipped back her head and sighed. This was not how she had expected power to feel. She dragged her feet away from the kitchen and up the stairs, Eren's voice increasing in volume as she went. She only had a few strikes before meeting her mother for dinner and she needed to debrief her team.

"WELL, THAT WAS a disaster," Anoor said, bursting into Gorn's room. She'd left her sodden shoes by the doorway, but still she trailed droplets of rainwater.

Gorn was sitting at her desk, a pile of papers stacked to one side, her notes in front of her. Anoor's eyes glossed over some of the book titles that lined a shelf above: *Criminal Logistics* and *Murders and Law.*

Interesting research for a chief of staff, Anoor thought, but dismissed her interest once she saw Gorn's open collar.

Though Gorn no longer wore the crimson pinafore required of Ember servants, she hadn't strayed from the same basic style of the uniform despite Anoor trying on multiple occasions to remake her wardrobe. She still wore stiff pinafores over a white shirt, but today it was blue instead of the Ember servants' red. She usually wore them buttoned to the neck, but now the collar flapped open, crumpled at the corners from her tugging at the fabric. It was a sign of how stressed Gorn was.

"You heard," Anoor stated, flatly.

"Kwame stopped by on his way to his lesson with Hassa. He'll be back soon. Are you all right?"

"Let's wait for him in the living room." Anoor turned on her heel and left.

Although she had a desk in her mother's office, Anoor had yet to use it. Being in such close proximity to her mother made her itch. The years of abuse hadn't faded; like a scar, the marks remained. But it wasn't a scar, not really, it was a wound that masqueraded as a scar, and being near her mother made it bleed all the more.

Anoor stomped through the living-room doors with a sigh loud enough to let the whole Keep know she was miserable.

"Oh!"

The room was not empty.

Staring at her with the biggest eyes Anoor had ever seen was a woman of middling years, though it was only the crinkles in the corner of her downward eyes that revealed her age. Her black hair was woven into twists that hung short by her ears. It wasn't just her presence that startled Anoor, but the uniform she wore: the bruised purple of the wardens' army.

"Disciple." The woman stood and clapped the back of her right hand against the back of her left in an opened-hand salute. The higher the hands, the higher the authority. As second-in-command to the head of the army, her mother, Anoor warranted a salute at chin level.

The woman held her saluting hand firm in front of her mouth. Anoor hovered awkwardly, not wanting to sit while the woman was still standing.

Then the right words came to Anoor; she'd seen her mother use the phrase enough times to know.

"At ease," she murmured, and the woman relaxed as much as she was able. Her back still seemed straighter than the chair itself.

Anoor sank into her favorite armchair and watched the guest from under her lashes. She let out a sigh of relief when she heard the clinking of the tea tray from down the hall. No matter how many times she reminded Kwame that he was no longer a servant, he still insisted on bringing up their food and drink himself.

"Hello," Kwame said, pausing in the doorway. "Who's this?"

"I was hoping you might know." Anoor frowned, her heartbeat quickening. Could this person be a spy? Or an agent of the Sandstorm here to kill her? Loot surely wanted her dead for stealing the title of disciple from Jond.

No, a spy wouldn't have just walked in off the street, in an army uniform no less. Anoor tensed her muscles anyway. They were already sore from her nightly Nuba practice. The formation-based exercise had become an important staple of her nightly routine, ever since Sylah had started training her half a year ago.

Half a year. Was that all?

Anoor found herself immersed in the memory of one of Sylah's rare smiles. The curve of her lips as they parted, how the left side was a little crooked, which made her all the more alluring, especially when the smile was made for Anoor. Just for Anoor.

Kwame placed the tea on the table with a clatter, rudely interrupting Anoor's thoughts. A teacup fell to the floor and shattered against the marble. Kwame ignored it as he rounded on the newcomer.

"Who are you and who let you in here?"

"Calm down, Kwame," Gorn said, her small triangle mouth pulled taut. She entered the living room and perched on one of the footstools. She began picking up the shards of the broken teacup. "Anoor, Kwame, meet Captain Zuhari. I hired her into your Shadow Court today."

Anoor's eyes widened, not quite as large as Zuhari's but close. "*You* hired her?"

"Yes, I told you I was conducting interviews. You told me to do as I see fit, and as your chief of staff I need, well, *more staff.*"

"And she's to join our Shadow Court as an adviser?" Kwame asked, reaching for the tea Gorn proffered.

Anoor held out her hand to Gorn. "No sugar, please."

Gorn started pouring a fresh cup as she continued, "We needed someone with actual military experience. I know you've been trying hard, Kwame, but we don't have the time to sit around and wait for you to catch up with the other advisers under Uka who've been working in the army for decades. I took a shortcut. I hired the best of the best."

The introduction seemed to be a cue for Zuhari. She once again stood and saluted.

"I trained as a foot soldier for ten years before becoming an officer. I was the head of security at your mother's first Aktibar, after which I was promoted to captain. I worked in the coal mines of Jin-Hidal where I fought against the miners' strike and the revolt of the hundred. Although I am no longer part of the wardens' army—"

"What? She's not even part of the army anymore. Why is she even wearing the uniform? What's the blinking point?" Kwame exclaimed.

Zuhari leveled her gaze at Kwame. "Although I am no longer a part of the wardens' army, I wear these colors as a reminder of a promise I once made. A promise to protect and uphold the law for *everyone* in this empire—"

"I doubt my mother was thinking of *everyone* when she had you pledge that vow on your initiation," Anoor said dryly.

Zuhari's mouth snapped shut and she turned a curious gaze on Anoor.

"This is nonsense." Kwame stood to further project his anger. "How can we trust her with our plans? With the truth?"

"Sit down, Kwame, I'll handle this." Gorn took a sip of her tea and looked at Anoor.

"Kwame's right. How can we trust her with the truth?" Anoor said.

"Aha," Kwame exclaimed, clutching at the last shreds of his pride. Here was someone with the experience to advise Anoor on the ins and outs of the military, not a former servant like him. Anoor gave him a kindly smile.

Gorn continued, "Zuhari was dismissed from the army for smuggling Dusters *out* of the coal mines of Jin-Hidal. It was only because the Dusters attested that it was the first time she had done it that she isn't rotting in jail right now. The Dusters, of course, well, they got the rack."

Anoor and Zuhari shivered in time with each other. Anoor thought of the last time she had seen a ripping. The popping of the joints as the rack's jaws opened still haunted her. The sound of flesh ripped as the prisoner was stretched across the device wasn't something she was ever going to forget.

"She might be sympathetic to our cause," Kwame said. "But it could kill us all if the truth got out."

Zuhari shifted, looking between Gorn and Kwame, her mouth

open, ready to interrupt. But no one was capable of interrupting Gorn.

"Kwame, can I remind you that Anoor chose me for this job because she trusts me? And in turn, my work?"

Kwame looked thoroughly chastised, his usual grin sagging.

"You can tell them," Zuhari said.

"Tell us what?" Anoor leaned in. Her love of literature and adventure hadn't been damped by the secrets that had ruined her life.

"My lover is a Duster," Zuhari said.

Gorn inclined her head.

"Oh." Anoor wondered how Gorn had found it out, then remembered Hassa. The Ghosting could get anywhere.

"And though we're not in the business of threats—you don't need to remind me, we are not your mother's advisers—Zuhari knows what can happen if the truth somehow . . . slips out of our Shadow Court," Gorn said.

Anoor nodded, pleased that they had some leverage. She inhaled deeply, steadying her heartbeat. It was never easy baring her truth, but it needed to be done.

Anoor said in a level voice, "Captain Zuhari, welcome to my Shadow Court. There are three things you need to know. One: the whole empire's in danger because the tidewind is only going to get worse. Two: the founding wardens learned bloodwerk from the Ghostings and stole their land. Three: the Ending Fire never happened and there's a whole world of other countries out there."

If Anoor thought Zuhari's eyes were wide before, now they threatened to swallow her eyebrows.

"Anoor, you're missing one tiny thing . . ." Kwame said quietly.

"I guess there are four things . . ." Anoor picked up a shard of the broken teacup and held it to the underside of her arm beneath her sleeve. She made the smallest of wounds. "I'm a Duster."

Zuhari watched the blue blood swell and sank back limply in her chair.

It took them four strikes to bring Zuhari up to speed. Kwame slipped out after the first strike claiming he had errands to run, but Anoor suspected he was visiting his sickly father. Gorn had told her that he hadn't been well, and Anoor didn't press him for details on where he was going.

After the initial shock Zuhari listened intently, asking intelligent questions and concluding that anyone could bloodwerk without Anoor having to explain it. She was reserved, but clearly tenacious, and Anoor soon found herself feeling pleased Gorn had hired her.

"I have to go, my mother's expecting me for dinner." Anoor shriveled within herself at the thought of dinner with her mother. "Zuhari, I have acquired the chambers next to mine for my Shadow Court—"

"I prefer to stay at my home, in the Dredge."

It made sense that she wanted to live somewhere that a Duster wasn't barred from. The Keep only allowed Ghosting servants and Embers behind the walls. Something else Anoor wanted to change: it was also a tenet of her Tidewind Relief Bill.

Anoor made her goodbyes and went to her bedroom to dress. She pulled down the shutters in anticipation of an early visit from the tidewind. One of the slats had become a little loose and she reminded herself to get it repaired before long.

Her dressing-room door was open, and she could see the two sides glinting in the runelight. One wall held her training weapons. On the other were her clothes. She could no longer train in the tower where she'd spent so many nights with Sylah. Every shadow looked like her, every sound reminded Anoor of Sylah's voice. So one evening she'd lugged all her gear back into her chambers.

Her journal sat open on her desk. It documented her day, along with her thoughts and dreams for the empire. Uka had given her the red-colored diary on the Day of Ascent. Journaling their days was a requirement of every disciple and warden.

"Tell the truth or Anyme will know you insult them," Uka had growled as she handed over the book.

"The truth? Everything?" *Even about my blue blood?*

"Everything," Uka said with the devout firmness of the Abosom. She never strayed from the path of righteousness, following the law to the word. Except when it came to Anoor—she hadn't given *her* up when the Sandstorm had swapped her for another.

"But the truth could ruin you." Anoor had always wondered why her mother had spoken the truth in her journals, knowing that the other wardens could read them in the future.

Uka laughed through her nose and it sounded like a snake hissing. "There is so much truth in the warden library, Anoor, your little secret is insignificant among the lies the empire has been telling. Write the truth. It is my only advice to you." She sneered. "Besides, no one will even read it. You think the wardens care what some disciple thinks? No, the law compelling us to document our days wasn't put in place to 'educate' future leaders. It was to unburden us. And to make sure that somewhere in this world of lies, the truth is written bare."

You want the truth, Mother?

Anoor sat at her desk and wrote.

My mother doesn't trust me. My mother doesn't care. She will plague my reign as disciple, and I can barely stand it. The Tidewind Relief Bill is one of the greatest pieces of legislation in the last ten years. It will make a huge impact on those most afflicted by the tidewind. She does not listen.

Maybe my mother should spend the night in the Dredge and perhaps then she would understand.

But she wouldn't survive one night in the Dredge. Though that wouldn't be a bad thing.

"Do you need help getting ready?" Gorn appeared suddenly in the doorway, making Anoor jump. She dropped her pen and shut her journal. As she closed the notebook, the gesture closed off her anger for the time being.

"No, I'm okay, Gorn, you don't have to do that anymore."

"I want to," she said, heading into the dressing room to retrieve a suit. "How about this?"

It was a bright blue blazer Anoor had recently acquired from a tailor in the Duster Quarter. Anoor gave Gorn a wicked grin.

Blue like my dirty blood.

"My mother would *hate* it."

Gorn chuckled and began to undo the buttons. It was more comforting than Gorn knew for Anoor to have someone here for her while she got ready. She hated being in her bedroom alone. The ghost of Sylah always slinked out of the folds of her clothes or the blanket on her four-poster bed.

Gorn tied a thin gold necklace around Anoor's neck. "There, all done."

Anoor looked at herself in the mirror. Hard, hazel eyes looked back at her. The blazer was corseted and pulled in Anoor's waist, adding angles she hadn't had before. She looked both frightening and fierce.

"I have to go out this evening. I'll be back before your dinner is over," Gorn said.

"Now? What do you have to do so late in the day?" Anoor heard the call of half a strike past six. She should leave soon.

"I have to take care of some personal matters. But I do have to go." Gorn's eyes moved skittishly.

"Okay, I'll see you soon." As Gorn turned to leave Anoor whispered, "How am I going to make any changes, Gorn, if she won't listen to me? If none of them listen to me?"

"We'll figure it out, but for now, just smile politely and eat. One strike, maybe two, and you'll be back home. A new zine came out today, I've put it by the bathtub so you can read it when you get back."

Anoor smiled; she'd been looking forward to this installment. Inquisitor Abena had just discovered the murder weapon at the eru races in Jin-Sahalia. Anoor wondered if the culprit she suspected would be revealed.

"Thank you, Gorn, I'll see you later."

LIKE THE REST of the wardens, her mother lived on the west side of the Keep. Her balcony overlooked the gardens and the cliffs above the Marion Sea. By the time Anoor got there she was well and truly late.

"Hi, Rasa." Uka's chief of chambers met Anoor at the door. Her hair fanned around her like a palm frond despite the hair tie that tried to tame it.

"You're late, Disciple." The title was bitter between her lips. Rasa knew how much Anoor's mother hated her, and she was ever the loyalist.

"I will apologize to the warden. Is she . . . ?"

"In the formal dining room. I will escort you."

"I think I can find my own way in my *family* home."

Rasa sniffed. "As you wish." She moved out of the way and Anoor entered her mother's chambers. The smell of lilies hit her like a physical barrier that she needed to wade through. Her mother always had the flower in her room, and now the scent was laden with the memories of pain and abuse.

Anoor noticed fewer carp in the pond in the foyer and wondered if the stink of the lilies had killed them. She moved through the corridors toward the formal dining room, lit by chandeliers that shone blood-red.

She walked past her old chambers and saw the oil painting of a child next to her bed. Few would notice that the image wasn't of Anoor, that in fact it was a portrait of Uka's true Ember daughter. Sylah had once believed it had been her, but the thin scar on the side of the babe's face had identified her as someone else.

Fareen, she'd been called. Uka had given Anoor the painting to remind her that she would always be lesser than her mother's true child.

How wrong my mother was.

Anoor knocked on the dining-room door, and after hearing no answer, she entered. The balcony door was open, letting in wind that billowed the gold curtains and sent a chill around the room.

Her mother sat at the head of the table, the food already laid out in front of her. She wore a gray dress with a bloom of red that spread from the neckline to the bodice. Her expression was one of anger, her lips pulled into a scowl, and Anoor involuntarily winced and looked to the floor.

"I'm sorry I'm late, Warden." Her mother couldn't abide being called "mother," even in private. "I know you must be extremely vexed with me and I understand it. But I didn't tell you for a reason: I do not need your permission to go forth in front of the court."

The balcony door rattled and then slammed wide open in the wind. Anoor kept speaking as she went to close it. "I will always approach things differently from you. As you well know, I am different from everyone else in that courtroom, and not just in blood color. The Upper Court needs to change. It is archaic and bigoted and based on a foundation of lies. Yes, I have been reading the other journals in the warden library. I know that the founding wardens stole the land right from under the Ghostings.

"So I know tonight you may want to argue about what I did, going behind your back. But the truth is, the Ghostings are the real victims in all your lies."

After she locked the balcony door, Anoor took a seat at the far end of the table. Her mother still hadn't said a word.

"No matter what you may think, I will keep pushing forward with my agenda, because while you tackle the small details of how many empty jail cells we have . . . I'm going to deal with the real problems at the heart of this empire." Anoor slammed her fist on the table—a gesture she had read about in her zines, had even seen her mother make once or twice, but never made herself. It felt *good.*

She looked up from the table and locked eyes with her mother. "Warden?"

Uka's eyes were as still as a beetle embalmed in resin.

"Mother?"

Anoor pushed herself away from the table, knocking over a

bottle of red wine. The wine stain bloomed on the white tablecloth until it slowly drip, drip, dripped onto her mother's unresponsive lap.

It merged with the blood that already pooled there.

Warden Uka was dead.

CHAPTER NINE

NAYELI

Yellow Commune is logical, leaders one and all
Green is full of passion, lovers standing tall
Orange Commune is clever, wise, and astute
Violet will tell no lies, truth sayers absolute
Indigo Commune will protect, friends they'll save
Red will lend their strength, fighters are the brave
Blue Commune will do their best, dutiful to the end
Clear will take care, reliable, you can depend.

—Lullaby sung by the Ancients on the Volcane Isles

Nayeli was ten when they first put her to work in the Foundry. She was a little younger than the other children there, but she had always surpassed her peers in skill.

The master crafter dragged his feet as he led the new cohort of novices through the Foundry, bored by the same routine. His speech was just as slow as his ambling feet as he said, "This here is the canteen."

Small windows tiled one side of the room. The glass was small enough to replace when there was an earthquake. Nayeli took a step toward the windows and looked down onto the town of the Yellow Commune. Huts dotted the black hills. The sea curved out beyond their yellowing palm-leaf roofs. Nayeli could see fishermen in the bay that separated the three isles. The smell of hydrogen sulfide wafted in from the volcanic craters that ruptured across the islands like boils. They were what gave her home its name: the Volcane Isles.

She stepped out of the weak sunlight streaming from the windows and brought her attention back to the Foundry. Built into the cliffside of the isles' rocky terrain, it was the center of machine production for the Yellow Commune. The air was filled with the sound of grinding metal and silent work, and Nayeli's fingers itched for her tools.

The master crafter spoke. "The canteen is where we have lunch at the noon bell. Food is served at that time only. If you miss your allocated time, then you go hungry." His mouth was like a puckered anus housing blackened teeth that made Nayeli wonder about his personal hygiene.

"What about the moon bell meal, is that also served here?" Nayeli asked. She caught the flashes of white as the other novices rolled their eyes.

"You are not required to work in the Foundry past sunset." The master crafter dismissed her and ushered the children further into the gut of the Foundry.

"But what if I want to?" Nayeli lifted her chin.

He let out an impatient sigh. "You are not required to work in the Foundry past sunset."

Nayeli cocked her head. Her hair was scraped back tightly into a practical knot at the top of her head, and she felt her scalp stretching from the tension.

"I heard you say that the first time. But I intend to be the youngest master crafter one day."

The master crafter looked as if he had swallowed his tongue. Nayeli was about to inquire if that was the case, but then he spoke again.

"The youngest master crafter? We shall see. We shall see." Nayeli didn't recognize the sarcasm in his voice; instead she heard the challenge she wanted.

"It *will* happen," she confirmed.

It hadn't really occurred to Nayeli that if she were to become master crafter, the current one would have to die, or be sacked by the commune leader. There was only one master crafter, and only one foundry.

"So will—" she was about to ask again, but the master crafter's eyes narrowed and he barked.

"No food will be provided after sunset. You stay late, you bring your own food."

Nayeli nodded sharply. That was fine. She was good at fishing, she could dry her own fillets and eat them while she worked. She wouldn't even need to stop working.

The master crafter led them toward the main warehouse of the Foundry. Rows and rows of workbenches filled the hall, and the scent of metal permeated the air. For the first time in her life Nayeli couldn't smell the sulphur from the volcanoes. Crafters moved like ants around the Foundry, their arms swinging up and down as they carved and manipulated the metal in front of them.

The flicker of yellow drew Nayeli's eyes to her right.

The Foundry's furnace burned at the far corner of the room. Far enough away that the heat didn't disrupt the crafters' productivity. An unlucky few were assigned the task of smelting the iron ore found beneath the Volcane Isles' surface. Just looking at them brought sweat to Nayeli's brow.

People often thought that fire was a destructive force, but Nayeli knew it for what it was.

Fire can forge. Fire can create.

"These are your benches." The master crafter pulled her from the hypnotic glow of the furnace as he waved to a cluster of small workspaces. "You will be given your assignments by your team leaders. Heed them. Because if you don't . . ." His eyes narrowed on Nayeli's. ". . . they'll send you to me, and I am not known for my kindness."

Nayeli wasn't listening. She was looking at the ball of metal on the workbench in front of her. She allowed herself to smile. She longed to feel the cold iron.

Her hands went to the tool belt at her waist. It had taken her years to trade enough fish to buy each slip of metal. But it was worth it. Her chisel was deft and light in her fingers, her carving knives sharper than the basic equipment given to the others. She knew her tools like she knew her limbs.

And she was ready to wield them.

IT TOOK FIVE years for Nayeli to become a team leader in the Foundry. She was the youngest team leader by at least four years, but she had earned her place. She had carved and sculpted more metal than anyone else in her cohort and made few mistakes. Her stellar record of both productivity and quality saw her surpass those with double her experience.

"You have served our God Kabut well. His blessing is upon you," the master crafter reluctantly praised her.

Nayeli didn't care about serving her God. All she cared about was being successful. Success and routine. Without that she was no one.

She didn't say that, though; she said, "Thank you, master crafter. Kabut's eye shines bright on me. To win we must begin again."

"To win we must begin again." He repeated the phrase with a knowing smile. "This is your new uniform."

He handed her the yellow robes of a team leader. Yellow of course, the color of her commune, the color worn by all Foundry workers, but these robes were softer, with wider sleeves and a wider collar. But the master crafter wasn't done.

"Here is your leather armor." He handed her a well-worn harness and breast plate. The brown leather was burnt at the edges. She wondered what had happened to the last owner. "You'll need it to protect yourself from the flames of the furnace."

"The furnace?"

The master crafter's smile grew.

"Yes, we're moving you to the smelting team."

It was a punishment, but she wasn't sure why she was being punished. The smelting team was in charge of extracting iron from ore. It was grueling, sweaty work.

Nayeli set her jaw.

"Master, why am I being assigned to the smelting team? You know my skill is crafting. There is no one who completes more assignments than I do. You said it yourself, I am touched by Kabut."

"You once told me you would be master crafter."

"Yes."

"To be master crafter you must understand every element of the Foundry. You must master every station."

Is the master crafter trying to help me? Is this a sign of his approval?

Nayeli frowned uncertainly.

"This is . . . a blessing?"

The master crafter laughed until tears sprang from his eyes.

"No one has ever called the smelting team a blessing, dear child. Few survive a year by the furnace. Survive three and I may consider you as an apprentice."

"I won't just survive," Nayeli said fiercely into the laughing face of the master crafter. "I'll thrive."

THAT NIGHT WAS a full moon. And like every full moon on the Volcane Isles, every citizen was expected to make their sacrifice to the endless flame.

"Shine bright under Kabut's eye," Nayeli's twin brother greeted her at the steps to the open temple.

"Shine bright, brother."

They both raised their fists to the silver moon, the emblem of Kabut's eye in the sky.

"Heard you were made team leader." He jostled her shoulder as they continued their climb to the temple. Her brother was taller than she was by at least a foot. Always exceeding her in everything. He was more loved, more beautiful, and quicker to smile than she.

But I have the brains. And the deft fingers.

He had only just been accepted into the Foundry the previous year but seemed content with his position. "A person without ambition is a happy person," he often said. To which Nayeli would respond, "A person without ambition is not a person but a ghost. For without a purpose, what are you?"

It had been the two of them for as long as she could remember. Their parents had died long ago and neither of them could even remember the shape of them in their memories. The terrain of the Volcane Isles was tough, and it took more than it gave. They had survived years of famine, poisoned waters, volcanic eruptions, and earthquakes that shattered their homes time and time again. But it was sickness that took their parents, leaving the twins in the care of the commune.

"I expected to be made team leader a year ago," Nayeli admitted to her brother with a scowl.

Her brother laughed, only stopping to greet an Orange Commune woman. She smiled widely at Nayeli's brother, but her eyes slipped past Nayeli's as if she weren't there.

Nayeli was used to it. She wasn't the friendliest of people. She didn't need friends. She had her brother. She had her work.

"Why do you do that?" he asked, tugging on her elbow.

"Do what?"

"Frown at anyone who looks your way. With your lip sticking out as if to say 'I'm better than you'?" He strutted up a few steps ahead of her, pouting and pushing out his chest.

Her laugh was sharp and barking. He looked so ridiculous.

"Look at me and my *scowl*, it's the fiercest scowl you ever did see," he shrilled.

"Stop it, stop it," she begged, her laughter giving her stomach cramps. But he didn't stop. He marched into the open temple with the same satirical stride.

Nayeli's chuckling rumbled to a stop as all eight of the commune leaders turned their gaze to the two of them.

Yellow, green, orange, violet, indigo, red, blue, and clear: eight leaders for the eight communes across the isles.

Eight sets of disapproving eyes.

"Eh . . . sorry," her brother whispered into the silence.

Nayeli snorted and tried to hide it with a cough.

"The Ilrase twins. Have you come to make your sacrifice to our God on this sacred night, when his eye is open?" the Yellow Commune leader, Andu, asked. His long white hair fell to his shoulders in soft curls, framing a face made only more striking by age. Andu had been one of the many people to help raise the twins after their parents died.

Of course we have, you dolt, we wouldn't have trekked up here if we weren't, Nayeli thought. Rather than saying that, she smiled and nodded. Nayeli could feign respect if she needed to, and though Andu wasn't the smartest person in the world, he had always been kind to them.

"Come forward then." Andu waved them toward the endless flame. His yellow robes flapped behind his small frame in the night's breeze.

The open temple was in the shape of God Kabut's preferred form, the spider. Eight legs had been carved into the ground, each ending in a plinth where the commune leaders stood. In the center, the body of the spider, was the endless flame. Firekeepers were tasked with keeping the fire burning throughout the year. They said the flame hadn't gone out for nearly four hundred years.

The twins approached the flame now.

Her brother spoke to the fire first. "Glorious one up above, you who knows no bounds or boundaries. Take my sacrifice this day. I give to you my last candle, that which I had saved for a dark night, but give to you now freely. For I need no light with your guidance."

"Pretty words," Nayeli muttered, and she saw him wink at her.

He withdrew a candle from his pocket and made to throw it on the flame, but Nayeli knew the candle had made its way back up his sleeve. There was no way her brother would sacrifice something as precious as a candle.

Nayeli stepped forward and removed the sticky rice from her pocket. She always made the same sacrifice. "Glorious one up above, you who knows no bounds or boundaries. Take my sacrifice this day. I give to you my food, for with your love I need no sustenance." The words were numb on her lips, losing all meaning in repetition.

The twins turned away from the endless flame and made their way back down the steps.

"Nayeli Ilrase," Andu called softly as she passed him. "Fasting is a sacrifice, but next time think how else you can satisfy our God. For without sacrifice, we fail."

Nayeli gritted her teeth. *I've been doing fine so far.*

"Yes, commune leader. I will think on your words."

Nayeli hurried after the shadow of her brother who was dashing down the steps two at a time. Streams of people from all eight communes were making the pilgrimage to the open temple and Nayeli elbowed past them to catch up with her brother.

"Kabut's eye. You just tipped over my crate of melons, what am I going to sacrifice now . . ."

"Watch out, young girl . . ."

"Stop running on holy ground . . ."

"May the moon smite you . . ."

She let their curses wash over her as she sped up. When she reached the bottom of the steps she was panting hard, but still her brother had sprinted off ahead.

She followed in the wake of his laughter, her stride elongating, her hair coming free of the rigid knot on her head. The ground beneath her feet went from rocky to sandy and eventually she kicked off her steel-capped boots and let her toes sink deep into the beach as she ran.

It was low tide, and the black sand was drying out to the faded ash color of her knees when she forgot to oil them. The sulphur was so strong it stung her eyes, but it guaranteed them privacy.

The waves rumbled and broke against the shore where a lone figure stood.

Moonlight illuminated his dark skin, the reflection of the water sparkling on the glass of his spectacles. He turned to look at her, a laugh on his lips.

"Took your time."

Nayeli moved to punch him, but he moved out of the way.

"You dare try and hurt your brother on this sacred night?" he teased.

Nayeli couldn't answer, as she was yet to get her breath back.

"Come on then, time for dinner," he said, withdrawing the candle. He pressed it into the sand and lit it with a box of matches.

Nayeli sat on the sand next to him and withdrew the other half of her lunch. Though she had sacrificed the rice, she had kept the whitefish. She split the fillet and handed half to her brother. Neither of them cared about the pieces of cotton and dirt that stuck to its flesh. They had survived on much worse meals.

They ate in silence, watching the waves under the moonlight.

"Do you think Kabut is real?" her brother asked, splintering the silence.

Nayeli cocked her head and looked at him.

"Yes."

"Why do you think that?"

"Because if he isn't, none of this matters." She gestured to the expanse of the Volcane Isles.

"Does it need to matter? Can't we just be?"

Nayeli didn't have an answer to that. She wasn't the most devout person on the isles, but Kabut had to be real because her work in the Foundry went toward satisfying the God. It was under Kabut's guidance that the Foundry even existed.

He had to be real.

"I'm getting married."

"What?" Nayeli choked on her saliva.

Her brother grimaced. "I'm sorry I didn't tell you sooner."

"But . . . you're only fifteen. *We're* only fifteen."

"And of age to get married," he said, adding, "according to Kabut's law."

Nayeli didn't know what to say. She'd had a few people bid for her marriage pact when she turned fifteen a few moons ago, but they had both laughed about it. Eventually she'd scared off anyone else from bidding.

"What about me?" She hated that she voiced the question. She hated herself for needing him.

"Nayeli, you'll be fine." He leaned in and tweaked her nose. She detested that. "One day you will understand. One day there will be someone that you will love so fully that all of this will make sense."

"No, I won't," she promised. "There is no one that I will love as much as I love you."

His expression turned sad. "I hope that's not true, sister. For your sake. You deserve more than just the Foundry. You deserve love."

She laughed bitterly. "Love? Who is it, then? Who do you love so completely that you must abandon me so?"

"A fisherman from Blue Commune."

Nayeli stood so quickly the candle went out. But it didn't matter, Kabut's brightness still illuminated her anger.

"A blue-blooded?" she hissed. "You are choosing to mix? That is illegal."

Her brother inclined his head. "Not illegal, but not encouraged. The Blue Commune leader has agreed to wed us."

Nayeli's eyes were wild. "And children?"

"He and I will bid for a child, as is the way."

"Which color will you choose to bid on? Blue or yellow?" Nayeli's mouth twisted with scorn.

Her brother met her gaze levelly. "I do not know."

"What is your husband's name?"

Nayeli saw a flicker of anger in her brother's face.

"I will not speak it if you are only going to twist it so in your mouth."

Nayeli wanted to scream. She wanted to run into the sea and drown in it.

"Are you moving to Blue Commune, then? Leaving the Foundry and becoming a fisherman like the rest of the blue-blooded fools?"

"Nayeli, sit down. These insults only serve to hurt you. I will not be pushed away."

She exhaled heavily through her nostrils.

"Nayeli, please. It has always been the two of us. My love for you is like the endless flame, but I can have more than one hearth in my heart."

He spoke so softly, so openly that she couldn't cling to her anger anymore. She sat back down on the sand.

"I should be happy for you," she said weakly. "But I am not."

Her brother nodded. "I know, but one day you will be. I am not going far. The east island is a short boat ride away."

Her brother reached into his pocket.

"I have something for you."

Nayeli's head snapped up from where it had dipped.

"A present?"

"I had some free time at the Foundry—"

"You used the commune's resources?"

"Divine's web. Calm yourself, honestly, you'd think I'd murdered a baby." He laughed, hoping it would draw out a smile from Nayeli.

Nayeli lifted her chin.

"Show me then."

Her brother's grin was wicked as he reached into his pocket and withdrew two glittering objects.

"My husband-to-be traded the black diamonds on a fishing trip, and I made the body out of silver scraps. See, there's one for each of us."

Nayeli's hand turned over the small silver spider in her hand. A miniature replica of their God. It was beautiful.

"Turn it over," he said.

On the spider's back was a pin, and behind it was an engraving.

"'Inansi,'" she whispered. "You engraved your name?"

His eyes shone.

"And look, see, this one says 'Nayeli.'" He turned the belly of the other spider upside down. "So, I will wear your name next to my chest and you will wear my name next to yours."

Nayeli smiled. It was a lovely gift.

"Thank you, Inansi." Her fingers curled around the brooch until the pin pierced her skin. "I will never part with it."

CHAPTER TEN

NAYELI

The vessel known as the Scowl *was lost at sea. None of the four passengers arrived at Souriland, and no trades were made. No survivors. All produce lost.*

—Message to Apprentice Nayeli

It had been the best day of her life, until Nayeli got the news that Inansi had died.

The master crafter had just told her he was going to apprentice her.

"I must admit I didn't believe you when you said you were going to become the next master crafter. This spindly little ten-year-old with ambitions of an Ancient. Now look at you. Eighteen and already my apprentice." He laughed and Nayeli grinned. It was a rare, genuine smile.

Apprentice, finally. This is what I deserve. This is what I've worked so hard for.

She had completed seven more carvings that day, seven more than anyone else. It was her personal record.

"Now you are my apprentice you will move your workbench into the office next to mine. Your time in the Foundry is about to increase. Lucky you're not married."

Nayeli's stomach soured. Andu, the Yellow Commune leader, had been pushing her for the last year to select a partner. He believed it was a slight to Kabut if she didn't do her part to procreate. Children were the most revered blessing on the isles.

Over the last few years as her reputation in the Foundry grew, more and more bids had come in for her marriage pact.

"You're dismissed for the evening. Why don't you go and visit your brother? He's at Blue Commune now, right?"

"He's on a fishing trip, trading with the Souri."

The master crafter waved her away; he wasn't listening anymore and clearly wanted to leave the Foundry himself.

Nayeli gave him a polite nod before making her way past the workbenches and out into the evening air.

"Apprentice Nayeli, Apprentice Nayeli." The shout came from the bottom of the hill.

Nayeli let herself revel in her new title; news must have got out already.

The messenger flagged her down with a slip of paper in their hands.

The commune leaders congratulating me already?

But when she read the words of the message they blurred before her.

". . . lost at sea? All four of them?" Her voice broke at the end.

But the messenger had already gone, running off to deliver other missives.

Her brother, his husband, and their two children . . . dead?

It couldn't be.

Nayeli began to run, faster and faster. She didn't know where she was going, the Volcane Isles a mirage behind her tears.

Her screams were silent, broken things, rupturing from her throat.

She kept running, up and up until she felt the heat of the endless flame.

"Why?" she screamed up to the sky. The open temple framed the waning moon above her. "Why did you take him from me?"

Kabut chose not to speak.

"Answer me!" she shouted, over and over again until her voice was hoarse, and she had no breath left to stay standing. She fell to the ground. The stone under her knees was cold and she willed the icy floor to numb her heart.

The ground shook beneath her feet.

The Volcane Isles suffered often with earthquakes. It was why all the structures on the isles except the Foundry were made of palm leaf and straw. Easier to rebuild that way.

"Kabut?" Nayeli asked as the earthquake ground to a halt.

"He makes his presence known."

The voice startled Nayeli, and for a second, she thought the God had spoken.

"Andu." She greeted the commune leader.

Andu tilted his head toward Nayeli and she could see the tears streaming down his face. The darkness of his beard contrasted with the white hair tied on top of his head.

"I'm sorry for your loss, for *our* loss. But I am more thankful for Kabut's gain. He will take Inansi's sacrifice and bless you anew."

The words, though shared in sympathy, rang hollow in Nayeli's ears.

"Why?" she whispered. "Why did he take him?"

"Nayeli, what did you sacrifice last full moon?" Andu came to kneel beside her. Though she didn't feel the heat from the endless flame, she was too numb, she saw the sweat bead Andu's wide brow in seconds.

"My lunch . . ."

"Nayeli . . ."

"Half my lunch . . ." she admitted.

"Kabut takes what we need. He took from you your greatest sacrifice."

Tears spilled down her face, but she saw more clearly.

"He has blessed you with many talents, Nayeli. But blessings come with a cost."

"What must I do?" she said.

THAT YEAR NAYELI got married.

The marriage pact was a ceremony that signified adulthood as much as a bonding of two hearts. Some even bonded to three or four. The idea of even one other person altering her routine was bad enough for her to contemplate.

Nayeli still lived in Yellow Commune, the largest village on the Volcane Isles. Her large straw hut was nearest the Foundry so she could work at any time during the day or night. Nayeli's craftwork was renowned across the isles. When word got out that she was intending to marry, offerings came in quickly. So much so that Nayeli hadn't traded or bought food for over three turns of the moon.

The Ancients of the isles flapped around Nayeli as the day drew nearer.

"Who will you choose? What about Aboba, the teacher of firefield?" As if she would dare to stoop so low. A teacher of all things.

". . . No, my son, my son, he's tipped to be commune leader one day, he is the one who left you the papaya."

The papaya had been sour.

"Ignore Aunty, you should marry my friends, Opo and Lopo . . ."

Over Nayeli's soulless body would she marry a couple whose names *rhymed*.

The truth was, though Nayeli understood the complexities of marriage, she still thought the only person she truly loved was her brother. But he was gone. Dead.

Nayeli swallowed down the grief and fingered the brooch on her chest. Toying with it was like pulling on a loose tooth; it hurt her, but she couldn't stop herself doing it. Though today wasn't a day for pain. Today she was to choose a partner and bring further glory to herself by bidding on multiple children in the years to come. Maybe she would even birth one of her own.

"To win we must begin again." She mouthed the prayer to herself.

She tugged on the hem of her skirt. It was large and impractical with no boiled leather on it to protect her from the sparks in the

Foundry. It would be useless beyond today. She looked into the cracked mirror that she kept hanging in the center of her hut. It had shattered during the last earthquake.

"The world shakes when Kabut makes his presence known," as Andu had said. She wasn't sure if her God was speaking to her, but either way Nayeli was listening to Andu more attentively than she had before. It was why she agreed to the marriage in the first place.

Nayeli rarely used the mirror so was surprised to see the gash running down its center. It split her lithe form in two. Everything about Nayeli was exaggerated. From the wide nose to the even wider chin, she was built like a warrior, a mother, a leader. The melodrama of her hair had been restrained with oils and gels, keeping the coils of her curls flattened against her large scalp.

She brushed the skirt flat, as flat as it would go with the underskirt ring puffing it up, but the Ancients had said it was a requirement. Nayeli doubted their God cared about what she wore. Even so, she liked the color. It was yellow, the color of her commune.

The color of her blood.

EACH OF THE eight commune leaders was present in the open temple. Those who had made offerings sat on their knees, only rising when Nayeli stopped by the endless flame.

She sighed, already impatient for the ritual to be over. She murmured a prayer to the flames.

"Glorious one up above, you who knows no bounds or boundaries. You who spins the web of my future, guide me in my choice this day."

Nayeli had refused any meetings with her suitors, had not made any offerings in return, but still they came, thick and fast. She lifted her gaze and scanned them, the people who would cling on throughout her rise up the ranks. For Nayeli was not stupid; her position attested to that. She knew these parasites for what they were. For what she represented to them—a future steeped in glory.

She circled the flame, nodding to the commune leaders.

"Nayeli Ilrase of Yellow Commune, last of her name. We amass beside this fire, in the full moon of Kabut's eye, our righteous one, our most holy God, to bind you with your partner in life. Have you made your choice?"

Nayeli rolled her shoulders and scanned the group again. She had never been attracted to men, women, or musawa. She could appreciate their forms, and the beauty in their work, but to love—like her brother had loved? No, that had never occurred to her, and she felt no less whole for its absence. She closed her eyes and pointed blindly, the act causing murmurs among the group.

"Is that how she's going to choose?"

". . . No, she can't be . . ."

". . . I heard she was a little strange, but this . . ."

Nayeli dropped her finger. Fine, she'd pick with her eyes open. She let her gaze roam over the waiting prospects. They all wore yellow, like her; of course their blood would run the same. She wasn't about to blaspheme like her brother. Segregation was one of the staple foundations of the Volcane Isles, each commune protecting its own. Besides, Nayeli couldn't imagine bonding with any of the lesser bloods. Though she supposed they'd say the same about her.

The Blue Commune leader coughed politely, and Nayeli scowled. The blue-blooded were always so focused on their tasks, they didn't condone dithering. It was why they made the best laborers; they would toil and toil until the work was done. They favored the attribute of duty above anything else. There weren't many people living in the Blue Commune on the isles, only the refugees who came back from their trading missions and decided to claim fealty to Kabut. They hadn't been part of the first settlers; their boat to the Volcane Isles had gone astray.

Nayeli, like all of those in her commune, relied on logic beyond anything else. So, when she saw the frail old man in the periphery of her vision, she knew he was the one. It wouldn't take him long to die. Marrying him would thus fulfill her duty to her commune, while preserving what meant most to her in the world, her routine and the freedom to carry it out.

Her finger uncurled a few yards from his face.

"I choose you."

The man smiled and reached out his arms to embrace her. He wore his hair cropped short. She realized the gray fuzz looked softer than it was as his arms wrapped around her and he pressed his head against her cheek.

Nayeli stiffened at the contact. He squeezed tighter than she expected he could. He smelled of pipe smoke and leather. The former was a familiar scent as Inansi had grown fond of the habit before he died. It made the embrace easier.

"You will be a good wife to me," Chah said.

Nayeli flinched at the word "wife." For some reason the word felt like a brand.

They were bonded before the eight commune leaders, the other prospects dispersing after Chah had been chosen. The moon was heavy and pregnant with light, casting shadows across the open temple. Nayeli dutifully said her prayers below Kabut's eye, while Chah clutched her hand, his nails far too long.

Once the final words were spoken, Andu, the Yellow Commune leader, handed Nayeli a knife. Gilded onto the hilt was a black diamond in the shape of Kabut. Eight legs and a body. Like the brooch on her chest.

This was the moment that sealed her fate to Chah's. A slash of the knife.

The wielder had the choice of where to cut themself. It was part of the ritual to Kabut, a God that traded in human pain and sacrifice. Some chose to cut themselves on their face, to show the depth of their commitment to Kabut. Others made a token sacrifice, merely slashing their wrists or cutting their legs.

Nayeli didn't suppose the God would care either way, so she went for the most logical solution—the underside of her arm. The cut wouldn't hamper her carving the next day, nor would it get in the way of consummating the marriage. She was looking forward to only one of those activities.

She plunged the knife into the soft skin near her armpit and winced. It reminded her of the time she'd fallen on a shard of glass as a child. The pain was clear and sharp.

Andu nodded and took the ceremonial knife, now covered in her blood, and plunged it in the flame.

Nayeli watched her blood sizzle on the knife and turn black while the blade turned red.

Her other hand held the wound closed under her arm. Her blood still seeped through the crack in her fingers. It dripped over her knuckles and fell onto the cotton of her dress.

Yellow on yellow.

"We, the commune leaders, welcome the partnership of Chah and Apprentice Nayeli. We pray that they are blessed with the Child of Fire." Andu's voice rang out.

The Child of Fire. A foretelling hundreds of years old, preserved in story. It was why children were so revered. So sacred. It was said the Child of Fire would start the final battle. A battle that would destroy everything, leaving behind a utopia for those favored by Kabut.

"Until that moment, we prepare," Andu continued. "We wait. For we are the Zalaam. So called by the first prophet. And to win we must begin again."

PART TWO

DISCOVER

Violet, red, green, blue, orange, yellow, indigo, and translucent. Today I learned there are eight blood colors. Eight.

—Journal of Elder Petra, year 237 B.W.

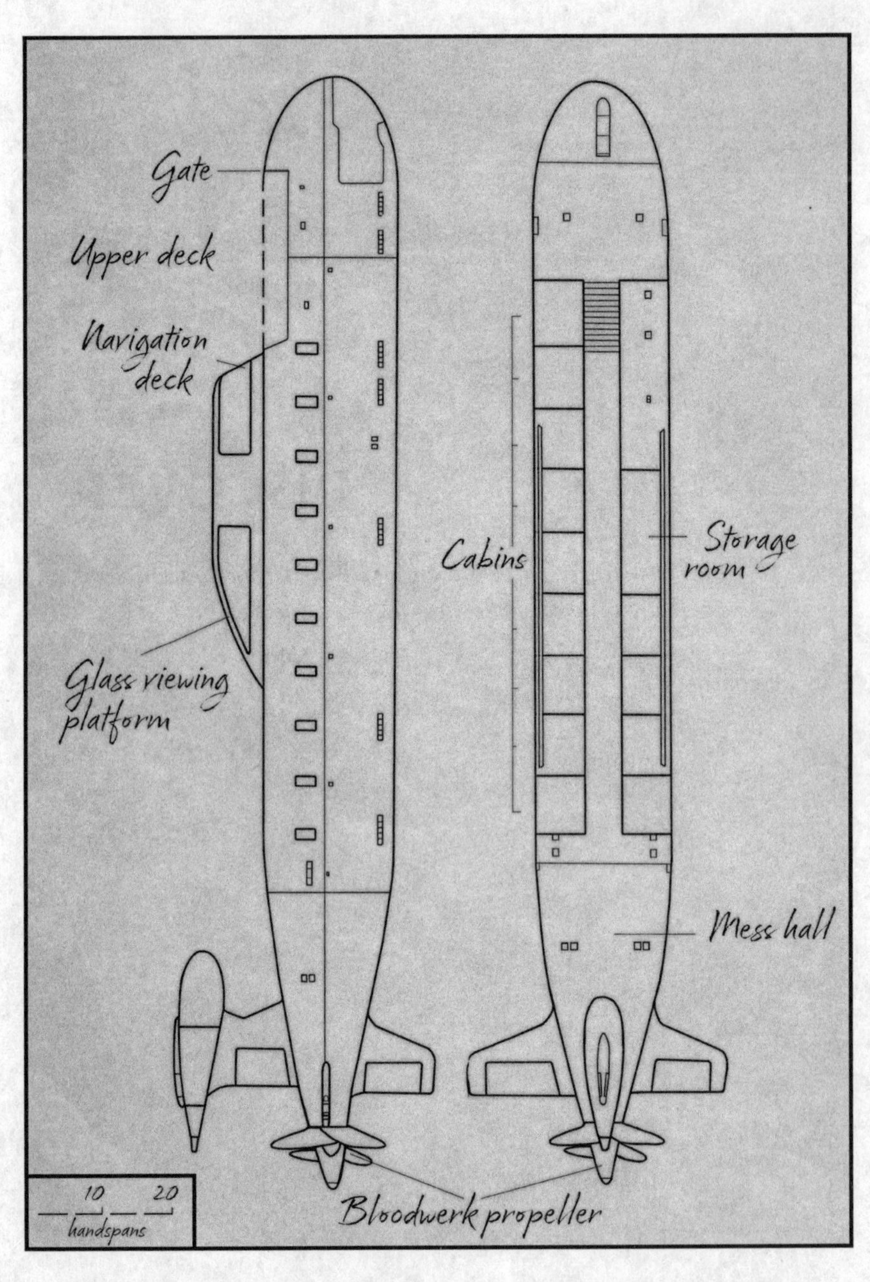

BLUEPRINT OF THE *BAQARAH* SUBAQUATIC SHIP AS DRAWN BY ADS NADER

CHAPTER ELEVEN
SYLAH

I will govern the people of my land with justice and mercy as my ancestors have done before me. A millennium ago, the mainland was an ungoverned home to nomad tribes until my family united all chiefs under one banner and the queendom of Tenio was born. As Queen I will seek no wars, I will reap no bounties, for Tenio will forever be a home to the homeless and restore faith in the faithless.

—Extract from Queen Karanomo's coronation speech

Sylah was standing on the deck of the *Baqarah* as it cruised through the ocean. Every morning, once the tidewind abated, the ship slipped up from the dark depths of the Marion Sea and rode the waves. It was Sylah's favorite time. Not only because it meant being free from the tin can that was her cabin, but because she loved the silence that dawn brought.

Good morning, Elder Zero signed as he joined Sylah by the railing. Like her, he rushed to freedom every morning. His company was always pleasant. He didn't hate Sylah, like Elder Reed, or pretend she didn't exist, like Ravenwing. Even Elder Dew turned every conversation into a lesson, making it hard to *truly* enjoy their company.

But Zero, he just liked to smile.

"Good morning, Elder Zero," Sylah greeted him and settled back down to her thoughts.

The sea is the color of indigo here.

Zero was chatty today.

A deep indigo, fathomless, he continued, signing to the sea more than Sylah. Then he rounded on her, his gaze penetrating, but a smile still hanging from his lips.

What is it that you see when you look at the ocean?

"Blood," Sylah answered honestly. "I see blood."

Indigo blood?

Sylah frowned. "No, the blood of Ghostings. Clear."

Zero seemed satisfied by the answer because he laughed heartily. *And so we cruise on the blood of my ancestors to an unknown land.*

Sylah shifted uncomfortably and let the silence fill with the clash of waves. The sun was rising, turning the waves violet. Though they were only three days away from the empire, the world around them was changing. The fish were getting bigger, the birds smaller with plumes of orange and green. Gone were the kori birds whose sweet song grew louder with the rising sun. Gone were the lava fish whose glittering scales adorned Anoor's dresses.

Anoor—

"Elder, why was Loot's blood yellow?" Sylah thrust the question like a knife through her thoughts.

Elder Zero's smile slipped. Frustration crossed his features. Sylah had asked Elder Dew the same question on their first day at sea, but their answer had been unsatisfying: *Loot was not a child of the empire.* When Sylah pressed, Dew had admitted that they didn't know more.

We know little of the life of the man who called himself Warden of Crime. Zero signed with a sharpness to his limbs. *We know of his involvement in running the Sandstorm, but I admit, we did not know his blood ran yellow. But that is not the question you should be asking.*

Sylah thought on Zero's words. That was not the question she should be asking . . .

"Elder Zero . . . are there other yellow-blooded on the continent?"

Zero's chuckle boomed across the sea, startling a shoal of fish near the surface. Sylah watched as they scattered, half going one way, half going the other.

Sylah grinned, feeling foolish. Of course, Zero found the question funny. There were only three blood colors in the world.

But Loot . . .

Look at the fish. What colors do you see? Zero signed through his laughter.

Sylah indulged him. "Yellow, a bit of orange. Some blue . . ."

And the birds?

"Red and green."

And the sea?

". . . clear . . . violet and indigo?"

Eight colors you have just named: clear, red, yellow, orange, green, blue, indigo and violet. That is the world beyond the Marion Sea.

Blood roared in Sylah's ears. She couldn't hear her own question, but Zero must have, because he answered.

Yes, Loot may have come from another island.

The truth sat heavy in Sylah's stomach. It bloated her with more questions.

"How . . . why?"

How? Zero snorted. *Why? How does the fish swim? Why is the bird orange?*

"Why didn't you tell me before? I need to be prepared . . . I need to know what's on the mainland—"

Zero's smile dropped completely. *We owe you nothing, Ember.*

That stopped Sylah's questions. Zero must have seen the hurt in her face because he signed with a more kindly expression when he resumed.

You didn't ask the right questions. Remember that in the end when you know all.

Zero left Sylah to her thoughts. Her mind churned like the sea, the truth a current dragging her along to yet more queries. But what was the right question to ask?

There was a scuffle behind her and Jond appeared, heaving over the side of the ship. His knuckles turned white as he held onto the railing, each retch ending with a groan louder than the last.

Sylah tipped her head back and looked up at the cloudless sky, asking herself, like she did every morning: *Skies above, why did I bring Jond? I'm punishing myself as much as him.*

They had been traveling for three days and each day Jond seemed worse than the last. His seasickness rolled in with each wave. He had spent every night in the small privy at the back of the deck, cradling the bowl like a child clinging to a security blanket. Though the crew were seasoned fishermen, not one of them had offered up a remedy. Sylah wasn't sure they'd tell him even if they had one.

"Any sign of the Tannin?" he rasped, wiping the underside of his hand across his lips. He still hadn't shaved off his beard and though it wasn't as bedraggled as it had been on their journey, it was now grazing the top of his broad chest.

It . . . suited him.

Jond had always looked dangerous, with sharp edges that only softened when he smiled. But now, with the beard, he looked outright lethal.

Sylah dragged her eyes away and back to the sea.

"No sign of the Tannin. But I still doubt we'll see it."

Jond looked at Sylah, his eyes sincere, his voice grave. "I . . . I don't think I'm quite finished."

And back over the railing he went. Sylah idly wondered whose cabin was below and if they could see the bile streaming down through their porthole.

"Monkey's balls," Jond shrieked. Somehow he had fallen forward, the railing giving way in front of him. His toes grasped for purchase on the deck as his chest swung toward the sea below. Sylah went to help him up, then chastised herself for caring. She flung him backward on the deck with more force than was needed.

"Who puts a fucking *gate* on a railing?" Jond panted and groaned as his stomach roiled.

Sylah looked back at the rail and realized he was right. The barrier hadn't given way. It was actually a gate that opened out to the sea.

"Maybe they need it to tie up the ship in the harbor or something." Sylah shrugged, not really bothered by it. There was so much about the ship she didn't know.

Her fingers yearned to inspect the bloodwerk runes that kept them moving. There were doors she had been asked to stay away from, but she left the elders with their secrets. She had to remind herself more than once that she was a guest on their journey, and she wouldn't put it past the elders to revoke that privilege if she didn't obey their rules.

Sylah closed the gate, securing it with a sliding bolt she hadn't noticed before.

"I think . . . the Tannin . . . urgh . . . is real, Sylah," Jond said behind her.

"Uhumm." Sylah rolled her eyes.

You'd think after the revelations of the last six mooncycles I'd be less cynical, she thought.

It wasn't just the last six mooncycles, it was the last few minutes.

Eight blood colors.

Sylah shook her head and smiled bitterly.

"What's so funny?"

"Nothing. I'm going to go get something to eat." Her peaceful morning had been ruined.

Sylah headed down the hatch that led to the main spine of the underwater ship. As soon as the metal lid swung closed, the claustrophobia that she'd kept at bay threatened to swallow her whole. There was just so much *metal,* she felt like a bullet rattling around a runegun waiting to be scoured with bloodwerk.

A sound made Sylah jump. It coincided with the lurch of a wave, and she was swung to the side. The latch on the nearest door struck her in the stomach and winded her. The handles were large enough for the Ghostings to slip their arms in and swing them upward. As she steadied herself, she accidentally pulled on the handle, opening the cabin door and tripping over the lip of the doorframe into the room.

"Ouch," she groaned. Collecting her limbs, she stood and looked around the dim room. "Oh, shit." It was the storage chamber, somewhere she wasn't supposed to be. There was a murmur and a movement in the darkness.

"Hello? Is someone in there?"

More murmurs. Sylah breathed out slowly and stepped forward. She heard a groan, like someone was in pain. Sylah shivered.

A runelamp turned on ahead of her, triggered by her presence. She let out a low hiss. The room was ten times the size of her cabin, sitting directly below the upper deck it encompassed the full width of the ship. Black boxes lined the walls. Sylah couldn't see how far they went, but she knew if she stepped forward, more light would illuminate above her.

There was a sound behind her, and Sylah spun.

Someone was knocking from the *inside* of one of the boxes. Sylah dipped into a Nuba formation stance, her knees bent, ready to pounce.

"Whilgh oo ghet meh oot?"

There was someone in there. They repeated the sentence over and over. Sylah inched closer to the sound.

"Whilgh oo ghet meh oot? Whilg you, ghet me out? Will you let me out?"

Sylah recognized the voice, dropped out of her defensive position, and ran fingers along the black surface of the box looking for the latch. When she found it, the door released a waft of stale air.

"I've been waiting for someone to open that door for ages. I'm *starving*. Oh, and don't go in any further, I had to pee in the corner."

There, standing in front of her, was Ads.

"WHAT ARE YOU doing here?" Sylah asked.

Ads shrugged. Her signature four plaits were a little more disheveled than Sylah had seen them before.

"Didn't want you all to have an adventure without me."

"You've been down here for three days?"

The girl was *stubborn*. For the first time, Sylah found herself liking her.

"Yes. I had to make sure we were far enough away so the elders wouldn't make me turn back."

Sylah smacked her hand against her forehead. "You are such an idiot."

Ads smiled a toothy grin. "Can we go get some breakfast? My supplies ran out ages ago. Plus, this place gives me the creeps. The ship groans like a person in here." She shivered and moved out into the hallway.

Ads knew the way to the mess hall. After all, she'd been one of the engineers who had made the ship. Sylah wondered how many Embers they had forced to do the bloodwerk.

She followed Ads through to the viewing platform where a simple breakfast was laid out on the metal table bolted down to the floor. Though the sun shone through the glass paneling at the back, Sylah longed for fresh air on her face.

"Hello, everyone," Ads announced as she walked over to the coffee pot. The elders looked up from the conversation they were having. The effect of Ads's appearance was explosive. Ravenwing stood, anger flashing across his face, Dew was the opposite; they seemed to shrink inward, as if shot in the stomach. Reed held a quivering wrist to her mouth, a cry escaping her lips. Zero was the only elder to remain composed. No laughs, no smiles, nothing. It made him seem more terrifying than the rest of them.

Ads had paused in pouring her coffee, shocked by the elders' extreme reaction. "Now I know you're mad, but you can't expect me to let you travel off in the thing I helped build and just be okay with it?"

Ravenwing turned to Dew. *We must turn back. The Tannin hasn't struck yet. We have time.*

Reed nodded slowly. *Yes, I think you're right.*

"No, no, I'm not going back." Ads's voice turned to a whine, and any fondness Sylah had for the girl dissipated.

The elders acted like Ads wasn't there.

Reed stood, though Sylah could see the arms by her side were still shaking before she signed, *I'll tell the crew.*

No, Dew signed with finality. *We stay our course. There is no guarantee the Tannin will not strike us on the journey back. The fishermen have seen it closer to the land before.*

We do not have enough. Ravenwing slammed his arm onto the metal table. The sound interrupted the heavy breathing in the room, bringing everyone to attention.

Sylah's eyes bounced from one elder to the next, fascinated by their reaction.

"I won't go back," Ads said, crossing her arms across her bosom. "I'll just sneak back on again and none of you will know how I do it."

We have enough, Dew signed, ignoring Ads's interjection.

We don't . . . Ravenwing began to sign but Dew cut him off.

She is my grandchild. I will take responsibility for her actions. I must. We are running out of time.

The elders looked between themselves. Sylah desperately tried to understand what was going on. Ads, too, had recognized the tone had shifted, as the elders looked pained.

Ravenwing sank back in his chair and glared darkly at Dew. *I respect your choice, but I vote we go back.*

Reed spoke up. *I agree, let us put it to a vote.*

Dew voted to continue on.

"I vote to continue too," Ads interjected, but she might as well have been made of glass; the elders didn't do so much as blink in recognition.

Zero? Dew asked. *As ever you are our deciding vote.*

Zero smiled softly, but the corners of his lips turned down. *We continue on.*

At his words Ravenwing stood again in anger and marched out of the mess hall, pushing past Ads and Sylah as he did. His black hair had grown on their journey, and it sprang up from his head, his anger made real.

Ravenwing turned to sign at Ads as he passed. *Foolish girl, you have no idea what you've done.*

Ads looked to Sylah. "Coffee?" A smug grin rounded her cheeks.

The grin didn't last long.

Ads spent the day talking. And talking. And talking. She didn't pause for breath, only for food, and even then it disappeared down her ever-contracting gullet in record time. Sylah had tried to escape her by slipping out to go onto the deck, but the girl had just followed, prattling on about the changes to the engine, the runes she'd recommended they use, the studying she had done to make the *Baqarah* just *perfect.*

Jond was still leaning limply over the side of the railing, his dark skin damp with the effort of being sick. It didn't take long for Ads's attention to migrate to him.

"Didn't anyone tell you to drink ginger tea?"

Jond perked up. "What?"

"Ginger tea. No vessel leaves the harbor without a stash somewhere. Even the most seasoned seafarer can fall prone to the wily nature of the churning ocean. Especially just before a tidewind. Come on, I'll show you how to make it. Better get it down you before nightfall."

Sylah looked to the sky at this. She couldn't believe the whole day had passed. But in some way, it felt like Ads had been droning in her ear for centuries. Sylah heard the latch close and breathed out a sigh of relief.

"Skies above, blessed silence." Her words were swallowed by the wind. It was picking up already, and it wouldn't be long before the *Baqarah* would sink beneath the waves, finding succor from the tidewind.

Two arms joined hers on the railing and Sylah looked up into the face of Elder Zero.

"Elder," she greeted him.

He didn't return the greeting, merely smiled and looked out to the sunset. The sun slipped out from behind a cloud, its final rays warming Sylah's face. She looked to the waves below and shuddered. The Marion Sea was ink-black. Sylah wondered what lived beneath the waves.

Zero exhaled, then signed. *You are a parasite on this journey.*

Sylah was shocked by his offensive words, though he didn't sign in anger and his face looked at her with his usual openness.

Not all parasites are bad. Some, like the liver worm, burrow into the host's body and feast on the cancers in the liver.

At first, the host will shed weight and lose their appetite. Their skin will turn clammy, their muscles weak. But if the liver worm is expelled from the body at the right time, the host will benefit from a cancer-free life. Expelled too late and the liver worm will continue to chew through the flesh of the organ, eventually killing both the host and itself in the process.

You are the liver worm. Remember to leave at the right time.

He chuckled and unwound the silver threads of his belt. He let the metal run across his wrist like a creature before passing the belt to Sylah.

You may need this to restrain Ads, he signed.

Sylah didn't have time to be shocked by his words as the ship swung violently to the left. Water sprayed up around them as the force of something large hit the vessel.

"Maiden's tits, what is that?" Sylah screamed. The tidewind had started too early—the sun hadn't even set.

Zero had started to laugh as he careened from one side of the railing to the other, delighted sounds gurgling up from his belly. The sea heaved up and down, settling for a moment. Sylah leaned over the railing.

The black water was flecked with bubbles and froth. Something was churning beneath the waves, Sylah could feel it. She saw a shadow. Then something large burst through the water and crashed back down toward the ship.

It looked like a tail, but it couldn't be, nothing was that large. Nothing except . . . the Tannin.

Sylah ran to the elder. "We need to get to the lower deck now!"

Zero pushed her off and shook his head, his eyes taking in the wonder of the Tannin as it broke the surface again. Sylah turned just in time to see the tail crash down two handspans away from the bow of the ship.

The tail was the width of Sylah's arm. And white, bone white, with scales of clear glass. She didn't stop to marvel and pulled open the hatch to the panicked face of Jond.

"It's here, isn't it?"

Sylah nodded. "Help me get Elder Zero down the hatch. He won't come."

Jond looked behind him on the ladder. There was some scuffling, then Jond said to someone else, "You don't want to come up here."

All of a sudden he was yanked backward and the face of Ravenwing appeared. He climbed onto the deck followed by Dew and Reed.

Are they coming? Ravenwing signed to Reed, who nodded curtly.

"What are you doing? You're going to die up here!" Sylah tried to shout, but the wind was in a frenzy, sea water spraying across her face.

Jond reappeared. "What's going on?" He climbed up onto the deck too. "Why aren't we going underwater?" He had to yell in Sylah's ear for her to hear him. She shook her head. The Tannin burst from the water again, but this time its face breached the waves.

That was when Sylah realized what she had thought was a tail was just a fin. The sea monster was impossibly large, the head half the size of the *Baqarah* with teeth of thick sharpened glass. Its snout hooked forward, ending in a point adorned with slanted nostrils the size of Sylah's whole body. Its triangular head ended in two white horns. And its eyes were as black as the depths of the ocean and shone with malevolent intelligence.

Sylah found herself holding Jond's hand as the head rose higher, higher, higher in the sky. The air was filled with the sound of rocks grinding together and Sylah realized the Tannin's vertebrae weren't bone, but whitestone.

What manner of creature is made of whitestone and glass?

A creature of nightmares.

Sylah still held Elder Zero's belt in her other hand, the metal scoring into her skin as she gripped it like a lifeline. The wind whipped around the beast creating a sea-spray hurricane. It wielded the tidewind like it was a part of it, its breath, its soul.

Jond's hand quivered in hers and Sylah dropped it.

The elders were moving, shifting toward the edge of the railing as the Tannin continued to rise.

Sylah tried to catch their conversation.

Are they coming?

Yes, I sent for them, the crew are bringing them up now.

It's time for me. I will make the first sacrifice. That was Elder Dew.

It was as if the Tannin could understand them. Its huge jaw opened wider, and Sylah suddenly realized what Elder Dew was going to do. They stepped out onto the edge of the bow and opened the gate that Jond had fallen out of that morning.

Sylah screamed and began to run forward, the wind and sea spray slashing at her skin.

Elder Zero was the only one who turned around at her scream. He looked at her and winked. Then without hesitation he pushed Dew out of the way and jumped into the swirling sea. The Tannin sensed a body in the water and lunged, the ship shaking in the wake of its movement.

Sylah rushed to the railing and looked for Zero in the water. Though she couldn't see his blood, she knew he was gone.

"Sylah." Jond tugged on her shoulder, his voice clear in the respite of the Tannin's dive.

She turned around. Lining the edge of the ship were eleven prisoners. Each of them looked half-starved, their eyes blurry from hunger, drugs, or both. Some had to be held up by crew members.

"Who arc they?" Sylah shouted at the elders. The *remaining* elders. Dew had slumped against Reed, tears streaming down both their faces.

"What's going on?" Ads appeared at the top of the ladder. "That's the overseer of the village."

Ads pointed to one of the prisoners shivering in tattered clothing.

Elder Ravenwing strode forward and began to herd the prisoners to the gate. He was signing angrily to the crew who hadn't yet seen the threat of the Tannin with their own eyes. Sylah watched in morbid wonder.

"They're sacrifices. Embers," Sylah said to Jond. "One for each of us."

"What are you doing with Yera?" Ads was shrieking, crying now. "Yera helped build this ship, her bloodwerk is why we're moving right now." Ads was screaming at Elder Ravenwing. He turned to Sylah.

You understand?

Sylah nodded.

Restrain her, please.

Sylah grabbed Ads from behind and clasped her thin wrists in one hand. With her other hand Sylah tied Elder Zero's belt across the girl's torso, pinning her arms in place. Then she knelt on her, pushing her head away from the gate in the railing. The girl bucked and screamed until her voice went hoarse.

The Tannin returned, the length of its body so frightening that the sight of it threatened to loosen Sylah's bowels. She wanted to cower from its gaze, this creature born of sacrifice, but she felt drawn to the depths of its eyes.

Who are you? Where did you come from? she thought.

It cocked its head as if it perceived Sylah too. As if it saw her for who she was: a murderer, a killer.

A kindred spirit.

Sylah felt the breath go out of her as it loomed higher before diving once more.

One by one the Ghostings pushed the Embers into the sea. One by one the Tannin devoured them.

The sea turned red as the sky turned black.

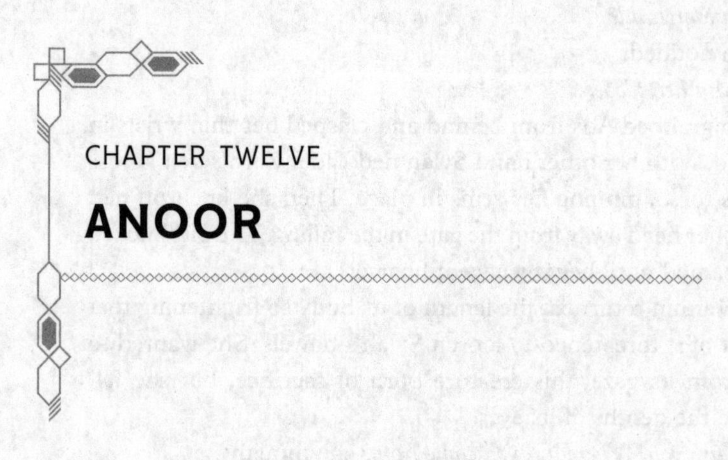

CHAPTER TWELVE

ANOOR

If you want to kill someone quickly, pierce their carotid artery.
If you want to kill someone quietly, sever their trachea.
If you want to kill someone in revenge, slit their throat.

—Master Inansi to the Sandstorm rebels

Anoor ran into thc hallway of her mother's home and screamed, "Get a healer, quickly!"

Even though the rational part of her mind had recognized her mother was dead, the fact that the body was still warm made Anoor think there was time for her yet.

Rasa appeared at the end of the hallway and frowned at Anoor's theatrics.

"It's the warden, her throat has been cut."

Uka's chief of chambers lurched forward like a palm tree pushed in the tidewind. Her slippers skidded along the floor as she ran to get a healer. Servants began murmuring and appearing out of rooms, their curiosity turning to horror as they watched Rasa running faster than they'd ever seen her move. Her screams of "Healer! By the blood, get a healer" echoed down the hall.

Anoor went back into the dining room, the door shut behind her. The sudden silence crept up the hairs on her arm and pressed down on her chest, stilling her breath.

Her chest spasmed and her lungs screamed as her body instinctively tried to grasp onto life.

"Mother." The words let in a torrent of air, tinged with iron, down her throat.

Am I meant to cry? Anoor wondered.

Her mother was dead in front of her. Dead. A laugh hiccupped out of her and Anoor held her hand to her mouth in horror.

"Warden. Oh, Warden Uka . . ." Rasa returned and Anoor wondered how long she had stood there staring at her mother's upright form.

She thought about what Sylah would say. In fact, Anoor knew what she'd say: *She finally has an excuse for looking so uptight—rigor mortis.*

Anoor stifled another laugh. Her right hand joined her left at her mouth, clamping her smile closed. Rasa was kneeling by Uka, murmuring a prayer.

"Returneth to Anyme, our God in the sky. We thank thee for what you give us, we praise thee for where you lead us. Anyme, we serve thee for how you punish us. The blood, the power, the life."

Rasa met Anoor's gaze with tear-filled eyes.

"What happened?"

"I don't know, I arrived, and she was already . . . dead."

A low moan escaped Rasa. The servant placed her head in Uka's lap.

Anoor heard the trudge of multiple footsteps. A healer entered the room with a group of orderlies.

"Let me see her." The healer's voice was deep and smooth. His expression held the neutral demeanor of someone unfazed by pain or danger.

Anoor knew what would happen next. She'd read it enough times in *The Tales of Inquisitor Abena.* First would come the medical investigation; then, when the officers arrived, they'd begin searching the crime scene.

On cue the healer started to examine the body.

Anoor, feeling qualified by the number of detective stories she'd read, began searching for evidence. First, she went to the balcony and pushed the door open. She stepped slowly into the outside air, the curtains billowing with her in the wind.

The view during the day would have been spectacular. Anoor knew this, because she'd grown up staring through the iron railings dreaming of the world beyond. The gardens at this time of year were full of summer blooms. But now, all Anoor could see was a dark gathering of shadows and the swirling red of runelamps.

She heard the healer confirm Uka's death behind her.

". . . Not long ago, half a strike, maybe less . . ." The healer's voice was soothing, and Anoor found herself feeling very sleepy. She walked back into the dining room and closed the balcony door. There were no clues out there that she could see.

"Rasa, inform the wardens, tell them I'll be meeting with the general." She barked the order, like Inquisitor Abena would have. "We'll need to begin a search for the culprit immediately." Another wave of tiredness struck her, and she couldn't stop the yawn that stretched its way out of her mouth and cracked her jaw.

Rasa's eyes widened. "You think the murderer is still out there?"

"Of course, unless they're in here?" Anoor said softly. The healer shifted his feet at that.

"Disciple, what would you like us to do with the body?"

"Prepare it for burning."

And with that Anoor left the room.

Anoor didn't know where the night had gone. She felt like she'd been whipped into the tidewind's heart, left grated and raw. Though she didn't remember the tidewind coming, she knew it must have done, as the officers' search had been contained within the walls of the Keep.

Anoor slumped against the front door of her chambers, her shoulders drooping downward. As soon as the tension released from her neck the door swung open.

"Agh." Anoor screeched and fell backward onto the floor of her foyer. For a moment she just lay there prostrate, the cool marble a welcome relief on her cheek.

"Anoor, where have you been?" Kwame's voice was higher than she'd ever heard it. Anoor sat up and looked up at his face.

"Anoor?" Gorn's footsteps preceded her worried expression appearing above Anoor.

There was a shuffle and Anoor saw Hassa appear in the doorway, out of breath, her uniform disheveled.

I heard what happened to your mother, Hassa signed from the doorway. Kwame and Gorn didn't see Hassa's signs at first. They were too concerned for the prostrate Anoor.

Hassa didn't offer condolences or congratulations. She just met Anoor's eyes and waited for her permission to show the emotion Anoor wanted her to portray.

Am I sad? Am I happy? The questions bounced around a vacuous hole in her mind. A hole of darkness where grief festered.

There was no doubt her mother was a cruel woman who had abused and mistreated her. "Maggot," she'd called Anoor in her journal. Anoor closed her eyes and thought, *At least maggots change. I transformed long ago.*

"Let's help her up. Obviously something happened at the dinner with Uka. I swear on Anyme, I will kill that woman someday," Gorn muttered.

Anoor giggled. She tried to contain it, but it wouldn't stop. It shook her shoulders and curdled in her stomach, bursting out of her in loud guffaws. She sat up, and leaned forward, holding her head in her hands both in horror and in delight. Gorn had taken a step away from her as if Anoor had caught a disease. Maybe she had.

She was certainly sick.

Hassa bent down beside Anoor and touched her limbs to Anoor's cheeks. She brushed away Anoor's tears. Because Anoor was now crying. Weeping, all-consuming sobs that felt as though they would shake the marrow from her very bones.

"Uka . . . my mother . . . is dead."

ANOOR CRIED FOR over a strike. The tears moved from hysterical to anguished keening until her eyes ran dry. It was only then that she explained what had happened.

"And so the army is sweeping the grounds?" Zuhari asked. Gorn had requested her presence so they could benefit from her expertise.

"Yes, we already searched every room and chamber in the west side of the Keep. We haven't found the murder weapon, and any evidence outside would have been wiped away by the tidewind."

"I request that I go join the efforts as your representative." Zuhari no longer wore the uniform of the army; in its place she had dressed in a lavender suit that more befitted a member of Anoor's Shadow Court. She tugged on the wide collar as if she wasn't used to the loose fit, preferring the choke hold of the army's garb. "There may be something amiss that I can assist with."

"Amiss? You think Anoor might have missed something?" Kwame's mouth curved with scorn. Anoor waved him down.

"It's fine, go, I will need to rejoin them shortly. I only came back to change."

Zuhari gave a firm nod, saluted, and then left the chambers.

Gorn turned to Anoor. "You shouldn't have walked through the Keep alone. You will need an armed squadron with you at all times going forward. If there's an assassin on the loose, you could be next."

Gorn was right. She'd been foolish walking by herself across the Keep. She'd just been so tired. When the general had offered her a guard, she'd dismissed them.

"Do you think it's him?" Anoor asked the question quietly to the room, but they knew who she meant.

Loot, the Warden of Crime, who had made his lair in the Dredge.

When Sylah had won the title of disciple for Anoor, she'd fought Jond—Loot's champion—for the win. Loot was also the leader of the Sandstorm, the group of rebels that had stolen Ember children and raised them to compete in the Aktibar. It was the organization Sylah had been a part of until she had inadvertently led the wardens' army to their hideout. The massacre had left Sylah the lone survivor, until Jond reappeared with Loot, the true leader of the Sandstorm all along.

The silence in the room shivered with the collective intake of breath.

Loot hasn't been seen in weeks. Neither has Jond. I don't think it was them, Hassa signed.

"Besides why would the Sandstorm kill Uka and not you?" Kwame said.

Anoor nodded slowly. Nothing was making sense.

There was a knock at the door, and they all jumped. Kwame sprang up to open it but the door flew open.

"You can't just barge in here—" Gorn started to raise her voice until she saw who stood on the other side. "Warden Wern, Warden Aveed, Warden Pura." Gorn bowed her head.

"Wardens, I said I'll meet you in the courtroom." Anoor pulled herself to her feet. "I'm just going to get changed."

"Search her chambers," Warden Aveed said, ignoring the greetings from the living room. Four officers filed into Anoor's chambers and started rummaging through everything they could see.

"What are you doing?" Anoor said. "Stop. At ease. At ease!" she shouted at the officers, who hesitated until General Dullah parted the gathered wardens with a hiss.

"You listen to me. Not her. She's the suspect and therefore her title is void."

Warden Wern nodded at Dullah's assessment. Her eyes were red-rimmed from crying, and a part of Anoor was pleased to see that someone else was truly upset at Uka's passing.

"Anoor, what is happening?" Kwame murmured beside her.

"I don't know, I don't know, I don't know." Anoor's words ran together as she chanted them out.

Warden Pura smiled and pulled the collar of his gold-edged

robe closer to the creases of his neck wrinkles. "You can thank your new adviser. She pointed out quite clearly that usually in these cases the people closest to the victim committed the crime. So we asked ourselves, who is closer to the victim than her own daughter?"

Zuhari moved past the wardens to stand by Anoor, wringing her hands. "I didn't tell them it was you. I promise, I was just doing my job."

"You," Anoor growled low. "You . . . you set me up. It was you who killed her."

Zuhari looked distraught.

"I didn't do this. I didn't mean to . . . I was just trying to help."

The reasonable part of Anoor knew it couldn't have been Zuhari; she hadn't meant to lead the wardens here. But Anoor wasn't rational today. She balled her hands into fists by her side.

"Why did you do it? Why did you set me up like this?" Anoor demanded.

Zuhari flinched, looking to Gorn with wide, pleading eyes.

Anoor threw Gorn a look of betrayal, but the woman was stoic, watching the scene unfold.

Before Anoor could launch herself at Zuhari an officer appeared.

"General, we found this on her desk." He held out Anoor's red leather-bound journal in his hand. It was open to her last entry.

"Give me that. I am the Warden of Truth," Pura sneered to the room. "The sacred journals are not for your eyes."

Pura's eyes widened as he read.

Anoor racked her brain to try to remember what she had written on the creamy paper that would cause Pura's eyes to bulge out so. Maybe she'd pondered how to replace the sentence of rippings? Or perhaps it was about the progress on the Tidewind Relief Bill?

Wern read the words over Pura's shoulder. "Arrest her," she said with a hiss.

The officer moved in to Anoor's side.

"Wardens, what evidence have you got to warrant this arrest?" Gorn spoke above the hubbub of disbelief.

"What evidence?" Pura spat, then he read from the journal: "'Maybe my mother should spend the night in the Dredge, and perhaps then she would understand. But she wouldn't survive one night in the Dredge. Though that wouldn't be a bad thing . . .'"

He flashed the ink forward.

"Anoor, did you write that?" Gorn asked urgently in her ear.

"Yes . . . but I was angry . . . we'd argued . . . I didn't mean it . . ."

Hadn't she?

Gorn looked to Anoor, but she didn't meet her gaze. She couldn't bear to see the disappointment in her eyes.

"The journal is not the only evidence we have amassed." Aveed spoke for the first time. They watched keenly for Anoor's response.

Pura took over the telling, his voice smug. "After your own adviser put us on the trail, we asked Uka's chief of chambers what happened. She said you'd been laughing. That you seemed amused by your mother's death. And then we asked the healer his thoughts, and you know what? He said you were acting quite strange, quite strange indeed. That you'd gone out onto the balcony." Pura leaned in and Anoor could see spinach in his long white beard. "And guess what we found in the bushes below the balcony?"

Anoor realized why he'd been holding his white cowl so close to his chest. He'd been waiting for this moment.

The big reveal.

Anoor gasped. Pura laid a jambiya on the ground. The curved blade was unembellished, with a leather band wrapped around the hilt.

She recognized it immediately. It had been hanging in her training room along with her other equipment just yesterday morning. Sylah had procured it for her mooncycles ago.

My tidewind shutter . . . it had been broken . . . Anoor suddenly remembered, and she tried to murmur the words, but no one was listening. They were all looking at Pura.

"And so, I asked around. Who fights with a jambiya? And do you know what, Yanis, runner-up in the Aktibar, had a lot to say about you. But most interestingly he said you preferred to fight with the jambiya."

An officer ran into the room holding an empty sheath. Pura grinned in triumph and spread his arms wide before plunging the jambiya into the sheath.

"It fits."

Anoor fell to her knees.

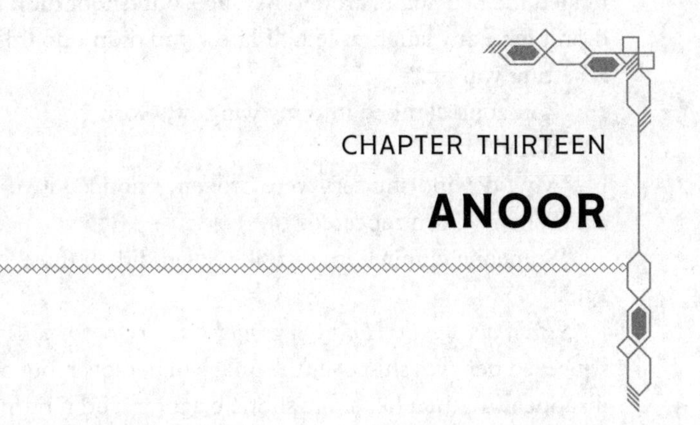

CHAPTER THIRTEEN
ANOOR

UKA ELSARI FOUND MURDERED IN HER CHAMBERS

WE HAVE IT on good authority that Anoor Elsari, Disciple of Strength, is spearheading the search for the killer. We also received a tip in the early strikes of the morning that the disciple was the first on the scene.

—*THE PEOPLE'S GAZETTE*, year 421

Anoor was still on her knees. Though she couldn't feel it, two bruises were beginning to bloom there.

The officer held her training jambiya in his hands, a triumphant grin across his face.

Someone must have stolen the murder weapon from my rooms.

"Move out of the way." The voice came from behind the wardens, and there was some murmuring as they complied. Anoor knew the voice, but it didn't fully register. All she could think was, *I'm going to be arrested for my mother's murder . . .*

". . . Don't you dare speak to me like that, Pura. You may be the Warden of Truth now, which I've always thought was deeply ironic, but I could spill secrets that'd make your precious Anyme fall from the sky . . ."

Gorn's hands clamped around Anoor's elbow.

"Anoor, Anoor, are you okay?" Gorn said in her ear. Her breath tickled the baby hairs around her face, but Anoor didn't laugh; she didn't have any laughter left. "I know you didn't do this. Someone is setting you up."

"Someone climbed into my window, Gorn."

"What?"

"My tidewind shutters were broken, I noticed it yesterday."

"What?" Gorn repeated.

"Someone climbed in, just like Sylah did all those mooncycles ago . . ."

Sylah, oh, Sylah. How you would hate to see me fallen so. Anoor squeezed her eyes shut over the image of her lover, but Sylah didn't disappear. Rather, her smile shone brighter, and it burned Anoor's heart.

"Get up, my kori bird. Get up and fly," Sylah said in Anoor's mind. It gave her the strength she needed.

Anoor pulled herself to her feet with Gorn's help. In the center of the cluster of wardens, Yona's tall form was gesticulating with a folder.

The veins in her neck bulged over the protruding muscles as she spoke: ". . . If you want to formalize it within the courtroom, I'm happy to make the journey, but I've already had to walk across half the Keep to get here, so can we all just agree, given the situation, I am the only choice."

"The laws say it should be the disciple's chief of staff."

Yona's chin took a step back and her body followed. "You want to give the wardenship to the chief of staff who has been working within the court for less than a mooncycle? I am the former Warden of Strength. For two terms, no less. I am not *taking* the role. I'm merely standing in while this mess is sorted out."

Yona looked to Anoor, and Anoor found herself wondering if it hurt her when she removed her wig, so seamless was the glue to her scalp.

Pura shifted his feet and looked to Aveed.

Wern cut them off before either of them could speak. "It's what Uka would want." She sniffed.

This assumption about the will of the deceased confirmed it. The four of them voted Yona in as temporary Warden of Strength. Anoor could barely process what was going on. *Was this a good or a bad thing?*

Yona turned to the general and smiled, showing all her teeth. Anoor noticed how sharp her canines were.

"Anoor Elsari, you are under arrest for the murder of Uka Elsari."

It was a very bad thing.

Anoor watched Kwame's mouth gape open and closed while the officers brought forward iron manacles.

"Stop," Yona said sharply. "Anoor will not be held in jail."

"What?" The wardens rounded on Yona.

Anoor dared to breathe.

"As Warden of Strength the jail is my responsibility, and I am putting Anoor under house arrest until her trial."

"Nepotism," Pura hissed.

"Oh, cry all you want, Pura, isn't your grandson being trained personally by the Abosom for the next Aktibar?"

"We will expedite her trial," Pura said, quivering with rage. "We will hold it tomorrow."

"Oh, will you? Have you read the documentation regarding Upper Court trials?" Yona dropped the folder she was holding to the ground, forcing Pura to bend and pick it up. "It seems that in the year 279 Warden Cera thought it prudent to instigate slightly different laws for us . . . rulers. Something about keeping the population calm. If a member of the Upper Court is accused of an 'egregious ill,' define that as you will, they have three weeks to clear their name *before* being put on trial."

Anoor's wrists were still held out toward the manacles. She couldn't believe what she was hearing.

Was she free?

"Three weeks," Pura barked. "She has three weeks until her trial." He spun on his heels and left. Wern was crying freely now and seemed less aware of the events than the other wardens. After a moment she followed in Pura's wake.

Aveed had watched the exchange warily. They twirled the ends of their long plaits in their hands.

"Be careful, young Elsari," Aveed whispered to Anoor as they passed. "I hope to Anyme you didn't commit this crime, because if you did, you will be prosecuted to the full extent of the law . . . and more besides."

With a nod from Yona the officers left too, leaving Anoor, Yona, Gorn, Kwame, and Zuhari standing in stunned silence.

"I think it might take three people to get three cups of tea, no?" Yona said bluntly. The members of Anoor's Shadow Court scampered away.

"Thank you," Anoor said, the words cracking.

"Did you kill my daughter?" Yona asked. Her voice was quiet and deadly.

"No, of course I didn't. I wouldn't . . . I couldn't—"

Yona waved for her to stop. "I just needed to hear you say it." Grief eked into the creases in Yona's face. She sank into a chair and indicated to Anoor to join her.

"You have three weeks, Anoor. Three weeks to find the *real* murderer."

Anoor dropped her head in her hands. Her mind went to the fictional Inquisitor Abena. Three weeks was more than enough time to solve a murder for her . . . but confined to her rooms? Maybe not.

And what about the tidewind? Nothing mattered beyond that. Who was going to support the Tidewind Relief Bill?

"Grandmother . . . the bill . . . I need it passed through the Upper Court."

Yona shrugged dismissively. "Easy, don't worry about that. Right now, you have no power. Nothing except your mind. Collect evidence, find the killer. Use your Shadow Court, well . . . I guess they're my Shadow Court now." She smiled thinly. "Three weeks, Anoor."

"How can I do anything from *here*?" Anoor hated that her voice came out as a whine.

Yona frowned, then understanding struck her.

"Oh, Anoor. You're under house arrest. Not room arrest."

"I can go around the Keep?"

Yona nodded. "But don't flaunt your freedom. And be careful. I heard what Aveed said. They are not a good enemy to have."

Anoor straightened her shoulders, like Sylah had taught her. "First comes posture, then comes power," she'd said all those weeks ago.

Anoor felt a flicker of confidence.

"Neither am I."

YONA HAD GONE by the time Gorn, Kwame, and Zuhari returned with tea. It was only then that Anoor realized Hassa was no longer with them.

"She left when the wardens arrived," Kwame said. He folded his long limbs onto the sofa.

"Disciple Anoor . . ." Zuhari hovered by the doorway.

"Don't call me that. It's no longer my title," Anoor snapped, letting her anger show.

"A . . . Anoor, I'm sorry, I didn't mean to . . ."

"Get out," Anoor said.

"Anoor, come now, you know she didn't—" Gorn tried to reason with her.

"Get *out*."

Anoor was past reasoning.

When Zuhari left, Gorn opened her mouth to complain.

"No, you don't get to question my judgment here. I don't want to see her right now. I don't trust her. She led them to me, Gorn. Someone you brought into the Shadow Court *led them to me*."

There it was: the accusation. Anoor knew it wasn't Gorn's fault, that it wasn't Zuhari's either, but she needed someone to blame.

"What's the plan?" Kwame broke the tension with a tentative smile.

Anoor rubbed her temples. "We solve my mother's murder."

Gorn looked to Kwame. They didn't have *any* clue. Anoor knew that because she didn't either.

What would Inquisitor Abena do? Anoor stood.

"Come with me, let's look at the crime scene."

Anoor led them down the corridor to her room.

"Eh, Anoor? The crime scene isn't here." Kwame tried to sound polite as he followed Anoor into her bedroom.

"Not where my mother died. Where my jambiya was stolen."

"Oh."

Anoor gasped as she entered. Her room had been ransacked. Clothing was spilling out of her dressing room and shoes lay flung about the place. The desk overlooking the courtyard had been upended with papers scattered among tangled bed sheets and bathing products that had been thrown to the ground. The officers had desecrated the safest place she had.

Despair threatened to consume her. How was she supposed to glean anything from this?

Gorn stepped forward into the mess and began to stack a nearby cluster of papers.

Anoor squeezed her eyes shut and thought back to her zines.

"Stop." Anoor's command rang out and Gorn froze. "We need to protect the scene." She spoke with the authority of Inquisitor Abena.

"Protect the scene?" Gorn repeated.

"Yes, don't touch anything. We need to analyze it as it is."

"But Anoor, this isn't a crime scene, it's a mess."

Anoor let a tentative smile spread across her face as she recited one of Abena's catch phrases. "Everything's a crime scene—"

"—when everyone's a suspect." Gorn finished the phrase.

Anoor looked at her questioningly and Gorn shrugged.

"I like to read the zines too."

Kwame looked between them and snorted, "What do you want us to do? Sit around and look at it?"

Anoor sucked on her bottom lip. "Pass me that paper, Gorn. And that pen please. But be careful, don't upset anything else."

The three of them moved systematically through the chaos,

Anoor documenting every piece of furniture out of place, every item that had been strewn from its home. By the time they got to the window she had three pages of notes.

The courtyard was quiet down below, but she ignored the view for once and tugged on the bloodwerk lever next to the glass. The little bloodwerk motor started to lower the tidewind shutters on the outside of the window.

She looked to the left corner, where she'd seen the broken piece of metal paneling.

"Wait . . . what?"

Gorn was silent as Anoor reversed the shutter.

"It was broken, there, can you see? Someone's fixed it . . ." Anoor couldn't believe what she was seeing. The broken panel had been replaced. She would have doubted her memory if the metal wasn't slightly shinier than the panel next to it.

"Who have you let into the apartment in the last day?" Anoor whirled on Gorn.

"No one, it's just been us." Anoor saw the flicker of doubt in her chief of staff's eyes.

"I'm telling you: it was broken just yesterday."

"Anoor . . ." Kwame shifted his feet. "It's not that we don't believe you, it's just that there's not much to go on here. Gorn's been here the whole time."

Anoor lifted her chin and looked levelly at Gorn.

"Not the whole time. Didn't you leave the chambers for a personal errand last night?"

Gorn met her stare.

"I was not gone long. Besides, they would have had to steal the jambiya, make it across the Keep, and kill Uka in the time between you leaving and arriving at your mother's door."

Anoor let out an exasperated sigh. "Maybe it was one of the officers when they were searching through my room."

Gorn and Kwame exchanged a look.

"You think . . . a *warden* set you up?" Kwame asked.

"No . . . maybe . . . I don't know . . ."

Anoor moved through the mess toward her dressing room. All

her fighting equipment was on the floor, and all of it accounted for except the jambiya. Anoor swallowed, trying to gain control of her wobbling lip.

"Wait . . . look." Kwame was pointing to the ground.

Anoor followed his gaze, but the hope that rose sank a moment later. "A footprint? It must be just one of the officers'. See, it's got some of my face powder in it, so the print could only have been left after they tipped over my makeup case. Not sure what they were looking for in there."

It was clear the damage the officers had done to her room had been vindictive. They believed she killed their leader, so in turn, they'd wreaked havoc on her home.

As Anoor turned away from the footprint something else caught her eye. A small smear of blue mud on the edge of the doorway to her dressing room

"Kwame." Anoor grabbed his forearm with growing excitement. "Did it rain this morning?"

Gorn joined them, drawn in by the tone of Anoor's voice.

"No," she said. "It only rained yesterday afternoon."

"I left my shoes by the door. Did either of you come into my dressing room yesterday afternoon?"

Gorn and Kwame shook their heads.

"And there'd be no reason for the officers to have mud on their boots today . . ." Anoor went on.

All three of them exhaled collectively.

"Someone was here yesterday afternoon," Kwame confirmed.

Anoor grinned.

"We have our first piece of evidence."

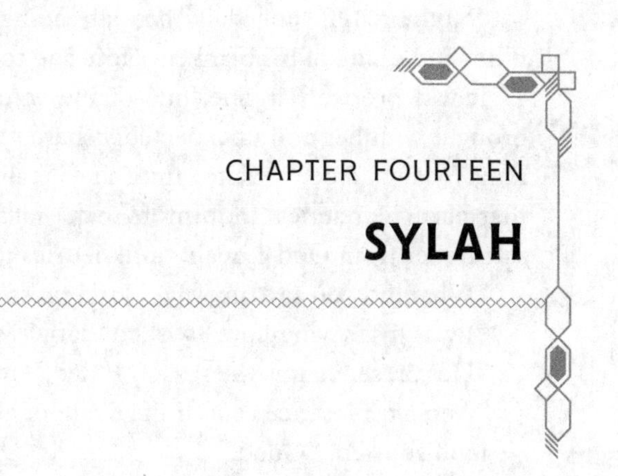

CHAPTER FOURTEEN

SYLAH

—"The Freedom Song" sung by the Ghostings

Ads had been inconsolable for days. Her weeping echoed down the corridor of the ship like the moaning of a pod of whales.

"By the hairiest monkey's bollocks, when will that girl stop her wailing," Sylah said in her hammock, to no one in particular.

When Jond didn't answer, Sylah lifted her foot and kicked his hammock, sending him careening into the cabin's wall.

"Aho, watch out," he said. On the return swing he added, "What did you do that for?"

"You didn't answer me."

Jond's seasickness had eased after he'd found the stash of ginger tea to treat it. Sylah wished Ads had never told him. She preferred him pliable and sickly.

"I didn't hear you," Jond replied.

"What were you doing?" Sylah peered over the lip of her hammock to his, less than five handspans away.

"Nothing." He looked like he was reading a book, but he stuffed it down the side of his blanket before she could read the title.

It was probably a zine, one of the volumes Elder Reed had brought with her and unexpectedly shared with the ship one evening. Sylah had been excited until she'd realized she'd already read that particular series. Inquisitor Abena falls in love with a rogue salt-trader from Ood-Lopah, until he tries to kill her.

"What did you say, anyway?" Jond pressed.

"I was just saying how I wished that girl would stop crying."

"Her presence was the reason Elder Zero sacrificed himself."

"And *our* presence caused the death of eleven other Embers."

Jond snorted. "Good."

Sylah brought her hands up behind her head. She no longer believed that all Embers deserved to die. It had been an ideology that Azim had indoctrinated all of the Sandstorm with. Though there were some Embers Sylah would still gladly see dead—Uka Elsari for one. She wondered if the elders felt any guilt toward the Embers they'd killed.

Sylah's own remorse was dulled as she thought of Anoor. She needed Sylah to go on this journey, and so Sylah was here.

Sylah pulled on the shell in her hair as she spoke. "Why do you think the Tannin required a sacrifice?"

"Because the world is fucked."

"Yes, I think you're right."

Jond guffawed. "That's a first."

Sylah kicked him, and he went swinging harder than the first time.

"Will you stop that?"

"No, I don't think I will," Sylah replied, kicking him again.

She saw the flash of his grin and got out of her hammock. The sight of Jond's smile pained her.

She turned away from him and reached down for her box of herbs and began to make Jond's tincture. She wondered if he'd figured out yet the potion she'd been giving him was harmless and not really the antidote she pretended it was.

"Drink," she commanded, passing him the little vial.

His eyes glittered as he swallowed the liquid in one.

As he handed her back the emptied vial she asked, "Jond, why?"

She couldn't form the full question, *Why did you betray me?* It hurt too much.

"Why what, Sylah?" He said the words with a sigh, letting her know he knew what she had asked. All she had to do was wait for his answer.

Sylah watched the black sea churn in the tidewind through their porthole. She noticed the hurricane had lessened of late and wondered if the elders' belief that the tidewind didn't afflict the queendom of Tenio was true.

Jond scratched his coarse beard. He was obviously sorting through the lies he had told her over the last few mooncycles. She couldn't wait to hear his excuses.

Finally, he spoke. "Sometimes believing in something else is all you have. Especially if you don't believe in yourself."

Sylah listened to the soft lilt of his words, savored them for a moment—and then burst out laughing.

"What a steaming pile of eru shit, don't come at me with that. Don't tell me some inner faith had you blindly following Loot like the puppy you are. I want to hear the truth."

"And what do you think that is?" Jond hissed.

"That you're a spineless fuck who is too weak to think for himself, too weak to consider his actions, too weak to question. You keep saying Loot told you nothing, that you didn't know he had yellow blood, and I'm starting to believe you. Why would Loot need to tell you anything? You're nothing but a dead man's weapon filled with a dead man's words." Sylah was shouting now, and it helped to drown out Ads's cries. "Azim and Loot are gone, and yet *you* are alive."

"If I am so abhorrent to you, why didn't you just kill me?"

At this Sylah smiled, and it soothed the flames of her anger. "Because I know that every day you wake up you find yourself being grateful to me. And like a cut from a hundred scythes, it'll slice you bit by bit until you find yourself coated in the blood of your self-hatred."

She turned to make a dramatic exit. The effect was ruined when she tripped on the lip of the doorframe on her way out. She let herself fall to the ground and lie there for a moment until the face of Elder Dew appeared above her.

Is your hammock not comfortable? Dew smiled, and Sylah felt her frustration from the conversation with Jond melt away.

"Thought I'd try sleeping out here." Sylah pulled herself up to standing. The ship swayed but no longer lurched. "The tidewind is getting weaker."

Yes, it is, we're nearing Tenio. Do you want some coffee?

Sylah nodded, wondering what the time was. She voiced the thought.

It is second strike in the morning, Dew replied.

The elders had a small clock in the center of the mess hall that only Elder Dew could read after studying it for many years. Sylah had been shocked to find another relic like the clock in Nar-Ruta. It had taken her some time to recall that the "relics" of the empire were actually items made by the Ghostings' ancestors. Sylah knew the Ghostings had recovered as many artifacts as they could from the ruins across the empire. It saddened her to think of all the histories lost during the Embers' conquest of the land.

They walked past the room where the Ember sacrifices had been kept. Dew had called it the "storage room," but really it had been a prison. The Embers had been drugged and kept alive only to feed the Tannin and ensure the *Baqarah*'s safe passage.

Sylah shuddered and reached for her braids. She had woven some of the metal from Elder Zero's silver belt into a plait by her ear. Sometimes the sharp wire stabbed her in the night, but she liked the pain of his memory.

"Elder Dew." Sylah took a breath while she figured out how to formulate her question. "Who were the Embers you killed?"

Dew's walking stick struck the metal floor. *Some were part of the governing family of Jin-Sukar; others were Embers we had captured during raids.*

Sylah nodded, blinking rapidly.

"How . . . how did you choose them? For the sacrifice?"

Dew smiled tightly and signed, *Get to the meat of the question, Sylah, let us not spend time chewing on gristle.*

"Do you not worry that by killing defenseless Embers you're becoming the people you are fighting against?"

Dew's gray eyes glittered as they looked at Sylah. She couldn't hold the intensity of their depth and dipped her chin to the floor, looking through her eyelashes as Dew signed, *Must not the oppressed become the oppressor in order to further change?*

Sylah wasn't sure what to say to that. It reminded her of something Azim would have said.

Then Dew signed, *Rest your conscience. Though we may use the tools of the empire, we have sharpened them to ease the sting. Every Ember had undergone a trial, and their crimes were tallied before being chosen. Execution was not a decision made by idle minds.*

Sylah let out a long sigh as the muscles across her back eased.

The mess hall was empty, and their breathing echoed around the room like wind through leaves.

Dew moved around the space slowly, setting the coffee to brew while Sylah got the mugs. She reached into the pouch at her waist and added a few grains of joba seed powder to her cup.

Does it still plague you so?

Sylah probed her tongue between her teeth, missing the bitterness of the joba seeds that once resided there. "Yes, it is something I must learn to live with. But it is a struggle. Each day I add a pinch of powder to my drinks to keep the symptoms at bay. But each day, I have to stay my hand from grabbing more."

Dew nodded as if they understood. But they didn't. They couldn't. No one who hadn't been through it could understand.

"I don't need it like I used to. I don't even want it anymore. But the memory of ecstasy is hard to forget. And each day I have to *choose* not to relive it. I have to choose to take just . . . a . . . pinch." Sylah held her thumb and forefinger in front of her. Just the gesture had her reminiscing about oblivion.

Then she thought of Anoor—a different type of addiction. One that was good for her, but now so far away. Her eyes moved to the fathomless black of the sea, swirling behind the panels of glass.

Dew moved to pour the coffee, their limbs deftly tilting the large kettle toward their mugs.

Sylah collected hers and took a seat on the metal bench in the center of the mess hall.

They sat in silence for a little while, each consumed by their thoughts.

The wariness that had entered Dew's eyes since Sylah had mentioned the Embers drained out of them. *I hope you have had some time to forgive our deception,* Dew signed. *That was my fault, I am afraid. I believed the fewer people who knew what had to be done, the less blame we would need to bear.*

Sylah thought about Dew's words and sipped on her coffee before answering.

"I know they were Embers and I know that you said they weren't good people. But I will feel the weight of their sacrifice for the rest of my life."

Dew nodded. *That is the way it should be. Now you understand the cost. We made a bigger sacrifice than we expected.* The creases under Dew's eyes sagged in the absence of tears. *But now you understand the price we pay.*

Sylah nodded.

And the price we must pay to get back.

Sylah thought of Anoor and knew that she would do anything to get back to her.

Anything.

"Can you tell me what you know of the queendom of Tenio?" She posed the question to distract her from Anoor's face in her mind's eye.

We know what our ancestors have told us. Before it was united as a queendom it was populated by eight tribes. The monarchy has ruled for hundreds of years, thousands possibly, and are a beloved family. Of the Zwina Academy we know a little more. The diary of one of our elders tells of a city filled with books and bursting with knowledge. I have studied the pages of the journal for many years. But the words are old. We do not know what will greet us when we get there.

"Are there erus with two heads and talking trees?" Sylah

snorted. Jond had joked that they were what faced them on the mainland.

Dew recoiled with a bemused expression.

They are your ancestors. Unless you know of any talking trees in your family?

Sylah laughed. "I don't think so . . ." Not that she knew who her family really were. Her smile slipped.

They are like you and me, but they use bloodwerk differently on the continent.

"How?"

The devices they use to transfer blood look very different from inkwells.

Dew didn't expand further.

"You learned about the Tannin from the journal too?"

Dew inclined their head. *Yes, though the creature did not roam the Marion Sea until the elder journeyed back. It was then that they discovered the sacrifice needed to cross its path.*

The conversation had gone full circle, and fresh grief entered the lines of Dew's face once more.

Sylah stroked the braid with Zero's belt.

"He made his choice. But we will always remember the price he paid," Sylah said to Dew as she stood.

Dew didn't respond so she left them there slumped forward in their chair, their chest concave as if carrying the weight of their grief on their shoulders.

It was a sight that haunted her dreams.

SYLAH WOKE LONG after dawn. She'd come to recognize the sun streaks on the water, and the time of day they represented. It was near noon she guessed.

There was an absence in the silence, and it wasn't just from Jond's empty hammock—Ads had stopped crying.

Sylah made her way to the upper deck. Now the *Baqarah* had breached the surface of the ocean, she would be free to walk there until the sun set. It was how she spent her days.

As she climbed the ladder, she heard laughter.

". . . no, you jump to the right. Yes, there you go. Then try and tap my toe . . . now my elbow. Aho. I got you first, do you see?"

Jond was teaching Ads how to play "Bow-clap-no." The sight of it struck Sylah in the chest, and she nearly toppled back down the ladder to the corridor below.

—"Fareen, you've got to go faster. See here. Elbow, clap . . . there. You got me." Sylah had made up a game to help improve Fareen's reflexes. Papa had been so mad to see her fail the reaction time test he had set.

"Sylah, this isn't a game." She laughed, trying to tap Sylah's elbow before she got hers.

"If it isn't a game, how did I just . . . win."

Fareen lunged out of the way, but too slow for Sylah. "Aho. Got you again."

"Jond," Fareen screeched. "Come and play this game Sylah's made up. It's called . . . ?"

"Bow-clap-no," Sylah said.

Jond appeared from the barn behind them. Though only fourteen, he was already corded with muscle, his small form stable at what would later be his maximum height.

"That sounds made up."

Fareen shimmied her shoulders and said, "I to-old you. You made it up." She pointed an accusatory finger at Sylah.

"No, Jond knows it, don't you, Jond?"

"Do I?" he replied. Sylah widened her eyes. "Oh, yes, of course I do. All I have to do is . . ."

". . . try and touch my elbow, but first . . ." Sylah filled in the gaps for him.

". . . first I have to . . ."

". . . clap and you can only lunge backward on one . . ."

". . . hand? Foot, no, foot. You can only lunge backward on one foot."

Fareen was belly-laughing on the ground, watching Jond's bemused expression as he tried to guess the rules.

"Demonstrate, demonstrate," her little voice demanded.

Sylah and Jond obliged, their eyes dancing their private jig as they faced each other.

"Ready?" Jond asked, his voice rumbling and low. It made Sylah's

tummy swirl, but it didn't distract her. She lunged, clapped, and tapped his elbow.

"I win," she announced into Jond's open-mouthed stare.

Fareen clapped and whooped.—

"What are you doing?" Sylah's voice came out deathly quiet. Everyone else on the deck turned to look at her.

Jond didn't raise his head. Instead he took the opportunity to clap, and tap Ads's elbow.

"Hey, that's not fair, I was distracted." She pouted.

"Jond, I asked what are you doing?"

At this he exhaled and looked up at Sylah. "I'm playing a game."

Something in Sylah sparked like the beginning of a flame. She marched toward him, pushing Ads out of the way.

"You don't get to play that game." Some spittle flew from her mouth and Jond blinked and wiped his eye.

"Sylah, I was just trying to make Ads laugh. Look, she's stopped crying, right?"

"You don't get to play that game," Sylah repeated, a slight tremble in her voice.

"Okay, okay, we'll stop." Jond held out two placating hands and stepped back from Sylah.

The deck had gone quiet.

Sylah stood there, her hot breath ragged. She ignored the stares and walked up to the railing.

"You don't get to own all the grief, Sylah. I lost her too, you know," Jond said softly. Sylah ignored him until eventually he walked away.

The sea spray was cold and welcoming.

ANOTHER WEEK PASSED and Sylah still refused to talk to Jond. She avoided him as much as she could, but the *Baqarah* wasn't large enough to hide from him completely. Ads had begun to follow him around like a love-sick bird that had imprinted on the nearest person. Wherever Sylah turned the two of them were there, playing shantra, cooking dinner, even fishing. Ads's laughter had a way of reverberating around the ship and Sylah almost wished she were still weeping.

Sylah still spent most of her time on the upper deck during the day. Although she'd never call them friends, she'd gotten to know the five crew members enough to comfortably slot into their daily routine.

How is it going? Petal asked Sylah. She was the youngest crew member and Sylah's favorite among them, maybe among the whole ship. She was bright and lively with wispy blond hair that had grown out into curly tufts around her suntanned face. Unlike most of the Ghosting crew members, Petal had chosen to ditch her drab uniform at the earliest opportunity, opting for bright colors and patterned fabric. She still wore the gazelle pin proudly on her chest.

I make my own clothes out of fabric that I can trade for, Petal had once informed Sylah. *The brown servant's garb is the cloth we can acquire the most of, but once a year I use my savings from the fish I sell, and trade whatever I can for the brightest cotton. I can only wear it in the Chrysalis, though. And now here.*

She'd twirled and Sylah had grimaced at the patchwork colors clashing in the sun. Sylah tried to muster a polite smile. She'd got a lot of practice with Anoor.

"I think I've nearly got it," Sylah said, twisting the rod of the fishing line, her stylus tipped red.

And you think this will help us catch more fish?

"Well, it'll make it easier to reel them in. I've also triggered the spear so that you just have to aim it and press your wrist against the rune." Sylah's bloodwerk wasn't flawless, but she'd learned enough to make small improvements around the ship.

Maybe we can catch a lava fish? Petal's eyes lit up. Lava fish had spectacular scales that could be used to decorate garments and add glitter to jewelry.

Anoor had worn a lot of sparkling garments. The pain of missing her struck Sylah like the spear she held.

"I'm not sure there are any lava fish this far away from the empire's coast," Sylah replied.

The fish have been getting bigger, you know. I wonder if it's because the tidewind has stopped. Petal sat down on the metal deck next to Sylah and brought her knees to her chest.

Sylah frowned. When had it stopped? Strange that something so constant could disappear without her noticing.

"Here, try this." Sylah handed her the fishing rod and watched Petal as she flung it over the edge. "Just press the lever to the right . . . yes, exactly, and it'll extract more line."

Petal smiled and nodded back to Sylah, letting her know it was working while her arms were occupied.

Sylah dozed as Petal fished. After some time, another crew member walked over, intrigued by Petal's impressive haul. He asked Sylah to modify his fishing rod, which she happily did. By the second strike of the day, all five crew members had taken it in turns to get Sylah to bloodwerk on their equipment.

As the deck began to pile up with fresh fish, the Ghostings began to sing. It wasn't singing as Sylah had known it, nor had she ever heard anything quite like it. They used their voice boxes as instruments, humming deep within their throats. One of the crew began to huff out a harsh exhale, adding a beat of percussion to their music. Petal sang an open-mouthed minor key that trilled up and down an octave.

Together it was a beautiful and haunting melody. The sorrowful tune caused the corners of Sylah's eyes to moisten as she watched the native people of the Wardens' Empire truly speak for the first time.

And they were saying: *Listen. We are coming.*

CHAPTER FIFTEEN

SYLAH

The city of Nsuo is one of the smallest port cities in Tenio. The lack of trade from the west means that the port is predominantly occupied by fishing vessels. Those who sail the waters of the Marion Sea are also subjected to vicious hurricanes and the threat of the sea monster that roams the far western depths, so only small vessels occupy the harbor now. The city still benefits from the fishing trade and has a lively and affluent population.

—Extract from *The Towns and Cites of Tenio* by Bole Oh-Nene

"Land, I see land," Ads cried.

And she was right. There it was, cleaved into the horizon: a hazy shadow of land just below the sinking sun. Sylah leaned forward on the railing, her chest pressed to the metal. She wondered if anyone else could feel her heart vibrating against the barrier.

"We should be there by midnight, maybe a bit before," Ads said, hopping down the hatch to share her excitement with those below deck.

Sylah nodded and turned her gaze back to the mainland. If the map they were following wasn't wrong, then they'd arrive in Port Nsuo. She watched the land get larger and larger as they approached. At some point Jond joined her.

"I want to come with you to the Academy," he said.

"No." The word was out of Sylah's mouth before Jond had finished speaking.

"Why not?"

"As soon as your feet touch the ground, you're in exile. I don't want to see you again."

"If I'm in exile I have the choice to go where I want, and I want to go with you."

Sylah looked at him, expecting to see the simmering rage that he always projected at her, but instead what she saw was softer, akin to the feelings he'd shown her before. Her heart contorted, and it felt like yearning.

This is what she'd been afraid of.

"You tried to kill me, Jond." She mustered the anger that had been cooling toward him over the last few weeks.

Jond sighed and looked down to the depths of the Marion Sea. The colors were shifting from dark blue to black. "No, I didn't."

"Jond, you swung your axe for my neck."

"No, I didn't," Jond whispered, and Sylah struggled to hear him over the rushing waves. Or was it the rushing of her blood?

He continued, "I had twisted the pommel so the flat side of the blade would have hit your temple, knocking you out."

Sylah tried to think back to that moment but all she could see was the unflinching obedience in Jond's moves.

"Great, thank you for trying to knock me out. I'm glad you had the presence of mind to delay my death a little longer."

Jond growled in frustration, his hair lifting in the wind.

"I would never have killed you, Sylah."

"I don't believe you."

His jaw jutted out with the anger she was more used to. She was relieved to see it. Anger between them was familiar territory. Safe territory.

But then Jond did something entirely unexpected. He told the truth.

"I was . . . jealous." He rubbed the shadow of his beard, the jut of his chin receding. "I was jealous of . . . of Anoor."

Anoor's name burned Sylah's throat, and she flinched with the heat of it.

"Sylah, I would never have killed you. Just like you could never kill me."

She snorted. But she knew it was true.

"I don't ever remember not loving you," Jond continued. "There was never a time when you weren't the person for me, no before, and no after. You made your choice, I know that, but . . ." he pulled in a ragged breath ". . . please will you let me come with you? I have nowhere else to go."

Sylah smiled and reached for the shell in her hair. She knew her journey would take her far, but her destination was always the same—back to Anoor.

She rolled her shoulders and drew her gaze level with Jond. She still felt it, the sting of betrayal.

"Do you remember the promise I made you? When I was bound in Loot's chambers? I told you that one day I would make you feel so alone, that the very darkness would be your only friend."

Sylah gestured out to the falling night.

"I will never regret not seeing you again."

If her words were true, why did they hurt her so much?

Jond stayed next to her for some time, barely breathing. Eventually he pushed himself off from the railing and made his way down to their cabin.

NSUO WASN'T WHAT Sylah expected from what she could see in the dark. Skeletal remains of ships haunted the harbor, and the crew were forced to navigate their way carefully into a docking station. There was a strong organic smell of decaying wood and something else, something bitter that singed her nose. The silhouette of the city could be seen in the distance, but Sylah couldn't make out any sign of life, just the silvered presence of the moon.

The tidewind had entirely abated in the last few days of their journey, and standing outside at midnight was a marvel Sylah would never not appreciate.

"Why isn't anyone here to greet us?" Ads asked the question everyone was thinking.

The entire crew and the three elders stood at the bow of the *Baqarah*, watching the darkness in silence.

Elder Dew breathed in and hummed softly.

We should stay the night on the ship. In the morning we will make our way to the city and see what we can glean from the townsfolk.

But Sylah couldn't sleep, or maybe it wasn't that she couldn't, she just wasn't willing to sleep in the cabin with Jond—with his words hanging heavy on her eyelids.

Zero would have known what to do. He would have plunged into the darkness without a second thought. It was Petal. She turned away from the railing and the moon illuminated the multi-colored pattern of her dress.

Sylah nodded at her comment.

"Indeed, he would have."

Petal turned to Sylah and smiled sadly.

Time for bed.

"I think I'll stay here a little while. Goodnight, Petal."

The woman's silver tooth glinted as she grinned her goodbye.

One by one the deck emptied as people went to their cabins on the *Baqarah* for the last time.

"What awaits us out there?" Sylah asked Dew. It was just her and the elder left now.

Morning will answer us.

Elder Dew inclined their head. Something caught Dew's eye in the movement, and they shifted to pick up what they'd seen on the deck. It was the fishing rod Sylah had modified.

I wonder what the world was like before. When we knew the runes. When we taught *the runes.*

"Do you think a lot of knowledge was lost?"

Yes, the Chrysalis is an example of that. How did our forebears create such a feat?

Sylah thought of the forged glass dune, and her eyes shone with possibility.

"Perhaps they managed to manipulate the friction in a runelamp to create a beam of fire or something that could forge glass."

You think that is possible?

"I think I'd like to try."

Dew smiled.

Sylah picked up the modified fishing rod. With a sweep of her hand, she removed the bloodwerk runes marring the pole. Blood recognized blood.

"This isn't the ideal testing surface for the theory but if I can concentrate the forces into a beam, then . . ."

She got to work, Dew watching over her with interest.

Her first series of runes nearly launched the rod overboard.

". . . that didn't work . . . how about I swap *Ba* for *Kha*."

But her combinations of bloodwerk runes failed time and time again.

Soon her blood was moving sluggishly, and she began to feel faint. She removed her stylus and returned it to the chain around her neck, and then shifted her inkwell. She couldn't remember when it had stopped feeling like metal and started feeling like skin. Always there, always ready.

"It was worth a try." Sylah gave Dew a crooked grin.

Indeed, Dew signed and turned their gaze back to the shadows of the harbor.

Dew and Sylah stood vigil throughout the rest of the night until the city began to take shape under the blushing rays of sunrise.

And what they saw made them gasp.

"What happened here?"

Dew didn't answer, though their eyes had grown moist, the wrinkles in their skin more pronounced.

Villas made of red stone spread out across a barren land of dead plants. At first Sylah thought the villas' melted forms were an aesthetic choice, but then she saw the caved-in roofs and crumbling remains of those truly decrepit. It was as if the red stone bricks had slipped into liquid. As if the land was bleeding.

"We need to go down there."

The sour smell had got worse as the sun rose, warming the decaying matter.

Wait, we need to be careful, we don't know what has caused this . . . destruction.

Sylah wasn't watching Dew sign. Instead, she slipped down the hatch to grab her pack which she'd stuffed with emergency supplies. She didn't look up to see if Jond was awake.

She headed back onto the deck and turned to Dew. "You have made many sacrifices. Let me scout for you, let me go ahead. I am the best warrior, so use me. Whatever happens we must return to the empire with aid. We must."

Sylah didn't wait for their response. She pushed open the gate that had been used to throw exactly eleven people to their deaths and jumped onto the rotting pier below.

The wood gave slightly against her weight, but she remained upright and ran toward the dockyard.

Sylah didn't stop running until she got to the edge of the town of Nsuo. A river of sticky red-brick water ran through the center of town. Sylah made sure to avoid it. The pungent smell that had assaulted her from the ship grew tenfold as she entered the city.

"Hello?" Sylah shouted, then covered her mouth with her sleeve. The cloth still smelled like sandalwood from Anoor's chambers. It gave her courage. "Hello?" Sylah coughed and covered her mouth again.

She stood silently, waiting for a response. When nothing came, she took a few more tentative steps into the city.

The buildings opened out to a square, and in the center were the rotted remains of a tree. Sylah could imagine it had been two or three times taller than it now was. But something had burned it from its tip, leaving ashen remains. Long gone were its leaves, but it was still high enough to give Sylah a view of the city.

She began to climb it.

"Shit." A branch dissolved to mush in her hand, and she swung outward, nearly falling to the ground below. She reached for another, her hands stinging from the bark. The branches were sticky with sap and rot.

"Skies above, this smell." Sylah cursed the tree. "As bitter as a moldy lemon."

When she reached the top, she stabilized herself as best she could before looking out across the city of Nsuo. Though the houses were red brick and the dirt black rather than blue, the resemblance to the Dredge was clear. Not in the architecture, as here, instead of domed roofs, the tops of the houses still standing were pointed and tiled. But what the two cities shared was decimation. Just like the Dredge, Nsuo had suffered from neglect and the onslaught of violent weather.

But there was supposed to be no tidewind here.

Sylah's eyes were drawn to a thatch of plants that must have once been a vegetable garden. Like the buildings the shrubbery had suffered a similar fate of destruction. The leaves that remained were skeletal, ghostly things with no color. Dead.

In fact, Sylah could see no evidence of life at all. Not one twitch of a curtain, not one shift of shadows.

But, as her feet touched the ground, Sylah felt eyes on her. She had learned early in life to trust her intuition. It was screaming at her now, *Someone is watching you*. Sylah dropped into a crouch and found herself slipping into battle wrath, her mind using anger to fuel her strength.

Then she heard it: the short sharp puffs of someone trying not to inhale too deeply. Sylah pressed herself into the nearest house, carefully not touching anything. She glanced into the dark room and noticed that everything had been cleared out, even the furniture.

Whatever happened here, happened slowly, she concluded. She turned back to the sound in the street and waited with her hand on the hilt of her sword until the person came into view.

Sylah sagged when she saw him, but still she sprang out at Jond anyway.

He leaped back with eyes wide as she arced the sword toward him. He tripped, his pack falling to the ground, the contents spilling out. She missed him by just a handspan.

"That, by the way, is what 'not aiming for someone' looks like," Sylah said dryly, sheathing her blade.

"Maiden's tits, Sylah. You still could have killed me by stopping my heart, though."

"If only," she shot back.

Jond began to repack his things. One of the items was a book, and she idly wondered where he'd gotten it from.

"Why did you follow me?"

"Well, Ads said that you'd gone scouting ahead and I thought I'd come along." He looped his hands through his pack's straps and lifted it onto his back.

"Return to the ship, Jond."

"Not until you're done scouting. Found anything yet?"

Sylah ground her teeth. If he wasn't turning back, maybe she could outrun him. She slipped into a sprint. The town whipped past her as she ran eastward away from the harbor. Her quickened breath filled her mouth with the bitterness of the smell, and it wasn't long before it began to burn in her throat.

She slowed to a jog, then a walk. Jond was not far behind her. He had taken his spare shirt and wrapped it around his mouth.

"It helps," he said, and she scowled, but followed his lead. It was easier to breathe after that.

"We must be near the edge of the town. The houses are getting sparser," he said.

Obviously. Sylah had already figured that out.

"Looks like a forest. The trees are so strange here," he added.

The bark of what remained of the trees was black like the soil they had grown out of. The branches grew more ashen the closer they got to the sky as if they'd been burned by the sun. Just like the plants in the city, the leaves were emaciated, stripped of their substance and color.

"They're dead. Husks of the plants they once were."

Jond perked up at the acknowledgment of his presence.

"Shall we go through it?"

Sylah didn't want to, but the question posed a challenge that she couldn't resist. She set off in a sprint again and only stopped once she was under the skeletal canopy.

"No birds," she said, looking up at the gray and rotting remains of the trees that had once grown here.

Sylah had seen a lot of horrors in the empire, but there was something truly haunting about a barren land so empty of life. Even the dunes of the Farsai Desert shifted with energy.

Jond had his hands in the black soil, a frown pulling his thick brows together.

"It burns, it's almost like . . . acid."

Acid. Jond was right. It explained why the red bricks looked as if they'd been . . . dissolved. Sylah picked up her foot and looked at the bottom of her shoe.

"Agh." The rubber was sticky, the structure of the shoe melting from the acidic ground. Her cry filled the silence of the forest.

"We should get back to the ship," Jond said urgently. "Before we lose our shoes."

Before we lose our skin.

Something moved behind them, coming in fast. Sylah turned a fraction earlier than Jond, but both of them were too late. Two of the greatest warriors ever raised in the Wardens' Empire were knocked out with a cudgel, at exactly the same time.

CHAPTER SIXTEEN

ANOOR

Inquisitor Abena felt a shiver of displaced air behind her. Someone was following her. Someone who wanted her dead. There was only one person it could be.

Her assistant, Duni, was the only one who knew she was going to be here. How foolish did he think she'd be?

The people closest to the victim often end up being the murderer. But she wasn't going to let herself become a victim anytime soon.

—"A Near Death, a Far Encounter" from *The Tales of Inquisitor Abena*, featured in *The People's Gazette*

Anoor stood by the window and watched her mother burn in the courtyard. An Abosom was chanting the final rites with the intention of guiding Uka's soul into the sky to reside with the God Anyme. The Abosom's hand waved the smoke from the pyre upward in a dramatic fashion. Sylah would have laughed at the ridiculousness of it.

Sylah would have held Anoor tight as she cried.

Why did I send her away? Anoor had never needed Sylah more than she did in that moment.

She pulled her arms around herself, trying to contain her conflicting emotions. The wardens had barred her from attending the passing-over ceremony. They didn't want the person accused of Uka's murder at the funeral. Anoor wanted to protest until Yona clarified that Anoor shouldn't attend for her own safety. People were angry.

Ash rose toward the setting sun taking with it fragments of her mother.

A tear slid down Anoor's cheek, following the tracks of many others.

She was a monster. She tore at my soul, ripped up my confidence, and tortured any sense of dignity I had. She doesn't deserve my grief.

It had been two days since her death, but it still didn't feel real.

"My teachings, my discipline . . . they were my gifts. I wanted to strengthen you . . ." Uka's words spoken on the day of the final trial of the Aktibar haunted Anoor now.

"No, they weren't *teachings*. They were punishments. You enjoyed it, you enjoyed being cruel to me," Anoor shouted out to the courtyard.

No one turned around at the sound. The wind was full of the murmuring of prayers as Warden Pura led all two hundred Abosom in worship. Pura had his back to Anoor, and she was grateful for it. She didn't want to see the man's puckered face right now. The two other wardens stood to the side of the pyre, their hands against their breasts in salute to their fallen comrade.

Warden Wern was crying freely, a low wail on the breeze. Aveed's face, so carefully blank most of the time, held a faint crease between their brows.

Anoor looked for her grandmother and found her in the shade of the joba tree, her grieving face cast in shadow. It was well known that Uka and Yona's relationship was strained. Anoor often wondered if the abuse her mother had subjected her to was learned from her grandmother. Either way, Yona was the only family she had left. And so far, she had been kind, almost caring, toward Anoor.

Crowds of Dusters peered through the black gates of the Keep. Some were keening with sadness, hands reaching through the iron as if the smoke could bless them. The death of a ruler did strange things to the citizens too. Reminded them of their own mortality, of the wardens' mortality.

Anoor scowled.

"She doesn't deserve your grief either. None of them do. They lie, every day they lie."

The day after she'd been made disciple, Anoor had wanted to scream the truth of the empire to everyone who could listen—that any blood color could bloodwerk.

But the truth would have brought riots and bloodshed. Instead, she tackled the most pressing issue first: the tidewind.

Anoor rubbed her brow and looked to her desk, once covered in notes for the Tidewind Relief Bill, now covered in notes to prove her innocence.

She turned away from her mother's burning corpse and looked at the case file she was building. She had less than three weeks before she stood trial in front of the wardens and a jury of Abosom. It was the Abosom who would ultimately pronounce judgment, but despite the sentencing coming from their lips, it would be the wardens' words.

She picked up her pen and glanced over her notes.

What we know:

The suspect entered my rooms twice. Once to steal the jambiya, once to fix the tidewind shutters.

They were able to climb the tower into my chambers, so they have some sort of training.

They were in my chambers between second and third strike.

They know how to use a jambiya to slit throats.

Anoor chewed the edge of the pen before she added:

They want to frame me for my mother's murder.

The list of people who wanted her dead was short. It started with Loot and ended with Jond. There was no one else who had the ability to get into the Keep, who had the skills needed to climb walls—and to kill Uka in her own home without leaving a trace.

But they had left a trace. A smear on the door to her dressing room.

Gorn had requested the list of visitors to the Keep during the rain shower for them to look through. She insisted on going through the names herself, and Anoor let her. She wondered if Gorn felt guilty about Zuhari.

Zuhari. Anoor's lips curled in an uncharacteristic sneer. The woman had sheepishly reported for duty that morning while Anoor was assigning work from her desk. As much as Anoor wanted to turn her away, she needed all the help she could get.

"Disciple . . . I didn't mean to, I didn't mean to cause you trouble—"

"I'm not a disciple anymore." *Thanks to you*, was the silent follow-up they both heard in Anoor's tone.

Zuhari hadn't dropped her salute, her right palm facing outward in the open-hand salute of the wardens' army.

"Is there anything I can do? To help you?" Zuhari asked.

Anoor ground her teeth; she didn't want Zuhari's assistance, but she needed it. She let out a breath of defeat.

"You can't mess up like that again. We have to be a consolidated front."

Zuhari's wide eyes looked earnest as she nodded.

"Would you be able to keep an ear to the ground in the army barracks? Maybe wear your old uniform to blend in. I don't trust any of them. I want to know if any of the officers who ransacked my room might have played a part in planting the murder weapon."

Zuhari gave a sharp nod.

"I no longer have my old army uniform, but I can procure a new one. I will let you know what I hear." But she didn't leave. Guilt still hung heavy on her features.

"Disci . . . Anoor, I'm so sorry for your loss. A mother's love is precious."

Anoor's smile was pained.

"Precious it may be, perhaps more so in its absence. I never had a mother's love."

Zuhari frowned.

"Uka," the name was sour in her mouth, "didn't love you?"

Anoor shook her head with a sigh.

"You know what I am. A Duster. And that disgusted her. I was always a reminder of her failure."

Zuhari didn't speak for some time. Her hand absently stroked her forearm as she pondered. She dropped her hand when she saw Anoor looking and tugged the sleeve over the bit of exposed skin.

But not before Anoor saw the start of a bloodink tattoo. Rare in Embers, the art form was mainly used by Dusters as a form of defiance against the branding they received. It allowed them to reclaim control of their skin in ways Embers could never understand.

Zuhari's bloodink was a word, drawn in exquisite calligraphy, though Anoor only caught the letter "r." She wondered why the bloodink had drawn Zuhari's focus during their conversation.

"I'd better get going. The sooner we know more, the sooner we catch the killer," Zuhari said.

Anoor nodded absently.

"Yes, go, please let me know what you find out."

Zuhari's smile was small and contained as she spun on her heel and left.

Next in was Kwame, whose lightness of spirit was always a balm to the soul. He'd started collecting statements from servants who might have seen anything. Despite his positivity he'd found nothing yet. She'd asked him about Hassa, but he'd got wary, flushing a little, and she wondered if there was more to their relationship than student and tutor.

Anoor hadn't seen Hassa since the morning after her mother's death, and she missed her.

Hassa was a connection to Sylah she so desperately craved. But she was also her friend.

Knock. Knock. Knock.

There was only one person who could knock in such a regimented manner.

"Come in, Gorn," Anoor called.

Her chief of staff entered her chambers.

"Are you all right? I brought you some kunafa."

Anoor's mouth filled with saliva at the sight of the sticky golden treat. Then she instantly felt shame for wanting to enjoy food during her mother's funeral.

"You can set it over there."

"I also brought you a zine. Inquisitor Abena's brother dies in this one, I thought it might help you . . . cope."

"Cope?" Anoor said softly. "Oh yes, I will cope very well now my mother is dead."

Gorn ignored Anoor's sour comment and placed the zine next to her papers.

"Have you found anything in the register from the Keep's gates?" Anoor asked Gorn.

The tall woman shifted her feet.

"No."

"I doubt the culprit would have used their real name, so you'll have to cross-reference every person who entered the Keep with records of their birth." Sylah had used a fake name when she'd visited the Keep the first time. Lylah of Ood-Raynib—a terrible disguise.

"I know. So far, I've found nothing," Gorn said. Her eyes were distant, drawn to the courtyard below.

Uka had been her master first. I wonder if she grieves too?

"Well, keep looking," Anoor said, more sharply than she intended.

Gorn placed a hand on the stack of zines on Anoor's desk.

"I was thinking back to one of the older Inquisitor Abena stories, from a few years ago. Do you remember the one with the griot who went missing?"

Anoor frowned and cast her memory back. There had been so many stories since then, she was surprised Gorn remembered.

"Vaguely, was it set in Jin-Laham?"

"Yes, that's the one. He'd had his throat cut and Abena was able to find the murderer because they'd abandoned their clothing."

Anoor nodded, not quite following.

Gorn spoke hesitantly. "Cutting someone's throat is messy. Whoever killed your mother wouldn't have been able to travel through the Keep unnoticed. They must have got rid of their clothes."

Realization dawned on Anoor, and she felt her heart begin to thud. This was another avenue to explore.

"Can you look into it? Check the launderers? The garbage?"

"I'll add it to the list." Gorn smiled thinly.

"Thank you, Gorn."

She turned to leave.

"Have you seen Hassa recently?" Anoor asked before she shut the door.

"No, though I think she's still giving extra lessons to Kwame. Shall I ask her to visit you?"

"Please," Anoor said without turning around.

The door shut quietly, and Anoor looked back to her notes.

The sun sank, merging with the dying flames of the pyre.

Knock. Knock. Knock.

"Gorn?"

The door swung open and in paraded Yona. Her grandmother's dress was a burnt red. The collar clasped her neck so tightly Anoor wondered if she could breathe. The sleeves were equally tight and cuffed at the wrist.

Anoor ran to her grandmother's open arms, realizing a second too late that she hadn't been expecting an embrace at all. Yona softened only marginally before Anoor broke the one-sided embrace.

"How are you?" Anoor asked her.

"Fine."

There was a tense silence until Yona's face cracked into a heartbroken grimace.

"Not so fine, but I will be all right."

Anoor nodded, understanding.

"How goes your investigation?" Yona asked.

Anoor shrugged.

"Don't shrug at me, girl. Speak, what is the matter?"

Whenever Anoor forgot to be frightened of her grandmother, Yona would always remind her.

"I'm yet to have a breakthrough in the case, but I'm confident I will."

Yona nodded and walked over to the window. She reached out a gloved hand to pull on the tidewind shutter lever.

The metal panels unraveled across the glass, and Yona peered at them.

"That's the new panel, on the right?"

"Yes," Anoor said.

"Have you spoken to anyone from the guild of duty? Found out who could have repaired this without your knowing?"

It was a good idea. One that hadn't come to Anoor.

". . . It's on my list for tomorrow . . ."

Yona smiled knowingly.

"Good." Her wig of choice today was a single thick braid that fell past her waist. She swung it in front of her before perching delicately on the edge of Anoor's four-poster bed. "I wanted to talk to you about the Tidewind Relief Bill."

Anoor's heart soared.

"Did you get it passed through court?"

Yona frowned. "Court was adjourned for today's. . . . event."

How quickly Anoor had forgotten her mother's funeral. The realization made her wince.

"Of course," she said quickly.

"What I wanted to say was, I'm impressed with the finished bill. It is ingenious, if a little naive."

"Naive?"

"There is no world in which the wardens will accept all twenty-five points. I will, however, make a start on introducing some of the actions, as I agree, protecting our people is paramount."

Anoor sucked on her bottom lip and waited for her grandmother to continue.

"I've already found a suitable building for the first tidewind shelter in the north of the city. Aveed has agreed to help with food and supplies and Wern has agreed to provide healers."

Anoor tried to contain her squeal but it came out as an awkward laugh. "How did you get them to agree to it?"

"Turns out it's hard to say no to someone whose daughter just died," Yona said dryly.

Anoor wanted to hug her, but she wasn't sure her grandmother would tolerate a second attempt at contact.

"I'm telling you this so that your mind isn't distracted. Concentrate on your trial. Leave the Tidewind Relief Bill to me."

"Thank you, Grandmother . . . or should I call you Acting Warden now?" Uka had always wanted Anoor to call her Warden when they were alone. "Mother" was just for the public facade.

"Oh, child, no, call me Grandmother."

It was better than any hug.

THE NEXT MORNING Anoor slipped out of her chambers and into the courtyard. It was early and the servants had only just begun to clean away the tidewind's havoc from the night before. A pair of Ghosting servants stood in the shadow of the cloisters, heaving pieces of debris from where they had been flung.

They looked up as Anoor neared. The taller of the two subtly turned to her and signed, *You are being followed.*

Anoor swallowed and tensed her neck muscles, refraining from turning around.

"Thank you . . ." she said, adding quickly lest her follower understand what had passed, "for cleaning up."

The Ghosting blinked once at her and went back to moving the debris.

Anoor moved more slowly through the courtyard, her senses heightened, and she tried to pick out the sounds of the spy. She paused by the joba tree and looked up to the white branches. Bursts of pink flowers bloomed in the canopy above, and she marveled at the beauty of them.

Then she spun. Quicker than she'd been able to a year ago.

She caught the flash of white robes and a delicately boned face. The Abosom dashed into the alcove of the cloisters, but it was too late. Anoor had seen them.

So, Pura has set his Abosom to spy on me. Their reports must be dull.

Anoor smiled grimly and tried not to let the Abosom's presence affect her. She had things to do.

The duty office was on the edge of the courtyard.

Thwum. Thwum. Thwum.

The sound of the duty chutes set the rhythm of workers within as they collected and delivered messages through bloodwerk-operated tubes. Anoor listened to the canisters zoom up and down the tunneling. There were twelve main chutes that ran under the city of Nar-Ruta to the other twelve cities of the empire.

The workers paused as Anoor entered.

"Good morning," she said brightly. "I was wondering if I could speak to someone about your repair services. Someone fixed my tidewind shutter three days ago and I want to see if it's documented."

A duty master with dark green eyes scowled at her.

"Why do you want to know?" He knew who she was, and he knew what she was accused of. This wasn't going to be easy.

"Is there a reason you can't share this information with me? The repair was done in *my* chambers."

"And where are your chambers?"

He just wanted her to say it.

"Above the kitchens in the eastern tower of the Keep," Anoor said, her smile refusing to fade.

The duty master muttered under his breath and began to flip through some papers.

"There's no record of it," he said after a moment.

Anoor's smile slipped. With no record she would struggle to prove to the court that the window had been broken.

"Oh, wait . . . here it is. The repair was made three days ago as you said. It was recorded by a metalworker."

Anoor's heart began to race. This was the breakthrough she needed. This evidence would lead her to the culprit.

"Do you have their name?"

"Kila, Metalworker Kila."

"And is Kila working today?"

The duty master narrowed their eyes, seeing that the end of their conversation was in sight.

"You'll find them in the armorsmith's near the barracks—"

"I know the place." It was where she'd had her armor made for the Aktibar.

Anoor ran out into the courtyard, her feet drumming on the cobblestones. The barracks weren't far, but she wanted to be back in her chambers before the Keep was fully awake. She hadn't forgotten what Yona had said about her safety.

Especially if Uka's murderer was Loot or Jond. The Sandstorm had never been afraid to breach the Keep's walls.

Anoor dashed into the armorsmith's and called out, "Kila, is Kila the metalworker here?"

A woman raised her head up from a bench on the edge of the large room and said, "Here."

Anoor jogged to her.

"Who told you to repair my tidewind shutter?"

Kila frowned, her thick eyebrows knotting together. An uneaten shawarma was held poised in her hand, garlic sauce running over her knuckles.

"Three days ago," Anoor pressed.

". . . your tidewind shutter . . ." Memory flooded her face. "Oh yes, I remember, I don't often recollect the things I repair, but this one was unusual . . ."

"Why? Who was it?"

"She was small, dark eyes. I didn't know what she was saying at first, but she wanted me to follow her, and so I did. She led me to your chambers and showed me the broken paneling. It didn't take me long. Maybe half a strike. Easy job . . . lots of shutters are breaking at the moment . . . tidewind getting worse, you know?"

Anoor did know, but that's not what she cared about. "Who was it?"

Kila shrugged. "Some Ghosting."

Hassa . . .

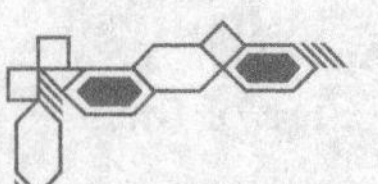

CHAPTER SEVENTEEN

HASSA

Uka Elsari, our warden no longer,
Protected the empire with no greater honor.
Fifteen she began, a disciple first,
Then twenty-five, a warden cursed.

Children taken, the Sandstorm born.
The Keep breached, families torn.
Children lost, the Sandstorm dead.
The Wardens' Keep sealed, Uka's bloodlust fed.

Uka Elsari, our warden no longer,
Protected the empire with no greater honor,
Thirty-five a disciple repeated,
At forty-five a Warden defeated.

—Submitted in evidence, a rhyme sung in the Dredge.
The singer was sentenced to the rack. Lot number 3288.

As soon as the wardens and officers flooded Anoor's apartment, Hassa scarpered. Her status as a servant ensured she was unlikely to be noticed, but being a Ghosting ensured she would always be a target in a room full of Embers. She had heard enough to know that Anoor was in trouble.

Hassa's fervent pacing led her back to the kitchens, where she found Sami, the Ghosting who had told her about Uka's death.

Sami, did any of the Ghostings see anything last night? They're accusing Anoor, but it wasn't her.

The old man drew himself together before he signed, *Are you sure it wasn't her? It was well known their relationship was bad. I heard they argued in the courtroom yesterday.*

No. Hassa cut him off. *It wasn't her.*

Sami shrugged. *I have heard nothing from the others, but if I do, I will let you know, Watcher.*

He used the title that the elders had given her. Acknowledging it was a sign of respect and a commitment to sharing his knowledge.

Thank you, she signed, turning away.

Sami touched her arm.

Watcher, I've been told an envoy from the elders has been spotted en route to the city.

Hassa's stomach lurched. *How far?*

Willow saw them on their way back from the coffee farm south of Jin-Eynab early this morning. She was on an eru bus and recognized the silver belt around the messenger's waist.

Foolish to let themselves be seen above ground. The tunnels are there for a reason. Hassa was signing more to herself than to Sami, but he answered.

Not everyone likes the dark as much as you.

She didn't respond, remembering that Sami had chosen to stay in the city rather than brave the journey out through the tunnels.

If the messenger was south of Jin-Eynab they'd only be a few strikes from the Dredge by now.

Hassa felt a stab of guilt toward Anoor's predicament, but the elders had to come first.

She ran through the courtyard and out into the Ember Quarter. She slipped by all the ostentatious villas like a fish in a river.

There was an access point to the underground tunnels by the cellar in the Sphinx Tavern. Hassa hated using it as the tavern was frequented by officers, but she needed to get across the city quickly.

Unlike the Maroon, the Sphinx Tavern didn't smell of body odor and blood, neither was it filled with the sound of laughter and dancing. Clusters of Embers sat quietly with their fine wines upon cushioned chairs. The runelamps were bright and unwavering, contrary to the cheap wax candles in the Maroon that trailed smoke.

Hassa kept her head down as she weaved through the tables. It wasn't unusual for a Ghosting to be there. The patrons probably assumed she was a servant, which was exactly what she was hoping for.

Thankfully, no one stopped her as she descended to the cellar around the back of the bar.

If her memory served her right, the ladder to the tunnels was situated behind a cask of wine underneath a loose floorboard.

She made her way to the back of the cellar quietly. Her residual limbs reached out to the ground feeling for the groove in the wood that would allow her to lift the floorboard with her wrist.

Got it.

She tugged on the plank with both arms until it gave way, revealing the ladder beneath.

"What was that sound?" The voice was softly spoken in the darkness.

Hassa froze. The question had been projected from the entrance of the cellar. She hadn't heard the newcomers arrive.

"Nothing, this building is old, it creaks like my mother's knees."

A third person laughed. "Smells like her too."

Three voices, and Hassa recognized them all. She peered around the cask of wine to confirm her suspicions.

There they were, Tanu, Faro, and Qwa, the three disciples of the Wardens' Empire.

What are they doing here?

She had a choice: descend the ladder, or wait to see if she could glean anything from their secret meeting.

Hassa hesitated.

"Why did you drag us here, Faro?" Tanu asked. She placed her hands on her hips and cocked her head to the left. The curls on the top of her head were so thickly coated in gel, they didn't move. The sides of her hair were shaved to the scalp, and she ran an idle hand over the skin there. "We could have just met in the Keep."

"Too many spies to talk freely," Faro replied, casting an accusatory glance at Qwa.

"Don't look at me, I don't direct the Abosom . . . yet." Qwa crossed his arms over his chest with a grunt.

Faro bit down on their top lip, grazing the thin mustache there, as they removed a slip of paper from their pocket.

"I received this yesterday." The three of them bent their heads over the letter.

Hassa would have traded anything to have a look.

"Help her? Why should we help her?" Qwa scoffed. "She killed Uka."

They are talking about Anoor.

"No, she didn't, can't you read?" Faro pressed, the warble of their voice strengthening with annoyance.

Tanu hadn't said a word; the two of them turned to her.

She shrugged. "Does it matter? We've been told to help her. So, we will."

Qwa mumbled something under his breath that Hassa didn't catch.

"We're disciples, we do as we're told," Tanu said with a hardness that Hassa hadn't heard from the woman before. Like Hassa, Tanu was small, but unlike Hassa, she exuded power.

Hassa held her power within.

"If they find out, it'll be a political disaster. We can't be seen to be helping her." Qwa was still being defensive, though some of the anger had slipped from his features. He pressed his palms into his eyes. They were small and puffy from tiredness.

Faro licked their lips with a darting pink tongue. Hassa thought they were getting ready to bicker some more with Qwa, but Faro reached for him.

"Are you all right?" they asked.

Something tender passed between Qwa and them. Tanu looked away. Hassa didn't.

Interesting, it seems that the disciples are more than allies.

"I know it isn't the first year we were expecting, but being a disciple was always going to be hard." Faro's smile was strained.

Qwa brought Faro's hand to his lips and brushed a kiss against their knuckles.

"Easier together."

"Easier together," Faro agreed.

Tanu let out an exasperated sigh.

"Are you done? Can we figure out how to help Anoor now?"

Qwa sighed.

"What do you have in mind?"

Hassa wanted to stay longer. She had so many unanswered questions. But the messenger would be in the Dredge by now, and kin always came first.

Always.

She slipped down the ladder with a racing heart. When she reached the bottom she pressed her limbs to her eyes and waited for her breathing to steady. First things first, she had to find the messenger. Then she could worry about Anoor, and then the disciples. A short list but a heavy one. It burdened her as she made her way to the Dredge.

HASSA PULLED HERSELF up from the hatch into the morning heat. Sweat instantly beaded on her brow and she wiped it away. The streets of the Dredge were empty. She had tracked the current patrol and ensured they weren't in the vicinity before she emerged from beneath the city.

She walked silently through the dirt road. A villa had been completely demolished by the tidewind, and its collapsed walls slipped into the street like strewn guts from a ripped corpse. Hassa picked her way through the debris, her eyes scanning left and right.

Something bone-white caught her eye. It was lighter than the limestone around it. She loped toward it and saw the signs of death straight away.

Their flesh had been shredded away in the tidewind, leaving only a few matted clumps of skin and sinew—enough to identify the body as a blue-blooded Duster, but not much else.

Hassa didn't gag. She was so used to the gore and horror of the empire that she'd become deadened to it.

I wonder who you were, she thought. *I wonder why you died.*

She reached out a limb and turned the body over.

She frowned. An incision had been made in the person's pelvis. A hole, larger than a needle, had pierced the bone.

Hassa thought back to what the Gummers had said in the Belly: "They think that the tidewind is covering their tracks, but we know the signs."

The Gummers thought that another crimelord had moved into the city. Hassa hadn't heard anything, but it was possible. She had been spending a lot of time with Anoor and not enough time listening.

Hassa growled and let the skeleton fall back down. She rubbed her limbs on her servant's attire, streaking it blue.

Another thing to add to the list.

MAIDEN TURIN'S WAS emptying, the night's clients disappearing into their eru carriages and back across the river to their riches. Hassa caught the eye of one of the men whose guilt hung in the sag of his lips.

He was an officer, Hassa could tell from the way he carried himself—back straight, shoulder blades pinned together. She wondered what violence he had wrought on a nightworker that evening. It must have been bloody to have stirred guilt in him. Officers were always the most violent.

He saw her looking at him, and his demeanor changed.

"I didn't see you for sale last night," he purred.

"She's not for sale," Maiden Turin said at the door with a scowl.

Hassa was surprised Turin came to her defense. The maiden barely noticed Hassa was there half the time, and certainly didn't like her. She'd made that clear enough times.

"Come, Hassa."

Turin waved her into her private bedchamber. Hassa had only been in there a handful of times.

The room was thick with radish-leaf smoke, but Hassa could see another figure in the room. They were sitting on the edge of Turin's velvet cover. She was another Ghosting Hassa didn't recognize, but she knew immediately that this was the messenger. She saw the silver brooch of the gazelle on their chest.

"I found them slinking through the shadows this morning in the dormitory. As you well know I do not know the Ghosting speak, but I know enough to understand they were looking for you."

She won't let me leave. She kept me locked in her cupboard all morning. I had to listen to her service three clients in quick succession. The Ghosting bared their teeth.

You come from the Chrysalis?

Yes, I am Starlight, a messenger sent from the elders.

Turin moved to stand between them before they could sign further. "Aho, now I've been so kind as to look after this . . . friend of yours, I think I deserve payment in kind. I need some information."

Ah, the catch. Turin wanted knowledge.

Starlight peered around Turin's shoulder and signed. *She doesn't speak our language so how does she wish for you to convey the information?* The messenger's mouth twisted in scorn.

"I might not be able to speak your language, but I am not blind. Wipe that smirk from your face before I cut it off."

Starlight's skin turned grayer.

Moderate your face as you speak. You have been among the free too long, Hassa signed.

"I will ask you questions, and I want you to answer me. I know you Ghostings know more than you let on. Especially that Marigold, may the tidewind take them. Leaving me short a nightworker. I have barely any left."

Hassa bristled but didn't show the grief on her face.

Let us play her game, Hassa signed to Starlight and turned to Turin with a curt nod.

"Do you know where Loot is?"

Hassa shook her head. Interesting that she wanted to know about *him.*

"Do you know if he's alive?"

He isn't. Sylah killed him, Starlight said to Hassa.

This time Hassa felt the shock flood her features as her jaw went slack.

"What is it? He's dead, isn't he?" Turin sounded excited.

Sylah killed him? Hassa ignored Turin.

Yes, and captured the other, Jond.

Hassa swallowed audibly. Turin grabbed her forearms.

"Stop talking and answer me. Is Loot dead?"

Hassa shrugged. As soon as her shoulders drooped back down, Turin slapped her hard across the face. Hassa could barely hear her over the ringing in her ears.

"Get out, you useless lout. Get out."

Starlight looped their elbow through Hassa's and pulled her up from where the slap had flung her. They were out of the maiden house in a few breaths.

That maiden is a very lovely person, Starlight said, and Hassa laughed. It felt good to laugh.

Come with me, let's talk in the Nest.

HASSA AND STARLIGHT talked all day, the latter filling her in on everything that had happened before the elders left for the mainland.

Memur has been left in charge of the Chrysalis. She will want a report from you before I return. She particularly wanted to know who was vying for power now Loot is gone.

Hassa's brow furrowed.

I will prepare words for you to send to her.

Starlight nodded and sucked on their teeth.

I'll leave in three days. I need to rest and replenish my stocks. Could you direct me to the nearest apothecary? I need to replenish my hormone herbs.

Hassa nodded and gave Starlight directions to the apothecary she used.

The shop token is a broken blade. It hangs above the door. The woman who runs it has a cane and a limp. Her name is Ren. She's the partner of our newest Shadow Court member, Zuhari.

Starlight's eyes widened. *Indeed? An Ember and a Duster. You like to collect your renegades.*

Hassa smiled feebly. She missed Sylah.

Starlight left Hassa in the dim light of the Nest.

The fire at the hearth still burned from the pile of wood she fed it in the morning. It banished the shadows of the room and the empty spaces where Hassa still felt the elders' presence.

She was lonely, she realized. Lonelier than she had ever been in her life. Having Starlight here made her realize how much she yearned for the company of other Ghostings. There were some in the city, but few who shared the ideals of the elders—if they did they'd be in the Chrysalis by now. Hassa had offered to stay here, as her spying, though no longer vital, could still help the elders, and definitely Anoor.

Anoor, Hassa sighed. All hopes Hassa had for Anoor's reign were dashed the moment Uka died. Not that Anoor would have brought true freedom to the Ghostings.

Only war could do that.

The carvings around the Nest flickered in the firelight. Hassa touched her arm to the wall and bowed her head in silent prayer.

Ancestors guide me, I succumb to Anyme. Show me my path.

Anyme had never been a God to the Ghostings. Anyme was the life-force of the world, the light and the dark, the sustenance of all living things. There was no fate, no destiny: only Anyme, like a firefly on a darkened path, showing you the way.

Like everything the founding wardens touched, the Ghostings' beliefs had been twisted to suit the Embers' needs. The wardens poisoned their teachings with the religion they had imported. This religion preached a new creed, with a new deity at its center that favored Ember values: strength, knowledge, truth, and duty.

But centuries on, the Ghostings continued to believe in their own version of Anyme. They didn't believe that when they died, they would join Anyme in the sky, like the Dusters and Embers preached. Instead, they believed your soul joined the energy of life itself, and that Anyme was composed of the spirits of their ancestors.

The grooves of the Ghostings' story carved into the whitestone felt familiar, despite the tragedy of it. And this was only a slice. Hassa had read some of the diaries they had managed to preserve from Before. Not only had the invaders pillaged, but they had also raped and murdered and stolen the very essence of their peaceful land.

Hassa's lip curled above her teeth, and she added another prayer to her forebears:

Guide the elders to the Zwina Academy so they might rid our land of the tidewind. Protect Sylah, and the elders. Bring them all home again.

The fire crackled and popped. Hassa doused it with water. No use lighting the dark if no one was there to see it.

She had three days to provide the elders with all the information she could muster, and she'd start with who was dumping those bodies. Anoor would have to wait.

Back through the tunnels she scuttled like the beetle she had been named after. After all, a beetle spent the majority of its life underground. It was a silent predator that hunted smaller prey at night.

I am the empire's hassa beetle, she thought. And like the predator she was, she roamed through her lair.

CHAPTER EIGHTEEN

HASSA

The shoemaker goes barefoot, and the weaver goes naked.

—Ghosting proverb, meaning to not neglect one's sense of self

Over the next three days Hassa found five more bodies. Each one had the same curious hole in their skeleton. She'd been unable to find the culprit for the murders, though, and no one seemed to know who the dead were or where they'd come from.

It frustrated Hassa. She'd spent strikes tracking Gummers and searching for signs of this rumored new crimelord but had come up short. The message she'd sent back to the Chrysalis with Starlight was brief, as she'd had little intelligence to share.

Hassa knew that the threads of secrets would eventually converge into a pattern. She just had to wait and listen.

"Hassa." Kwame's smile was waiting for her in his chambers.

While she'd been collecting information for the Ghostings,

she'd limited her time in the Keep, but she couldn't stay away from Kwame. Their lessons had become the highlight of her day.

Hello, Kwame.

His eyes flickered left and right nervously. His chambers weren't large. In fact, Hassa was sure they'd originally served as an extra storage room for the kitchens below. He had, however, filled the rooms with the gaudy decorations he favored. One wall was lined with crude paintings of stick figures drawn out of charcoal.

"It's an original Gochoo," he had said. "I bought it exclusively from their art dealer in the Duster Quarter." He had pushed out his chest proudly.

Got you? Hassa had signed back.

"No, Gochoo."

Hassa snickered. Realization dawned on him.

"Oh, bollocks. I was swindled." He tipped his chin to the ceiling with an exasperated sigh.

When she pressed him, he sheepishly told her that a lot of his "decorations" had been bought on a solo trip to the Duster Quarter. When the Duster artisans realized he had money, each stall began thrusting goods upon him and he'd been unable to resist. So he'd ended up bringing home a carriage full of things he didn't want. He now had fifteen different terra-cotta vases lining his window.

It was also why it took Hassa a moment to spot Anoor standing among all the junk.

"Where've you been?" Anoor demanded, her hazel eyes blazing.

Hassa frowned. *I've been busy. What's wrong?* Hassa knew Anoor had been working on her trial. Now that Starlight was gone, Hassa was free to help her.

"She didn't do it," Gorn said to Anoor from the doorway.

Hassa had heard Gorn arrive but didn't turn around to look at her. She was watching Anoor closely. Her friend seemed to be battling with her next words.

"You . . . you . . . got my tidewind shutter repaired . . ." Anoor was trembling.

Yes, I did. I noticed it was broken a week ago; the tidewind pulled up one of the panels. I had someone come in and fix it. Hassa was always there in the morning opening Anoor's shutters. She felt a bit guilty that it had taken her so long to get someone in. In truth, it had slipped her mind until she'd seen Kila fixing another broken shutter in the kitchens.

"It was broken a week ago? But my jambiya was only stolen that night . . ." Anoor sank to the ground next to the vases. Kwame dashed forward to steady one of them that was teetering on its base.

Understanding hit Hassa like a whitestone brick.

You thought I stole the jambiya? You thought I murdered Uka?

"No," Gorn said. She had noticed the rising anger in Hassa's face. "She doesn't know what she's talking about, she hasn't slept for three days."

Anoor was crying now, a painful wail that nearly pierced Hassa's anger. But her wrath stayed fast like armor. She couldn't believe Anoor had really thought she had stolen the jambiya.

"Anoor, come on, let's go talk in your chambers." Gorn was trying to help Anoor up, but it looked like her limbs had turned to jelly.

Hassa went across to one of the terra-cotta vases and kicked it over. The sound of the crash on the tiles brought silence. Anoor looked up miserably.

"What did you do that for?"

Look at yourself. Sylah would be ashamed of you. You're acting like the spoiled brat you used to be. Stop accusing your friends and start fighting for yourself. Because you're the one who's meant to be fighting for the rest of us. And we need you.

Something clicked in Anoor's mind. She stood with dignity and wiped away her tears.

"You're right. I'm so sorry, Hassa. Do you forgive me?"

Forgiveness should never be requested. Only granted. Work for it.

Anoor flinched, but she understood.

"Shadow Court meeting in my chambers," she said with authority. "Hassa, will you join?"

Yes.

Anoor went to clean herself up, and Gorn left to fetch Zuhari.

Hassa helped Kwame pick up the pieces of terra-cotta.

Sorry, she signed to him. *I needed to get her attention.*

"That's okay, I get it," he said warmly, and her stomach turned over. "Besides, I probably didn't need fifteen vases."

Hassa laughed. She could always count on Kwame to soothe her anger.

She looked at him sidelong. His brow furrowed in concentration as he plucked the smaller shards up from the floor.

"Ouch." A splinter of terra-cotta punctured his palm.

Hassa reached for him and cradled his hand between her limbs before pressing down on the small wound.

Kwame's mouth parted in a soft "o" before he looked away shyly.

Hassa made a small sound in the back of her throat, and he turned to her. When he did, he wasn't smiling anymore. Something blazed behind his eyes, hot and alive like the shifting sands of the Farsai Desert. Hassa shivered, and he withdrew his hand from underneath her limb.

"Sorry, I didn't mean to . . ." he mumbled and stumbled backward, knocking another vase over with a crash. "We should go, leave this, I'll clean it later. Anoor will be waiting."

Hassa frowned, wondering if she'd mistaken the desire in his eyes.

She looked down before he could see her hurt expression. Red blood marred the raised scars of her wrist where she'd put pressure on his cut.

Ember blood. The realization of it made it burn.

She wiped it away and pushed any thoughts of passion from her mind.

Let's go, she signed with finality.

Kwame didn't meet her eyes again, and she was glad of it.

ZUHARI, GORN, AND Anoor were waiting in silence as Hassa and Kwame entered.

Anoor stood by the window, her back to the sofas. "It is unlikely the murderer climbed in through the window, and though it is still a possibility, it isn't as sure as it once was."

"So, we're back to where we started? No evidence?" Kwame said.

"No." Anoor whirled around. "We still have the mud smear, the fact that the jambiya was used, and that the murderer was able to climb up to my mother's balcony. Gorn, did you find anything at the launderers?"

Gorn shook her head.

Why the launderers? Hassa asked.

"I thought someone might have remembered bloody clothing being cleaned," said Gorn.

"Clever," Zuhari said. "But the murderer could have just as easily taken the clothes with them."

Gorn let out a tired sigh. "Yes, but I had to try."

Anoor took a seat on the sofa and turned to Hassa.

"Have you heard anything about Loot? Or Jond?"

Hassa lowered her eyes in guilt. She hadn't even told them Starlight's message. She'd been too consumed by the murders.

A Ghosting messenger arrived from the elders. Sylah made it to the settlement. They successfully left for the mainland a mooncycle ago. They should nearly be there by now. Hassa cleared her throat.

A cry escaped Anoor. "She's alive."

Jond is with her.

"What?" Hassa saw jealousy fracture Anoor's relief. "How?"

She has taken him prisoner and intends to exile him from the empire. To eliminate the threat to you.

"Oh." Anoor took that in, then shook her head. "Why was he with Sylah in the first place?"

Loot and Jond attacked Sylah during her journey.

"What?"

Sylah fought them and won. Loot is dead.

"Loot is dead? Are you sure?"

The messenger confirmed in the report from the elders that Sylah killed him.

Kwame clapped his hands. "Well done, Sylah."

There was silence as everyone waited for Anoor to formulate a reaction.

"This is a good thing, Anoor," Gorn said. "One major threat eliminated."

Anoor nodded slowly.

"What's wrong?" Kwame asked.

"I am . . . glad that Loot is no longer a threat, but if it wasn't Loot . . . and it wasn't Jond . . . then who framed me?"

No one had an answer to that.

THE MEETING DISPERSED with the setting sun. Hassa still held her rage clenched in the crook of her elbow. She squeezed it tight, her limbs held under her chin as she walked toward the door.

How dare she accuse me? I, who have helped her, I, who have protected her?

Hassa flinched at the stab of shame she felt from withholding the information about Loot's death. She didn't realize Anoor's investigation had hung on the belief that he had been involved in Uka's murder. Hassa had simply forgotten to tell Anoor the news. With the bodies turning up in the Dredge and Starlight's visit, she had been busy.

"Hassa, will you join me in my chambers?" Kwame called after her.

She stopped and turned around.

I can't. I have things to do in the Dredge. Hassa's limbs sliced through the air quickly. She wondered if Kwame could read her full sentence.

Kwame blinked slowly, his head dipping. He understood, but still he asked, "Please?"

Hassa ran her dark eyes over Kwame's features. His narrow shoulders were held tight to his ears, and his lips that were always so full of smiles were turned down at the corners.

She nodded once.

He led the way out of Anoor's chambers into the corridor and back into his rooms. Hassa followed him, her feet silent on the tiled floor.

Kwame turned on the runelamp. It was a hideous thing, poorly constructed from lumps of glass cast-offs. Hassa wondered how much he had been charged for such a creation—it was no doubt the work of a grifter in the Duster Quarter.

"Hassa, I'm so sorry. She found out from Gorn that we were having lessons still, and because she hadn't seen you . . ." His words came out in a rush.

He thought she was angry at him for the ambush with Anoor? So quickly he had forgotten her touch. She must have conjured his feelings from her mind.

"Anoor commanded me . . ." Kwame continued. He stepped toward Hassa until he stood a mere arm's length from her. She could smell the rose oil in his hair, but she didn't let it distract her as she listened to his words.

"I didn't believe you had anything to do with Uka's murder. You know what she's like. First, she was convinced it was Zuhari, even with everything Zuhari is doing to help the investigation . . . and now you . . ."

Hassa didn't say anything, though her eyes glittered. Silence was the best way to get people to talk.

"Anoor's breaking apart, Hassa. Her mother's death . . . the tidewind . . . it's all too much. It's all too much for *me* . . . And with my father sick and no medicine working . . ."

Hassa struggled to keep her features smooth. Kwame's father was sick? Hassa hadn't known. She knew Kwame visited his father sometimes in the Ember Quarter and that he was a retired kitchen servant.

"The healers aren't sure how long he'll have."

His hand reached out then, as if to touch her. Hassa leaned forward but he snatched his hand away all too quickly.

"Please don't hold it against Anoor. She's our disciple and she's good at it. It was just a lapse of judgment."

He clasped his hands together as if restraining himself. He waited, using his silence in turn as a way to draw her out. Hassa realized he was learning more than the Ghosting language when they trained together.

I will not hold it against her. She signed slowly so he understood her meaning clearly.

Kwame sagged and stepped back, the lack of his body heat leaving her cold.

"Thank you—"

But I will correct you. She is not our disciple. She is yours. Ghostings bow to no leader of this empire.

Kwame swallowed.

However, she is a friend, and friends may earn forgiveness.

He gave her a weak smile.

She thought then about telling him of the bodies in the Dredge. But when she recalled the forlorn cast of his features as he said, "It's all too much for me," she knew she couldn't add to his burdens.

We missed your lesson today, get the book. It's time to learn all about the difference between directional verbs and the nouns they mimic.

Even if he didn't feel the same way, Hassa would still take pleasure in teaching him. There were so few pleasures in her life.

Kwame laughed and said, "Learn the difference between what and what?"

His laugh filled the room with joy, and Hassa closed her eyes to savor the sound. No, she'd tell him about the bodies another day.

CHAPTER NINETEEN

NAYELI

We do not speak our prophet's name.
He who spoke Kabut's words.
He who gave us worship.
He who taught us sacrifice.
—Teachings of the Zalaam

Nayeli was married for seven years before she killed her husband.

Chah had moved into her hut the night of the wedding, claiming his was too small and humble for the likes of her. Nayeli wouldn't have had it any other way.

Her hut was still full of marriage offerings, and Chah didn't have any qualms in searching through them and laying claim to anything he took a liking to, which was most of it. Nayeli didn't mind. The food had value because it sustained her, but the trinkets and treasures she had little use for. If only someone had bought her a new tool set, she might have chosen them instead of Chah and fallen in love. If not, she'd at least have found the present useful.

"The bed is too small," Chah announced after stuffing his pipe and lighting what he claimed was the "best grass in the world." Nayeli didn't even know grass was one of the wedding gifts.

"There has only been one resident until now," Nayeli replied.

"Yes, well, that's going to change, isn't it?" Chah sat on the bed and patted his lap. Nayeli wasn't sure what he meant by that, so instead she perched on the footstool by the bed.

"Your parents informed you what must come next?"

"I have no family," Nayeli said, tilting her head. "They are dead. But yes, I know what is to come next."

Chah nodded deeply and puffed on his pipe. Nayeli did not like the smell; it stung her eyes and made her feel cornered, without air.

"This is not my first time," Chah said.

Nor was it hers, but she didn't voice it. Two mooncycles ago she had taken a boat to Green Commune and lain with one woman, one man, and one musawa, just to see if the physical act would rouse any feelings for her. Instead, she'd found it sticky and uncomfortable. The rubbing of their skin on hers had repulsed her and made her feel trapped within her body.

"I was married once before," Chah continued.

This she had not known.

"She died young. Weak of heart, the healer had said."

Nayeli didn't pry. Instead, she got up from the footstool and placed her hand in his in an effort to hasten things along.

Chah seemed to understand her meaning and his gray bushy eyebrows crept up his forehead. *He must be sixty, or older*, Nayeli found herself thinking. So, he had twenty years, maybe even less if she could get him to smoke more grass.

His fingers gripped hers tightly and he leaned in for a kiss. He pulled his hand toward his stomach and pushed her fingers down onto the protruding hardness in his crotch. Nayeli cursed her luck. *Why wasn't he afflicted with failing manhood like I've heard about from the Ancients?*

"It won't bite," he said, his hot breath on hers.

"I know." The ridiculousness of it—biting? Of course not. Still, she grimaced as she moved her fingers along the shaft through his yellow pantaloons.

Chah huffed out a laugh and began roaming his hands around her body. Was this part of her sacrifice to Kabut? Nayeli wasn't sure, but for the second time that day, she began a silent prayer.

Days turned into weeks into full moons that bled into years. Chah smoked more, drank more, and wanted more. Every time he took her to bed Nayeli prayed and offered up her sacrifice to Kabut. The sacrifice was surely working because that year the master crafter had taken ill, and Nayeli stepped into his role running the Foundry as acting master crafter. She was now the youngest master crafter there had ever been. Though she had never doubted her ability to achieve her goal, it was still a relief when she reached it. Each day she grew more formidable in both skill and power. If it wasn't for Chah, she would be content. Nayeli was now the highest-ranking person in Yellow Commune, except for the commune leader, Andu.

Since Inansi's death Nayeli took tea with Andu once a moon turn, after the sacrifice at the open temple. He had proved a good source of advice, leaving Nayeli more devout with each visit. She told him of her struggles with Chah.

"Kabut tests you, he tests your union," Andu said.

Nayeli clicked her tongue. "Have I not proved my devotion? I have produced more structures in the Foundry than any of my predecessors. For we will be ready." Nayeli squeezed half a bitter lime into her tea. Most people used sugar to season the native bark tea, but Nayeli preferred hers sour.

Andu bowed his head, his soft white hair now more silvered with age. "There is no limit to the pain we must suffer, there is no end to the devotion we must feel."

Nayeli thought she understood. Andu continued.

"When Kabut is satisfied with your sacrifice he will bless you with a child."

Nayeli lowered her eyes. She had been inserting the juice of the loffa flower throughout their marriage, killing off Chah's seed before it took root.

Children were not important to her right now. She had only just taken charge of the Foundry. There were processes she wanted to install, crafters she wanted to train.

Surely the final battle was more important than giving Chah a child?

The silence was filled with her thoughts, and she realized Andu was waiting for her to respond.

"As Kabut wills it," she murmured.

Andu seemed to sense her reluctance.

"There is no battle without the Child of Fire, and it is our duty to give birth to them. You need not keep them. You can relinquish the babe to the commune for bidding."

Nayeli scowled. She thought of the bloated women she'd seen walking up the steps of the temple, each full moon growing larger in the stomach and gaunter in the face. To Nayeli it was as if the babes were parasites.

No, I will not carry a babe. But she didn't say those words to Andu.

"Thank you for the tea, Andu." She had stopped calling him commune leader long ago. "I will continue to do my duty, and will be blessed with a child, should Kabut will it."

Andu's eyes glittered as he followed her to the door of his hut.

"Remember that our God takes. And he will take and take, and then he will take some more. Do not defy him."

Nayeli allowed herself a small feeling of guilt, but it disappeared with the rising of the sun.

IT WAS DURING their fourth year of marriage that Chah struck her for the first time.

"Smile, why don't you smile?" he said this while rutting above her, his sweat dripping down on her bare chest.

Nayeli wasn't sure what to say to that. She had been deep in thought about the schema of the next structure she was going to make in the Foundry.

"Wife?" he shouted, the word spat out like an insult. He always called her Wife, not Nayeli.

"I am sorry, *Husband*."

The slap shook her teeth and knocked her head back against her pillow. She lay there stunned, pinned down by the man above her.

"Why do you not take pleasure from this?" He thrust in fiercely and she cried out. The pain in her sparked something dark in him and he struck her again.

The slap split her lip, and tears sprang in her eyes.

Chah had apologized the next morning once he saw the damage he had done to her face. He was more careful the next time to strike her below the neckline. Over time Nayeli began to notice the pattern of his behavior. Her pain fueled him, and so all she could do was act like the hurt he wrought on her body didn't affect her. Instead, she went to a place in her mind that replicated the open temple in the center of the Volcane Isles. And there she placed her pain before Kabut.

Nayeli knew that her offerings were pleasing her God. The previous master crafter died suddenly in the night, making her the youngest leader of the Foundry since its inception. Then, after a particularly brutal night with Chah, an unclaimed shipment of steel washed up on the shore. The metal was the finest quality Nayeli had ever seen.

Glorious one up above, you who knows no bounds or boundaries. You who spins the web of my future, take my pain and bless me anew.

Those words became her mantra, and though she still used the loffa flower she knew her pain was enough to sate the hunger of Kabut.

Pain and success became one and the same.

IT WAS A normal night like any other, the night Chah died. The lights were dimmed in the Foundry, low enough so the surrounding huts didn't complain, but bright enough for Nayeli to see her work. She moved the chisel back and forward on the structure she was working on. The sound of metal being gouged away was her favorite type of music. Sometimes the chisel created a spark of friction, and the screech of metal thrummed through her veins.

Nayeli had taken to spending most of her evenings at the Foundry just to avoid Chah. He had lost his job of knitting fishing nets, because his fingers were too gnarled to keep up with the younger contenders, though that wasn't what he'd told Nayeli.

"The master fisherman is too ashamed to keep me on," Chah shouted, no longer caring who heard them through the thin walls of the hut. And in turn no one else seemed to care either.

"Too ashamed, Chah?" Nayeli said quietly. She was tired, and Chah was drunk.

"Because of you, *Wife*." Spittle struck Nayeli in the eye, directed by the quivering finger Chah held in front of her face.

"Because you are barren," he continued. "Because you refuse to bid on a child and refuse to give me one either."

For a second, Nayeli thought he'd figured out she was using loffa flower, but there was no intelligence in the watery depths of his eyes. If he knew, he'd have taken the truth to the commune leader, and she wasn't sure Andu would have protected her.

"It is not that I don't want to have children, Chah, it is simply because I want to keep trying." She recited the lie with waning conviction. It was past midnight, and all she wanted was to sleep. "I want them to have your eyes and my skill for crafting. That is the child I want, not some abandoned brood with dirty blood we can't trace. You know how the green-blooded like to sow their seed in other communes."

Chah scowled and spat on the floor. The effort seemed to tire him, and the anger went out of him fast enough for snoring soon to follow.

Nayeli had let out a shaky breath. These excuses had bought her time. But not enough—Chah was still alive.

Nayeli went back to her work, pushing all thoughts of her husband aside. This was what she was good at, this was all she needed to be happy.

There was a sound in the far end of the workshop, and Nayeli looked up to see the yellow-cloaked form of the Yellow Commune leader, Andu.

"Nayeli, you have worked from dawn until Kabut opened his eye. Tomorrow will be a big day. We are sending for the harvest to begin testing the structures."

Nayeli hunched over the dome of metal she was working on. She knew how important tomorrow would be: she was Master Crafter—she had been the one to organize the experiment.

"Go home, Nayeli," Andu pressed.

Nayeli wanted to suggest the same thing to him, but Andu was now one of the Ancients, those who had seen over eighty years—and disrespecting an Ancient was like disrespecting Kabut.

"I will finish here and then take my leave," Nayeli said, still not looking up, but knowing all the same that Andu's lined face would be puckered in disapproval.

"Unless there is a reason you avoid your marriage bed?"

At this Nayeli stopped her grinding and placed her chisel back on her tool stand to rest among the other gleaming implements.

She met Andu's gaze. It was concerned, but she knew it wasn't for her personally. It was concern for the order of things, for the continuation of Yellow Commune's reputation.

"What are you suggesting, Andu?"

Andu's shoulders lifted and then fell. "Remember that there is no prosperity without sacrifice. And sacrifice is painful."

Oh, Nayeli knew that.

"But out of that pain will come our rebirth. Out of the fire we will be made anew. Kabut has spoken it to our prophet. Once we purge this land, we will be Gods. We will join Kabut in the web of life."

Nayeli felt her eye twitch backward. She knew all this, *she* was the one leading the battle preparations, *she* was the one readying the stage for them to burn it all. Having a child wouldn't affect that.

"You doubt me?" Andu said with uncharacteristic annoyance.

"You doubt the importance of your child? Know this, Kabut took no partner, took no man, woman, or musawa. But one day when we are made Gods he will look upon us and choose. So be sure to be the wife you want him to see."

There it was, that word again. *Wife.*

"I will," Nayeli murmured and packed up her things.

CHAPTER TWENTY

NAYELI

All people of childbearing age must sacrifice their body, as is Kabut's will. The Child of Fire will one day be born and each day we pray that their time on this land will begin anon.

—Writings carved onto the wall of the open temple in the Volcane Isles

Kabut's eye followed her as she made her way to her hut a short distance away. The silver tendrils it cast set the commune in shadow. She liked this time of the night most; it soothed her knowing her God was watching.

Tomorrow was a big day. The first harvest from the Shariha was arriving, and Nayeli was going to demonstrate the new weapons she had developed for the commune leaders. She needed a restful night's sleep. Hopefully Chah wouldn't be awake when she returned. With Chah's joints plaguing him more and more, she had not suffered from his violence in recent weeks.

But when she pushed open the reed door to their hut, he was waiting for her.

"Wife," he said.

"Husband."

"Tonight, we make a child."

Nayeli knew that wasn't possible, but she nodded anyway. "Yes, husband." She went to his open hand.

"Uhuh, you smell," he hissed. It was a poor insult, unoriginal, like him. When you lived on an island afflicted by sulphur you always smelled. Still, he nuzzled into her neck and began to take his fill of her.

Nayeli began her prayers to Kabut.

Glorious one up above, you who knows no bounds or boundaries. You who spins the web of my future, take this sacrifice as your own—

"Divine's web. Look at me." He punched her stomach.

—Take my pain and forge it anew and bless me on this day. Guide my hand and my tools as I bring forth the final flame, so that I may be molded in your eye, an infinite spirit, a God—

"I said look at me." Chah punched her stomach again.

—I am your servant, but I will be your equal. When the time of the purge comes, I will find my way into your many arms and find solace among your wisdom—

"Look. At. Me." He punctuated his words with fists, the force of which made Nayeli's body contract in on itself, but she couldn't move. She was pinned below him.

—Take my offering and in turn build me up.

With the breath knocked out of her, Nayeli had no chance to warn Chah of the vomit that was about to spew from her mouth.

"Argh," he cried. She felt the suction of him leaving her body. Now freed, she could curl into the ball her body so craved.

—Like the metal I carve every day, give me strength to be solid. Give me strength to be his wife.

Something was happening inside her body. She could feel it pulling her organs downward, an aching pain between her legs and a wetness that wasn't just the lubrication Chah used.

"I'm going to Green Commune," he murmured, and Nayeli knew that he would find someone to feed his appetite there.

Cramps racked her body but still she chanted.

God almighty, God above, take this sacrifice and build me up.

Nayeli wasn't sure how much time passed, but she must have

fallen unconscious. When she woke, the bed was sticky with her blood. She gasped and began to bundle up the bedsheets, hissing as pain still doubled her over.

Then she saw it.

Cradled in the folds of the blanket and enveloped in a thin film of blood. The size of her finger, no more, no less. A cry escaped her.

She hadn't even known she was pregnant. It shouldn't have been possible with the loffa flower she'd been taking.

She reached for the clotted blood, her lips parting as she recited the prophecy seared into every person of the Zalaam:

A Child of Fire whose blood will blaze,
Will cleanse the world in eight nights, eight days,
Eight bloods lend strength to lead the charge
And eradicate the infidel, only Gods emerge,
Ready we will be, when the Ending Fire comes,
When the Child of Fire brings the Battle Drum,
The Battle Drum,
The Battle Drum,
Ready we will be, for war will come.

The prophecy was the reason every child-bearing adult was encouraged to procreate. Nayeli hadn't wanted to, hadn't considered that her own brood might have been the one chosen by Kabut to lead the war.

If they had lived.

"My child," she whispered.

Her fingers brushed the impossibly small form of the babe that had been growing inside her. Now dead.

And for the first time since her brother had died, Nayeli knew love.

NAYELI DIDN'T REMEMBER walking to the temple. But she found herself there, the small embryo clutched to her chest, cocooned by both her hands. The endless fire was always lit, its talons reaching up to the full moon in the sky.

A full moon. A sacred day.

She approached the fire. The sacrificial blade sat on a plinth beside it, unsheathed. It had been the tool she'd used during her marriage ceremony. The small cut hadn't even scarred. She had been so foolish back then. She should have known Kabut would demand more from her.

And she from him.

She knelt before the endless flame.

"Kabut, take this offering. Take my pain and carve me anew." Tears streamed down her face as she placed her child into the flames. The fire devoured it in moments, and the smell of her own flesh and blood burning was the sweetest sharpness Nayeli had ever felt.

There were footsteps behind her; she knew the heavyset tread, the movement slurred by alcohol.

"Wife, where have you been? I realized my foolishness and came back for you, my bonded one."

Wife.

That word. She knew what she had to do. It struck her like a shard of light during a storm. She knew the thought had come from Kabut. Her God was speaking to her, not in a language she knew, but she could feel his presence in the conviction of her thoughts. Her mind was focused on two clear words that flashed beneath each eyelid as she blinked away the smoke of her blood and flesh.

Kill Chah. Kill Chah. Kill Chah.

Nayeli didn't turn from the flame. As much as she yearned to join her child there in that moment, there were other paths she needed to walk first.

"Chah." Nayeli called him near.

"Wife? Oh, Wife, how are you bleeding so?"

He knelt beside her, and finally Nayeli turned to look at him.

The orange glow of the fire danced in his amber eyes. Those eyes sagged in the corners like the rest of him. His dark skin, tinged ever so slightly ochre in the light of the flames, was sweaty and dirt-speckled. His hair hadn't receded, rather disintegrated into old age, wispy like the seeds of a thistle flower.

Sometimes flowers need to be pruned.

Nayeli reached for the sacrificial dagger and in one fluid motion plunged it into Chah's heart. His mouth opened in a silent "Oh," but it was too late. He was dead.

"Kabut, take this offering. Take his pain and carve me anew." Nayeli twisted the dagger before pulling it out and plunging the blade in the flame. Once her husband's yellow blood was cleansed away, she returned the dagger to the stand.

She stood and pushed Chah's body into the hungry fire with her foot. He was lighter than she imagined, but it was never his strength that kept her down, it was hers.

"No one will sway me from my holy mission," she promised to the flame. "To win, we must begin again."

NAYELI WATCHED CHAH'S form burn away into skeletal remains until the licks of fire blended with sunrise. Today was the big day. Today all the commune leaders would congregate to watch Nayeli's crafters at work. They were meant to meet in the open temple before being escorted by Nayeli to the Foundry where the harvest from the Shariha would have arrived by boat. The crafters would be busy preparing the structures so when Nayeli escorted the commune leaders through the Foundry, they'd see the crafters' weapons at work.

Nayeli still knelt before the endless flame, her hands pressed into the ground where the white-tiled image of Kabut lay. His spider form filled the open temple, the endless flame sitting in the belly. His eight legs stretched outward, branching out across the large space, each limb ending in a plinth that represented one of the blood colors. Each commune had decorated the white marble of their plinth with carvings that represented their villages.

A woman danced in silk robes on the Green Commune plinth, as the green-blooded folk were known for their entertainment and festivities. Spiky cacti sprang from the base of the Violet Commune's, the plant native to the east island where they resided. Fishing vessels swam across the Blue Commune plinth, rudimentary fish drawn into the grooves of the marble. It made her think of Inansi, though it sparked no pain. Her heart was now numb.

The wind pulled up some of the ash from the fire, stinging her eyes. She blinked away the tears, streaking her face black.

She heard the gritty footsteps of people ascending the crumbling stairs to the open temple.

"Master crafter." Andu entered the open temple and saw Nayeli's prostrated form before the fire. Behind him stood the other seven leaders, each wearing their formal robes for the occasion in the color of their commune. The Violet Commune leader's dress was offensively bright, dyed with flowers imported from off the island.

I wonder what they sacrificed to Kabut for such an indulgence.

Andu hissed through his teeth as he grew nearer.

"Nayeli?" He sounded scared. "What happened?"

Nayeli raised her head and locked eyes with each of the commune leaders in turn. Cloaked in only her yellow blood and the flecks of her husband's ash, Nayeli knew she cut a terrifying sight.

Fear was good, fear she could use.

She pulled herself to her feet. Dirt clung to the drying blood that ran down her legs.

"Commune leaders. Please take your positions." Nayeli's voice was strong.

Andu took a step toward her. "Nayeli? Is this . . . is this essential for the demonstration of the new weapons?"

Her crafters would be preparing the harvest from the Shariha and testing the mechanisms before she led the leaders to the Foundry. But that would have to wait. There was something she needed to do first.

"Please take your positions by your plinths," Nayeli repeated. The Indigo Commune leader hissed in indignation but was the first one to follow Nayeli's order. The indigo-blooded were always so weak-spirited.

Once they were all stationed at their relevant sections, Nayeli reached for the ceremonial dagger. It felt warm as if it had been passed from her God's grasp to hers. She had never been so convinced of her purpose.

"I welcome you all to my wedding."

There were shouts and guffaws from the congregation of leaders. Nayeli held up a hand to silence them.

As Kabut's eye had set and the sun had risen, Nayeli had felt her God's will once more. Again, it wasn't in words but a conviction of feeling.

Today was to be her wedding day.

The thought struck her between the eyes, and she knew it to be from her God. He had taken her sacrifice and granted her a boon in return.

"I understand you may be confused. But last night Kabut spoke to me." Nayeli held the dagger high before bringing it down on her forearm, slicing a line through her skin. She knew the pain was there, but she felt detached from it, an outsider looking on. It was as if her God was protecting her. It gave her all the more faith that she was doing the right thing.

She continued, "Once Chah made his passing to the other side, I knew I would live to marry again." She kept slicing with the blade. The cuts crisscrossed up her left arm and she began on her right. "And it was Kabut who told me who I shall be bonded to next." She began on her legs, savoring the shock from the leaders.

Andu began to walk toward her, his expression worried. "Nayeli, stop, what are you—"

"From this moment on, Nayeli Ilrase of Yellow Commune does not exist," she shouted at him, and he faltered in his steps. "Forever more, I shall be known as Wife. Wife of all, and wife of one. Kabut's partner in the sky."

There were cries of blasphemy and mutters of scorn. The Green Commune leader spoke up, her emerald cloak so fine you could see the curves of her body.

"Nayeli—"

"Wife," she interrupted, starting on her torso.

"Indeed, this offering of pain is . . . impressive, but I urge you to stop, you will not survive much more blood loss."

"Kabut will protect me." She took the dagger and carved away the locks of her hair, digging the blade into her scalp. Slowly, she scoured her flesh into a web starting from the crown of her head. Matted, bloody hair fell around her, and she found it freeing, shearing away all that had come before. Her own blood was cleansing, forging her anew.

The pain felt like ecstasy now, and she laughed as the blissful feeling soared through her veins like the most exquisite of drugs.

"Yes, I am your wife, Kabut, love of mine." She breathed her thoughts out in wonder.

"Nayeli—Wife—please stop this nonsense," Andu shouted.

Nayeli didn't exist anymore. Instead, she had shed the remains of what she once was. Blood dripped down every surface of her. It was hard to see any skin that had not been marred by the blade, but still she slashed at it.

"With sacrifice comes prosperity. Will you refuse Kabut's will?" she said.

It was in that moment the ground shook.

Those who lived on the Volcane Isles were used to the unstable nature of the land. It had been afflicted by earthquakes since the Zalaam had settled there four hundred years ago. But this was an earthquake like no other. The ground roared as it shifted, clouds of debris and dirt bloomed as the plinths fell to the ground cracking the tiled image of Kabut. The sea in the distance churned and retreated in an impending tsunami that would crash against the rocks of the open temple, chipping away at the cliff face.

The leaders called to one another as they dropped to the ground away from the edge of the temple. The motion was practiced.

Nayeli let the dagger fall to the ground, but she didn't cower like the others. She rode the shaking earth as if it were her steed, her power to control.

As the earthquake reaped chaos and destruction, Nayeli whooped and cheered. Here was Kabut at work, here was her God's will on show for all to see.

A fracture had formed through the middle of the likeness of Kabut, the white tiles cracked like an egg. Nayeli's feet stood on either side of the fault line.

Chaos was hers to mold.

Nayeli looked the commune leaders each in the eye. Some were bleeding from small wounds; Andu was cradling what looked to be a dislocated shoulder. All were crying and fearful as they looked up at her.

She was the only one still standing.

"Will you refuse his will?" the Wife said.

PART THREE

RENOUNCE

They say the mad prophet foretold what is to come. But I have found no evidence that there is any truth in prophecy. The only way foretelling harks true is if those who believe make it so. It makes me wonder, is faith a type of madness?

—The First Councillor of the Zwina Academy

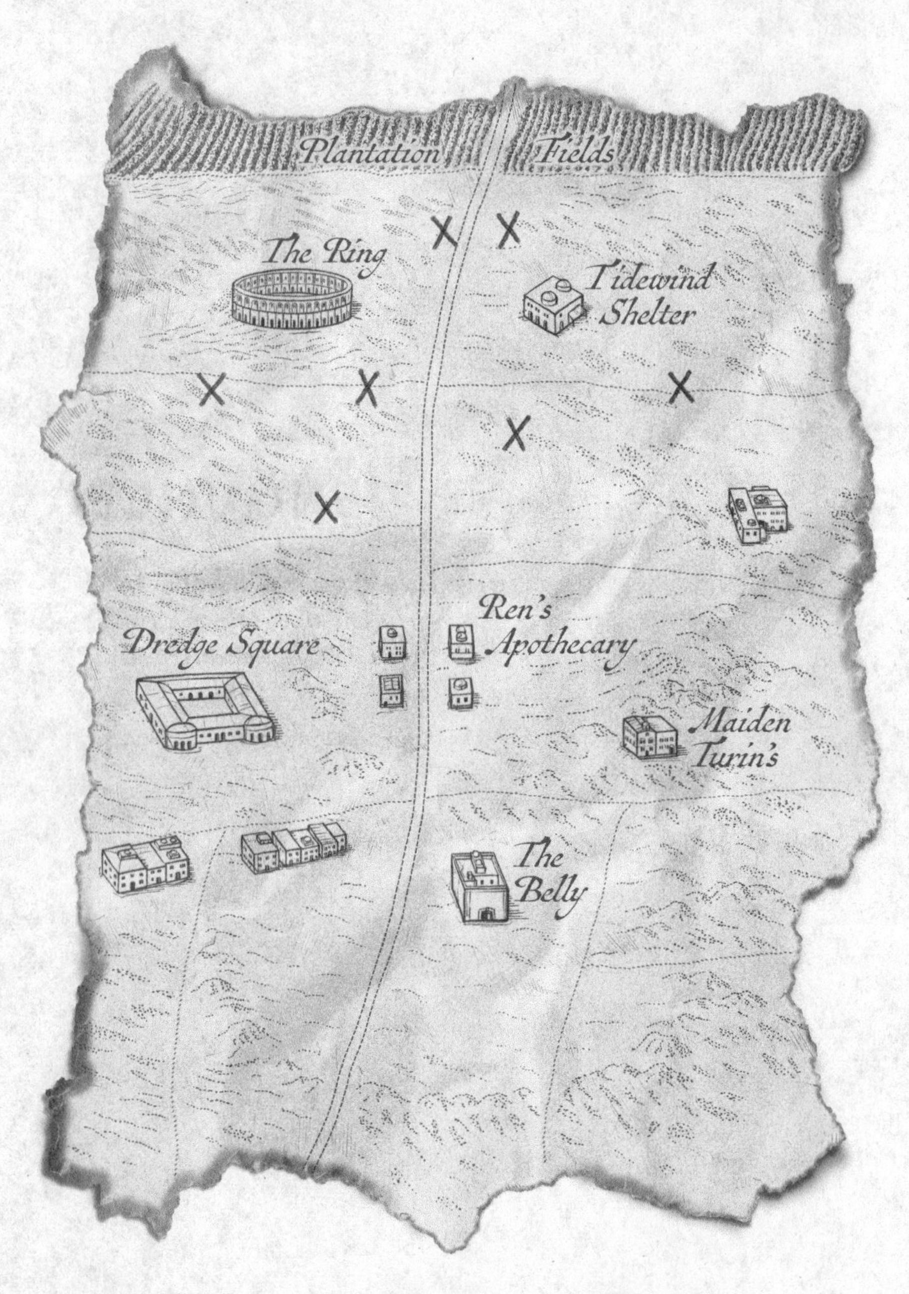

Map of the bodies found in the Dredge by Hassa

CHAPTER TWENTY-ONE

SYLAH

Sea Lords govern the shores and Earth Lords govern the inner land of Tenio. Each jurisdiction is provided with a squadron of officers the size of which is reflective of the population where they are stationed, in order to maintain law. Both titles make up the Chamber of Lords that advises Queen Karanomo on matters of state.

—Extract from *Monarchy in Modern Times*, by Rubo Oh-Kinsha

The last time Sylah had been knocked unconscious was when she had triggered the bloodwerk trap in Anoor's chambers, causing a paperweight to fall and strike her on the head. The aching in the back of her skull blurred those memories with the present.

"Anoor?" she murmured. He eyelids fluttered in the darkness as she fought to regain wakefulness. She shifted and realized her hands were bound at the wrist, like they had been in Anoor's dressing room all those mooncycles ago.

"Anoor?" she called again, though she was less certain that her lover was nearby.

She couldn't smell the sandalwood oil she used or see the flicker of the runelight that hung in her dressing room. Instead, she smelled unwashed bodies and waste, and all she could see was darkness.

"Anoor?" This time her name was a plea.

But Anoor wasn't there. Anoor had sent her away.

Sylah searched the darkness for the brightest object to clutch onto until her eyes adjusted. She detected a sliver of light through wooden slats and flashes of ivory: teeth. Then the alabaster of a hundred eyes.

Mainlanders.

Sylah took them in. People of every gender and every age sat upon the two benches lining the cart. Some were crying, water tracks running down their glossy black skin, slick with sweat. Others hissed at Sylah when her gaze settled on them. Their clothing was less structured than that worn in the empire, with flowing fabrics that draped across their torsos. Their clothes looked like they had been patterned once, but they were so faded the swirls could just as easily have been streaks of dirt. Some wore hair wraps in intricate styles, the fabric falling like hair on either side of their face. Unkempt curls sprang from behind the more threadbare coverings, revealing curls as shiny and as black as hers. A few hooked the edges of their headwraps from one ear to the other, protecting their noses from the smell. As the odor assaulted her, Sylah threw them envious looks.

She felt the sharp pang of disappointment, which coincided with her locking eyes with Jond. They were just ordinary people. Not one of them was a talking tree.

"What happened?" Sylah asked him from the opposite side of the cart. He was ten prisoners down.

"I'm not sure, I woke up not long before you. No one will talk to me, though. I'm not sure if they speak the common tongue."

Someone clicked their tongue at them.

"Does anyone here speak the common tongue?" Sylah shouted.

There were moans and murmurs, until a voice cut through it all.

"We all do, obroni." The voice was deep and harsh.

The mainlander accent was more guttural than Sylah was used

to, but she knew an insult when she heard one, even if she didn't know the word.

"I am not an obroni."

"Be quiet or you'll bring the Shariha down on us," another voice said.

"Will someone tell me what's going on?" Sylah shouted.

"Sylah, maybe you should be quiet," Jond said as more prisoners grumbled their dissent.

"No, I want to know why I'm suddenly tied up, my pack missing, my inkwell gone, and on some sort of massive cart with people who haven't washed for years." Sylah began to bang her head against the wall behind her. "Hello? Someone free me, please!"

She made the request without expecting a response, so when the cart stopped moving, she froze in the sudden silence.

The man next to her was sobbing softly, his eyes flicking to the back of the carriage in anticipation of whoever was coming. The door at the back of the cart opened, and half of the prisoners flinched.

"Who say they wantin' to be hurtin'?" The woman framed by daylight was older than Sylah was expecting. A scarf hung across her mouth and hooked behind her ears while her coiled hair reached for the cloudy sky above. Gold rings pierced her graying eyebrows. She brandished a spear of pure metal, its tip lovingly sharp. But that wasn't what made Sylah's blood run cold.

It was the fresh cut by the side of her eye that oozed violet.

The woman was purple-blooded.

Sylah involuntarily cowered before straightening her shoulders and shouting, "Where are you taking us?"

The woman was tall, at least as tall as Sylah, but Sylah knew she could put up more than a fair fight against this woman even while wearing manacles.

"Ina," she called. "Talush achram be abbeh."

She didn't recognize the sing-song lilt of the woman's language, but she understood the finger pointing steadfastly at Sylah's chest.

Another face appeared, presumably "Ina." Sylah watched the boy jump up into the center of the cart. He too wore a scarf over his mouth but Sylah barely noticed as she had spotted the sword hanging by his waist.

"That's mine," Sylah hissed through bared teeth.

Ina followed her line of sight and ran an idle finger down the blade. Mirth flashed in his eyes as Sylah's manacled hands balled into fists.

The sword was almost the same length as the boy's leg, and it was clear from the way he grasped the hilt that he didn't know how to use it.

"Mine now, picked for picking. Far it was for Ina to see obroni. So now mine mine mine."

Her last gift from Anoor, stolen.

Sylah's frayed temper snapped, and she lunged for the sword but the chains held her fast.

A sharp slap rang out, and it took a few seconds of shocked realization for Sylah to comprehend the pain spreading over her cheek. In that moment, Ina bent around her and pulled a key from his pocket. He unlocked the chains around her waist that tied her midriff to the wall of the vehicle. Now freed, Sylah stood and held her hands out so the manacles could be removed too.

Though she towered over the boy, Ina just winked.

"Nah, nah," he said. "Not till good copper you are sold."

Sylah tried to swing for him with her manacled hands, but he skipped out of the cart, cackling.

"Festa blud be hutish," Ina said to the woman, and she joined in with the boy's laughter. Sylah knew she was the butt of the joke but didn't know why.

She stood and moved through her prison. Sylah thought she heard Jond whisper, "Be careful," as she passed him, but she wasn't sure. Sylah jumped down as gracefully as she could, but her feet were held together by a metal bar.

The ground was as black as the forest they'd been captured in. The acrid smell that had been present in Nsuo was just as strong, though at least out here it didn't smell like shit and body odor. She lifted her head following the copper bar that was towing the carriage. She expected to see an eru attached to a harness at the end.

Instead, it was something far more monstrous.

"What the fuck is that?" she screamed.

The beast had two lips protruding from an almond-shaped head. Black eyes with eyelashes too long for its features. And a neck, a neck that angled out from a body that carried two *humps* covered in thick, shaggy hair.

Ina smirked. "Obroni, seen not a camel 'for?"

"A camel?" Sylah repeated the unfamiliar word. She then took one manacled step back, forcing the other foot along as well. She peered around the edge of the carriage and saw at least twenty of these "camels" pulling other carts behind them. And "cart" was an understatement. It was more like a gargantuan cage, hauled on giant metal wheels. There were so many of them that they curved around the road behind Sylah until they were dots on the empty horizon.

There was a sound ahead of her, and Sylah spun around, nearly falling over her irons as she pinned her eyes on the creature in front of her.

The camel's mouth was moving unnaturally, the two sides of the jaw going in opposite directions until the lips puckered and spit flew out.

"What is it doing?"

Ina cackled as Sylah stumbled away from the camel spit.

There was a crack: a sound Sylah would recognize anywhere. A whip.

The older woman who was wielding the weapon had caught the camel on the rump. The creature made a guttural trill and shifted its hooves, moving away from Sylah. It was then that she saw the metal shoes that protected its feet.

Acid. She remembered the dissolved brickwork and panicked. Was it on the ground?

She tried to lift her feet to look at the soles of her shoes, but it was impossible with the manacles on.

"Thinkin' she crazy," Ina reported to the older woman in the common tongue. This was an insult that he wanted Sylah to hear.

Sylah met the woman's gaze.

"Free me," Sylah said.

"See, crazy. Free she wantin' before a storm. Death her be callin'," Ina confirmed.

The woman turned to Ina and murmured a few words in their language. It clicked and shrilled with pronunciations Sylah hadn't heard before. When the woman finished speaking, Ina scowled and slinked off.

"You got firebelly, child," the woman said to Sylah.

"Free me."

"Copper child, you be free when we get copper." The woman lifted her scarf to scratch her nose, and Sylah was shocked to see darkness where her teeth should have been.

"You can't do this. You have to take me back. Back to Nsuo—"

"—What in Nsuo that have you wantin' back? More obroni?"

"I don't know what obroni is." At least it meant they probably hadn't found the Ghostings.

"Obroni." The woman waved her hand up and down Sylah's body like an explanation.

Thunder rang out up above them and Sylah jumped.

"You want free?" the woman said softly, her scarf moving with her breath. "Go."

Sylah looked around, confused. Was it going to be this easy?

"Go." The woman snapped the whip at Sylah's feet, lifting some of the black dirt.

Sylah needed no other encouragement.

SYLAH DIDN'T FEEL guilty about leaving Jond, not really. If he saw that she'd escaped, then maybe he could do the same thing.

But none of this makes sense, why would they just let me go? She pushed the thought to the back of her mind.

Her capturers cheered and whooped as she set off, some of them laughing and calling out in that language she didn't know. Thunder added percussion to their cries, but Sylah paid it no heed.

The landscape was flat, just black dirt and dying trees for as far as she could see. Sylah thought she could see the ocean in the distance to her left, so that's where she was shuffling toward. It took her a while to get any sort of momentum with the metal stick separating her legs, but eventually she picked up speed.

Her thoughts turned to the elders back on the *Baqarah*. Did they know Sylah and Jond had been taken? There had been no Ghostings in her carriage of chattel, so hopefully they were still free.

The Shariha, the other prisoners had called them.

"Shariha." Sylah hissed the word between her teeth, committing it to memory. Committing a pledge for revenge. "No one enslaves one of the Stolen."

She laughed, the sound reaching no one, not even the ears of any creatures, because all life had long ago died in this barren land.

There was a final crack of thunder before the rain. Sylah didn't notice it at first. She concentrated instead on putting one foot in front of the other. She moved to push a wet braid out of her eye with her manacled hands. When she dropped them down to her waist again, she saw that the rain was red. She gasped, and then looked up. Was the sky bleeding?

Then the pain came. The searing pain of her skin being burned away. The rain wasn't red.

"No, no, no."

It was her blood.

Sylah now understood the death sentence they had given her. She pulled her arms and head into the fragments of her shirt. She didn't have long to decide what to do next. Her clothes were being shorn away with every raindrop. The rest of her skin would be the next thing to go.

She had only one choice.

Go back.

JOND WATCHED AS the prisoners huddled into the center of the truck. He saw the hisses of pain as droplets of rain made their way through cracks in the walls. He saw and he understood.

They had sent Sylah into a storm of acid rain.

He squeezed his eyes together and tried not to think of it. Of her. *She could survive it. She could survive anything.*

The door at the end of the carriage opened. Through the rain Jond could see the copper sheet that had been pulled out from the top of the cart to cover the animals that dragged them. There were a few of their capturers there too, and Jond leaned over to garner what he could from them. The prisoners had murmured their name enough times for Jond to learn that the people who had made him prisoner were called the Shariha.

A silhouette topped with braids was thrown into the center of the cart, and the prisoners scattered as far back as their manacled limbs would allow them. But Jond leaned forward, his strength dragging down the prisoner he was shackled to. The chains by their waist connected them to the cart, but also to each other. His neighbor was sturdy—but he was no match for Jond.

"Oh, oh, oh. Stop that," the man groaned, pushing out with his gnarled hands as Jond dragged him and two more prisoners forward.

Jond reached as far forward as he could. His fingertips skimmed the top of her braids, and he tried to get a grip of them. One of the plaits broke away in his hand, and he yelped. He lunged again and managed to grab her shoulders.

He couldn't see much in the dim light, made dimmer still by the storm outside. But what he saw was reflected in the gasps of the others around her. Sylah's skin was covered in open wounds. Some were small, droplet-sized, but others had spread and converged and were doing serious damage.

"She won't survive," the man said. Jond turned to look at the other prisoner, his jaw set in defiance, ready to argue. The man was older than he expected, in his fifties, though as muscular as someone in his prime. He looked at Jond with one eye. Smooth scar tissue covered the one he had lost. An old wound.

He continued, ignoring Jond's stare. "Too much blood loss. Too much pain. Infection will settle into her not long from now."

Jond looped his manacled arms under her head and pulled her forward onto his lap. Even her chains had rusted some.

"She'll survive."

"Salamander's shit. She won't. You must listen to me, I know these things, I was a healer in my town. I have seen more acid burns than you can ever imagine. Better to kill her." The man spoke clearly now the sound of the storm hid their conversation from the Shariha.

Jond growled low in his throat and bared his teeth. The man didn't flinch. He'd clearly seen too much for Jond to scare him.

"I will not kill her."

"A flying goat is still a goat," the man said with finality.

Jond looked at him incredulously.

"You do not know this saying? I mean to say, you are being stubborn, boy. But it does not dispel the truth."

Jond squeezed his eyes shut against the man's words and held tighter onto Sylah's bleeding form.

"I will not kill her."

He thought of the box of herbs Sylah had used on the ship and wished he had it with him. There might have been something in the "poison" mixture that could help her now.

Sylah had thought the ruse was working. But Jond had worked with Master Inansi—or Loot, as Sylah knew him—for years, and his skill in poison study was unmatched. Jond knew how to detect all the major toxins, and there was no way the tincture she had given him had anything harmful in it.

But he played along for her. To give her the peace of mind she so craved.

So fractured is your trust in me. But trust me once more, Sylah, I will see you survive this.

THE STORM DIDN'T stop until the morning. Jond stayed awake holding on to Sylah's body, watching her rattled breathing. At some point during the night the Shariha shuffled the prisoners out one by one to take a piss in a bucket above a metal canopy. Jond left Sylah with Niha, the healer, when it was his turn.

"They will give you a cup to reuse for water." Niha jiggled the metal cup clasped to his waist chain. "Piss in it and bring it back."

"What?"

"Just do as I say." Niha brushed a braid off Sylah's face. It had settled into the beginnings of a scab across her cheek.

As Niha predicted, they gave Jond a metal cup filled with gray water. Jond drank it in full. Others held on to it for some time, knowing they had to ration it throughout the night, and possibly the day, but Jond needed the cup as a vessel.

It had been difficult to angle away from the guard to pee in his cup, and his manacles had not helped. There had been a bit of spillage, but he'd done it.

"You got it?" Niha asked.

"Yes."

"Good, now use it to cleanse the largest wounds."

"What?"

"I said I was a healer, now do as I say." Niha flicked his fingers forward in a grabbing motion and Jond handed over the urine. Jond saw a circular scar in the center of Niha's palm, too perfect to be a simple wound. "Water would have been better, but you needed that to stay alive yourself. If you mean to keep her breathing it'll be a hard battle." Niha began to wash Sylah's wounds with Jond's piss. Without hesitation, Jond joined in.

The damage done by the acid rain was worse than Jond had imagined. There was one wound on her arm that was so deep Jond could see the yellow tissue of fat. When they were done he thanked Niha.

"Why are you helping me if you believe she is going to die?"

"It's the way of a healer."

"Did you train at the Zwina Academy?" Jond asked.

Niha barked out a stilted laugh. "Oh, no, I am not so grand. The healers there are probably the only people in the world that could have saved your friend here." Niha chewed on the side of his cheek, pronouncing the hollows across his wide face.

Sylah began to spasm, her arms trembling by her chest.

"Hold her down. We don't want her to hurt herself even more," Niha said.

Jond grasped her shoulders, stabilizing her until the tremors passed.

"It's the joba seeds," Jond said softly. "It's a drug where I come from. Sylah . . . she used it for a long time. Now she needs to take a little bit every day to temper the withdrawal symptoms; her body relies on it."

"Ah, she has substance dependency."

Jond nodded.

Niha rubbed his eye.

"That makes things even more complicated. Her body is the battleground and right now she is fighting against infection, withdrawal, and substantial blood loss. The only positive I have for you is that she isn't feeling anything in her current state."

Jond had to look away from Sylah, his eyes hot and prickling. He could see the Shariha moving around a campfire beyond the slats in the carriage wall. The boy, Ina, was sharpening Sylah's sword by the fire, sparks raining around him.

After a time he asked Niha, "What are they going to do with us?"

"Trade us to the Zalaam for copper."

"What? Who are the Zalaam?"

"You are an obroni for sure."

"Obroni?"

"It means 'other' in the speak of the Shariha. Where are you from?"

"An island far away." Jond continued quickly before Niha could ask more. "They're going to trade us for copper?"

"Lasts the longest in the rain."

"Has it always been like this?"

"No, only in the last year have the storms become so acidic, it's made most of the coastline uninhabitable. The Shariha know to hunt here because the Sea Lords and their infantry have vacated. It is a lawless land now."

"And what do the—Zalaam, did you say? What do they do with the people they trade for?"

Niha shrugged. "The Shariha have been trading with them for years. But no one knows what they do with the slaves they trade.

The Shariha were exiled from Souriland in the northwest. Some say they traded all their own people before coming to the mainland."

Jond looked around the cart. Some of the prisoners were too old for labor. So what did the Zalaam do with all the people?

Sylah twitched, and Jond felt himself tense up in response.

"Now I'm going to get some sleep. I suggest you do too."

There wasn't an easy way to sleep. The chains around their midriffs that held them fast to the wall of the cart also kept them mostly upright.

But Jond couldn't sleep, wouldn't, not while Sylah lay there dying. Instead, he immersed himself in memories of her.

"Jond, stop being such a dung beetle." Sylah ground her teeth together. She'd just won a bout of wrestling.

He laughed and poked his elbow in her ribs. "How am I a dung beetle?"

"Well, you're holding your legs so far apart it's like you're clutching shit between them."

"And you smell," Fareen chimed in from across the room. She smiled happily to herself, having formulated a half-decent insult and interjected it at the perfect moment.

"Thanks, Fareen, aren't you meant to be practicing Nuba foundation three? Azim won't be happy to see you sitting down."

Fareen sighed into her hands and stood. Azim rarely disciplined Fareen like he did the other Stolen; there was something special about her. Not her ability to fight, oh no, she was a poor contender for Disciple of Strength, but the way Azim sometimes watched her, like she had something that others lacked.

"Let's go again," Sylah said.

"Sylah, you've bested me every time, let's take a break."

"No, come again." Her thirteen-year-old form slipped into a defensive stance. Two years his junior, and she could still pummel him to the ground.

"Enough, Sylah, enough."

"No," she barked, and this gave Jond pause.

"Why are you so angry? You're winning."

"Exactly, Jond. We do this together, remember?"

She meant the Aktibar—the trials they'd been trained for their whole lives. Jond smiled and closed the gap between them. He placed the flat of his palm on the center of her chest where they had learned the largest artery—the Akoma—pumped blood around the body. It became his nickname for Sylah when they were in private.

"We do this together, my Akoma."

They fought like that day after day until eventually she dragged up his skill level. He regretted what the past few mooncycles had done to the love that they had once shared.

And he regretted even more the secrets that he kept from her still.

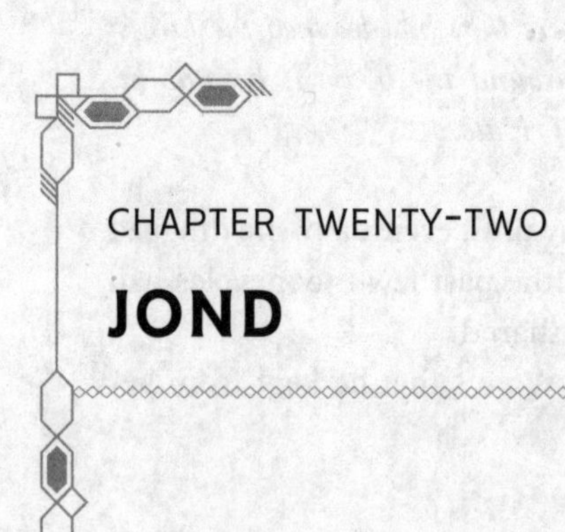

CHAPTER TWENTY-TWO

JOND

The acid rain is getting worse. Aid and resources will no longer do. I will be evacuating my settlement for safer territory inland on the next full moon. I will not be the first Sea Lord to make this decision. Prepare for coastal refugees.

—Missive from Sea Lord Nafina to Earth Lord Telata

Once the storm abated, the morning breeze blew away the acidic smell left over from the rains.

"Jond?" Sylah's croak was hoarse.

"Sylah? I've got you, don't worry, you're going to be okay."

Her eyelids fluttered for a moment, sticky with blood, before she slipped back into unconsciousness.

I've got to get her to the Zwina Academy, Jond thought. Niha had let slip this bit of information, and Jond had tucked it away. He knew that the Academy resided in the southeast of Tenio. He'd read it in the diary he had stolen from the Ghostings. It had been risky to slip out during the night in the Chrysalis, riskier still to read it in the same cabin as Sylah during the journey. It didn't matter now. The book was lost to the Shariha. He mourned it, missing the feeling of the cover in his hands.

Jond had always loved books; they had been his escape in the Sanctuary, though the library was small and restricted to what the Sandstorm could steal. The subjects were also limited, selected for their benefits to the cause rather than enjoyment. It was why he could name every plant in the empire from reading a text used to teach those training for the Aktibar of Knowledge. From then on Jond had consumed every book he could find, often hiding his reading habits from Sylah lest she mock him.

It had been fascinating to read the diary of Elder Petra. Though Jond had only read half of the journal, restricted to reading it when Sylah wasn't around, he had committed to memory the route to the Academy as much as he could. He'd intended to go with Sylah no matter what she'd said.

The door at the end of the cart opened and the boy, Ina, who had unchained Sylah the day before, stepped among the prisoners like he owned them. Jond spotted the keys that hung on a chain around his neck as he swaggered around. His mouth scarf was loosely dangling toward his chin now that the air was clearer. He smiled as he began to unchain each prisoner from the back wall, one by one.

"Is it a toilet break again?" Jond asked Niha.

Niha pretended he couldn't hear him and kept his head low, his one good eye fixed to the floor.

When it got to Jond and Sylah, Ina sneered.

"Days be dead they."

Jond knew better than to contradict him, but when the boy reached for Sylah's unconscious body, Jond leaned in with a snarl.

"Leave her alone."

Ina jumped back in surprise, then his eyes crinkled, and he cracked a laugh.

"Better for the birds be leavin' 'er."

"No."

That laugh. It was somewhere between a snort and a hiss. It made Jond want to pummel the boy to dust.

"Choosin' to stay in hotpot." Ina shrugged. "Suppose maggots good to eat." Ina kicked Jond in the stomach with his copper-tipped boots. It winded him, allowing Ina to haul Sylah up by her armpits. With deft fingers, he chained her back to the wall. She slumped against it, her skin oozing blood.

"Now out." Ina kicked him toward the outside air.

Jond couldn't help sighing with relief when the sweetness of the fresh air tousled his beard. He joined the line of prisoners waiting for their cups to be filled. He looked down at the procession of carriages and saw the same events happening over and over. The road wound back on itself, the full view of the landscape distorted by the blistered wood of the carts. But what Jond could see was bleak. Black soil, barren land, no help in sight.

Jond was pushed forward in the queue. A handful of misshapen, crumbling biscuits was thrust into his hand.

Breakfast and lunch, he supposed.

He peered around the chained-up prisoners and looked behind him. Like the head of a snake, the next carriage along was wider than the rest and reinforced with metal sides. He could see a campfire in the distance with fresh meat roasting over it, and Jond imagined the smell of its sizzling fat. He swallowed and leaned farther forward.

There were around thirty Shariha camped around the fire, bringing their total to approximately sixty if he included the guards at each of the other carriages. Jond homed in on the group ahead of him. They were laughing, their mouth scarves billowing as their eyes pressed together. Something gold glinted in the watery sunlight, and Jond crept farther away from the shuffling line to see it better.

The clunk of a metal boot behind him was all the warning Jond got before the whip caught him between the shoulder blades.

"In line get you be." One of the Shariha dragged Jond back from where he'd strayed. He had moved just a few steps.

Jond's back stung with an all-too-familiar pain. Azim had often resorted to the whip. Jond dragged his gaze forward, his fists clenched in anger, because he had realized what had caught his eye.

One of his captors was wearing his inkwell.

THE TRAIN OF carriages set off not long after the captives got their morning rations. Jond came to recognize the grunts and blurts of the camels that hauled the carts, the sound of the metal wheels pressing down in the acidic soil. A day and a night passed and still Sylah didn't wake. Her breathing had become shallower, her wounds crustier. Jond pressed water to her lips, saving most of his ration for her.

"The clouds are not hurt by the baying of dogs," Niha said. He only spoke at night once most of the Shariha had gone to sleep. When he did speak it was in proverbs Jond didn't understand.

"What you are doing is pointless," Niha explained. "She's not going to make it."

"She has to." Jond reached forward to grasp her hand. "I'm going to get her to the Academy."

Niha laughed, then stopped as Jond's black eyes bore into his.

"Boy, you can't escape the Shariha."

"I will." He wasn't sure how, but he'd figure it out. All he had to do was get the inkwell. Whoever the Shariha were, it didn't seem like they knew how to bloodwerk.

There was a wet cough from one of the prisoners, and Niha flinched.

"Pneumonia," he whispered.

"What?"

"Lung inflammation caused by infection. They will die within three days." Niha shook his head sadly.

The prisoner coughed again, and this time Jond saw the shade of their spittle as it hit the carriage floor. It was indigo.

Jond hissed and recoiled.

"Indigo blood."

He'd read in the Ghosting diary that there were eight blood colors in the world, but to see his long-held belief shattered so completely struck him like a spear in the heart.

"Oh, oh, you're not one of them that castes blood color?" Niha scolded.

"What do you mean?"

"You know, think red bloods are fiery, blue bloods are maudlin, purple bloods are always loyal . . . You get me?"

It was a simplistic view of things, but it still rang true in his mind.

". . . I suppose I was taught to think like that . . . that Emb—red bloods are more powerful, blue bloods better for labor, and clear bloods are good as servants . . ."

"Servants? Ha, if you talk to one of the Crystal Tribe, they'd have your ear for that."

"The Crystal Tribe?"

Niha shook his head in disbelief. "Where have you come from?" When Jond didn't answer he continued, "The Crystal Tribe were one of the eight aboriginal tribes on the continent. The Tharis family united all tribes under their monarchy a millennia ago. The Crystal Tribe were clear-blooded. Though there are few of them left who still follow the traditions of their ancestors. Harder to be a nomad now the world is ending—"

"Jond?" The croak was quiet, broken-sounding.

"Sylah? I'm here, I'm here."

"Water," she whispered through cracked and trembling lips.

He leaned as close as he could and dribbled the dregs of his water ration onto her lips. Her tongue darted out to moisten her mouth.

"Jond, my hair."

Jond looked at her hair; a few of the braids had been singed, but she'd protected it mostly with her forearms. She was such a proud woman.

He smiled. "It's fine, Sylah."

"No, Jond." She coughed and winced. "My hair." She began to shudder, her breath coming out in rasps. She tried to speak again, but she slipped back into oblivion.

A small sound escaped the back of Jond's throat. He cupped her face in his hand, a movement she would have killed him for if she'd been awake. He stroked her braids, the chains across his stomach straining.

Something scratched his hand. He leaned forward and saw the slip of metal wire entwined in a braid. She had woven in part of

Zero's silver belt. And in that second, he understood what Sylah had meant, what she had given him in those few seconds of wakefulness.

She had given him a means to escape.

NOW THAT JOND had a way to pick the locks he could plan their next steps. There were three things he needed to do, and he made a mental list:

1. Find a way to carry Sylah
2. Figure out how to get his inkwell
3. Try to get their packs with the Ghosting's diary and Sylah's joba seed powder in it

It took Jond a day to plan. A day that Sylah didn't have. Step one was easy. Though Jond wasn't looking forward to it, he'd seen the Shariha gallop on top of the large beasts' backs in between the two humps. Just the sight of it made his bollocks twitch.

Step two was harder. The guard who wore his inkwell only worked at night. He seemed to be a supervisor of sorts that wandered between the carriages, the inkwell glinting in the moonlight. That meant waiting until nighttime.

Jond knew that the Shariha must have kept their packs. It seemed like too good an opportunity for them to miss. He did worry there might be nothing left in them, as he was sure he'd seen one of them wearing his spare shirt in the distance. Jond knew that if they had kept their bags, they'd be stored in the carriage at the front of the procession. Jond didn't have a clever plan to retrieve them. So, he'd have to rely on brute force rather than strategy. He hoped that once he was armed with his inkwell it would be easier.

It would be the grand finale to their escape.

All Jond had to do was wait for Sylah to wake again.

"Jond?" It happened on their third night of capture.

"Sylah, listen, I'm going to undo your manacles, okay? I've already picked the locks of mine. But I need you to try and walk today. I need you to try and make it to the toilet queue. Sylah, are you listening?"

"I can help her," Niha said softly. He'd been watching Jond play with the locks for some time. "If you free me too."

Jond thought for a moment. He liked Niha; he had been kind to him and Sylah. But the risk of escaping as a threesome was exponentially higher.

"No."

"She can't walk alone. She won't make it out of the carriage."

Jond tugged on his beard. It was ragged and dry. Sylah's eyes had opened, the slit of her pupils blearily watching the exchange.

Niha went on. "I can lead you to the Academy. I've been there before."

Jond didn't say that he didn't need his help. If it all went according to plan he'd find the Ghosting diary. If not, he had the route to the Academy committed to memory.

"Fine. Help her out, keep her standing. Keep the manacles on, though they won't be locked. There's something I need first. Once I get it, it'll be easier for us to escape."

"A weapon?"

"Of sorts."

When the toilet break came, Jond took center stage. The camels from the train behind them had folded themselves down for sleep close enough for him to see their breath in the cold night air. Niha had helped Sylah down from the cart toward the water queue. Jond looked behind him to check they were still there.

Sylah's eyes were closed, and she leaned heavily on Niha's stocky form. Some of her scabs that had formed had cracked and were bleeding freely.

When Ina poured Jond his water ration—always less than the other guards—Jond bucked forward in his manacles and smacked Ina in the head with his forehead. The crack rang out across the queue, and a hush of terror descended on the prisoners. Ina blinked and fell to the ground in a pile.

"Fuck," Jond murmured. He hadn't meant to knock him out cold, just wanted to make a scene.

"What are you doing?" Niha hissed.

"Trying to get the supervisor here," Jond replied before proceeding to scream into the wind.

That should do it.

And thankfully it did. The Shariha with Jond's inkwell cantered up on his camel.

"Doing what 'ere?" He looked toward the crumpled form of Ina and back toward Jond. "Whip be getting ya."

Jond watched the Shariha jump down from the camel and pull out his whip. He was taller than Jond had hoped, and wider too. His mouth scarf was a pale pink, like a flesh wound barely healed.

"Ten and ten again," he said and raised back the arm that held the whip.

Jond unbuckled his manacles from his hands and rolled to the left. The movement allowed him to unhook his foot restraints. The chain around his stomach, although no longer locked into the cart, was wound too tightly for him to spend the time unwinding it. He had an inkwell to retrieve.

The Shariha watched Jond's movements, his eyes growing wider as the manacles came off one by one. Jond watched him inhale to shout for help, but before he could, Jond used the flat of his palm—a Dambe fighting technique—to thrust the Shariha's head back, breaking his nose.

With his capturer down, Jond leveled a kick to the man's head and then his neck, designed to put the man to sleep. But the guard wouldn't oblige him. So Jond reached for his inkwell. The Shariha clearly thought it was mere jewelry, as on the other arm he wore Jond's stylus on his wrist, held in place with a metal cuff like it was decoration.

The Shariha started screaming, and Jond knew he didn't have much time left. He broke a few of the man's fingers as he pulled off the inkwell. Getting his stylus was equally difficult, and Jond had to resort to stomping on the Shariha's head to get him to stop moving. Jond ignored the sickening crunch under his feet.

With his inkwell and stylus rightfully reclaimed, Jond stood in time to see twenty Shariha cantering toward him on their steeds.

"Get her on the camel," Jond barked at Niha and pointed to the supervisor's lounging beast.

Jond riffled through his mind until he found the bloodwerk runes he was looking for. Using his discarded manacles, Jond drew a combination of runes that would trigger once he threw them. They weren't much, but they would be enough to distract the Shariha and buy them some time.

The prisoners behind Jond mewled and cowered in fear as they watched him work.

"Deathcraft," someone whispered.

Jond paid them no heed. The Shariha were approaching. The first manacle Jond threw triggered before it hit the ground, the force of the rune *Ru* knocking the riders closest to him to the ground.

Jond aimed better the second time and the bloodwerk runes burst open the ground, spraying acid soil across the rest of the cavalry. Taking advantage of the distraction, Jond turned away and joined Niha and Sylah on the back of the camel.

"Go, go," Jond said to Niha, who had the reins. "Go toward the front of the train."

"Why?"

"The joba seed powder, it's in our packs, I need it for Sylah."

"No, we can't, it's too risky."

"She'll die."

"She'll definitely die if we're caught."

Niha kept riding away from the Shariha's vehicle.

"Turn around," Jond commanded, but the old man wasn't listening. Jond looked behind him and saw that some of the Shariha had laid chase.

The camel screeched beneath them. The saddle lodged against Jond's groin uncomfortably, but however he felt, he knew Sylah felt worse. He held her sleeping form against him and finally conceded.

"Take us to the Academy."

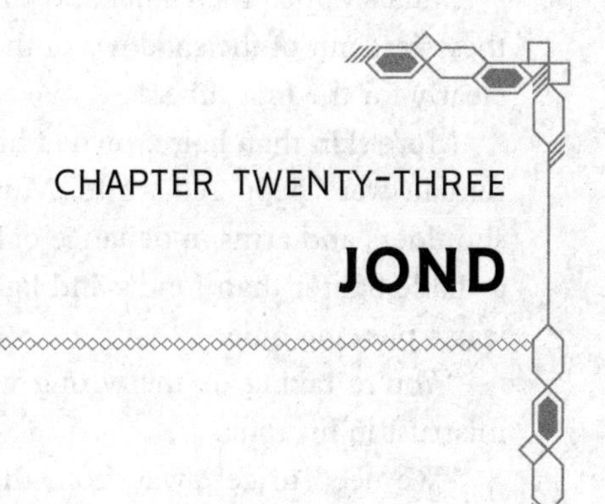

CHAPTER TWENTY-THREE

JOND

I have requested an additional harvest from the Shariha. They are moving on from Souriland to Tenio. Hopefully we can continue our testing. Ensure our copper yield is increased in order to make the trades.

—Message to Andu, Yellow Commune leader, from the Wife of Kabut

The Shariha gave up the chase when the sun began to rise. Three escaped prisoners were not worth expending their resources. Especially when one was close to dying.

No, I cannot think like that. I will not give up on her. I will not. Jond clutched Sylah closer to his chest. She jolted with the movement of the animal beneath them.

Niha had been riding the camel hard. Its breathing was as labored as Sylah's.

"We need to slow down, I need to get Sylah off this camel," Jond shouted at Niha's back.

Niha didn't stop his pace. It was then that Jond noticed the direction of the sunrise. They were going northeast, not southeast, which was where Jond knew the Academy to be.

"Stop." Jond pulled violently on Niha's tattered shirt. It broke in his grip, but it had the desired effect.

Niha stopped the camel and turned to look at Jond. Now that they were out of the shadows of the carts, Jond could see the man clearly for the first time.

More skin than hair crowned his head and the strands that did remain were peppered white. Muscles corded around his broad shoulders and arms in defiance of his aging features. His skin was a shade lighter than Jond's and lightly freckled. His one good eye was a piercing blue.

"You're taking us the wrong way," Jond said, laying bare his mistrust in his tone.

"We need to get away from the coast. Away from the risk of acid rain. And the Oarigha Plains are the quickest and safest route to stretch the distance between us and the Shariha."

Jond jumped down from the camel, his arms holding Sylah steady, as she slipped to the side. He lowered her to the ground.

"She needs rest and water. The camel is chafing her wounds."

Niha's jaw clenched.

"We need to continue northeast until we reach the Souk. The Shariha won't come for us there."

He was still on the camel, and Jond wondered if he was considering riding on without them. His arms quivered on the reins from adrenaline. He looked at them and exhaled.

"Salamander's shit, that was a close one." Niha jumped down from the camel with the ease of a man half his age.

"We didn't get the joba seed powder," Jond whispered, more to Sylah than to Niha.

Niha walked over to Jond and rested a hand on his shoulder.

"You don't know if it would have still been in your packs anyway."

"Will she be all right?"

Niha's hand dropped away.

"I don't know. We are forcing her mind through an extreme detox while her body is already failing her. If she makes it through it is likely she won't have the dependency she once had."

If.

"I don't suppose you have joba trees here?"

Niha shook his head sadly.

Sylah, you have to make it through this. Please.

Jond tore his gaze away from Sylah and looked around them. The ground had gone from black to pale yellow. The dirt under their feet was littered with rocks and cracked earth. There was not a speck of civilization in the distance.

"This is the Oarigha Plains? Any water you know of nearby?"

Niha laughed. "No, that's why we need to keep going. The Souk is the safest place to be."

Jond laid Sylah on the ground, and Niha knelt over her to inspect her wounds. Jond clutched his elbows and refused to give in to the despair that threatened to overwhelm him.

"What is the Souk?" Jond said.

"An area to the northeast. Where we can get resources safely." Niha interrupted himself by tutting at one of Sylah's wounds. Then he continued, "Before Tenio was a queendom, the eight tribes were often at war. The Souk was the one place of peace where people could trade. To dishonor the tranquillity was, and still is, the greatest offense. The Shariha won't go there."

"How far is it? And how much will it delay us?"

"Half a day's ride. But the provisions we can gather will save us having to forage later. The journey from the Souk to the Academy will be two weeks."

"Will she make it?"

"With extra provisions, yes." Niha didn't sound confident.

Jond inhaled, his mouth drier than the Farsai Desert. He desperately needed water.

"Okay, let's go."

"BY ANYME, THIS is incredible . . ." Jond breathed.

The Souk sprawled out for as far as he could see. Stalls selling spices and cloth piled higher than an Ember villa lined narrow streets filled with bustling people. Shouts of bartering rang in the air, and music drifted on the wind. Jond let Niha lead the camel through the throngs of people.

"Anyme?"

Jond gave a sheepish laugh. "Ah, our God."

"Indeed? You have a God in your lands? How . . . archaic."

Jond didn't ask what *archaic* meant. He could tell from Niha's tone.

Niha continued, "Each of the eight tribes had Gods once. But their religions were lost, diluted"—Niha coughed—"or disproven."

"How can you disprove something you can't see?"

"How can you prove it?"

Jond considered Niha's words. He had always been devout to the God Anyme. Azim had raised the Stolen to fear Anyme, and Jond was nothing but obedient, both to Azim and to God.

"Either way, I choose to believe," Jond said. "What's that?"

The stall to their left was roasting a dark fruit, and the sweet smell filled Jond's mouth with saliva.

"Dates," Niha said without looking, as he kept his head lowered, his one eye moving skittishly. His thumb absently rubbed the circular scar in the center of his palm.

It was then that Jond realized. They had no money, nothing to trade for provisions.

"How are we going to buy anything?" he hissed, mistrust filling his tone once more.

"There's someone here who owes me a favor. Come on . . . this way."

Jond was tense as they moved through the Souk. He kept checking on Sylah, but few people looked at her slumped form on the camel.

Music tinkled on the scented breeze, from an instrument Jond couldn't name. Everyone wore diaphanous fabrics in swirling colors, in shades he hadn't seen before.

Niha led them down a side street, where the laughter faded and the colors dulled. Jond flexed his muscles and moved to the balls of his feet. He knew the signs of danger. "Tranquillity" be damned, this alley was trouble.

"Niha . . . where are you leading us?"

"Shh," Niha said. He stopped them in front of a boarded-up stall. "Do not speak. Stay here with the camel. I will be right back."

Niha slipped behind one of the boards.

"I do not like this, Sylah," Jond grumbled to her. The camel huffed in response. "Not much choice, though; I have no idea how to get to the Academy from here . . ."

Half a strike passed, then another.

"Monkey's bollocks, I can't wait any longer." Jond tied the camel up behind the remains of a vacant stall. "Look after her, camel."

Jond didn't want to leave Sylah for a second, but time was running out, and Niha had been gone too long. He followed where the man had gone.

The corridor smelled stale and pungent, an aroma that was also somehow familiar. Jond didn't recognize it until he followed the cacophony of voices. The corridor opened out to a wide space, full of the sound of glasses clinking and people cheering.

Alcohol, the smell was alcohol. If he closed his eyes, Jond could have been back in the Maroon.

"A fucking tavern . . ." He saw Niha among a group of scantily clad people with a glass of liquid in front of him. They all had the same look in their eyes, a look born of mischief and chaos. They reminded Jond of Master Inansi: everyone carrying themselves with the same righteous power.

The tiled floor was sticky, and Jond's sandals stuck to it as he marched toward them. Patrons at rickety tables paused in their drinking and watched him as he walked past. The bar itself was circular, with the staff standing vigil within it as they served a cloudy yellow liquid from wooden casks. The barkeep nearest Jond narrowed her eyes at him. Jond didn't notice as he rounded on his target.

"Niha," he barked.

Niha looked up, and for a moment pure fear painted his features. It was smoothed over moments later. "Jond. Come and join me. I'll get you a pint of ale." He held open his arms with an arrogant swagger, at odds with the person Jond had come to know.

"What is going on, Niha? We need to go, you said the route was two weeks, she's not going to make it to the Ac—"

"Sit down, sit down, my young friend," Niha interrupted him, a bite to his tone. The people around him quieted, watching the exchange warily.

"Who is this you've brought us, hunter?" a woman with orange eyes said, her voice like butter.

"A companion," Niha said. "Jond, sit." Niha's eye bulged a little as he spoke. Jond wasn't sure who was the real Niha, the one from this morning, or the one sitting in front of him.

Jond sat, playing along.

"Here, have some ale."

"Ale?" Jond asked, accepting the frothy piss-colored liquid.

"Just drink," Niha hissed under his breath. He turned back to his companions. "As I was saying, I will provide you with half my findings, if you just front my resources."

Skies above, what has Niha got himself into? Jond wasn't foolish enough to voice the question.

"No," the woman said.

Jond watched her over the rim of his glass as he swallowed. He winced as the bitter ale filled his mouth.

"Argh, tastes like soap."

All eyes turned to him.

"Where did you find *him*, hunter?" Her orange eyes glittered as if she was weighing up Jond's worth.

"Ignore him," Niha growled. "You cannot expect me to hunt for you, without resources to carry out the task. You must pay for my supplies."

The woman winked at Jond. He bared his teeth at her.

She turned to Niha and said, "I recently made a good investment and I no longer need to partner with another hunter to trade with the Shariha."

"The Shariha?" Jond spat at Niha. "You traded with the Shariha?"

"The queen's word. Be quiet, you fool." Niha didn't bother lowering his voice.

"I tell you what . . ." The orange-eyed woman interrupted their exchange. "I will give you all the resources you need, if you tell us a waxing fable."

"What's a waxing fable?" Jond wasn't going to be quiet anymore.

"A waxing fable is a tale that you add to every time you hear it. No retelling is the same. There are hundreds, thousands of waxing fables circulating across the queendom, all starting from the same seed, but blossoming into different flowers," the woman purred.

"But what is the truth?" Jond asked her, ignoring Niha's kicks under the table.

She frowned. "Truth? There is truth in every story."

"Not if everyone's changing it each time."

"*Especially* if everyone's changing it each time. Because what is truth but collective belief?"

It made sense in a strange way.

Niha cleared his throat. "What fable do you want?"

"Tell me the waxing fable of our queen," she said.

"And I have your word? You will provide us with resources?"

"You have my word as a hunter: deals we stitch, until we grow rich."

Others around the room echoed the saying while drumming their tankards on the wooden tables.

Niha nodded once before speaking, "O what there was, in the time when Queen Karanomo was born. O what there wasn't, in the time prior."

The tavern quietened as people heard the sing-song sound of a story. They moved their chairs and leaned in.

Jond shivered, the spider legs of a memory crawling up his skin. Here he was in a tavern on the other side of the world, and if he closed his eyes, he could be back in the empire listening to a griot.

All rivers lead you to your own reflection, he thought, then scowled as he realized Niha's proverbs were rubbing off on him.

Niha spoke. "A long line of ancestors built the steps so our queen could rise. The first of her dynasty unified the eight tribes of the continent. The second of her dynasty built the Shard Palace so they could reign. The third of her dynasty implemented a financial system. The fourth of her dynasty—"

"How many fucking queens are you going to go through?" Jond muttered and Niha shot him a dark look.

"The fourth of her dynasty founded the Zwina Academy. And so it went, for forty generations."

Jond gritted his teeth. He'd never had any patience for griot stories, and he had even less patience for Niha's waxing fable. Sylah was dying.

"I will speak of her mother first," Niha said. "Before Queen Karanomo was queen she was a princess. The daughter of Queen Togla, a monarch known for vibrant parties and overspending the treasury's riches. When Karanomo was thirteen, Queen Togla fell from the balcony of the Shard Palace onto the plain of slate below. To this day no one knows if she threw herself or fell.

"Oh, oh, oh. Our Karanomo was grief-stricken. She sent for the healers at the Academy, but Queen Togla had no flighters in her employ to carry the message to the councillors. And by the time they sent a healer it was too late. Karanomo was princess no longer, she was queen."

Niha's eyes glossed over with devotion as he continued. Those around him were enraptured with the same loyalty.

"At sixteen it is rumored she trained covertly for a time at the Zwina Academy, learning the fighting skills that could have saved her mother. At twenty she spent a season on the coast with her Sea Lords, learning to govern the navy. At thirty she worked the fields on the soil governed by her Earth Lords. She is a woman with talents aplenty. Her beauty is unmatched, though unwed she continues to be. Twenty-two years she's reigned, granting Tenio prosperity."

Niha stood, his voice booming outward. He pulled Jond to his feet, encouraging others to do the same.

Niha said they had no God, yet they sermonize their leader with the same gusto as an Abosom priest preaching about Anyme.

"But o what there wasn't before Queen Karanomo reigned. O what there is now she sits on the throne." Niha raised his glass high among the cheers.

His one eye locked with Jond's. "Never trust a hunter's word."

It was all the warning Jond was given before Niha smashed the glass of ale into the face of the orange-eyed woman. Jond stood open-mouthed as the scene erupted as if in slow motion around him.

Gurgled screams. Purple blood gushing. Her nose shorn in half. Ale dripping from the curls around her ears.

There was a beat of confusion until the room burst into anarchy. Other hunters at nearby tables withdrew weapons as they saw one of their own laid low. Some drinkers took advantage of the disarray to settle other scores, lunging across tables to wreak their own violence.

"What the fu—" Jond started.

"Run!" Niha shouted. The one word triggering the movement of the other hunters.

Jond dodged as a dagger flew through the air toward him. Niha was one step ahead, carving a path by shouldering his way through. The barkeep that had eyed Jond before lunged at him now with a metal baton, her lips held in a growl. He skidded across a puddle of upturned ale, and out of the way of her swing.

Jond's frustration with Niha tapered off as adrenaline pumped through his veins. He laughed, savoring the feeling as he leveled a kick in the groin of his nearest attacker.

Niha had made it to the door. Jond was a step behind, a manic smile across his face, tinged with blood where someone had managed to nick his lip with a blade.

"Where's the camel?" Niha asked.

"There."

Niha took the reins, Jond jumping behind Sylah.

And then they were off. Cantering through the Souk, leaving upturned stalls and chaos in their wake.

THE JOY OF the fight drained from Jond as quickly as it had come, leaving him cold and annoyed.

"What was that about?" Jond rounded on Niha once they were far enough away from the Souk to stop.

Niha winced. "That didn't go to plan . . ."

If Jond hadn't been so spent from the brawl, he would have punched Niha. The old man saw it in his eyes.

"Look, I didn't mean for that to happen. I was trying to make a deal with a hunter—"

"With people who traded with the Shariha?" He pointed to Sylah, the product of the Shariha's cruelty. "And you knew them, like they were *colleagues* . . ."

"I admit, I used to trade with the Shariha too." Niha shrugged without shame. "I have never been a man of means. When the acid rains began to fall on the west coast, I turned my skill to salvaging. At first it was easy: Wear rubber clothing. Sneak in and out under the cover of the storm. Steal what I could, then escape.

"It was easier once the cities were abandoned, but others soon followed suit and so I targeted the most acid-damaged cities for I knew few dared to enter them. I traded with anyone who would buy my goods. I grew a reputation among the other hunters, and they sought me out to request certain materials or items from cities they knew had fallen. I was fulfilling a contract when the Shariha caught me and enslaved me. My reputation didn't help me there. I was chattel, worth more to them as a product than a scavenger."

Niha sighed.

"The woman, Feri, with the orange eyes. I suspected she was the one to sell me out to the Shariha. I saw one of her agents slip away as we were discussing. She asked for me to tell that waxing fable to give her agent time to return with backup."

"But I thought there was no crime in the Souk?" Jond dabbed at his split lip. Now that the adrenaline had faded the pain had come.

Niha laughed. "Indeed. Everyone in that tavern with an injury would have testified that they'd done it to themselves. There are always loopholes for those looking for trouble. The hunters would have escorted us out of the Souk and then resold us to the Shariha in days. I'm sure the Shariha have put a bounty on our heads. Camels aren't cheap."

Jond kicked a rock across the dry ground in frustration. They were back on the Oarigha Plains.

"And now we have nothing. Less than nothing, because we wasted half a day."

Then Jond noticed the soil underneath the rock was darker. He bent down and pressed his fingers deep within the dirt. It was moist, and not at all acidic. An idea came to him.

Jond crossed his legs and inserted his stylus into his inkwell. The rock's surface wasn't smooth, and he struggled to be precise with his blood strokes. He was light-headed from a lack of sustenance, and the excess blood loss wasn't helping.

"What are you doing?" Niha asked, marching over. The man seemed to be made of stronger stuff than Jond, and he idly wondered if Niha had grown accustomed to the acidic air.

"Trying to get water . . . ah." Jond had pushed the rock into the moist soil and *pulled* what he could out of the ground. As runes could only be used on non-living things, fragments of dirt and water were sucked toward the rock. Jond reached for the mud now covering the rock and sucked on it. Dirt and his blood and water. Sweet water.

"Those runes, they look like deathcraft," Niha growled, reaching for Jond's stylus. "You are not licensed to practice deathcraft."

"What are you talking about, get off that."

"That's illegal."

"Says who? I don't see anyone around who is about to arrest me, so if you want some water, get out of the way."

Niha was shaking with fear. More fear than he had shown in front of the Shariha or the hunters.

"You can get water?" he whispered, as if it were a secret. He smacked his lips together, and dry as they were, Jond saw blood seep from the cracks. It was blue. Niha was a Duster.

"Yes, I can get water."

Niha stepped away from him then, as if being too close to the illegal deed would implicate him.

It took some time for Jond to fashion the well. It required a combination of runes and a filtering system to remove the larger particles of dirt. By the end the water that pooled on the surface was brown but drinkable. He drank his fill before calling Niha over.

Once their stomachs were bloated with water, together they cleaned and fed Sylah. Her breathing was surer, though she didn't wake. Jond was quietly hopeful.

"Where did you learn those runes? I have never seen the implements you use before," Niha asked. His fear had abated to a fervent curiosity.

"I was taught by her." Jond jutted his chin at Sylah. She had curled her knees up to her chin in her sleep, the wounds on her skin there cracking, feeding the soil red.

"Where?"

"To the west." Jond remembered what the Elder Ghosting's diary had said about the empire. "You people call it the Drylands."

Niha sat up. "The Drylands? No one has traveled from there in years . . . not since the Tannin."

"What do you know of the Tannin?" Watching the Embers screaming in the face of their death should have delighted Jond, but their sacrifice sickened him instead. Sylah was changing him more than he cared to admit. He blinked away the memory.

"It is a creature of death. It haunts the Marion Sea. No one has crossed it for over four hundred years . . ." Niha said.

"Four hundred and twenty-one years, precisely."

Niha raised an eyebrow.

Jond continued, "That was when the wardens founded the country. They came from the mainland . . . red bloods and blue bloods. They—they *stole* the land from the clear bloods."

Niha hissed. "I heard rumors from the Earth Lord of Truna that the land had been colonized, but no one could prove it. No one could cross the sea . . ."

Sylah spasmed, and the two of them sprang to her side. The tremors turned into a hacking cough, and Jond cradled her head until it subsided. She remained unconscious throughout.

"Give her more water," Niha said, averting his gaze from the bloodwerk well.

Jond began the process of extraction again. "You told me never to trust the word of a hunter. Yet you promised you would lead me to the Academy. You are a hunter, are you not? That's what they called you? Why should I trust you?"

Niha's gaze turned thoughtful.

"You know, I was relieved when I was finally caught. I was tired of the contracts, the risks, the loneliness. I didn't know what the Zalaam did to their prisoners once they traded them for copper, but at least I had a purpose. Even if that purpose resulted in death."

Niha took in a ragged breath and swallowed. "You and your girl, Sylah. You reminded me of something I fought hard for once. Something I lost everything for but would still do again. I have long lived in shame for my expulsion, but I won't die with that shame. I refuse to."

"Expulsion?"

Niha rubbed a thumb over the smooth circular scar in the center of his palm as he spoke.

"You may not trust the word of a hunter. But trust the word of a scholar. I used to train at the Academy."

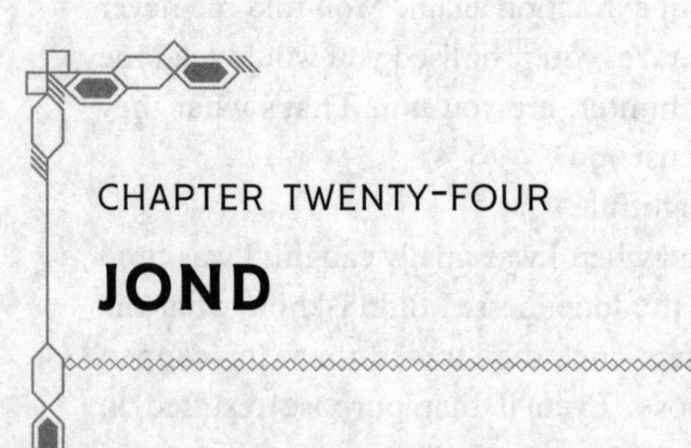

CHAPTER TWENTY-FOUR

JOND

The construction of the Blooming Towers took over fifty years. It became the sole work of Councillor Ubba of the first charter. There are three towers altogether, one sprouting, one blooming, and one just emerging from its bud. The tallest stands at 1,567 feet above the ground.

—*The Life Blood of Councillor Ubba* by Hula Oh-Jobo

They walked through the night trying to regain the time they had lost. Niha had found some edible shrubs that they ate while they walked. The roots he'd distilled to make a mild sedative to keep Sylah asleep and "let her body heal."

Jond had been pressing Niha for more information.

"You were expelled from the Academy?"

"Yes."

"And you didn't tell me this . . . because?"

"Because, boy, I didn't think it was any of your business." His voice grew gruff.

Jond shrugged.

They didn't speak for some time, the only sound the clopping of the camel's hooves. They had fed and watered the beast twice since setting off.

It's eating better than me, Jond thought.

He tipped his face to the night sky and sighed through his teeth. The moon pushed its light through a broken cloud in the silence.

Finally, Niha conceded with more of his tale. "Twenty years ago, my love lay dying from a cancer on the coast of Tenio—a city in the north, where I was raised. Though we had not seen each other for many years, we still exchanged letters and tokens of affection. When I graduated it was my intention to wed him. A delay I regret on long days like this one." He coughed and looked to the ground. "I requested the use of a flighter to go and administer aid to him."

"A flighter?"

"A flighter is a graduate of the fourth charter who has completed their orb."

"Fourth charter? Orb?"

Niha smiled at Jond's naivety, then stilled as some painful memory crossed his mind. He let out a breath and held out his palm. It was shaking slightly.

"You see this scar? It is where my orb used to be. The ball was engraved with hundreds of small runes. The orb itself was held in place by a metal cuff, allowing me to roll the ball in my blood and transfer runes onto objects."

He clenched his hand into a fist and brought it to his side.

Jond instinctively reached for his stylus around his neck.

"You have runes here?"

Niha's lips curled into a grimace as he eyed up Jond's inkwell.

"Of course, though their use is illegal for those not granted permission by the Academy. It is strictly . . . policed." The swallow that followed this statement made Jond wonder if the name "deathcraft" was in part influenced by the sentence for the crime.

"How does an . . . orb . . . transfer runes?"

"Do you have printing presses in your country?"

Jond nodded.

"Okay, so you know how they have stamps that they paint over with ink? Then press onto paper?"

"Yes."

"Well, the concept is the same. The runes are engraved on the orb, and the wound in our palm creates the ink—our blood."

"But how do you know what combination you need? You said there were multiple runes on the orb?"

"Precision." Niha grinned. "The Zwina Academy is grueling. Only ten people of each charter are accepted as students. Of those, less than half make it through their first year. You are only taught one rune in your first year and it has to be perfect. One orb is given to each student and if they don't craft it correctly, their orb is destroyed, and they are sent unhappily on their way."

"One rune in your first year?"

"Yes, on average, though there are those people who excelled and completed their orbs quicker than the standard twenty years."

"Twenty years? That couldn't be all you learned."

Jond had learned to bloodwerk in less than twenty *weeks*.

Niha smiled, and it was full of the pure joy that only a happy recollection can bring. "I learned the art of healing, with and without deathcraft." He stopped, took a breath, then returned to the story. "I tried to visit my love . . . to say goodbye. But my request for a flighter was denied. I was . . . adamant I needed to see him." He let out a shaky sigh. "So I decided to steal a complete fourth charter orb."

"Why would a fourth charter orb help?"

Niha's eyes glinted with the anticipation of a reveal. "Each charter specializes in a different form of deathcraft. Graduates of the fourth charter become flighters. They carry urgent messages or transport people when needed. They can travel instantaneously."

"What?" Jond stumbled as all the blood rushed to his brain to unpick what Niha had said.

"They transition across distances in the blink of an eye."

Jond's mind reeled at the implications.

"Then why are we *walking*?"

Niha chuckled. "No, no. Didn't you hear what I said? Most

people have to train for twenty years for a completed orb. There were few flighters back then, fewer now."

"What are the other charters?" His neck felt hot as something akin to panic rushed through him. It was a panic of the unknown.

"The first charter is the law of growth. The power to grow what is given.

"The second charter is the law of connection. The command of mind communication.

"The third charter is the law of healing, putting back together what was once broken.

"The fourth charter is the law of presence. Flighting from one place to another."

Jond was silent. He couldn't speak. Shock held him frozen. Elder Petra's diary had referred to charters, but Jond hadn't known what they entailed.

"Anyway," Niha continued after shattering Jond's mind.

"Wait, you said four charters? Not five?" Jond thought the diary had said five charters.

Niha's eyebrow twitched, almost imperceptibly.

"Only four."

Maybe Jond had got it wrong. Niha continued.

"I tried to steal an orb." Niha's voice turned bitter. "Suffice to say I failed. My career as a healer of the third charter was over. I was exiled from the Academy. They destroyed the orb I had lovingly created for twenty years. The wound I had cleaned every night and pierced every morning healed over. All because I wanted to see my dying lover for the last time. I never saw him again. I was told that they burned him at sea—which he would have hated. So, I became a wanderer, I took jobs from anyone who would take me."

"You willingly come back to the Academy now?"

Niha smiled a smile of sad memories. "I have nowhere to go."

"WE'RE NOT FAR, three or four days through the Mistforest," Niha said.

Jond was trying to pour water into Sylah's cracked lips. She was asleep, like she had been for the last ten days.

"Did you hear that, Sylah?" Jond whispered into what used to be an ear. "We're not far now."

There was a small mewl from her, and Jond's heart leaped.

"Sylah?"

Nothing.

The whole journey had been like this. She would make a sound or whisper his name, sometimes *her* name, the Disciple. Each time it gave Jond hope, until he saw the look in Niha's eyes. It seemed to Jond that he saw what Jond didn't, or perhaps couldn't admit to. He saw that she was dying. Slowly, but surely.

"Can we get there quicker?" Jond asked, refusing to accept what Niha said with his gaze.

"The Mistforest is difficult to navigate, but if you want to walk through the night, we could arrive there in two days."

Jond nodded. "We walk through the night."

Plod gargled beside them as Jond began the process of strapping Sylah between his humps. Niha had named the camel on their second night. Jond had rolled his eyes at the concept of personifying a tool—because the camel *was* nothing but a tool, just like erus. Jond scowled as he recalled Boey, the eru that had led them to the Chrysalis, and how Sylah had sat with the creature every morning sharing stories about Anoor Elsari. As if the animal could talk. As if the beast was worthy of her love.

Unlike him.

Jond pushed the sour thought away as he finished tying Sylah in place on top of Plod and set off.

The landscape had changed over their journey. Niha said the acid rain was limited to the coast, and it was true that the farther inland they got, the sweeter the breeze became. A few days in and trees had begun to appear in clusters amid the dust of the Oarigha Plains.

The trees there were taller and wider than any in the empire. The bark was a rusty brown, the leaves dark green with large fronds. Eventually the clusters grew denser, the ground going from brown to green. Bushes and flowers sprouted in meadows and on the horizon was an impenetrable mass of foliage that could only be the Mistforest Niha had talked about.

They came across an abandoned farmhouse on their fourth day. Neither of them acknowledged that the inhabitants had probably gone to their death, captured by the Shariha. Though they didn't find any food, Niha found a small pot of dried-up balm, which he claimed would help with the infection in Sylah's wounds. Jond had used the balm on Sylah's biggest gashes, the ones that wouldn't heal and oozed with yellow pus.

The balm had long been used up. And it seemed Sylah was worse than ever. She sagged forward in the saddle, her face gaunt, her bones light.

Jond slapped Plod's rump to speed the camel up. He trotted alongside the creature, as carrying Sylah was the most economical way to use the beast's strength.

Niha led them to a parting in the dense foliage.

"Into the Mistforest we go."

JOND DIDN'T NEED to make a well again. Instead, the rains came.

At first it was a welcome change, a weak spitting drizzle that was more wind than water. It sated their dry throats.

Jond would tip his head to the canopy every morning and drink to break his fast, the sweet rainwater running past his cracked lips. Sylah's wounds began to improve, the water moistening and cleaning out the infection. But by the second day, the rains had not stopped.

The Mistforest was filled with the incessant percussion of water hitting waxy leaves. The plants in the middle of the forest were different from the ones on the edge of the Oarigha Plains. The trees here were skinny, lacking the girth of the joba trees Jond was used to. But they made up for it in height, reaching up into the sky. Their branches, laden with leaves the size of his face, weaved together to blot out the sun. Small shrubs that Niha called "ferns" sprouted between their knobbly roots in lighter shades of green and red. Every now and then they'd come across a cluster of yellow berries growing from a thorny vine that they'd harvest and eat. The berries were sour but sated some of their appetite as they walked.

One morning Jond found a bush of them near where he'd relieved himself. He collected them, popping two in his mouth before returning to the main path where Niha was waiting.

"Tell me you didn't just eat those."

"I did," Jond said uncertainly. The pride he'd felt at foraging by himself was ebbing away in the face of Niha's horrified expression.

"Make yourself throw up, now."

Jond did so. Apparently, the berries he'd found were not the same *shade of yellow* as the ones they'd been eating.

"Yellow is yellow," Jond said between bouts of retching.

"No it is not. If you'd have noticed, these berries have a slight green tinge to them. They will give you diarrhea for a week."

Jond's stomach had lurched at the thought, but thankfully the symptoms never manifested. From that moment on Jond took more care, and Niha spent every moment teaching him the names of plants and their purpose.

"That bush there is the hudir. Its flowers are a dark blue and are very nice in salads. Though be careful, snakebirds feed on the sap and their sting is poisonous. Kill you quick."

Jond faltered, and Plod bumped into him with a grumble.

"What?"

"You don't have snakebirds? They're about the size of my forearm, look like snakes with butterfly wings. They're an insect."

"A *snakebird*, that's an *insect*." Jond shook his head in bafflement, raindrops flicking outward.

"You wouldn't believe such a small thing can take down a man such as I. Well, as they say, a pebble can support a barrel or crack an iceberg."

Later that evening Niha made a fire "to keep away things even worse than snakebirds." He had dug up some sweet potato roots which he roasted directly on the flame. The fire crackled as droplets of rain landed on the burning wood. Even the kindling here smelled different, fresher, a bit tangy.

When the sweet potatoes turned black, he handed one on a stick to Jond.

"Peel away the charred flesh and eat the insides. It's good. Better with a bit of lamb, but good nonetheless."

"Thank you."

Jond let out a sigh of pleasure as he swallowed his first mouthful. Then he shot a guilty look at Sylah's prostrate form. Niha must have caught his expression as his next question was pointedly a distraction.

"Tell me, what's the most dangerous animal in the Wardens' Empire?"

Jond responded straightaway. "Scorpions."

Niha raised a gray eyebrow in question.

"They're hard-shelled arachnids, like spiders, but with a pointy tail full of poison."

Niha's mouth went slack.

"The queen's word," he breathed. "Our spiders are harmless."

"But your snakebirds aren't," Jond snorted.

Niha's eyes widened and he went tense.

"Wh—"

Niha pressed a hand to his mouth to indicate silence.

Then Jond heard it. A snuffling, snorting sound coming from just outside their clearing.

"Move closer to the fire," Niha mouthed with a bit of breath to give his voice sound.

Jond edged forward, his muscles tense.

Sylah lay farther away from the light of the fire's glow. Jond retreated to reach for her.

"Leave her," Niha hissed.

But Jond wasn't leaving her, not again.

He began to drag her body closer to the flame. The sound was a beacon to the predator that circled them.

Plod started to shuffle his feet, a low whine emanating from his long neck.

Jond wrapped his arms around Sylah, cradling her closer to the fire.

"The queen of fools you are," Niha growled; he had dropped the whisper. The beast had found them.

Jond followed the direction of Niha's wide eye. He expected something small, something like the snakebird but with bite. No, this creature was not small at all.

It was twelve handspans tall while crouching. Four legs with paws the size of both Jond's hands together ended with claws the length of his fingers. Its wolf-like jaw hung open, drooling sticky saliva. Two white horns grew like blades from its forehead, made for charging.

No, this creature was not small at all.

Its fur was a dark brown, perfect for camouflage against the bark of the Mistforest. And its eyes were a mossy green, which narrowed as they spotted Jond. It stood on its hindquarters and grew even taller.

"Anyme give me strength to survive this."

"Plod," Niha whistled to the camel. "Plod. Come here."

The camel reared its head at Niha's beckoning and shuffled a few steps toward the fire. Unfortunately, the movement caught the predator's attention.

"Get ready to carry Sylah," Niha said and then continued to coax Plod toward them.

"What are you doing—"

The beast jumped through the air as if on springs and landed on the back of Plod's hump. The camel shrieked and fell onto his knees. Plod was done plodding.

"Quick, grab her."

Jond didn't need further encouragement. He lifted Sylah and ran in the direction where Niha was heading. They ran for as long as their legs would carry them, exchanging Sylah halfway.

The sound of Plod's keening filled his mind long after they had left the camp.

After a strike or two the foliage began to clear.

The forest thinned out and they found themselves panting and dizzy on the corner of a green field with villages dotted across the horizon where the sun was rising. It reminded Jond of Jin-Gernomi and the green meadows that had been irrigated there, except for the constant rain. He felt a pang of longing for the home he'd left behind.

"What the fuck was that?"

Niha lowered Sylah to the ground and fell to his knees. Neither of them were in the best of health after weeks of malnutrition.

"A . . . mist . . . bear," he panted.

"A mistbear? Why didn't you warn me of them earlier?"

"So . . . rare . . ."

Niha lay on his back, his face tilted up to the rain, which had grown worse now they were free of the canopy.

After they had regained their breath, Niha made to stand.

"We need to keep going, need to find Sylah shelter. Her wounds need drying out or she won't make it."

When they reached the first homestead in the distance, they realized that the rain that had been their savior was becoming their enemy just as quickly. The village was flooded and abandoned.

"She still needs shelter," Niha pressed.

Jond looked at the drenched Sylah in his arms. The pus in her wounds had returned with ferocity in the last day.

They camped on the top floor of a barn that night. Though Jond was exhausted he barely slept, as every so often he would look out of the glass window to watch the water level below them rise.

Thankfully they didn't drown in the night. In the morning the rains broke, and a watery sunlight leaked through the white clouds above.

"We'll be there in half a day," Niha said quietly, his eyes slipping to Sylah and away again.

"If this is the main trade route into the Academy, why aren't there any other travelers or merchants?" Jond asked.

Niha looked back and forth up the unending cobblestone road. It was wide enough for two erus, maybe three. Jond wondered if they even had erus here.

"It's been a long time since I came to the Academy. They might have another more well-traveled path." He didn't sound certain.

Jond shivered in his damp shirt. He only hoped Sylah's wounds had dried better than his clothes.

A strike in, the rain started again. Rain was too light a word. Jond had been in bloodwerk shower units that had produced less water. It poured down, soaking them in seconds. A strike later the cobbled road became sodden, the gutters to the side filling with debris and rainwater. There was no thunder or lightning, just the steady stream of water pattering down on the ground. First Jond's feet disappeared, and then the rain reached his calves. Eventually it rose to his waist and he felt himself being tugged beneath the water.

"We're nearly there, I can see the gateway. It's up ahead," Niha shouted in Jond's ear.

Jond lifted his head and looked through the sheets of water falling from the sky. He could see stonework in the distance, the archway disappearing as the water rose. The words "Zwina Academy" were preserved in marble.

"We'll have to swim," Jond shouted.

Niha splashed ahead, the water reaching to his navel. Together the two of them shared Sylah's weight and waded through the water. Something brushed his leg and Jond looked down to see the tail of a water snake happily making its way downstream. The road had once been tree-lined, but Jond could no longer see the plants that grew there.

The water was up to his shoulder now. Sylah's weight lessened as the water rose and it helped carry her load. It panicked Jond not to feel her presence in the strain of his muscles, like she was slipping away, her soul finally retreating.

He had to resort to swimming, the crack below the archway of the Academy growing ever smaller. Niha swam confidently up ahead as Jond held Sylah's head above water. Niha's head disappeared underneath the archway, and for a moment Jond thought he'd drowned. Two minutes passed, and Jond lugged their bodies toward the words "Zwina Academy," the "y" slowly disappearing beneath the flood.

Niha burst through the water ten handspans ahead. A blur of a man against the backdrop of so much water.

"Quickly," Niha yelled. "There's a doorway on the other side."

Jond reached him and together they pulled Sylah under the

small gap beneath the marble archway. But the doorway Niha had seen was welded shut. Jond could see there was no getting in. Niha jutted his chin to the left as his head bobbed above the brown water. Jond looked in that direction and saw the stairs. They snaked up the left-hand side of the stone wall that protected the Academy. In a few jerking lunges they were there. Jond noticed how the metal on the doors was much more silvered and less worn than the railing on the stairs; they had clearly been a more recent addition.

The rainfall had begun to lessen but the steps were still slick. And small—only wide enough for one foot at a time. Jond took the entirety of Sylah's weight in his arms while Niha went up ahead. Though it took only a handful of steps to reach the top of the stone wall, Jond was breathing heavily.

Niha looked stricken.

"What is it?" Jond asked, laying Sylah on the stone wall.

"Look."

Jond stood, his heart swelling with hope, only for it to burst with disappointment a moment later. He took in the Zwina Academy.

What was left of the Academy, that is.

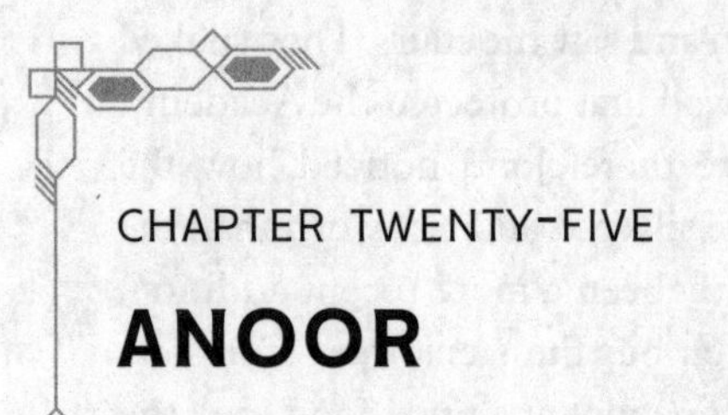

CHAPTER TWENTY-FIVE

ANOOR

Inquisitor Abena circled the weapons store. She needed a weapon that would kill someone quickly. Silently.

She spotted the bow and arrow. Such a death would be neither quick nor silent.

Maybe that would do . . .

—"A Crime, Committed" from *The Tales of Inquisitor Abena*, featured in *The People's Gazette*

Anoor rocked back and forth on her heels. The dressing room had no window, just a low hanging runelight that never turned off. She reached up and tapped the glass globe, her nail making a satisfying clink on the lamp as it began to swing backward and forward, lighting up the corners of the room with red flourishes. The friction caused by the runes blurred the light ever so slightly, the shadows quivering.

Two weeks she'd been investigating her mother's murder. She'd followed up on every single person who'd entered the Keep, but they all had alibis. It should have delighted her to discover all the sordid affairs that had been accruing under the Keep's roof, but her mind was too occupied to enjoy gossip. Two weeks and she still had nothing.

Anoor moved into Nuba formation three. The exercise based on strict movements tested a person's mental and physical capabilities. Anoor slipped into the state of battle wrath and let anger fuel her movements. She thrust her hands upward to the ceiling, her right leg flexing in a half-twist behind her.

She breathed in and out, trying to retain focus. *Anger is a tool, anger is a tool.* The problem was, she had so much of it. It filled her up, flecks of it flashing behind her eyelids as it boiled beneath her skin.

"Arrrgh." The scream tore through her, leaving her a quaking, crumpled heap. She let the sobs out.

"Sylah, I wish you were here," Anoor whimpered. But as she said the words she wondered if they were true. "No, I don't want you to see me fail so completely."

Sylah didn't fail, and if she did it was because she chose to. There was nothing her lover didn't do out of choice.

Lover.

The word was a gentle caress in her mind, like the unfurling of fingers in the softest part of her.

Anoor closed her eyes, her hands slipping beneath her trousers to feel the heat that had pooled there. The tears on her cheeks turned to sweat as she explored the warmth.

Sylah's form moved through her mind in rhythm with her movements. She imagined Sylah's hand curving over her breasts as she explored the contours of her body. Anoor's back arched at the memory of Sylah's deft fingers, and her mischievous glance as she lowered herself to taste Anoor.

Sylah always started slow, her tongue parting her gently, leaving Anoor crying for more. Then the tension would build, plying Anoor with pleasure with each suck and lick until she couldn't take the pressure anymore and she'd explode like the tidewind.

Her mind scattered into grains of sand as pleasure burst through her at the memory.

"Oh, Sylah," she whispered again. Though the name held more passion than helplessness now.

The aftershocks of bliss abated with her breathing.

There was a knock at her door, the space between each rapping precise. Anoor jumped to her feet, pressing a hand to her beating heart.

"Come in, Gorn," Anoor said, wiping the sweat from her face.

She walked over to her desk and crumpled in the seat in front of her useless notes, the momentary quest for pleasure already forgotten.

"I heard crying, are you okay?"

"I'm fine, Gorn," Anoor snapped.

Gorn inhaled sharply; Anoor never snapped at her.

"I'm sorry," Anoor continued. "My investigation has come to a dead end. I think I'll be spending the rest of my life in jail."

"No." Gorn's response was adamant, so adamant Anoor turned around. "You will not. We won't allow it. No one will allow it."

Anoor's heart swelled. "Thank you, Gorn. Sometimes I need to hear that."

"Take a break. It's late anyway."

"I can't sleep." Anoor waved a hand across the writings on her desk.

"Then go to the library, read a few zines, play shantra, anything. You need to get out, think of something else."

Anoor pushed the heels of her hands into her eyes.

"Yes, you're right. I think I will go to the library."

"Good, and while you're gone, I'm going to . . . clean up a bit in here."

Anoor looked around the room and was shocked to see the mess. She spotted at least four empty plates, a cluster of mugs—one tipped, spilling coffee on the floor—and a growing pile of dirty clothes.

"Oh, I didn't realize it had gotten this bad."

Gorn barked out a laugh. "Go, I will enjoy some respite from the work Yona has me doing. She's moving quickly through your tidewind bill."

Anoor was glad to hear it. Her grandmother had been as good as her word, fighting for the bill like she'd promised.

"Thank you, Gorn. I'll be back soon."

The Abosom was waiting outside her chambers as she left. The wardens no longer bothered to hide the fact they were monitoring Anoor's every move.

"Hello, nice evening for a stroll, isn't it?" Anoor said to the surly man.

He didn't respond, but she heard him follow her slowly through the Keep.

The clockmaster called tenth strike. The library would close soon, so Anoor picked up her pace, rushing through the business district with light steps. She was practically jogging when she bumped into Faro, Disciple of Duty. Faro tripped over their feet, falling headfirst to the ground.

"By the blood, I'm so sorry." She offered a hand to help them up. They smiled and waved her away.

"It is my fault for not looking where I was going," Faro said, their eyes crinkling with an apology.

Anoor had spoken so rarely to Faro that she'd forgotten the light cadence of their voice. Like the song of a kori bird, it set her at ease.

"Are you okay?" Anoor was assessing them for injury, and Faro laughed, a small hiccupping sound.

"I should be asking you that." They looked behind her, locating the Abosom. "I see you've got . . . company."

"Yes, just in case I kill any other wardens." She was aiming for sarcasm, but it came out sounding bitter. She realized her mistake. "No, no, that was a joke, I didn't actually—"

"I know what you meant, don't worry . . . but maybe save the jokes for when you don't have a spy in earshot."

Anoor smiled nervously. This was the longest conversation she'd ever had with Faro. Usually they had little to say to her. Their crooked nose was always lifted when they gazed at her as if Anoor's very presence brought on a mild feeling of disgust.

Today, their chin was downturned, their gaze open, if a little discerning.

"I was going to the library, before it closes," she said by way of explanation.

"The warden library? I'll come with you. There was a journal there I wanted to pick up."

Anoor didn't want to correct them. The zines she was after were located in the public library, a place few people ventured into, given its level of disrepair.

Faro dropped their voice. "Plus, the Abosom isn't allowed in the warden library."

"That's true." She returned Faro's sly smile.

Faro led the way, their thin curls frizzing around them as they walked. If they were friends Anoor would have recommended the oils she used in her hair. But they weren't—yet.

Anoor was thankful for the kindness they were showing. Her reputation wasn't as tarnished as she had thought. If Faro was being nice to her, then maybe Aveed, Warden of Duty, was sympathetic to her cause too.

"Allow me." Faro drew the access runes on the slate across the warden library door. She watched their red blood flow into the combination that would give them admission. Anoor hadn't been in there since she'd snuck in with Sylah. The smell of ink and paper threatened to lead her back to that memory, but she didn't want to think of Sylah right now. She was worried she'd start crying in front of Faro and lose all the credibility they were currently affording. The room was already lit with the red glow of runelamps as they walked in. It made the floor-to-ceiling shelves of red journals glow even more crimson. Blood lighting blood.

The door shut with a satisfying thud, blocking out the Abosom who was following her. She let out a sigh of relief, only to catch her breath again as shadows moved to her right. Anoor jumped, swinging her head toward the movement.

The faces of the three disciples looked back at her.

"Now we can talk," Tanu said.

"What are you guys doing here?" Anoor said.

Qwa, the Disciple of Truth, was leaning on the shelves, his wide chin tilted to the side.

"Waiting for you," he grunted. A strand of his straightened hair fell forward over his perfectly circular bald spot.

"Tanu?" Anoor asked her old friend to explain.

"I brought you allies," Tanu said. A wry smile hung across her lips.

"Allies is pushing it . . ." Qwa said, ending the sentence with a yawn.

Faro nodded, adding the question Anoor was waiting for. "But first, did you kill Warden Uka?"

Anoor summoned as much conviction as she could muster in response.

"No."

She fought the urge to squeeze her eyes shut as she chanted in her mind: *please believe me, please believe me.*

No one said a word.

She looked around the room at the future leaders of the empire, imploring them to believe her with her eyes. Tanu's smile hadn't faltered, her soft lips curling upward toward the shaved sides of her hair. Qwa's features were bland, almost bored. Faro was looking between them, their brow furrowed.

"I didn't. I would never. Yes, we argued, and yes, I wrote those things in my journal. But I said them in anger, without intent. I am not a murderer." Anoor jutted her chin outward.

"You are either a very good liar and a very bad murderer or an honest person and a very bad daughter," Qwa said, his stare penetrating hers.

Anoor flinched. "I'm the second, that's for sure."

"I believe her," Tanu said. "Now can we get to the point?" She waited for the other disciples to nod before continuing. "We want to help you. We have some information that might help your investigation."

Anoor was dumbfounded.

"Why?"

Tanu smiled. "Because you're one of us."

Faro cleared their throat. "Because if you are convicted then the balance would be off. The next Aktibar would have to result in the disciple becoming warden straight away, without any training."

Tanu mimicked the sound Faro had made with their throat. "Blah, blah, blah, blah. Always so *practical,* Faro."

"But you'll be going against your wardens' wishes . . ." Anoor still couldn't understand their motivation. The three disciples had gone out of their way to avoid Anoor for the last few mooncycles; why were they helping her now?

"Exactly, by Anyme. I hate Wern, the old crone is the worst." Tanu ran a hand through the cluster of black curls on the top of her head. "It'll be the four of us in the end. Leading the empire."

Anoor looked at the three people surrounding her, and she felt her eyes sting with tears. She looked away before the droplets fell.

Remember, you are their equal, she reminded herself, all despair being pushed away.

"What information do you have?" Anoor asked.

Faro went to stand by Qwa, and Anoor noticed a glance between them that suggested there was more to their relationship than mere colleagues.

"That's why we had to meet you here and not in your chambers. We think that the person who murdered Uka Elsari is someone close to you, very close indeed," Faro said, crossing their matchstick arms over their chest.

Anoor's heart began to race.

It definitely wasn't Hassa, she knew that for certain. But what of Kwame . . . Gorn?

"No."

It couldn't be either of them. They were loyal to her.

But how far did that loyalty go, a thought whispered in her mind. *Did it extend to eliminating Uka altogether?*

"We have reason to believe that your chief of staff was the person responsible for Uka's death."

Anoor lowered herself to her haunches, the weight of their words pushing her down.

"Gorn? No, it can't be . . ."

A memory flashed behind her eyes. The night of Uka's death, Gorn's sudden departure just before seventh strike. And the books on Gorn's bookshelf, *Criminal Logistics* and *Murders and Law.* She was the only one who had access to her dressing room to take the jambiya.

Did I know this all along?

"Oh, Gorn. No, it can't be true."

Tanu pulled out a sheet of folded paper from her pocket. It looked like a list of records. Library records.

"I was auditing the public library as part of my educational duties and spotted a shelf of books that looked truly worn out," Tanu said. "And I thought to myself, that's odd, no one ever really comes here, and few take out the same book over and over."

She handed the list to Anoor.

"So, I thought I'd look to see who was borrowing them. There was only one name against the list. And guess what the subject matter was?"

Anoor didn't need to guess, the book titles were there in front of her: *The Mind of a Victim*, *The Acts of a Killer*, *Criminal Logistics*, *Murders and Law* . . . the titles went on. All borrowed from the library in the last few weeks.

"But that doesn't prove anything, she might have been reading up on . . . you know . . . stuff."

"I went through the files of who left the Keep that night," Faro interrupted, presenting Anoor with the original document with an element of smugness.

"So did I," Anoor confirmed.

"Gorn left the grounds shortly after seven on the night of Uka's murder," Faro added.

"Yes, because she had a personal errand . . ." Anoor's voice was thinner than Faro's.

Qwa withdrew his own report from the folds of his white Abosom cowl.

"While Warden Pura had an Abosom following you, I had one following Gorn. Did you know she leaves the Keep once a week to meet a woman by the printing press in the Ember Quarter? She hands her a folder, and leaves. We suspect the woman might be the assassin, and the notes Gorn's instructions. We were unable to find her to . . . question her, however." Qwa looked so bored his eyes had almost closed.

Tanu collected the pages and handed them to Anoor. They were heavy, so heavy in her hands. Gorn wouldn't be so reckless, wouldn't let Anoor be blamed for something she'd done herself.

Anoor thought back to all their conversations about the murder. Gorn had been the one to suggest she look into the culprit's clothing. Was it a ruse to cover her tracks, knowing that the soiled dress was at the launderers?

"She wouldn't do this to me . . ." Anoor mumbled with numb lips.

But what if Gorn didn't intend for Anoor to be caught, what if Anoor had been approaching this completely wrong? The murderer hadn't been trying to frame Anoor, they'd been trying to protect her. And who else had seen Uka's cruelties firsthand?

Anoor felt the trust she'd had in Gorn tearing apart like broken skin, the blood seeping away, robbing her of her life-force.

She lowered her head to the floor. The cool tiles soothed her cheek and dulled the panic that surged up from her stomach. Someone was above her, patting her with stiff hands.

Anoor looked up.

"It's all right, this is a good thing," Tanu said, attempting to be soothing. "Now you'll be able to clear your name and you can return to the courtroom to talk all that crap about the tidewind."

This is a good thing.

A solitary tear fell from her eyes and splashed onto the spotless floor.

No, this was not a good thing at all.

ANOOR FELT A fresh wave of grief press down on her shoulders. Not for the mother she had lost, but for the mother she was about to. Qwa said she'd be locked up in jail for decades, unlikely to see the world beyond her cell before she died. When he'd seen Anoor's horrified expression he had shrugged and said, "She killed a warden."

Anoor left the library more desolate than she had been when she'd entered it. The disciples had encouraged her to seek out more proof before accusing Gorn. Until then, she couldn't confront her, it'd be detrimental to the trial. Maybe even scare her into hiding. Anoor felt a flash of rage simmer beneath the surface of her grief. If Gorn had done this, then she would have to suffer the consequences.

The information from the disciples was helpful, "groundbreaking," as the fictional Inquisitor Abena would say. But she needed to make sure the case was solid before presenting it to the wardens at her trial. She needed more evidence.

Anoor barely noticed the Abosom following her back to her chambers. She clutched the journal Tanu had thrust into her arms. She had folded all the notes into the pages so no one could see them. "It'll also look like you were actually here for something." Tanu winked. "We'll stagger our exit. But go, get more evidence. Take her down."

Take her down. Anoor shuddered.

"Granddaughter."

Anoor jumped, a screech escaping her lips.

"Grandmother, sorry, you gave me a fright."

Yona was wearing a looser gown than Anoor was used to seeing on her lithe form. It fell to the floor in shades of green. The sleeves billowed but were cuffed tightly at her wrists.

"It is not the first time I have been told I am frightening." Yona's smile was as small and sharp as a dagger. She turned it to the Abosom following her. "Take yourself and your false God far from here before I throw you in jail myself."

Anoor couldn't contain her laugh as the Abosom dashed away, his slippers slapping the tiled floor as he went.

"That's better," Yona said. "I went to your chambers. Gorn told me you were out."

"Yes, I had to clear my head."

"And?"

Anoor knew Yona was asking her about the investigation.

"I have some solid leads."

"Indeed?"

Anoor's mouth pressed into a grim line.

No, I will not accuse Gorn without more evidence. Not after what happened to Hassa.

Yona filled the silence with a disappointed sound in the back of her throat.

"Time is running out, Anoor."

"I know." Anoor fiddled with the hem of her skirt. "How is the Tidewind Relief Bill going?"

"Well, the curfew will come in next week, and hopefully you will be around to manage it."

"Hopefully."

"You've been in the warden library, I see. Is that Warden Biq's diary?"

Anoor felt a surge of panic. Truthfully, she had no idea; she'd just taken it from Tanu's outstretched arms.

"Yes."

"And reading that is helping clear your head?"

Anoor heard the disapproval in Yona's voice. It was like salt in a wound.

"Yes," Anoor said, her voice small.

"You might have some questions after reading that. Normally your warden would guide you through the truths of the empire, unraveling them through the years. Come to me if you have any thoughts. Though I'd rather you spend your time solving your case."

"I will."

"Good night, Anoor, I will check on your progress tomorrow."

"Good night, Grandmother."

Anoor held the journal out in front of her.

Whatever secrets this holds, I don't have time for it. I've a murderer to catch.

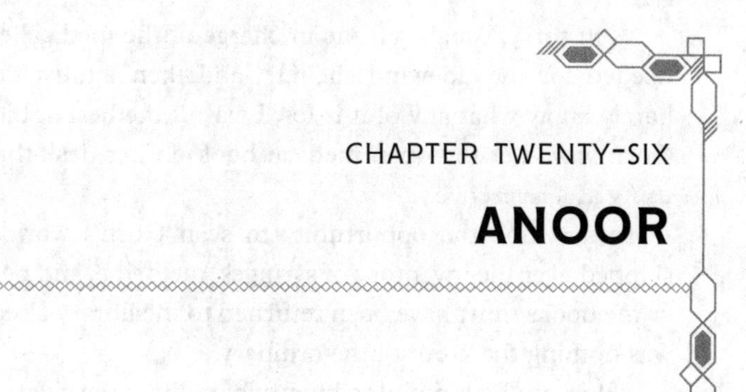

CHAPTER TWENTY-SIX

ANOOR

Remember that anger burns like coal, long and slow, and it takes but a spark to reignite the flame.

—Griot Sheth

Anoor spent the next day watching Gorn's every move—so much so that the woman grew irritated.

"Anoor, why are you hovering by my doorway again? Is there something you need?"

A thought came to her.

"Yes, actually, could you go to the market and get me some chocolate?"

And give me a chance to search your room.

Gorn's eyes narrowed. "Anoor, I am no longer your chief of chambers, I'm not even your chief of staff anymore, I'm Yona's and I have *a lot* to do."

Anoor smarted. Gorn rarely spoke so harshly.

The large woman exhaled and pushed her hands through the

gray curls on her head. Her hair was the longest Anoor had ever seen it, so used was she to the shaved head of Gorn's servant uniform.

"I'm sorry, Yona's put me in charge of the medical equipment needed for the tidewind shelters, and then I must deliver it. I barely know what any of it is for, I wasn't the best at biology . . ." Gorn waved at the open medical book on her desk that she was using as a reference.

Anoor took the opportunity to scan Gorn's work. Her eyes skipped over the inventory of syringes, medicine, and needles. The crime books must have been returned to the library already. There was nothing there out of the ordinary.

"How am I supposed to know what tube is the right size for the bloodletting contraption?" Gorn said, a little flustered.

"Why don't you ask Tanu to help?" Anoor said distractedly, still looking around the room.

"Tanu?"

"Yes, she's Disciple of Knowledge, she'll be able to advise you."

Gorn tilted her head to the side. "Yes, you might be right. I'll suggest it to Yona. She and Wern were arguing about the number of healers needed at the tidewind shelter. Maybe Tanu will be a good go-between."

"Maybe, though she probably hates Wern more than Yona does."

Gorn's head snapped to Anoor's.

"Oh, yes?"

She didn't press further, and Anoor was grateful for it.

"You only have six more days until the trial. How are you feeling?"

The question sounded sincere and full of concern. It cracked Anoor's theory into doubtful shards.

It can't have been Gorn, it can't.

"I'm beginning to think that the person who did this wasn't trying to frame me," Anoor said softly.

"Is that right?" Gorn turned back to her work.

"Yes, I think they might have actually been trying to help me. Remove Uka so I could become warden."

Was it you, Gorn?

Gorn's face was passive, expressionless. Anoor searched it for a flicker of emotion.

"That's an interesting theory."

Did her eyebrows just twitch?

"It might have even been an act of love, and now they're too ashamed to take the blame." Inquisitor Abena would say the statement was "leading."

Gorn made a frustrated sound, and Anoor took a step forward, her eyes narrowing.

"Oh, Anoor, you're not going to blame Hassa again, are you? I don't think she's fully forgiven you yet."

"No, not Hassa." She hissed out Hassa's name and Gorn flinched.

"Anoor? Are you all right?" There was a touch of worry in her voice.

I can't scare her off, not until I know more.

Anoor forced out a small laugh.

"I'm fine, light-headed. Probably low sugar . . . nothing a bit of chocolate wouldn't fix . . . ?"

Gorn let out a small laugh herself. It sounded genuine but Anoor couldn't be sure.

"Anoor, I don't have time to go get you chocolate."

"All right, all right," Anoor conceded.

"Now, I'm sorry to be rude, but until I have Tanu's assistance, I'm going to have to continue on my own."

"Okay, bye then."

"Bye."

Anoor lingered for a moment longer, wondering if the woman in front of her, who raised her like her own daughter, had killed her mother.

THE NEXT DAY Anoor heard Gorn leave her chambers. Anoor ran into the corridor.

"Where are you going?"

Gorn held a folder of notes in her hand. She jumped at being caught by Anoor, and at first tried to hide the papers.

"I'm going out. Personal matter."

"What personal matter?" Anoor said lightly, though rage had started to rise from her toes.

"Something I need to attend to at the market. I won't be long. Zuhari is taking care of some of my work in my room. See you soon." Gorn practically ran out of the door.

Anoor's stomach sank. She hadn't heard Zuhari come in, and now she couldn't search Gorn's room like she had intended.

Zuhari was sitting at Gorn's desk. Though her frame was smaller than Gorn's she still somehow filled the room with her presence. It was the same aura of power that Anoor had come to associate with higher-ranking officials in the army.

"Morning, Zuhari."

Zuhari jumped up, her hair twists swinging by her ears. She clapped the back of her right hand against the back of her left in the opened-hand salute of the wardens' army.

"Good morning, Disciple."

"At ease. And I've told you, you don't need to call me that anymore. Maybe not ever again."

Anoor had come to like the woman over the last few weeks despite her earlier error of judgment. She was reliable and helpful.

Zuhari frowned. "You will always be my disciple."

Anoor looked warmly at the older woman and leaned over to see what she was working on.

"Ah, back on the inventory?"

"Yes, it appears Yona is doing a lot of good in the Dredge. The supplies here are more than we had in the mines in Jin-Hidal. Especially after the revolt of the hundred."

Anoor detected the bitterness there. She had forgotten that Zuhari had served during one of the largest uprisings in the empire's history. Anoor pressed her for information, while she once again let her eyes roam around the room.

"Tell me about it, the revolt. I was taught the basics, that a hundred Dusters rose up and were then slaughtered. But that is all."

Zuhari's large eyes seemed to shrink as she returned to the memory.

"There was a young girl . . . Rola." The name was filled with a deep sadness. In fact, Anoor had never heard another Ember place as much emotion in a Duster's name before. Except Sylah. When Sylah said Anoor's name it was like fire raced across her skin, burning with warmth and love.

"She was ten, only just. Like all the Dusters at Jin-Hidal she was branded with the guild of duty and sent to the mines the day after her nameday. There were few other opportunities for Dusters. If you were really lucky, you became a rubbish collector or sewage cleaner."

Zuhari pulled in a quick short breath, bracing herself for the rest of the tale.

"Rola got hungry and stole a sandwich from an overseer. I . . . I didn't see it happen . . ." All emotion fled from her voice, as if the memory was too painful to bear, and she had to speak plainly or not at all. ". . . but I saw her body afterward."

Anoor felt her heart mourn for the girl, her investigation forgotten.

"The Dusters rose that night and turned their chisels and axes on their Ember overseers. They held the mines for two weeks before the army arrived. I tried to save as many of them as I could, but when the army realized what I was doing I was dismissed. They shattered my weapon and stripped me of my titles. The officers couldn't navigate the mines as well as the Dusters. So, instead, the army had a better idea . . . they herded the Dusters over the course of a few days, setting dummy traps and false trails. Then they collapsed the tunnels they were in. Buried them alive."

Anoor gasped. She hadn't known any of this.

Zuhari's voice changed from matter-of-fact to hard and hate-filled. "You know what I think is the worst thing? They call it the revolt of the hundred, but over four hundred Dusters died. Even more injured. And Embers? Four, only four overseers killed in retribution for what they did to *four hundred*. All because Rola stole a sandwich as her mother had forgotten to pack her lunch that day."

Zuhari looked away from Anoor, but she caught the tears in her eyes. The woman had a hard outer shell, a bit like Sylah in many ways, but it was just a front. Underneath it she was rage and emotion.

"That's awful, I'm so sorry."

Zuhari's face relaxed back to neutral, and she rubbed at her eyes as if a speck of dust had landed there.

"That's why you have to keep fighting, Disciple Anoor. You're a Duster. You can change things around here."

Anoor thought for a moment.

"Zuhari . . . have you seen anything . . . unusual in Gorn's room before?"

Zuhari's eyes glittered. Anoor had to be careful here; it was time to strain Zuhari's loyalty to Gorn.

"What do you mean, unusual?"

"Anything that might implicate her in anything . . ."

"Speak plain, Disciple."

"I think Gorn is hiding something from me," Anoor said cautiously.

Zuhari didn't react, but her jaw clenched.

"Now, I'm not accusing her of anything," Anoor added quickly. "But it would set my mind at ease if I knew someone else was keeping an eye out."

"I will do that for you, Disciple."

Anoor smiled gratefully.

"Thank you, Zuhari, I will leave you to your work now. But thank you for sharing your story with me. I will never forget Rola's, nor the sacrifice those Dusters made."

Zuhari flinched at Rola's name and bowed her head to try and hide it. She saluted once more before Anoor left her to her work.

IT WAS THE day before the trial. The tidewind raged outside, a screaming reminder that the world was ending.

Anoor held a cup of coffee in her hands. It had long since cooled. Notes were scattered across her bed. She'd found nothing beyond the evidence the other disciples had found. It was all circumstantial, more hearsay than fact. Not enough to pin Gorn to the crime.

Part of Anoor was glad. She didn't want Gorn to be the murderer.

There was a soft tap on the door.

"Disciple?" The whisper came. There was only one person who still called her that.

Anoor padded to the door and opened the door a crack.

"Zuhari, what is it?"

"I found something."

Anoor ushered her in.

It was well past second strike in the morning. Zuhari must have waited until the tidewind reached its zenith before making her way to Anoor's chambers. It was risky, as Gorn was asleep in the next room. She wondered when Gorn had given the woman a key but was glad that she had.

Zuhari held out a page of writing.

Anoor began to read, her stomach sinking. It was unmistakably Gorn's handwriting.

The fastest way to kill is by piercing the victim's carotid artery which is easily located in the throat. But if she uses the bow, she'll have an easier escape. Need to figure out weapon before next delivery.

"She did it. It wasn't her, but she hired someone to do it." Anoor was crying, but they were tears of anger. "She let me spend the last three weeks compiling a case when she knew all along exactly who had done it."

Zuhari bowed her head.

"I'm sorry, Disciple."

"You are not the one who should be sorry. Thank you for this. It was the last piece of the puzzle. Now go, don't speak a word of it to anyone. I will expose her tomorrow before the court."

Zuhari left.

Anoor didn't sleep that night.

Anoor was standing by the window when Gorn entered her room the next morning with breakfast on a tray. Steamed milk bread drizzled in honey, her favorite.

I'll be sure to send her some in jail, Anoor thought bitterly.

"Oh, you're already up," Gorn said, resting the tray on her now-clear desk.

"Yes, I didn't sleep."

"I can imagine." She made a sympathetic sound. "Anoor, I wanted to talk to you."

A confession is too late. But still, Anoor turned away from the morning light and looked at Gorn, who perched herself on the edge of Anoor's four-poster. There was no one else who could look more uncomfortable on a four-layered duck down mattress.

"I know you haven't got a case, and I know that today will probably end in a guilty sentence. I'm so proud of you for persevering, but I think we need to think about alternative options."

"Other options?" Anoor's voice was cold. *Was this her plan all along?*

"Escape. I'm sure we can figure out something."

"You want me to run away?"

"Not run away, preserve your freedom. What if you bleed in jail? They'll find out you're a Duster, then they'll sentence you to the rack, Anoor. I won't have them take you from me." There was real emotion there.

"You should have thought about that before."

"What?" Gorn said, confused.

"Nothing. I'm not running away, Gorn. I will face what happens. And so will you."

Gorn frowned, her face a mask of worry. She wasn't concerned for herself, but for Anoor. It caused a pang in her heart. Anoor tried to steel herself against it but failed.

"I need to go back over my notes," Anoor said, her voice fracturing at the end.

"Anoor?" Gorn asked.

How could you? She wanted to scream.

Instead Anoor turned away, refusing to face her. Eventually Gorn left, leaving Anoor to her grief. It spilled out of her and down her cheeks.

CHAPTER TWENTY-SEVEN

HASSA

We lost another last night. But we will continue to experiment. The longer we keep them alive, the more we can harvest.

—Notes found in the tidewind shelter

Hassa stood by the window in Kwame's chambers looking out over the courtyard. The joba tree flowers had long stopped blooming. The blood-red petals had gone, leaving the hardened shell of the joba fruit behind. Hassa thought of Sylah and wondered how she was doing on the other side of the world.

I hope she's still alive.

Hassa shuddered as she remembered Sylah's last words: "Will you look after her for me?" she had asked, with eyes like black marbles. But Hassa had failed. They still didn't know who had killed Uka.

Hassa let out an exhausted sigh.

"Are you cold?" Kwame was beside her in a moment, the scent of his rose oil cloaking her in a familiar warmth.

No, just worried. Anoor's trial is tomorrow, and she has nothing.

He nodded.

"We don't need to do a lesson tonight."

No, she signed quickly, *I want to.*

His returning smile was filled with heat, and her chest fluttered to see it.

They sat together in his chambers, a pot of coffee between them, alongside the book they used to aid translations.

"What shall we learn today?"

Emotions, Hassa decided.

"Emotions?" he repeated to confirm the translation.

Yes. The way Ghostings show emotion is unique. We cannot always convey our feelings on our face in front of a master, so occasionally, we sign them.

Kwame seemed to be following. He had improved remarkably in the last few weeks though she still signed slow enough for a Ghosting babe.

This is frustration. She slid her two forearms over each other in a slashing motion.

"Anger?"

No . . . more—Hassa thought of a word to lead him to the translation—*tight.*

"Oh, I've seen you use that in front of Gorn before, does she know what that means?"

No, and don't tell her. Hassa's eyes glittered with mirth. *She makes me sign so slowly sometimes.*

That made Kwame laugh, and she enjoyed the sound of it.

This is happiness. Hassa lifted her arm across her face in a wide arc.

"Hmm . . . so you're signing a shape like a smile . . . happiness?"

Yes. You, Kwame, make me happy.

For a moment she wondered if he'd understood, then he grinned, and it was full of teeth.

"Stop teasing me."

She didn't return his smile, her attempt at flirting dashed.

Kwame reached for the book between them. He flicked through the pages until he found the word he was looking for.

"And what does this sign look like?"

Hassa leaned forward.

Oh, she thought. Her gaze caught his. Gone was the mischievous glint, gone was the nervous energy. In its place was smoke and coal.

Desire. She crossed her arms over her chest and felt the roughness of her servant's garb beneath her skin and grimaced. Kwame saw it and misconstrued her meaning.

No, that wasn't about you, she signed.

"No, it's okay, I understand. It was a poor attempt . . ." He gave a halfhearted laugh.

Kwame.

He turned away from her. "You know, I'm finding myself quite tired. I also need to stop by and see my father this evening . . ."

Kwame. Hassa tapped his arm. *You make me happy. And I desire you too.*

"Can you repeat that, I didn't quite get it . . ."

Hassa laughed and shoved him, knowing full well he had understood every word. He grasped her by the arm.

"Hassa." His voice was rough as he leaned in, closing the distance between them. "Can I?" His hand trailed her collarbone and up to her neck. A soft mewl escaped her as his thumb ran over her lips.

Yes, she mouthed against it. *Yes*.

His lips pressed hers and she shivered against him. She savored it for a moment before breaking apart.

"What is it?"

Hassa led him out of the sitting room and into his bedroom.

Time for the rest of the lesson. She slinked out of her servant dress and undergarments in quick motions and stood naked before him.

"You might be my favorite teacher," Kwame growled before lifting her onto the bed.

HASSA COULDN'T STOP smiling. Her lesson with Kwame had gone better than she could have hoped. She looked at his face in the shard of moonlight, smooth with innocence and dreams. Kwame was a capable bed fellow, giving her time to sign her needs while also clearly taking pleasure in it.

But the night was calling, and Hassa needed to leave him for the darkness.

She crept out of the bedcovers and padded to where she had dropped her clothes. A brazen move that she'd enjoyed executing. Sweat still cooled on her skin and stuck to the garment as she dressed, but she reveled in the sensation. It had been a long time since she had bedded someone. Growing up in a maiden house, it was hard to not see the act as a transaction.

But this had been different, special. Kwame had a piece of her heart.

She snorted softly in the darkness. Oh, how Sylah would laugh to hear her friend so sentimental.

"Hassa?" Kwame's voice was groggy with sleep. He turned on the runelamp by his bed. "Where are you going?"

I have to go, there are a few things I need to sort in the Dredge.

He pushed himself onto his elbow, the covers slipping from his chest. It was lightly peppered with tight curls. Though he wasn't overly muscular, each muscle was clearly defined, every one earned by a life in the kitchens. His smile dipped to the side.

"Can't it wait until morning?"

She answered with a grin of her own. She couldn't help it.

I want to stay, but I can't. I'm . . . investigating something.

"Sign that again please . . . oh, investigating?"

She nodded.

"Tell me," he asked softly. "Please."

Hassa looked out of the window. The night darkened the edges of the city making it hard to see the Dredge in the distance. She looked to the sky. The tidewind wasn't far away. She'd stayed too long in Kwame's chambers.

I've been finding bodies in the Dredge.

"What do you mean? As in dead bodies?"

Hassa walked deeper into the pool of light created by the runelamp and sat on the edge of Kwame's bed.

Yes.

"Is that . . . unusual? I know there are a lot of drug users in the Dredge . . ."

Hassa flashed her eyes at him.

These bodies all have holes in their skeletons.

She told him what she had found, and how she'd been monitoring it these last few weeks.

"Why didn't you tell me? Tell Anoor?"

Hassa exhaled, answering Kwame's questions with two words.

The trial.

Kwame nodded, understanding. "Who do you think is responsible?"

I don't know. That's what I've been trying to find out.

"Tomorrow, we tell Gorn. We'll wait until after the trial to tell Anoor."

They didn't acknowledge that Anoor would probably be in jail by this time tomorrow.

"Come back to bed?" He pulled back the covers, revealing the rest of his body.

She let out a low sound in her throat, and Kwame's grin turned feral.

Yes, tomorrow. She'd tell Gorn everything tomorrow.

There's something going on in the Dredge. Hassa and Kwame walked into Gorn's chambers the next morning.

"Sign slower please," Gorn said, her lips taut. Hassa knew how much it galled her that of the three students, she was now the worst at grasping the Ghosting language.

Will you translate for me, please, she signed to Kwame, her movements clipped with frustration.

"People are dying in the Dredge, Hassa's been monitoring it. Every corpse has a hole in its skeleton," Kwame said.

"What?"

Hassa untucked the map from the bosom of her servant's garb. She and Kwame had made it that morning. It sprang into a roll and she used Gorn's stacks of papers to keep it flat. Hassa was surprised to see so many zines on the desk, and it made her feel more fondly toward Gorn.

This is where I found the bodies. Blots of ink surrounded the north of the Dredge. *Every night, just before the tidewind, they're dumped on desolate streets. So, in the morning it looks like a tidewind death, not a murder.*

Gorn leaned back in her chair, though the movement was incremental as the straight-backed wood had little give.

"This is all very strange."

What shall we do?

Hassa was shocked to find Gorn's face crumple into tears. Few droplets fell, and her shoulders shuddered as she tried to contain even those few.

Kwame and Hassa exchanged an incredulous look.

"I'm sorry, it's just that Anoor's trial is in two strikes. She's going to jail. I want her to escape, to leave, but she's refusing. She's given up all hope."

Hassa perched on the edge of Gorn's desk.

You suggested she escape?

"Yes, what other option does she have?"

Where would you have her go?

"I don't know, somewhere out of the city."

No, they'd search all the nearest cities.

"Where would you suggest?"

Keep her here, in Nar-Ruta. In the Duster Quarter or the Dredge.

"Do you have somewhere in mind? The tunnels maybe?"

Not the tunnels. She would not jeopardize her people's safe haven. *But there is someone who would be willing to shelter her, I think.*

"Wait, wait, wait." Kwame's voice sliced through their discussion, making Gorn jump. "Are we really considering this? Kidnapping Anoor, our friend? Our disciple?"

Gorn set her jaw. "We have no other choice."

Hassa looked deep into her eyes. *Are you willing to break her trust?*

Gorn looked away, tears still in her eyes. "I must," she whispered with doomed resolution.

Kwame laughed, a little hysterically.

"So how do we do this?"

HASSA STAYED IN the shadows of the corridor as Anoor Elsari was escorted across the Keep to her trial by an Abosom. Anoor had dressed on her own, refusing anyone else's help.

While she kept herself holed up in her room, Gorn, Hassa, and Kwame had been busy sorting out her escape. Everything was set.

Anoor wore a long flowing yellow dress, high-necked and long-sleeved. It looked like something Yona would have worn, and Hassa knew that was intentional. Her white makeup was extravagant, swirling and dashing across her face and eyes like warpaint. She held a red eru-leather satchel with her notes inside. Her chin was raised, as if she were walking up the five hundred steps to become warden, not to a trial where she'd most certainly be condemned for murder. Her expression was so resolute, it made Hassa worry what was happening under the surface.

Kwame and Gorn stood on either side of Anoor, the perfect picture of loyal advisers. Though they had helped to set up the escape plan, the execution was down to Hassa. Neither of them could be implicated.

They reached the corridor nearest the stables.

"Ouch," Anoor said suddenly, clutching her wrist.

The laudanum syringe had been Gorn's idea. It had been easy to strike it off the inventory for the tidewind shelters. Kwame had administered it in Anoor's wrist as they walked.

It didn't take Anoor long to fall to the floor.

"Anoor," Gorn cried. She turned to the Abosom. "Get a healer, quickly."

The Abosom hesitated. If he didn't go, or sent Kwame in his stead, then this was all over.

"Are you deaf? Go," Gorn barked. Hassa wasn't sure if the

Abosom was swayed by the urgency or their fear of Gorn, but either way it worked.

As soon as he was out of sight, they got to work removing Anoor's dress. Gorn pulled it free from her sleeping form and Kwame tugged it over Hassa's head in one quick motion. It pooled around her feet. She pushed her arms through the sleeves and signed, *I can't run in this.*

"Here." Kwame ripped off the bottom layer. It left it frayed, but that wouldn't matter from afar. "You know what to do?"

Yes, she nodded.

"Kwame, I need help over here." Gorn was trying to lift Anoor's body down the nearest staircase toward the stables. Hassa had already ensured that another Ghosting servant would cause a distraction, loud enough to draw away any Ember servants in the stables. They heard it now as screams and shouts erupted from somewhere outside.

Sami's let an eru loose in the courtyard; the stables are empty of people. Quickly, now.

Gorn and Kwame shuffled Anoor down the stairs as Hassa led the way.

"Have you got the wig?" Kwame said while lowering Anoor to the floor.

What do you think's been chafing my bits for the last half a strike?

Kwame's eyes lit up with barely contained amusement. Hassa winked and pulled it out from under her dress and then pressed it to her shaved scalp.

Kwame cocked his head, surveying her new look. The curly wig was shorter than Anoor's hair, but it was all they could find at short notice.

"I don't hate it," he said, and Hassa laughed because it was so clearly a lie. His nose pinched upward like when he drank Jin-Eynab wine, which he pretended to like because it was what nobles liked to drink.

Gorn shouldered her way between them with a sound of frustration.

"Help me get her in here."

Hassa ducked ahead and pulled open the carriage door Gorn was pointing at. The carriage was full of medical equipment for the shelter.

Gorn and Kwame laid Anoor in an empty crate and closed the lid.

"Where's the satchel? With her notes?" Gorn said, wide-eyed.

They looked between themselves for a breath before dashing back up to the corridor.

The Abosom would be back any moment, and each of them had their parts to play. The infirmary was at the farthest point from the stables, but not so far that he wouldn't return soon.

"Fuck," Kwame whispered behind her.

The Abosom was already back. Hassa could see him rushing down the corridor ahead with a healer. She had to run before he came too close and realized she wasn't Anoor.

But the satchel. It was there, ten handspans ahead.

Kwame saw the risk she was about to take, but he couldn't help her. He had his own task.

Hassa dashed forward and pulled the satchel to her chest. She didn't look to see if the Abosom had noticed the woman dressed like Anoor didn't have hands. Instead, Hassa fled.

"Anoor, what are you doing? You can't run away. It's your trial today," Kwame called after her. Each sentence was stilted with forced concern.

Oh, dear, Kwame was *really* bad at acting.

"Anoor, stop, where are you going?" Gorn said with more conviction. "I'm not sure what happened, she fainted then got up . . ."

Hassa dashed back the way they had come, down the kitchens' staircase and out into the courtyard. A crowd of people who had been drawn to the excitement of an escaped eru lingered.

Hassa was glad—she needed lots of people to see her. She made sure not to get too close, as the ruse only worked from afar. Next, she ran toward the duty office, and then circled back via the joba tree. She heard the cries of the Abosom as he followed her snaking steps.

Now came the tricky part.

There were a few sets of tunnels under the cloisters in the Keep that were used during the tidewind. Hassa hoped no one else was in them during daylight.

She ran down the steps two at a time, shedding her disguise as she went. Thankfully the basket they had placed at the bottom of the steps was still there and the tunnel was empty. She shoved the wig and dress underneath the soiled clothes they had procured.

Then she steadied her breathing.

Flip-flap. Flip-flap.

The Abosom's slippers slapped the stairs as he ran.

"Did you see her? Anoor Elsari? Did she come this way?" he shouted in her face.

Hassa shrugged then pointed slowly back up the steps.

"Fool. She came down them, not up them." He looked like he was about to strike her, but she held the basket of clothing to her chest.

Then he smelled them.

"Urgh, is that . . . dung on those clothes?"

Yes, indeed it is. Anything to stop you digging through them.

"Be on your way, you useless servant." The Abosom ran past her, holding his cowl in his hands as he went.

It had worked. It had actually *worked*. The plan had been like something out of a zine. And they had pulled it off without issues.

Hassa was so relieved she let her face fall into the basket of clothes with an exhausted sigh.

Oh, shit.

Despite the dung smeared on her face, she couldn't help but laugh in relief.

CHAPTER TWENTY-EIGHT

HASSA

Father, try this medicine, it was hard to procure but I hope it helps. Anoor tells me it should ease the pain. I will come to see you soon.

—Message sent with a vial of medicine from Kwame to his father

Hassa watched the eru carriage hiding Anoor begin to cross the Tongue. Officers swarmed across the metal bridge stopping every cart and carriage. Even the trotro had been stopped, the goods for the day's market going rotten in the sun and lacing the air with their pungent odor.

Hassa was careful as she made her way through the streets. She had burned the contents of the laundry basket that had concealed Anoor's clothes and hidden her satchel in the Nest.

It had been three strikes since Anoor's disappearance, and Nar-Ruta was in uproar. The wardens had ordered the capital city be searched, including every villa. Messages had gone to the twelve cities and patrols sent to monitor every route out of Nar-Ruta. The worst thing was, Anoor's disappearance had resulted in the certainty of her sentence. The whispers followed the carriage through the Dredge.

". . . The daughter, she killed Uka."

"I heard she planned it for weeks . . . wanted to become warden herself . . ."

"I was told she was found in the dining room with a glass of red wine in her hand, smiling. But it wasn't red wine, it was her mother's blood . . ."

Hassa was a step ahead of the carriage as it neared the north of the Dredge. The crowds of gossipers were easy for her to slip through, but harder for a carriage to navigate. She located the meeting spot to the left of Ren's apothecary. A shattered jambiya hung above the doorway of the shop. Hassa smiled at the occupant as she passed.

Ren sold Hassa her daily hormone herbs. She also offered surgical procedures for free for anyone who wanted them. Neither surgery nor hormone herbs were a requirement to affirm your gender in the empire. Simply put, Hassa was always a woman. There were many such places in the empire, but Hassa liked Ren's apothecary the best; the woman had kind eyes and knowing now that she was Zuhari's partner made Hassa like her more.

Hassa stopped by the second villa along. It was opposite the tidewind shelter and where she had agreed to meet Kwame. He wasn't there.

"Out of the way." Anoor heard Gorn's gruff voice at the front of the carriage as the eru pulled up. "Supplies for the shelter coming through."

Hassa watched Gorn park the eru carriage outside the tidewind shelter and jump down from the driver's seat. She was flanked by two officers, but that wasn't unusual. The tidewind supplies were always guarded, just in case overzealous Dredge-dwellers chose to ransack the carriage.

Two healers came out from the loading bay of the shelter and began to remove the supplies.

"Leave that one in." Gorn pointed to the crate with Anoor in it. "That needs to go back to the Keep."

No one questioned her; the supplies were Gorn's remit and so the crate was left in the carriage.

Anoor would be waking up soon. Gorn knew that she herself would likely be questioned after Anoor's "escape" but three strikes was longer than they'd anticipated. They didn't have long.

Where is Kwame? The thought struck Hassa with a whip of panic. He was meant to be here by now to help her carry Anoor.

Gorn looked to her right, spotting Hassa in the shade of the villa. She gave her a grim nod.

It was now or never.

But Hassa couldn't carry Anoor's dead weight on her own.

There was a cough beside her, and Hassa turned to find a man looking down at her. A man she recognized.

You're late.

Kwame was wearing a fake mustache. It peeled up at the corners ever so slightly, where his uneven skin had lifted it off his face. He had abandoned the court fashion that he had grown to love and instead wore the drab blues and limp patterns more synonymous with the Duster Quarter.

Do you really need the mustache? Hassa asked. *It's not like anyone knows you on this side of the river.*

"I was going to borrow Zuhari's old uniform and pretend to be an officer, but she said she'd thrown it out."

Dressing as an officer would have been an awful idea.

Kwame's mustache twitched. "Well, good job I decided on this disguise," he said, his voice pitched an octave lower than usual. Hassa saw he had blackened one of his teeth with paint. She muffled her laugh. Somehow, she *still* found him attractive despite all the absurdities of this new character. Kwame would be Kwame no matter how he dressed. His spirit was too bright to be concealed.

"Are you ready?"

Yes, they've nearly finished unloading. As soon as Hassa finished signing, they saw the last crate touch the ground.

The officers that had escorted Gorn stayed at the shelter to continue guarding the supplies while the healers finished sorting through them. Gorn climbed up to the driver's seat and began to lead the eru back toward the Keep.

Hassa and Kwame had to run to keep up, but the crowds that on the way there had been merely annoying were now the perfect cover. The plan was for Gorn to stop the carriage and leave it open so that Kwame and Hassa could jump on and retrieve Anoor.

"Inspection!" The cry came out from ahead of them. A patrol of officers flagged down Gorn.

"Oh, Anyme above, this isn't good," Kwame muttered, the mustache fluttering from his breath.

Hassa had to agree.

Then Gorn did something unexpected: she tried to keep riding. But erus weren't stupid creatures, and when the patrol didn't move, the eru balked at being urged forward.

When an eru balks, it thrusts its tail up and rears its forearms. Few riders survive a balking eru.

The carriage snapped off the leather harness tied to the animal as its tail propelled the carriage, and Anoor, backward. Gorn was similarly thrown forward over the eru's almond-shaped head and landed hard on the ground in front of the officers.

But Hassa and Kwame didn't have time to check on Gorn, because her fall had given them the chance to rescue Anoor.

In the chaos that ensued, Kwame and Hassa chased down the carriage and slipped into the back. The crate had fallen to the side, and Anoor was blinking up at them with half-lidded eyes.

"Whatisgoingon?" she slurred.

They each hooked an elbow under Anoor's and heaved her up, pulling her to her feet and out into the street. Some people looked their way, but Hassa doubted they knew who Anoor was. They probably thought the three of them were chancing a steal.

"Hassa, I got her. You go open the hatch to the tunnels."

In this area of the Dredge there were few access points that Hassa could use safely. Pockets of explosive gas, disrepair, and shifting villa foundations meant there were some places that even Ghostings didn't go. Thankfully this particular route was clear.

Hassa let Kwame take Anoor's weight. She was walking a little herself, but it was clear she didn't have full control of her body yet. Anoor mumbled something that sounded like "get off me" as Hassa jogged away.

The hatch wasn't far, just to the right of the shelter. Hassa had been using it frequently, because it was where she'd found a lot of the bodies.

She stumbled, an idea striking her off balance. She thought back to the map she had drawn that morning with Kwame. The bodies: they were all within one or two streets of the tidewind shelter.

How had she not realized this before?

She was torn from her revelation by the sound of someone talking to Kwame.

"What's going on here?"

Hassa turned to see an officer pointing a rune gun at Kwame and Anoor.

Anoor lolled forward in Kwame's arms. She was still in her undergarments, a thin satin dress that was now grubby from the inside of the crate.

Kwame's eyes widened in fear as the gun was leveled at him. His eyes flickered to where Hassa was before returning to the barrel of the runegun. Then, as was Kwame's way, he improvised in the most unpredictable way. He started to sing.

"Here's to you, my friend and foe,
Be merry now, come high, come low.
Let's drink to the end while we have breath,
No regrets we'll take in death."

He began to jig, his feet bucking out, while throwing Anoor further forward so her face was more concealed by her curls.

Kwame, you genius.

"Get back to the maiden house with you. I don't want to see you on the streets," the officer barked, using the runegun to direct Kwame away.

Kwame swayed and careened in the direction the officer pointed. But as soon as their eyes were averted, Kwame guided Anoor out of the crowds and back toward Hassa.

That was very close.

"Very. She kept mumbling to the officers, so I thought singing might help." Kwame's grin was full of amusement and Hassa wanted to kiss him.

Come on, get her down here. We still have a long way to go.

It's the third house along, Hassa signed then pointed with her limb.

"Will she be in?" Kwame asked.

She's always in.

Together they guided Anoor up the steps toward the villa. Kwame knocked.

The door crept open slowly.

"Hello?" Her voice was raspy with disuse. "What do you want?"

"We need your help," Kwame said, adopting the deep voice he had used earlier.

"What?" Lio asked, opening the door wider. "Why are you talking to me in a fake voice?"

"This isn't a fake voice." Kwame's pitch wavered up and down.

"Go away." Lio began to shut the door then she caught sight of Hassa.

"You." The door flew open, and Hassa could see all of her for the first time. The woman had wasted away. She had always been thin, but now she was gaunt, and her signature shaved hair had grown out in tufts. But as Hassa could see all of Lio, Lio could see all of them.

"Who is that?" Lio whispered the question, knowing the answer.

"Your daughter, and we need you to hide her. Now," Kwame said.

Lio leaned out into the street and looked around.

"My neighbor . . . she's nosy. Come in." It was an order and not an invitation.

Lio hadn't taken her eyes off Anoor's as they entered the villa.

"What happened to her?"

"It's a long story, but before we tell you, we need to know you're not going to turn her in." Kwame's face was grave as he lowered Anoor onto the sofa.

"Your fake mustache has fallen off," Lio said dryly.

Anoor laughed and all eyes turned to her.

"This is a very strange dream I'm having," she said, her laughter growing. Lio's eyes softened as she watched her.

"Laudanum," Kwame said by way of explanation. "She wouldn't have come willingly."

"There is a story here, a long one. I will put on the coffee."

I hope she has firerum, Hassa added, collapsing onto the wicker sofa next to Anoor.

It had been a very long day.

CHAPTER TWENTY-NINE

NAYELI

The Wife has taken full control of the Foundry. She oversees all the preparations and has increased production. She says war will come this generation, but we are yet to find the Child of Fire.

—Message from the Green Commune leader to Orange Commune

It had been three years since Nayeli named herself Wife of Kabut. Her hair had never grown back. She wore the scars there proudly, a crown of silver webs that marked her as chosen by the Spider God.

In that time they had prepared for the war Kabut had foretold. At the center of their preparations was the Foundry where Nayeli was master and Wife both.

Before she began her search for the Child of Fire, Nayeli went to the open temple to hold vigil. When the crescent moon rose, Kabut's eye blinking, she took to her knees next to the endless flame.

The wind was laced with specks of rain, and it hissed as it struck the fire.

"Husband, I come seeking success. Preparations continue. A new harvest arrives from the Shariha tomorrow."

Nayeli withdrew from her robe one of her most intricate creations: a miniature structure that perfectly replicated the Spider God's larger form. It had taken her three moon turns to complete. She threw it into the fire.

She would get no help from Kabut without sacrifice.

The rain was pouring heavily now, but Nayeli didn't feel ready to leave the quiet world of the temple. She stood and walked toward the back of the pillars where the cliff face looked over the sea.

There was a sound beside her, and Nayeli called out, "Come out, little one, I see you there."

The boy was small and a little malnourished. In his hands he clutched a notebook that he kept shielded from the rain.

"What are you doing here so late? Where are your parents?"

The boy mumbled something into the tattered remains of his sleeve.

"Speak up."

"Forgive me, Master-Wife, I like to come here to draw at night." His lip was quivering, and Nayeli felt a rare stab of sympathy.

"Show me." She didn't mean for her words to come out like a command. The boy flinched and offered up the notebook.

His drawings were meticulous and deftly done.

"You drew the Zalaam's exile from the continent?"

"Yes," he said in a small voice. "My mama used to tell me the story, before she died."

Nayeli ran her fingers over the ink drawing of eight boats.

"Tell me it." Again, a command. "Please," she added.

"The prophet was expelled from the Zwina Academy for speaking Kabut's truth." The boy spoke with the surety of memorized words. "But the prophet drew people to him, for truth is powerful and it cannot be unheard. The communes were born, growing in numbers and wealth. But the queen of Tenio did not wish to hear the truth, her ears were closed. So she executed our beloved prophet, the one with no name, and exiled Kabut's believers from her land.

"Eight boats for the eight colors. All took to the Marion Sea. But a storm separated them and four went north, while four went south. Yellow, orange, green, and violet made it to the Volcane Isles, the others were lost to the sea. But truth cannot be unheard, and over the years those who listened made their way to the Zalaam. And so, the communes grew once more, reinstated. Ready for war."

Nayeli smiled and patted the boy on the shoulder.

"You told the story well. Your mother would be proud."

He ducked his head, but Nayeli saw the tears in his eyes.

"What is your name?"

"Chah."

Nayeli started. She hadn't heard that name for a long time.

"How old are you?"

"Nine."

"How would you like to use your talent in the Foundry? You're a little young, but I could do with someone with deft fingers like yours."

"Truly?" He gave her a shy smile.

"Truly." She gave him back his artwork. "Now it is time for rest. Come to me in the morning."

"Thank you, Master-Wife."

"MASTER-WIFE, HAVE I carved this correctly?" Chah called to her.

Nayeli leaned over the workbench and squinted at the metal tube. He was following one of the easier schemas used to train the children.

"You've missed the second dash above the central line," Nayeli said, pointing to the flaw in his work. "Here, let me show you."

Nayeli took the scalpel and leaned over the workstation. Those carving around them paused to watch their master at work. She rarely took up the scalpel anymore. Her pursuits were more focused on the experimental side of the Foundry's products.

With quick strokes she completed the combination of runes.

"You see, you missed this here." She blew on the metal, pushing the shavings she had created away.

"Oh, yes, I don't think I saw that before," the small child said.

"Come, let me show you something."

The boy smiled, glad to be chosen by the Master-Wife.

Nayeli led him down the rows and rows of worktables. She had expanded the Foundry as much as she had been able, increasing their production tenfold. Now more than three hundred yellow-bloods worked day and night. The mines in Violet Commune had to work overtime to supply the metal they needed in order to keep up. It had caused an explosive argument in the council.

"You can't just demand more supplies," the Violet Commune leader had cried, clutching her purple robes to her chest.

"The Wife has increased production and therefore—" Andu said, closest to the fire. It cast his yellow robes in a sickly glow.

"'Therefore' nothing. You cannot just claim more metal, it is the main export of this island. No, no, it is the *only* export."

"Excuse me, do not forget our fishing haul—"

The Violet Commune leader scowled and tilted her head to the blue-robed leader that had spoken. "'Excuse me,' indeed, I forgot about the handful of fish we trade to the nomads. In fact, let us compare. How much wealth has the fish brought in, Nori?"

"Well, I—I—I was just saying that . . . it isn't the *only* export."

Blue-blooded are always so docile, Nayeli thought idly. She twirled the ceremonial dagger through the flickering shadows of the fire.

"It is the only export of note." The Violet Commune leader's lips were so tight, Nayeli was impressed words could even be formed.

"I understand your concerns, but the Wife is preparing us for battle as Kabut foretold. You must increase production."

"How?" she shrieked, violet robes flung open, her hands flailing. "I have everyone in my commune working in the mines."

"Use the blue-bloods." Nayeli spoke softly, but they all heard her.

"What?" Both violet and blue recoiled.

"If the fishing export is as weak as you say, why not consolidate our efforts?"

There were hisses—it was never truly a good council meeting if there weren't.

Andu stepped toward Nayeli, the only one brave enough to do so. "That is against our basic principles. We are stronger segregated."

Nayeli nodded deeply, and there was a collective exhale of relief. But then she spoke, circling the fire in the center. The fire that had burned her child's body. Her husband's body.

"The eight legs of a spider are separate but work as one. I concede, it is a principle we have long stood by, in honor of our God." Nayeli stopped in front of the Violet Commune leader. "But I ask you this. What is our purpose in this life?"

No one answered her.

"We preach this to our community, so why can you not answer me now?"

Andu sighed. "To prepare for the Ending Fire in order to cleanse the world."

"To *bring* the Ending Fire and *burn* the unbelieving. It is this path and only this path that will lead us to utopia," Nayeli said. "I know some communes say 'purge,' but there will always be small differences in the retelling of Kabut's final words to our prophet. One thing we all know for sure. War is coming, because we will bring it. To win we must begin again."

"To win we must begin again," the leaders reflectively murmured.

"What of the Child of Fire? Are we not to wait?" A red-blood. Of course. They believed the child would be of their ilk. A literal child of fire.

"Generations we have waited. And for generations they have not appeared. But there is something different now, it rumbles in the earth and blows in the wind. Now, we have me. I will guide us to the Child of Fire."

Feet shifted under different color robes.

"I tell you again. War is coming. Because we will bring it. We must end."

Her words shivered across the open temple, ruffling their minds with possibility and anticipation.

Violet Commune and Blue agreed to work together after that. Nayeli rarely spoke at council meetings, but it was a tactic she exercised so that when she did speak, she held their attention.

"Master-Wife, where are we going?" the small child in front of her asked, and Nayeli was brought back to the present moment. He wore a yellow shift dress that his frame barely filled—a garment that held the echoes of its previous owners in the split seams and fraying edges.

"I'm going to show you the orb."

Chah gasped and held up his hand to his mouth. Nayeli saw the blisters there. He had been working hard.

"The orb, Master-Wife? Not even some of the Ancients have seen the orb."

"Well, I don't like to show it to everyone. It is very precious."

They reached Nayeli's private quarters. These too she had expanded, absorbing the land where her hut had been to create an annex for her personal experiments and her sleeping quarters.

She unlocked the door with a heavy metal key and pushed it open. The metallic smell of blood permeated the air like a welcome kiss. She lit the gas lamp, illuminating vials of every blood color congealing in their glass tombs on the wall. Her carving tools lay stacked on the wooden desk in the center of the room along with reams of notes. Metal structures, half-built, protruded from wooden crates in the corner. The gas lamp darted out shadows as she moved through the space.

"Chah, hand me that box on the second shelf."

The box was a little heavy for him to handle, but there were no grunts of effort, just the unblinking gaze of devotion as the box was handed over.

Nayeli withdrew a second key, a smaller key, and unlocked the box. Inside lay a large bead of black obsidian. She carefully held it out into the lamplight so the grooves in the rock's surface could be seen.

"This was our prophet's orb. He worked hard to claim it, succeeding at the Zwina Academy before they expelled him. It is nearly four hundred years old."

"The runes, they're so small."

"Indeed, it took three generations to transcribe them onto the texts you work off today. It took a generation before that to understand what each sign did."

"Why did they draw them on the orb? Why not do what we do?"

Nayeli smiled. "Because they were foolish. The mainlanders believe runes to be sacred. That one must earn the knowledge to wield them. They believe that the world needs balance."

"And we don't?" Chah said uncertainly.

Nayeli laughed bitterly. "No, Chah, there is no balance in this world. It must be burned down. Balance comes later, once death has taken its fill. The world must be sacrificed so that we can live as Gods."

Chah reached out to touch the orb, but Nayeli snatched it away from the light.

"This is more precious than you can ever imagine."

Chah hung his head low, chastised.

"It is the reason we can go to war, do you understand that?" Nayeli said.

Chah nodded.

"On the mainland they call these signs 'deathcraft,'" Nayeli mused, running her fingers over the grooves in the rock. "I have a better word for them—battlecraft."

"Battlecraft," Chah whispered.

"The Ending Fire comes." Nayeli shut the box with a snap.

CHAPTER THIRTY

NAYELI

My people, go forth and find a new land. Do not let this exile stop our purpose. Kabut is watching. Kabut is waiting. Bring forth the last battle and purge the world of the nonbelievers.

—Last words of the prophet of the Zalaam,
recorded prior to his execution.

Nayeli had promised the council she would find the Child of Fire; without them the war would not begin. Could not begin. The truth of it had been preserved in their history, passed down from the prophet and in their spoken prayers:

A Child of Fire whose blood will blaze,
Will cleanse the world in eight nights, eight days,
Eight bloods lend strength to lead the charge
And eradicate the infidel, only Gods emerge,
Ready we will be, when the Ending Fire comes,
When the Child of Fire brings the Battle Drum,
The Battle Drum,

The Battle Drum,
Ready we will be, for war will come.

At first, she began her search in Yellow Commune. Though there was little foretold of the Child of Fire, Nayeli believed she would know when she saw them. After all, she had known with absolute certainty that she was the Wife—she must recognize her Child when it came.

But the children in Yellow Commune had not been any different from the snotty, dribbling mess of regular children. Despite the hopeful look in their parents' eyes as they presented them to Nayeli, there was nothing special about any of the yellow-blooded children.

In Green Commune, on the west of the isles, Nayeli had been welcomed with a singing procession of children. Their screeching was enough to send her running to Orange Commune without looking back. Over her dead body would the Child of Fire *sing*.

The orange-blooded had set up a feast for Nayeli. Close as they were to the only major port of the Volcane Isles, their food was the freshest. With each dish they presented another child to Nayeli to inspect, but none of them seemed inclined to be the Child.

"What are you looking for exactly?" Mira, the Violet Commune leader, had asked Nayeli quietly, albeit pertinently. Violet-bloods, always so curious.

"I will know them when I see them," Nayeli had replied ominously.

But by the time she had seen all the indigo-blooded children in her fifth commune that day, Nayeli was beginning to doubt herself. She left them and their incessant posturing behind her.

It was Red Commune that got her really riled. The red-blooded weren't a big community, having not been part of the original settlers on the land like the first few communes, but they had a righteousness bred into them.

"You will find the Child here," the leader said. "Child of Fire" had been interpreted in many ways, but every red-blooded believed it would be one of them, given the color of their blood. They thought the "fire" could be a metaphor for red.

Nayeli conceded that maybe they were right. They had fifteen children in their settlement. The leader had lined them up proudly and called their names as Nayeli inspected them. She asked them questions—those that were old enough to speak—but still felt nothing. Kabut had always made his will clear to her, and she didn't doubt he'd do it now if she saw the Child of Fire.

She left the commune frustrated and miserable. The blue-bloods were hostile to her, and many refused to present their children, but eventually the leader got the children in line—grubby with dust from the mines in Violet Commune. They had even fewer children here. Nayeli dismissed them without talking to them.

Finally, she got to Clear Commune. The transparent-blooded. They were the smallest commune on the island and only had the one child. The leader presented it swaddled within the type of sheer fabric the commune preferred.

"She was born two weeks ago," the leader said, revealing a tongue-size gap between their front teeth that Nayeli thought would have once been endearing on a small child, but on an adult just made them appear unkempt.

Nayeli was sick of looking at children. Her tour of the Volcane Isles had eaten into her important work in the Foundry. But still she mustered her lips into a twist that was somewhere between a grimace and a smile.

"Let me hold them."

The small brown baby cooed and gurgled in her arms, and the soft silk of its blanket warmed Nayeli's chest as she clutched the child close. It was the first time that Nayeli wondered whether her own baby, if given the chance to survive, would have been the Child she was looking for.

Tears began to well in her eyes as Nayeli looked into the gray eyes of the baby. Those watching thought they saw the Wife weep in joy for the blessing of life, and love swelled in their hearts for her. Some thought the tears were a confirmation that this child, the only child of Clear Commune, was the one they foretold.

But only Nayeli knew her tears were a product of the effort she wrought on her muscles, clenching them tight so as not to crush the baby under her fingers.

The Child of Fire was not on the Volcane Isles.

NAYELI WASN'T SURE what she was going to do. On her journey back from the Clear Commune she was plagued with doubts that rarely afflicted her. The commune leaders would have surely heard by now that she had failed. The Child wasn't coming this generation.

She took a small fishing boat along the coast of the isles to return to Yellow Commune. It was the island farthest south. The leader of Clear Commune offered to escort her, but Nayeli needed the respite from other people. She found the subtle movements that conversation required loathsome, but she feared nothing—not even Kabut himself—more than *small talk.*

Her muscles rippled as she rowed across the shoreline. Her time in the Foundry had built a foundation of muscles underneath her scars and the rowing was soothing.

The open temple came into view, and Nayeli turned the nose of the vessel toward it. She tied the little boat up and made her way up the steps to the endless flame. She could see it had recently been fed, the flames bright red, the wood smoking upward through the open roof and to the sky beyond.

Nayeli fell to her knees beside it. There she sat for three nights and prayed. The council tried to convene while she fasted, but she ignored them until they went away and left her to her prayers. She got to know the footsteps of the people who fed the fire, the girl in the morning, the old man at night.

"Kabut, my husband, know that I am your servant first. Advise me on my failures, show me wherein lies the truth among calamity. Know that our path is clear: we will end and we will begin again."

Nayeli trusted in her God so completely that she would have stayed there for innumerable days until she wasted away, for if death was what Kabut required as a toll, she would give it gladly. But it was on the third day that he came to her. Not as clearly as on that night three years ago, but it was his touch all the same.

"Wife, you must come. There has been word of your brother."

Nayeli closed her eyes and blocked out the messenger's calls. A few people had come to join in prayer or to tempt her from her vigil.

"Wife." Someone touched her arm, but still Nayeli refused to acknowledge them. The messenger whispered urgently in her ear, their hot breath smelling faintly of chicken. "Inansi, there's been word from Inansi. He's alive."

The messenger pressed something into her hand. It was cold, sharp.

Nayeli opened her eyes and looked down at the shining black spider brooch with her name inscribed on the inside. The matching one sat on her breast with the name of her brother written on the inside.

Inansi was alive.

PART FOUR

RECLAIM

Soon everyone will know our name. We have hidden away for too long.

My husband urges us to fight so ready the army.

We will win and we will begin. The Zalaam are coming.

—Letter from the Wife, sent to the Volcane Isles by messenger

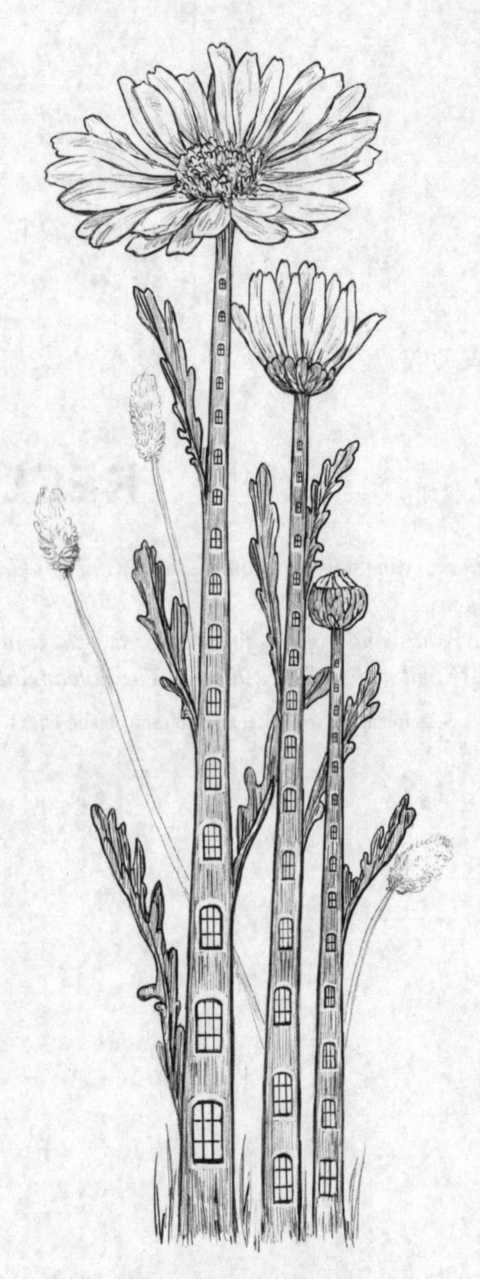

Sketch of the Blooming Towers
drawn by Elder Petra, 237 b.w.

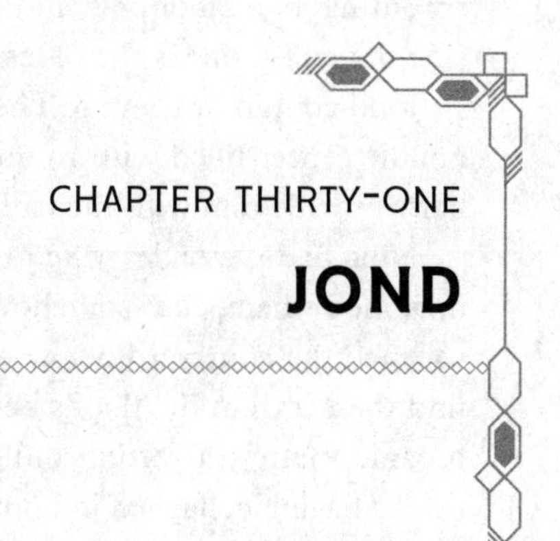

CHAPTER THIRTY-ONE

JOND

It takes three years to sustain the open wound required to use an orb. Each engraving of a rune includes small spikes to perforate any scabs the body may have developed. A tincture of camblo root is recommended. A few drops into the palm each night will deaden the nerves, prevent infection, and counter healing.

—*On Orb Power* by Vulo Ah-Ro

Jond stood at the top of the stone wall that surrounded the Zwina Academy. The walls that protected the citadel were also the cause of its destruction. They cradled the rainfall like two cupped hands flooding every street and building as far as Jond could see. He frantically searched for life, his eyes determined but his knees giving up. He fell to the ground beside Sylah.

Niha had told Jond of the wonders of the Zwina Academy, of the Blooming Towers that grew from the center of the city.

"You're telling me the Blooming Towers are *real* flowers?" Elder Petra had referred to them in the diary, but Jond hadn't considered for a second that they were real plants.

Niha smiled with the memory Jond couldn't see. "Yes: the wonders of the first charter. The legendary Councillor Ubba grew the towers over the course of their lifetime. They have stood for seven hundred years. There are three towers altogether, one sprouting, one blooming, and one just emerging from its bud. Inside the tallest one is the oldest library on the continent."

Jond couldn't believe it. The building was really a flower with a hollow center filled with rooms and books. Books that would finally provide him with the truth of his ancestors.

Niha had never described the color of the petals but Jond had imagined them red somehow. A beautiful rich crimson that warmed the courtyard below when the sun shone. He strained to find the petals in the floods below. All he saw were the remains of organic matter, a rotting mulch of brown and gray, the hollow center having collapsed in on itself.

"It's all gone, all of it." Jond wondered about the books, the truth that he longed to find there. Then he looked to Sylah and thought of her salvation, the healing he had hoped to give her.

"The rain, it's stopped. Maybe we can find something in the medical supplies that can help," Niha said, though his heart wasn't in it.

They sat side by side watching the water slowly retreat and the buildings emerge from the murky depths of the flood. Jond hung his legs over the edge of the wall and saw the distance grow and grow, until eventually the cobbled street appeared, the pink marble gleaming in a watery sunlight.

"Let's go," Jond said and picked up Sylah for what he expected to be the last time. She was so much lighter despite how sodden she was.

Jond had to stop twice in the journey down the steps. Niha was waiting at the bottom to transfer Sylah's load.

"Her breathing is really shallow," Jond said.

Niha's lips thinned as he leaned in to listen to the rattle of her breath.

"Let's hurry, the hospital is in the center of the Academy. Hopefully there'll be something we can use."

Jond refused to see the empty houses, the broken windows, or the looted stalls; instead he saw the citadel how he had imagined it. Bursting with color and culture, languages trilling on the wind and laughter humming through the streets.

"Over here," Niha said, and Jond noticed for the first time the tears pouring down his face. He had studied here. This had once been his home.

The pink cobblestones were smeared with the debris and mud of the flash flood.

Sylah coughed. "Jond?"

"Sylah, Sylah, we're going to get you better, we're at the Academy." Jond rushed to say everything he wanted before she slipped back into unconsciousness.

"This way. Let's hope there's something salvageable," Niha said. He led them through the broken glass doors of a domed structure that had once been an infirmary. The ground floor was decimated.

"Let's go to the higher floors."

They climbed up two flights of stairs before finding anything worth using.

"Put her down over there, no, not there, here, wait, let me put down a blanket." Niha spread out a threadbare sheet he'd found. "I've found some antiseptic and some pain blockers, this is a good start, boy, a good start indeed. Why don't you go look for food while I work on her?"

Jond didn't want to part with Sylah.

"It's best that she's out cold for this as it's going to hurt some. I'm going to give her some sedatives. Go, there's nothing to do here." Somewhere Niha had found some latex gloves, and Jond wondered where the rubber tree plantations were on this side of the world.

"I won't be long," Jond said, hovering by the doorway.

"Go. But if it starts to rain get back here quick. We're high enough that it looks like the flood doesn't get here."

Jond nodded and looked to the sky. It was clear again, a soft blue.

JOND WENT STRAIGHT toward the stumps of the Blooming Towers. He wanted to see them up close. The stench of rotting plant matter reached his nose well before the sight of the remains did. There was only one stalk that hadn't completely turned to gray soup. Jond approached it with a hand over his nose, his footsteps light though they still squelched on the decomposing remains.

The stem was gargantuan, as round as the great veranda in the Wardens' Keep. He closed his eyes and saw the dappled light the petals would have made. He could even feel the warmth of it on his cheeks. When he opened his eyes, he half expected the Blooming Towers to be standing, but no, this was no illusion, they would never stand again.

He could see the congealed stairs that once spiraled through the hollow center of the flower, and with cautious steps Jond made his way toward them. He reached the stem and placed his hand to vault over it, but his fingers slipped through what remained of the structure and the section in front of him collapsed in ooze.

"Gross." He gagged as he flung the gelatinous remains off his fingers. The collapsed wall had made an opening large enough for Jond to get through. He was careful not to touch any more of the stem as he made his way toward the stairs. They were harder than the outer plant, suggesting they hadn't been exposed to the rain as long. He stood on the first one, testing its strength, and was surprised to find it was reinforced with bark.

Jond knew it was foolish, knew that he should be getting back to Sylah, but he wanted to see what remained of the council chamber. There were sections of Elder Petra's diary that Jond had read over and over, and the description of the council chamber had been one of them.

THE COUNCIL CHAMBER was in the roots of the flower and my guide led me down on steps made of bark. As I entered the room, I became aware of my attire and how drab the cotton milled from the fields of Jin-Noon looked among the rich silks of their land.

The five councillors are the greatest minds in the world. Or so they said. They have studied their professions so completely that all they had left to do was teach.

Five councillors. Not four like Niha had said. For some reason, Niha had lied, and Jond wanted to find out why.

A sweeter smell merged with the rotting plant, a smell of earth and sap. There was more structure to the rooms as he descended, and though the light grew dim, Jond could feel his way down the corridor toward what had to be the council chamber. He tried the door.

"Monkey's bollocks." It was locked. "The whole city is massacred by floods, and they lock *this*." He felt his way around the doorframe. It was water-damaged and primed for breaking. He leveled a kick at it; nothing happened. With a sigh he inserted his stylus and pierced his skin. It was risky using bloodwerk with the building already in disrepair; any use of force could bring the whole thing down. He drew the bloodwerk runes quickly, the doorframe cracking instantly beneath their force. The door burst off its hinges and fell flat on the ground. The vibration of its collapse reverberated up the walls. Jond heard another side of the stem collapse above him.

"Well, I'm not getting out that way." But that was a problem for later.

Jond stepped into darkness. His hand groped the wall for a runelamp lever until he found a small switch. He turned it, and a small hiss of gas escaped before a spark ignited the flame. The council chamber was bathed in the glow of the gas lamp. This new dim form of lighting was alien to Jond. He tried to peer at how it was made but the light hurt his eyes.

Blinking away the illumination, he turned to look at the chamber beyond and saw, like Elder Petra had seen, the councillors in his mind's eye sitting around the wooden table, grown from the very roots under his feet.

There were five carvings, one on each of the backs of the five chairs. Jond ran his finger over the closest one.

"The first charter is the law of growth." The carving was of a small sprouting seed. "The power to grow what is given."

The second charter was an intertwined rope. "The second charter is the law of connection. The power of mind communication."

"The third charter is the law of healing, putting back together what was once broken." Carved on the third chair was a beating heart, the arteries embalmed in wood.

"The fourth charter is that of presence. Flighting from one place to another." There were two figures carved identically side by side.

"And the fifth charter . . ." He stopped by the final chair. Jond hissed as a splinter pierced his skin. Angry slashes gouged the wood rendering the image and words unrecognizable. He sat down, trying to read what had been carved away.

There was a sound behind him, and Jond turned in time to see the point of a blade leveled at his chest.

"How did you enter this chamber?"

Jond tilted his head around the blade and took in the hooded figure of his assailant. Her voice was light, well-balanced, like the dagger in her hand. She was tall, wearing sheaths of shiny-looking material in tones of gray. Water rolled off the waxed surface and onto the floor. It must have started raining again.

"I broke down the door."

"I can see that." She flashed the blade to the door on the floor. "But how?"

Jond shrugged. "Don't feel the need to tell you while you have a blade pointed at me."

"I will never talk unarmed to one of the Zalaam."

"I'm not one of the Zalaam," Jond said. He propped himself on the armrest of the nearest chair.

"Yet you sit on their prophet's chair." She pointed to the chair belonging to the fifth charter.

The prophet of the Zalaam? There was so much Jond still didn't know. But he didn't want his assailant to figure out his ignorance.

Jond shrugged and crossed his ankles. "Closest one."

The person smirked.

Jond tried a different tactic. "Now I think *you* are one of the Zalaam to know so much about the prophet."

The hood dipped backward, and the woman spat on the ground by Jond's feet before retreating into the shadow of her mouth scarf. Jond caught the sharpness of a long nose and black skin a shade darker than his. "You know not of what you speak." She let the scarf fall beneath her chin, revealing more of her fox-like features.

"Look, I am a traveler, and I came here to see if there was anything worth salvaging," Jond said. "Besides, you're holding that dagger wrong. That grip would do more damage to you than me."

The woman hissed and spun. She was there in the doorway one second, and then she was standing by Jond, the blade pressed against his neck before the end of her hiss reached his ears.

"Do you still think this would cause more damage to me than you?" she whispered in his ear. He smelled the mint on her breath.

"You're a student of the fourth charter," Jond said. He heard her smile, her lips pulling over sharp teeth.

"I am the *councillor* of the fourth charter."

Jond felt a flutter of fear. He had underestimated her so totally.

"Can you help us? Can you help my friend? She's dying, we need to get her medical help. Please, if you can take her to the councillor of healing, I will do anything you want. Please."

This change of tone from Jond made the councillor pause.

"Tell me how you got in here."

"I used bloodwerk."

"What is that?" The blade dug into Jond's neck creating a hairline cut.

"The inkwell, the cuff on my arm, it lets me write with my blood. I used it to open the door."

The blade dropped to the woman's side.

"You're from the Drylands."

"The Wardens' Empire," Jond corrected her, and she laughed.

"So, you're Zalaam after all."

"What?" Jond spun to face her, but she didn't answer. It was then that he saw the orb in her palm. It covered the wound that he knew remained open underneath. It was surrounded by a circlet of silver that kept it in place. The orb itself was metal and finely carved with minuscule runes. She saw him staring and slipped her hand behind her back.

"I will help your friend, if you show me how you . . . bloodwerk."

"Fine."

"Promise me."

"I promise."

"Then show me the way."

JOND LED THEM back through the deserted streets toward the infirmary.

"Where are the rest of the councillors? Do they live here?" Jond asked.

The woman didn't answer.

"Can you tell me your name at least?"

Nothing.

Jond cracked his knuckles. "Fine, well, I'm Jond Alnua."

"May peace uphold you, Jond Alnua."

"And you are?"

"The councillor of the fourth charter." Jond thought he heard her laugh, but he wasn't sure as the face scarf was hooked back over her ears.

They entered the broken infirmary doors, and Jond led them up the steps to the second level. Niha was bent over Sylah's body and didn't look up when Jond entered.

"Did you find any food?" Niha asked.

"No, I found something better, though."

"Dry clothes?"

"Step away from the patient, outcast," the councillor growled to Niha.

He jumped up quicker than Jond thought he could.

"Councillor." Niha bowed his head.

"Was not part of your punishment exile from the citadel?" She rounded on Niha, who tripped over a broken chair but steadied himself.

"You know each other?" Jond said, swinging his gaze between

them. Despite their age difference, the contrast in power was clear. Niha cowered under her gaze.

"This student was expelled from the Academy ten years ago for trying to steal rather than earn their knowledge."

"Ten years ago?" She was older than Jond thought. "How do you remember his face?"

"I remember his face because it was my orb he tried to steal. Niha, outcast of the third charter. Healing was never enough for you."

Niha's wide shoulders slumped. "The patient, she needed help. We were captured by the Shariha . . ."

Sylah coughed, and it was a wet gurgle. Jond ran to her and as he did her body began to spasm.

"Her vital organs are shutting down," Niha said to Jond's questioning glance.

"Please," Jond said, tears streaming down his face as he held Sylah's quivering body. "Please can you take her to the councillor of the third charter? Please help me get her healed."

The councillor looked at Jond's devastated face and nodded once. "You remember our promise."

"Yes, I'll do anything."

"Then head south toward the Truna Hills. Look up, and there you will find us. I can only take one other. Niha, outcast of the third charter, you must come before the council for breaching your banishment." The councillor brandished her left hand, the black orb glinting in the weak sunlight. Jond watched as she rolled the orb over Sylah's brow in incremental movements that created a pattern of runes. Jond saw the blood there was violet. He gasped but the sound clogged in his throat as both Sylah and the councillor disappeared.

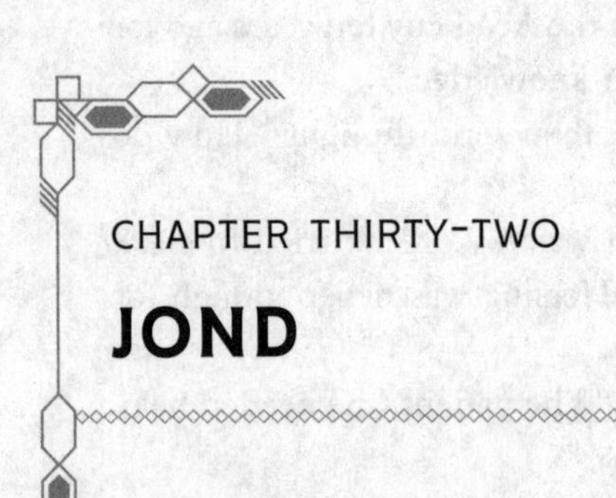

CHAPTER THIRTY-TWO

JOND

Those found to be practicing deathcraft will be executed under the queen's law. Only those with completed orbs and a license from the Zwina Academy have permission to compose runes.

—*The Decree of Deathcraft* issued by Queen Karanomo

"Will she be safe?" Jond asked the question for the third time. They had left the walls of the Academy and were making their way to the Truna Hills.

"Yes, the councillors will protect her," Niha grumbled. He had spoken even less than usual in the last few strikes of their trek.

"What will they do to you?" Jond asked.

Niha shrugged and looked down. "I'm not sure."

"You don't need to come with me. You can leave now."

"I'm not running anymore."

"Fine," Jond grunted. After a moment he asked the question that had been turning over in his mind. "You told me there were four councillors, but in the council chamber, there were five seats. Why?"

"You went to the council chamber?" Niha asked, surprised.

"Yes, it was where the fourth charter councillor found me."

"Kara." Niha said the name with defeat. "Her name is Kara. And yes, you're right, there were once five councillors, but I'll let them tell you that story. As graduates we are sworn to secrecy, it is not my truth to tell."

"More secrets . . ." Jond murmured. "How much farther, do you think?"

"I'm not sure, I have only traveled to the Truna Hills once, many years ago." Niha breathed out sharply. "But the councillor's power is limited; no one can travel all that far with the fourth charter. A few leagues at most, less with a second person."

"Doesn't sound worth stealing to me."

"And yet, I would do it all over again. There is nothing that I would not have done to see my love one more time. Is that not true for you?"

Jond didn't trust himself to voice the words, but he nodded. *Yes, there is nothing I would not do for you, Sylah.*

The ground beneath their feet was thick with mud. Though the floods had clearly brought destruction to this part of the land, there were pockets of beauty too. They came across a lake, teeming with fish. Unaware of the rising water of their home, the fish wriggled with happy delight, casting flashes of color in bright yellows and greens. Large birds, which Jond didn't know the names of, swooped low, filling their beaks with shoals.

And though nature bloomed in the water and skies, it withered on the land.

Jond lost count of the number of dead animals they passed. At first Niha named them: "That's a mongoose . . . a squirrel . . . a forest wolf cub . . ." Eventually he went silent, tears prickling his eyes.

After a time he said, "There is something so heartbreaking about seeing an innocent animal's home displaced," Niha said. "The people . . . you can explain, reason with them, get them to safety . . . but an animal is like a child. You cannot explain. You cannot cajole a wild animal."

"But why are there floods? Why is this happening?"

"Balance. Something is wrong with the balance of things." Niha paused. "Did you hear that?"

"No."

"Listen."

Mewl.

Jond heard it that time.

"Wait—" But it was too late. Niha dashed away looking for the animal in distress.

Jond ground his teeth, anxious to see Sylah, to see she was okay. He ran after Niha and found him bent over, his knees in the mud.

"Niha, we need to keep going," Jond said, reaching out to him.

He peered over to see what Niha had found. Cradled in his large hands was a small kitten, completely covered in mud. Jond could see it wasn't going to survive much longer. It was too small, and its mother and the rest of its litter lay dead on the ground.

"It's a sand cat," Niha whispered. "They're so rare."

"Great, good. Okay, now can we go?"

Niha turned incredulously to Jond. "I can't just leave her here. She'll die."

"She's already dead." Jond had learned this lesson early on as a child. The memory was a deadened nerve from his childhood.

"Jond, hurry up, we need to collect the firewood and get back before Papa gets home."

Jond ignored Sylah's calls. Because something else was calling louder. Though its tweets were small, it held Jond's attention.

The fledgling struggled to stay upright. And Jond eased it into his palm.

"You'll be okay, little one. You'll be okay. I've got you." Jond abandoned his task and began to look for the chick's nest in the trees.

"Jond, what are you doing?" Sylah demanded. She was ten years old, but already she towered over him despite being two years his junior.

"Shh," he said, trying to soothe the baby bird. "I found a kori fledgling."

"Let me see."

He cracked open his palms and revealed the beautiful blue feathers of his new ward.

"I can't find its nest, so I think I'll take it home and look after it."

"I don't think Papa will let you."

"Well, don't tell him then, Sylah."

It was then that they heard the shifting sand of an eru cantering through the desert. Azim was home. Jond scrambled to collect the firewood he'd already cut into the crook of one arm. Sylah moved to help him, panic written across their faces. They didn't want a beating that day.

They made it back to the barn but Azim noticed they were late. When he asked them why they had taken so long to complete a basic task, the bird had been the one to give them away. It chirped in Jond's closed fist.

"Show me," Azim said.

Jond opened his hands reluctantly.

"Go put it back where you found it. It is already dead."

"No, it isn't, it's alive—" The slap shook Jond's teeth.

"It is dead. You altered nature. Without its mother it will die. Go now."

Jond had cried as he put the little bird back where he had found it.

He had cried harder when he found its cold body the next day.

"I will not leave it," Niha said.

"Fine, but I'm not stopping so you can feed it, we need to keep going."

Jond didn't check to see if Niha was following; he just marched straight ahead, the birds above chirping.

"I NEED TO urinate," Niha announced.

They had just started the climb up the Truna Hills. The ground turned thick with moss, and Jond's feet sprang as he walked. The hills weren't like the cultivated grass of Jin-Gernomi; in fact this land was closer to a mountain than a hill. It rolled out across the horizon reaching high peaks that Jond hoped he wouldn't have to scale.

"Thank you for the announcement."

"I need you to take her." Niha held up the kitten. He had been cooing to the creature for the last strike as if his words would somehow keep it alive.

"Leave her on the ground."

"No, she needs warmth. Just hold her for a few minutes, please."

Jond sighed and looked up at the clouds that now filled the sky. It had started to rain *again*. "Fine, but hurry up, we must be nearly there."

The kitten's fur was claggy with mud, and Jond scowled as he tucked it into his shirt.

"That warm enough for you?" The kitten looked up at him with wide, fearful eyes. "Stop that, it's not my fault you're going to die soon."

Mewl.

She licked his chest hair and Jond screeched. "Stop that, you rascal, that tickles." She did it again, and he realized she was drinking the rainwater off him.

"Rascal, here." Jond held out his hands and cupped some of the rain. He offered it to the little cat. She looked at him, still clinging to his chest, before reaching forward, sniffing it and then darting her pink little tongue in and out to drink.

"Good little Rascal."

"Rascal?" Niha had returned and was watching the exchange with a bemused expression.

"It's as good a name as any," Jond said. "Until she dies, that is. Do you want to take her back?"

"No, she looks quite comfortable."

Jond looked down. She had stopped drinking and had settled both paws over the edge of his shirt, her eyes closing in sleep.

"Fine. Let's keep going."

They walked a little farther, the rain getting worse. Every so often, Jond would look up, searching for the buildings the councillor had promised.

"She lied."

"She didn't lie. They'll be here somewhere," Niha said.

"Where? I don't see a building for leagues, just these mountains wherever I look." Jond looked down at the ground with a scowl, sick of the same shade of green.

Wait, that's odd.

A deep red dust covered the moss in front of them. Jond bent down to get a closer look.

"Jond."

"What?"

"Jond, look."

Niha was pointing upward. There was a break in the clouds above, and Jond saw what Niha was referring to.

Domed structures pushed through the sky above them held up by thin towers. So thin Jond marveled at how the structures were staying upright. There were twenty of them at least, all strung together by swaying bridges that moved in the wind.

"So clever, so very clever." Niha breathed out heavily. "They created mushrooms to live in."

"Mushrooms?"

"They're a type of fungi that people eat. They're quick-growing and thrive in wet conditions. The powder on the ground, it's spores from the cap above."

"You're telling me the councillors of the greatest academy in the world live in a type of fungus?"

Niha's grin was wide.

"That's exactly what I'm telling you. Come on, let's go. I think I can see a pulley lift on that central stalk."

Niha set off at a run.

"Well, Rascal, I think we're about to climb some fungus."

The kitten opened a bleary eye and chirped.

"Yes, I agree, this world is fucking wild."

The closer Jond got to the mushrooms, the less inclined he was to get in the lift. The stalks were gray, mottled things that smelled like earth with a sweetness that lingered in the back of his throat.

They weren't as wide as the Blooming Towers, a fraction of their size really. Jond estimated they were the diameter of his height. He reached out to touch them and recoiled. Rascal grumbled deeper into his shirt.

"That is disgusting. It's soft, like skin. And spongy . . . you eat these things?"

"Yes, you've eaten many on the journey. I often put them in the broths we fed to Sylah," Niha said.

"Oh, I thought those were snails."

"They were, sometimes."

Jond shuddered, more repulsed by the idea of eating the fungus than the mollusk.

"Shall we?" Niha opened the metal cage by the side of the stalk. Jond had never been in a crank-operated lift before, as the ones in the empire used bloodwerk to harness the forces required to move. This one had a lever-and-pulley system that looked like a lot of work.

"Let's go."

They took it in turns to turn the lever. The mushrooms were tall, and neither of them were even close to full strength. It had been a long journey.

Niha took them the final distance. The lift pushed up through the ribbed gills of the underside of the mushroom into a hollow cavern.

Jond's pulse began to race. He hoped Sylah survived the healing. He didn't know what he would do if she didn't.

Rascal pressed a cold nose to Jond's collarbone.

"Stop that," Jond hissed at her. She didn't shy away, just blinked up at him with wide eyes.

"We're here." Niha opened the cage door and stepped out on to the spongy platform.

They were in the center of the mushroom's cap. Above them gas lights swung from the small breeze created by the hole where the lift had come up. The earthy smell wasn't as overwhelming as Jond had feared, but the texture of the floor under his feet wasn't pleasant. But at least it was dry and warm.

A figure in the same gray metallic material as Kara was there to greet them. He wore his blond hair long, in soft waves that were highlighted a strange green. As Jond got nearer he realized it was a type of paint, layered into the hair like makeup.

"Welcome to the City of Rain. May peace uphold you." The

man held his palm out wide in greeting, revealing a circular wound, empty without an orb. "I'm to escort you to your rooms; follow me."

The man took a step back and Jond rounded on him.

"Sylah, the woman, is she all right? Did she survive?"

"I have been informed that the healers are still working on her. You will be updated of her status as soon as possible."

Jond let out a shuddering breath.

She's still alive.

"May peace uphold you, Lune. You are still a student, I see?" Niha stepped into the light, greeting the man.

"Niha? Is it truly you?" Lune's eyebrows shot upward. "I heard an outcast was coming, I didn't know it was you."

They clapped hands, making Rascal jump. Jond stroked the top of her head absently.

"I hope our rooms have water and a change of clothes." Niha laughed.

"And food, good friend. Come, this way."

THE TWO MEN huddled together as they walked ahead. Jond was so mesmerized by the environment around him that he only dipped in and out of their conversation. The ceiling of the mushroom was a mottled brown, like aging skin pulled taut. The corridor they walked down was flanked by walls that had been grown upward from the flesh of the floor.

At first, Jond thought he was imagining the breeze, but then he saw the sunlight coming through a small arched doorway up ahead. Through it he could see a bridge swaying in the wind.

"I'm not getting on there . . ." Jond growled, but the two men ignored him, so engrossed were they in each other's stories.

". . . six weeks, we had to evacuate quite quickly . . ."

". . . the mushrooms, ingenious . . ."

". . . fewer students than we would have liked . . ."

". . . and the Zalaam . . . they are growing stronger . . . war is coming."

"Zalaam?" Jond drew level with Lune and Niha. "Did you say the Zalaam?"

"Yes, the Zalaam." They had reached the archway, and Lune paused in his telling. "You'll need to harness yourself to get across the bridge when the wind is this bad. Here, take these belts."

Lune pulled them off the hooks on the wall and helped Niha and Jond strap them to their waists.

"Why's your chest moving . . ." Lune started, staring at the gap in Jond's shirt. Rascal popped out her dirty face. "Oh, hello there, little one."

"She's his." Jond tilted a head toward Niha, who only laughed.

"Always saving creatures, that's the Niha I used to know," Lune said with a fond expression. "Shall I send for some goat's milk?"

"No, no, she's not going to survive," Jond said quickly, and Niha rolled his eyes.

"Right . . ." Lune said. "Let's get going. Use the clip on the front of the belt to attach yourself to the top of the bridge."

"Why didn't you just make the bridge out of metal?"

Lune looked at Jond as if he were a fool. "Because it's too rigid: the mushrooms move in the wind, and the bridges must too."

"Right. Obvious," Jond muttered darkly.

The three of them crept out into the gale force of the pouring rain. The droplets were flung at them so fast they felt like pellets. The ground below was flooding, rising slowly up the mushroom's stalks, but still far enough away to not reach them.

Jond clipped himself onto the rope bridge and slowly shuffled along, plank by wooden plank.

"Argh." Jond slipped on the wood, slick as it was. His hand went instinctively to his chest, clinging to the little creature that resided there.

She might be about to die, but that doesn't mean I have to kill her, he reasoned with himself.

The bridge swung and he veered off the edge, the harness saving his life. Niha and Lune stopped and clung onto the rope, waiting for it to stabilize before they continued on.

When they reached the other side after what felt like an entire strike, Jond panted out, "Please tell me we don't have to go on another bridge."

Rainwater dribbled down from his hair into his mouth.

"No, your rooms are in this mushroom." Lune smiled. "You'll also find waterproofs like mine in your rooms. I recommend you wear them."

They walked a little farther through the plant. It was similarly structured with a corridor down the center and walls on either side.

"Here we are."

Jond looked for the doorway. It wasn't until Lune separated a section of thin, fleshy wall with his hand that Jond realized *that* was the opening.

"Through there, you'll find everything you need. I recommend you don't do any wandering. There are over thirty-five mushrooms and some of them are yet to grow into stability. It is easy to fall to your death. The councillors will come for you when they need you."

With that Lune left them.

Jond pushed himself through the limp skin-like opening and shuddered.

"It's like being birthed all over again."

Niha laughed. "It is ingenious how they've grown walls into rooms. Ingenious, I say."

Jond found a gas lamp and it flickered to life. The room was small, but full of everything he desperately needed.

There were two washbasins, two beds covered in thick sheep's wool, and a table full of food. Jond ran for the latter.

"You stay there." Jond set Rascal on the side of the table, her dirty paws leaving muddy prints as she tried to get back into his shirt. "No, stay. I need to eat."

Niha sat down opposite Jond. "Why don't you give her a bit of meat, she might settle."

Jond shot him a scathing look. Rascal was *not* his pet.

"Fine." Jond gave her a small piece of white meat, maybe chicken? And left her to it while he began to take his fill.

"You finished that already?" Niha said in a cooing voice. "Jond, give her more."

"You give her more. She's not my problem."

Jond looked away from her pleading eyes. Niha sighed and gave in, giving Rascal a few more ribbons of meat and eventually a slice of cheese that Jond had taken a liking to.

"I wanted to eat that," Jond growled. "And you gave it to the dying cat."

Niha paused in his stroking of Rascal and looked at him. "Why is it that you're so determined for this cat to die?"

"I don't want it to die. It's just that it *will* die."

"And how do you know that?"

Jond shrugged.

Niha sighed. "Let me rephrase the question. Why are you afraid for this cat to live?"

Jond stood, the chair digging into the spongy ground.

"I'm going to wash."

It took a long time for Jond to get all the dirt off him. He wasn't just dirty, he was filthy. They had left him a shaving set, and though it was a strange double-bladed system, he hacked away his beard with only a few mishaps. He looked in the mirror when he was done.

He had always been lean, but now his skin stretched over his wide jaw with a boniness he wasn't used to. Bags of exhaustion layered under his dark eyes. He had pulled his overgrown hair into twists after washing it and they hung over his brow.

I look like I did when I arrived in Nar-Ruta for the Aktibar.

Before the Aktibar he had trained with Master Inansi for years. Every few mooncycles Inansi would send a new tutor to perfect the skills he had lost through the injury he had sustained at the Sanctuary. He touched the runebullet scars on his chest. They never faded, nor did he want them to.

But there was something he'd had then that he wasn't sure he had anymore: belief. In himself. In the cause.

What is the cause anymore?

He scowled and turned away from the mirror. The sheepskin bed was calling.

Jond got under the covers. He hadn't spoken to Niha since he'd asked that ridiculous question, though he'd heard him talk to Rascal as he gave her a bath in the leftover water. As soon as his head touched the pillows he heard the soft padding of feet on the blanket.

Jond looked up in confusion. Was the sheepskin moving?

Then he saw the bright blue eyes immersed in a dandelion-puff face. Rascal was completely white without a streak of dirt on her. The only color was the pink of her nose and the azure of her gaze. She began to knead his stomach, purring softly.

Niha got under the covers of his own bed and didn't look Jond's way. Jond gave Rascal a tentative pet before he spoke.

"I didn't come to Tenio willingly."

Niha turned in his bed but didn't respond.

Jond continued, "I was sent here in exile. She . . . the person who made the decision, she couldn't execute me in cold blood, but the expectation that I wouldn't survive on Tenio . . . was there. I began to think it was the nature of things, to let me die here. It's hard sometimes, waiting for death. But if that isn't my purpose, I don't know what is."

"To live, Jond. To live," Niha said before rolling over.

Rascal crawled under the covers and Jond let her.

CHAPTER THIRTY-THREE

SYLAH

Like all laws, the third charter is based on four foundational runes: restore, *to heal what is broken,* harmonize, *to regulate what is erratic,* banish, *to expel the unwanted, and* induce, *to increase what is given.*

But sometimes this still won't be enough, for we can only do what is possible with the power that lies in our blood. We cannot deny death.

—Teachings on the third charter, Zwina Academy

Sylah woke to the sound of a low buzzing in her ear. She swatted it away with an irritated wave, but it continued.

"Jond, will you shut that up?" Her tongue felt swollen and dry, like she had eaten a handful of sand.

Sylah opened her eyes, and reality came slapping down on her like an unannounced shit falling from the sky. The buzzing she had heard was the sound of distant chatter, and it paused as she sat up.

The room she was in was circular, painted a drab gray with speckled dark spots. The two speakers were watching her with worried expressions as she pulled off the flower-scented blankets and stood up.

"Careful. You might be a bit unstable," one of them cried out, reaching for her despite the ten paces between them. The figures were draped in swathes of unstructured shiny fabric that covered their heads. The taller of the two had rolled-up sleeves that exposed muscular forearms and dark skin.

The floor beneath Sylah's feet was springy and cool.

"Who the fuck are you, and where the fuck am I?"

"Polite," a woman who moved with the lightness of running water said. Her accent was clipped, the words sounding strange to Sylah's ears.

"You're in the City of Rain," the other figure said. He lowered his hood revealing an unlined face of about forty years with a cropped afro and large ears that had Sylah wondering if he could pick up Anoor's voice from across the sea.

Anoor. Panic struck her. How long had she been unconscious? Was she too late to save the empire from the throes of the tidewind?

"You'll need to be more specific. Where in the world is the City of Rain?" Sylah stumbled forward, her weak legs buckling like a newborn lamb's.

"The Academy has flooded. You're in its new location."

Sylah clutched the hem of the pale pink nightdress she was wearing.

"You mean to tell me we made it? We actually made it?" She whispered the words quietly to herself. *But not we . . . me.*

"Where's Jond?" Unwelcome panic rising again.

"Who?" the man said.

The woman exhaled with a note of irritation. "Her companion."

"He's safe, he arrived not long ago."

Sylah didn't feel relieved. She looked for a doorway out of the room, but the smooth gray substance circled the space completely.

"Why am I trapped in here?"

"You are not trapped."

Sylah reached one of the walls and tried to beat her weak fists against it. They bounced back, her hands unable to penetrate the substance.

"Let me *out*," she shouted at the two strange people.

"Calm down. You've just been healed," the woman said.

"Who are you? Where am I?"

"I told you, you're in the City of Rain." The man crossed his arms over his chest. "I'm Zenebe. You were brought here to be healed by the Third Councillor."

"Clear as piss." Sylah found herself clenching her fists.

"What do you remember?"

Pain, endless burning pain like her whole body was being branded. She automatically reached for her wrist to run her fingers over the raised brand of the guild of duty, but it was gone.

"My scar . . ." Sylah mumbled and raised her wrist to the light. She ran her thumb over the smooth brown skin.

"You may find old wounds have been healed," Zenebe said.

Sylah thrust her hand down the back of her collar, searching for the raised scar from the wound she had received on the day her family had been murdered. It was gone. The skin where it should have been ached all the way to her heart.

Wide-eyed and a little more terrified than she cared to admit, Sylah turned to Zenebe. "I want to talk to this Third Councillor."

"You're talking to him."

Sylah hesitated, thrown by his gentle smile.

She reached for her hair to settle her mind with the familiarity of her trinkets. But instead of braids, she found soft, conditioned curls tied up in a bun. "Where is my stuff?"

"Pardon?"

"The things in my hair, where did you put them?"

"Don't fret," Zenebe said lightly.

"Fret?" Sylah spat the word. She bent her knees and assumed a fighting stance. But her body gave up beneath her, and she fell to the spongy ground.

Zenebe appeared above her, a frown of concern striking his face. "I told you to be careful." He helped her up, and she tried to swat at him with a Dambe martial-art move. The punches were weak, and he led her to the bed unconcerned.

She collapsed onto the covers.

"I kept your charms here." Zenebe moved to the side of the bed and withdrew a lacquered wooden box. "You can keep the container. My daughter makes them from salvaged wood."

Sylah opened it to find the Anoor-shell, the metal wire from Elder Zero's belt, Loot's spider brooch, and the small piece of bone from the Sanctuary. She released a breath and narrowed her eyes at the other woman, who was now leaning on the wall of the room. Something about the wisp of red hair curling out of her hood was familiar.

"Are you the person who brought me here?"

She nodded, "I am the Fourth Councillor."

"Do you have a name?"

"Not one I give to strangers."

Zenebe tugged on his ear. That was when Sylah saw his palm for the first time.

"What is that?" she said. A black ball was in the center of his hand. "Are you people born with your nut sacks on your hands?"

Zenebe chuckled.

"No, this is my orb; it allowed me to heal you."

"What?" Sylah was gulping in air at a rapid rate.

"Oh, locust plague, she's a fool," the Fourth Councillor muttered.

"Try . . . saying . . . that . . . to . . . my . . . face. I'll . . . knock . . . your . . . teeth . . . into . . . tomorrow," Sylah panted out.

Zenebe shot the other councillor an irritated glance. "You need to try breathing slower, you're hyperventilating."

Sylah tried, but the room was bursting with black spots.

"I need my joba seed powder." Though it didn't quite feel like one of her episodes, the tremors were smaller and the unfamiliarity made her panic more.

"What is joba seed powder?" Zenebe asked.

Sylah tried to speak again, but she couldn't.

"Count your breaths now. Eight in, eight out. There you go," Zenebe said with a soothing tone. "Breathe with me. One, two, three, four . . ."

Sylah followed his commands, letting her breathing ease. She didn't take her eyes off the other councillor in the room. Though she was hidden behind the darkness of her shiny hood, Sylah could just make out the sharpness of her features and the red hair that curled around her chin.

When she was once more in charge of her breathing, she asked the question she needed the answer to most.

"What happened to me?"

THE COUNCILLORS DIDN'T know much. Only the state Sylah had been in when she got there. And even then, she could tell they softened the truth. A look passed between them that said she had been in a very bad way indeed.

They explained the orb to her, and the student in her, the one Anoor had uncovered, was keen to know more. She only wished Anoor was here to learn about it too.

"Growth, healing, connection, and presence," Sylah murmured. *They must be able to fix the tidewind with one of those.* "And you don't have the type of runes we use in bloodwerk? To move objects?" she asked.

Zenebe shook his head. "No, and we call it deathcraft here, not bloodwerk. How are you able to move objects with runes in your homeland?"

"Enough," the woman said. She hadn't said much, and Sylah was grateful for it. "We will question her with all the council present."

Zenebe nodded, deferring to her. Sylah wondered at that significance.

They led Sylah out of the room and down a windowless corridor that ended in an arched doorway. They had given her thin rubber-like slippers and a cape of shiny fabric, belted at the waist. Zenebe pulled one of the folds of fabric over his head and indicated that Sylah should follow suit. The other councillor was already wrapped up.

"Use the belt to hook yourself to the bridge," Zenebe explained.

The wind and rain barrelled into them with ferocity as they made their way onto the swinging bridge.

With a hand on the rope and the other clutching the fabric at her chin, Sylah looked around at the City of Rain. Gargantuan mushrooms sprouted from the ground beneath her, strung together with bridges like this one. Sylah looked over the edge and laughed in exhilaration. The highest she had ever been was at the top of the five hundred steps of the Wardens' Keep. This was double that in height, at least.

A gale swooped under the bridge, and she felt herself being lifted up. Sylah whooped, laughing at the adrenaline rush it gave her.

She was alive, she was whole again, and the councillors had *deathcraft.* Deathcraft that could save the whole empire.

I didn't let you down, Anoor. Tears pricked at her eyes at the thought that she was a step closer to returning to her.

Zenebe stayed close to Sylah as they walked along the bridge toward the opposite mushroom. She wondered if he was worried at her laughs of glee because he gave her a look of relief once they slipped under the archway and off the bridge. There was no corridor in this mushroom, just an open space filled with a table in the center.

"Jond!" Sylah felt herself rushing to him despite the anger she had been nursing toward him over the last few mooncycles. He had saved her life.

He looked thinner than she'd ever seen him. Thinner than when Azim had made them survive out in the wilderness for three days. His beard was gone, leaving just a shadow of stubble, which brushed her skin as she hugged him.

Something squirmed under the material of his coat. Sylah's eyes widened as a small ball of white fur burst through his collar. Its head was half the size of her fist, and its eyes took up most of its features, blue and bursting with life.

"What is *that*?"

Jond gave Sylah a small smile. "This is Rascal, she's a sand cat."

"What? Why?"

Jond waved away the explanation, pushing Sylah to arm's length, surveying her, healthy and whole. "You're alive." His voice cracked.

"I am." Sylah hadn't taken her eyes off Rascal, and reached for her now. The kitten licked the rainwater off Sylah's fingers with her small sandpaper tongue. "Hello, Rascal."

There was some murmuring behind them, and Sylah turned, noticing the others in the room for the first time. There was an old man whose silhouette she vaguely recognized from the chattel cart.

"You. You helped Jond. You helped me. Why?" she demanded of him.

He dropped the gaze of his one eye and laughed.

"So fiery you are. I often daydreamed what would be the first thing you'd say to me as I was cleaning all those cotton diapers we swaddled you with, and *thank you* was always in there."

He attempted to embarrass her, but he didn't realize who he was talking to. When you were a former joba-seed addict, you'd shit yourself more times than you could count.

Sylah smiled; she liked his barbed jibe at her.

"What is your name?"

"Niha."

She stepped closer to him; she was taller than him by a handspan, but he was wider by the same amount.

"Thank you, Niha," Sylah said gently. "Thank you."

His eye shimmered as it met hers and he nodded deeply.

"My queen's blessing on you."

"I don't know what that means, but on you too."

He laughed.

Sylah looked over his shaking shoulders and saw that there were two people standing behind with impatient looks on their faces. Both were dressed in the same shiny material. The woman was more light-skinned than Sylah had ever seen, and she thought she could see green veins running down her neck. The man was shorter, more petite, with a beard that fell to his navel. Both had seen more than sixty years. Sylah looked to their hands and saw the black orbs there.

They must be the other two councillors.

"Shall we sit?" Zenebe said into the silence.

There were no chairs next to the table in the middle. Instead, there were cushions surrounding it and a recess in the floor underneath for their feet. Sylah sat down next to Jond and Rascal.

"Have you asked them about the tidewind?"

Jond shook his head and looked down. It was a sign of defeat she had got to know well at the Sanctuary.

"What is it?" she asked him, but he didn't look up.

"I don't think they're going to be able to fix it, Sylah . . . they seem to have their own problems." The councillors took their seats.

Zenebe spoke, "First let us deal with the accused: Niha of the third charter. Do you accept that as an exiled member of the Academy you breached the very rules you pledged your life on?"

"I do," Niha said.

"And are you willing to accept the consequences for your actions, on this day, before the council of the Academy?"

"I am."

Sylah began to shake with rage. "What is going on? You can't be serious? We have important matters to discuss. Life and death of an entire continent. And you are squabbling over some old man helping us to get into the Academy? The Academy that, if my blurry memory serves, is in ruins under a sea of water?" Sylah stood. "If I have to be subjected to one more ounce of bureaucracy, I swear to whatever God you believe in that I will get very, very, violent."

There was silence, then a small chuckle from the Fourth Councillor. A slip of red hair curled around her chin as she spoke. "Maybe we should have let her die after all."

Jond stiffened at her words.

"We know of your plight," she continued. "The rest of your entourage arrived a week ago."

"What?"

Sylah fell down on her backside.

"The elders are here?"

"Yes. Along with an irritating girl who talks more than she breathes."

"Ads." Jond smiled.

"I will tell you what I told them. The forces wreaking havoc in your lands have plagued the mainland too. It manifests in different ways: acid rain on the coast, flash floods here, hail and unseasonable snow to the north. It has caused devastation across the world, to the farthest corners of this realm. It is slowly killing us all off one by one."

"What is causing it?" Sylah pressed.

The woman held up her hand to the light, revealing her orb.

"We call it deathcraft." Her palms came together, the orb transferring the blood-printed runes onto the other side. She vanished. Sylah jumped as breath tickled her ear as she appeared beside her. "You call it bloodwerk."

CHAPTER THIRTY-FOUR

SYLAH

Councillors,

I have entered the Zalaam commune at your behest. What I have found I can barely put into words. They worship the Spider God so completely that the town itself is split like the legs of a spider—every blood color is segregated.

And councillors, the Zalaam are preparing for war. Tomorrow I will enter the war tent where I have seen so many people enter and not leave.

Send me strength.

—The last letter from Student Raha

"The tidewind is caused by bloodwerk?" Sylah whispered. Then reality hit her. "Did you just disappear and reappear next to me?"

"The fourth charter means traveling from one place to another instantaneously," Jond said, distracted. "How is the bloodwerk causing these world phenomena?"

"It drains the earth's essence," Zenebe said.

"What do you mean?" Sylah demanded. She didn't cope well with ignorance.

"There is an invisible energy that the runes drain from the world. I have been in deep conversations with the elders of your land, and it seems that they have a word for it: Anyme."

"Anyme the God?" Jond said.

Zenebe tilted his head. "It seems that they believe that Anyme is less than a God and more of a power fueled by their ancestors. It's where they believe bloodwerk power comes from. We have a more . . . tangible . . . understanding of the power."

"You think invisible energy is a more *tangible* explanation?" Sylah drawled out. "Wait, if bloodwerk is what drains the energy, then why did you just use it?"

"It was frivolous," the woman with green veins said. She was the Second Councillor. Connection was her power, Sylah recalled from the conversation with Zenebe. She wondered what that meant. "But Kara has always enjoyed theatrics."

Kara hissed. It was unclear whether it was because her true name had been revealed or because of what the Second Councillor had said.

"The action was minimal. Besides, the councillors are the only four permitted to practice deathcraft anymore."

"What of the students?" Niha asked.

"Their orbs have all been confiscated. No one beyond this chamber is permitted to use deathcraft," Kara said.

Niha settled down into an uneasy silence.

"And the Fifth Councillor?" Jond said. His words were met with a jolt around the room.

"There is no fifth," the Second Councillor said.

Jond frowned. Sylah would question him later.

"So only the four of you can do bloodwerk—deathcraft, whatever you want to call it. Then why is it so bad over here? That still doesn't make sense."

Zenebe nodded. "Indeed, because the truth of the matter is that even your empire had a balance, if a tenuous one. But there are bigger powers at play. There is a group who have been draining the resources of the world at an alarming rate. It has accelerated in the recent years, throwing our world into turmoil."

"The Zalaam." Sylah said the words, and the room seemed to grow colder.

"Yes," Zenebe said. "The Zalaam. They are a cult, a religious organization founded by a prophet nearly four hundred and fifty years ago. Their core belief is that it is their duty to purge the world in what they call 'the Ending Fire'—a great war triggered by the coming of a Child of Fire."

The Ending Fire? A Child of Fire? Sylah's thoughts churned.

"Everything, every single thing that you just said, needs further explanation," Sylah growled. She felt on the cusp of understanding, like there was something she was so close to grasping but it was slick with oil.

"Start from the beginning, Zenebe," the Second Councillor said, giving him a pointed glance.

"The Zalaam were founded on the mainland by a prophet who believed that a God from an old religion, the Spider God Kabut, had spoken to him in prophecy. It is claimed that Kabut spoke these words:

"A Child of Fire whose blood will blaze,
Will cleanse the world in eight nights, eight days,
Eight bloods lend strength to lead the charge
And eradicate the infidel, only Gods emerge,
Ready we will be, when the Ending Fire comes,
When the Child of Fire brings the Battle Drum,
The Battle Drum,
The Battle Drum,
Ready we will be, for war will come.

"The Zalaam made it their life mission to prepare for a war that they would one day start. Their numbers grew and they settled on a piece of land not far from here. They introduced communes that segregated the blood colors as the prophet believed Kabut's words praised the strength in separation. At first no one paid them any heed. They were fanatics, religious heretics that had twisted the word of their fake God to suit their needs. But then people began to start disappearing. One by one they were sucked into the commune never to be heard from again."

Here Zenebe paused.

"A student of the Academy was drawn to the Zalaam to study their beliefs. What they found was worse than anyone could have ever imagined. They were harvesting humans to fuel their experiments in their attempt to prepare for a war. They were using deathcraft."

"They were harvesting blood? That's what happened to the people who disappeared?" Sylah asked.

"Worse. They were harvesting bone marrow. The substance more potent than blood could ever be."

Sylah whispered, "Bone marrow?"

"Yes." Zenebe sighed and pulled his shiny fabric closer to his chest. "Needless to say, the queen did not take this lightly. Their prophet was put to death, and the rest of the Zalaam exiled from the mainland. They left on eight ships, one of each blood color packed full of the riches they had accumulated, for the Zalaam had powerful allies. They set off west."

"West?" The truth was there, close, so close, but the slippery bastard wouldn't give Sylah any purchase.

Zenebe nodded deeply. "West. Eight ships left Nsuo. Four were waylaid by storms and settled on the Volcane Isles: those with yellow, green, orange, and violet blood."

"What happened to the others?" But Sylah knew, she knew.

"Two were sacrificed to the Tannin, the sea monster that has separated our land for centuries. And the two that were granted passage for this sacrifice . . . settled on what we know as the Drylands."

"The red- and blue-blooded ships," Sylah whispered through numb lips.

"The founding wardens," Jond added.

Sylah turned to him wide-eyed.

"We're Zalaam."

Kara's smile was triumphant. "You are Zalaam."

"BUT WE KNOW nothing of the Spider God. Our Abosom preach of Anyme." Sylah was indignant.

"So it would seem. But what we have gathered from the Ghostings, though a lot of their histories were destroyed, is that the Zalaam took advantage of the world they had landed on. With their prophet gone, over time the beliefs of the Ghostings were bastardized, twisted to their purpose," Zenebe said. "They preached that the battle at sea *was* the Ending Fire and that they, the red-blooded, mind you, were the Gods left behind. That the Drylands was their utopia."

"Why were the Embers able to claim righteousness over the Dusters, the blue-bloods? If they were both Zalaam?"

"Well, that's where the Child of Fire comes in. The red-blooded Zalaam, like their prophet before, believed that 'Child of Fire' meant red-blooded. So as malleable as the blue-blooded were, to believe in the scripture so completely, they let the Embers—as you call them—reign."

"What of the rest of the Zalaam?" Though Sylah wasn't sure she could take any more truth.

Zenebe's eyes turned forlorn.

"What you see outside is the beginning of their battle with the rest of us." Zenebe ran a hand across his jaw. "They have grown in numbers once again, thriving on the Volcane Isles and trading with Souriland in the north. Their marrow techniques are draining the world's energy like never before. Whatever they're creating will destroy everything we know—"

"It has already drained everything we know," the Second Councillor growled, her sharp teeth flashing. "At first, we thought the weather phenomenon was us. We dropped our student numbers to fifty, then ten, then five. But when it persisted, we sent scouts out to all corners of the land—even to the Drylands, sacrificing one of our own in the process. They all returned with similar reports: that the weather was changing. The scout we sent to the Volcane Isles didn't return. We suspected, but we couldn't be sure; it had been hundreds of years since we'd heard from the Zalaam. Then the Shariha appeared on our shores and confirmed our suspicions. They had been trading slaves with the Zalaam for years, using the bodies to harvest bone marrow. Our old enemies were stirring, they were making ready for the final battle."

"The slaves sent to the Shariha are used to harvest . . . bone marrow," Niha murmured, his expression slack with horror.

Sylah ignored him. Rage made her voice quake. "You're telling me there's a whole population of fanatics ready to start a war with the entire world, and at one stage you just *exiled* them."

The councillors shifted. It was Kara who answered.

"There were children, families, communities. Our ancestors couldn't have executed them all. It would have been genocide." Her tone was defensive. Her hood slipped backward revealing her face for the first time.

Jond stiffened beside Sylah, and she knew why. Kara was beautiful. Not just attractive, but truly ethereal. With glossy dark skin and red hair that coiled in large ringlets to her chest. Her eyes were a striking violet. She looked like she was in her mid-thirties, the youngest councillor by far.

Kara sensed all eyes on her, and she went to pull forward her hood. Sylah hid her smile as Jond's breathing went back to normal.

"The way I see it, seems like we've got a lot to blame our ancestors for," Jond said. Rascal had crawled out from his shirt and now lay asleep, curled up on his lap.

"What of the queen?" Niha said. "What are her orders?"

The councillors looked at each other before the First Councillor spoke for the first time. His voice was soft, and he spoke haltingly, as if the common tongue wasn't his first language.

"The queen has made her position clear. Tenio must survive. She is putting her resources into protecting her people."

Sylah snorted.

"Protecting? Not defending?"

"We cannot. We don't have enough students to fight them, and even if we did, the energy required to battle them would ensure there's no world to live in after."

"Wait, so the most powerful people in the world are in this room, and you have no idea how to take down the Zalaam? What the fuck have you been doing for the last few years? For the last few *centuries*? You knew this was coming. They told you this was coming."

With each word Zenebe seemed to shrink in on himself.

Kara spoke up. "The last few mooncycles we have been working on survival, building these towers where we now live and preserving the knowledge from the flooded citadel. That survival is the very reason you now breathe. So, do not dare to judge those who you have no understanding of."

"I need to get out of here." Sylah stood and made her way toward the door.

THE RAIN HAD stopped, and Sylah was grateful for the slice of sun beaming through the clouds. She ran her fingers over the rope railing as she walked, her feet weaving through the lattice of bridges until she was truly lost.

She saw two people up ahead, their shiny clothing shadowing their faces.

"Excuse me?"

The smaller one jumped as they turned around.

"Oh, sorry, I didn't mean to startle you," Sylah said, reaching a hand forward.

They flinched. Two sets of wide eyes met Sylah's.

"I was just wondering if you could tell me how I get down from here."

"Down?" The smaller person stepped forward, the light illuminating their face. Their skin had an ochre tone, and Sylah knew they had yellow blood, just like Loot.

Had he been one of the Zalaam from the Volcane Isles? It was the only explanation. "To resist and sow chaos" had been his mantra. A clue, maybe, to the God he prayed to.

"I was wondering how I get down there." She pointed over the railing.

"Why would you want to go down there?" the yellow-blooded asked, their lips twitching.

Before Sylah could reply, the other person spoke.

"There is a lift. Cross the third bridge on your right and it will lead you there." Their blue eyes and monotone voice did nothing to reveal their feelings.

"Thank you."

There was an awkward pause as Sylah contemplated an appropriate goodbye. She had no idea of the customs of this land, so she resorted to a small wave before shouldering past them in search of the lift.

What Sylah hadn't appreciated was that the lift wouldn't be operated by bloodwerk like the ones in the Wardens' Keep. Instead, she had to manually crank a lever to lower herself to the ground notch by notch. She was sweating and breathless by the time she got there, but she didn't wait around, and instead set off toward the citadel on the horizon.

"Maiden's tits, I think I'd prefer sand to this mud." Even though the rain had stopped, the mud splattered her clothing and ran down her leg in rivulets.

It didn't take her long to reach the Academy walls.

Black iron, just like the Wardens' Keep, she mused.

She began to scale them, her weakened muscles slowing her progress. When she got to the top, she cursed herself.

"There was a set of stairs *right* there."

Tearing her gaze away from the concealed staircase, she surveyed the ruins before her. A lump formed in her throat.

The floods had decimated the city. Buildings had crumbled and homes were destroyed. The breeze smelled of earth and rotting plants. But there was something familiar in it too.

"The Dredge," she whispered to herself. The weight of missing Nar-Ruta took her unawares. But the city had been her salvation, her home. She pushed her tongue between the gap in her teeth, and for a second, she craved the ecstasy of a joba seed.

Once Sylah's hyperventilating had subsided earlier, Zenebe had asked her what she had meant by "joba seed powder." When she explained her affliction, he had looked at her thoughtfully.

"It may be you are no longer beholden to the powder due to the forced detoxification." Zenebe withdrew a notebook and wrote as he talked. "I did notice some damage to your synapses, but I did not heal them. Brain healing is complex and given the injuries you sustained I concentrated on your body first. If you would like, I'd be happy to take a look in another session?"

Sylah had said no immediately. Her addiction was as much a

part of her as the trinkets in her hair. Even if the majority of the physical effects were gone, the cravings and memories lingered still.

No one could ever take that from her.

She stood in the weak sunlight for some time, reminiscing in the feeling of oblivion. A tear fell down her cheek to join the wet earth below. She wiped it away, shaking the longing for joba seeds free, and set off into the heart of the citadel.

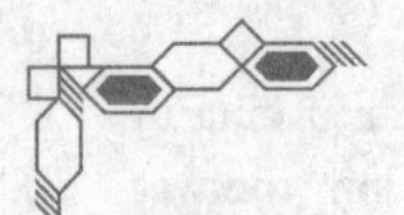

CHAPTER THIRTY-FIVE

SYLAH

The fourth charter is arguably the most powerful, but the hardest to yield. The four foundational runes have basic properties: dissipate *to remove oneself,* appear *to add oneself,* navigate *for spatial awareness, and* transfer *to carry one other.*

The fourth charter runes do not work individually, but must always be part of a combination. There are many students who have suffered from this error. We know not where the dissipated go. So be warned. Craft the rune combinations carefully.

—Teachings on the fourth charter, Zwina Academy

Sylah turned the nozzle on the gas lamp, and the room came into view.

This must be the council chamber, she thought.

At first the decaying flowers had frightened her, until she realized their purpose. They had been buildings.

She took a seat in one of the council chairs and put her feet up on the table. There were drawers built—no, *grown*—into the table, and Sylah opened one to find thin strips of paper and pointed pieces of lead.

She laid out a page on the table and began to write.

Anoor,

I have reached the Academy, but the news is not good. They are plagued by the same, though different, issues as the empire. They say the world is ending. I worry that the task you have given me is harder than either you or I can comprehend.

I wonder what you would say if you were here. The powers they wield are so very different from bloodwerk. They healed me, Anoor. They healed what the acid rain had done to me. Maybe they can heal the world too. I refuse to give up.

I miss you, my kori bird. I wish I could see your reign in flight.

I will come home to you.

Sylah.

Sylah folded the letter in trembling hands. She knew the words wouldn't reach Anoor; how could they with the Tannin between them? She placed the letter in her pocket anyway.

She stood, making to leave.

"Wait, there's a fifth chair but only four councillors." Her words slipped out unbidden.

She went to the chair and inspected the symbol on the back. Despite the slashes through the carving, Sylah recognized the shape of it.

It was a spider.

"But why would the symbol of the Fifth Councillor be a spider?"

"Sylah!" The shout was far away but it reached her nonetheless.

"Down here," she called back to Jond. He appeared wild-eyed not long after.

"What are you doing? You can't just disappear."

"No, I can't, though I'd very much like to try. Do you think Kara would teach me?"

Jond's lips drew into a line.

"Sylah."

"I didn't go far, did I?"

"The rains could come back at any moment."

"I know, I just wanted to see it. Properly see it. You know."

He nodded and looked around. "I came here before."

"You did? Did you see the spider on the back of this chair?"

"What—" Jond bent down to get a closer look. His eyes widened. "You're right, it is a spider, I didn't realize it before."

"I think the councillors have some explaining to do."

Jond sighed wearily.

"The truth is murkier than ever."

"Muddier."

"Huh?"

"The truth is muddier than ever."

He glanced down at his speckled attire and gave a halfhearted laugh. "Yes, I suppose you're right."

Rascal pushed her head out of his shirt and chirped.

"At least someone's still clean."

Jond sighed. "Yes, I think she lives in my shirt now."

The rains had begun while they were underground and though it was only a drizzle Jond grew agitated.

"We need to hurry up."

"I'm trying," Sylah grumbled. She didn't want to admit she was tired from the unnecessary climb up the wall. "I should have stolen Kara's orb."

"She studied for twenty years before she completed her orb," Jond said through clenched teeth. "I don't think you'll be able to figure it out in the next few minutes. Come on."

He half-dragged her all the way to the City of Rain. She let him crank the lift all the way to the top. And to his credit, he didn't comment on her slumped position against the cage.

Skies above, she was tired.

Then she heard the distinctive voice of Ads, and exhaustion threatened to render her unconscious. Did the girl ever stop talking?

". . . You see the way the clouds dip on the horizon? They say that happens a strike or so before the flash flood, though there is no pattern to it. It does make me wonder why the tidewind is patterned so. It seems odd for there to be a nightly occurrence. Don't you think, Elder?"

"Stop cranking. Take us back down," Sylah hissed at Jond. She was too drained to deal with Ads's energy today.

"Sylah!" The scream could be heard for leagues around. "You made it."

Ads hurtled down the corridor toward them and squeezed the air out of Sylah's lungs.

"Hello, Ads. How's it hurting?"

"Sylah, you're really here."

"I am." Sylah peered behind Ads to see Elder Dew. She greeted them with a nod.

Welcome, Sylah. I am to understand you had quite a journey getting here.

"Something like that."

"Were you really taken prisoner?" Ads asked.

"I was."

"And did you nearly die like they say you did?"

"Yes. I'm healed now." Something scratched her hand, and she looked down to see the letter she had written for Anoor peeking out of her pocket. She reached for it, and her stomach sank. The rain had blurred her already-poor handwriting into smears. Sylah held back the sudden tears that threatened to fall.

"Their bloodwerk is amazing, isn't it? The orbs, so clever, no need to wait to draw the whole sequence, it's there carved in already," Ads continued without pausing. "They have no idea about the system of runes the Embers use. When I describe it to them, they're as shocked as me when I see Kara disappear and reappear. And Zenebe, he healed my arm when I broke it on the journey. No scars, can you imagine? I asked him if he could heal Dew's hands back, but he said he can't grow limbs, which is a shame, I guess. So I asked Elyzan, the First Councillor of Growth, and he, he said he can only grow plants from a seed. I think he got the shortest scythe in the skills department, but I suppose the greenhouses wouldn't work without him and we'd have no food to eat."

Ads, breathe, Dew commanded. *You're going to tire Sylah out and she's only just been healed.*

"How was your journey?" Sylah asked.

Less painful than yours, I gather. Come, the others are eager to see you. You must also be famished. I have noted the councillors here are not the best hosts, but little do they know, I've found the kitchens. Dew winked before leading Sylah, Jond, and Ads off the bridge.

NEITHER RAVENWING NOR Reed looked "eager" to see Sylah but at least they acknowledged her with a curt nod as she joined them at the table. Both looked more haggard from their journey, but whole at least.

In the center of the table was a plate of couscous, which was like small grains of potato mixed with vegetables. Sylah was dubious but began to fill her plate after the second bite. Rascal kept trying to climb onto the table, but Jond kept taking her down.

"Try the tea. They make it out of a flower called hibiscus. It's red."

Sylah tried it under Ads's expectant gaze and grimaced.

"Add sugar."

Sylah did as Ads had bidden.

"Better?"

"Much."

We didn't think you'd make it. When you disappeared we assumed you had abandoned us, Reed signed. The lines of her face were harsher than when Sylah had seen her last.

"I told them you wouldn't leave us," Ads said, adding a third spoonful of sugar into her tea. "But then we saw the tracks of the Shariha and their carts. Did you see the camels? I wish I'd seen one."

"Well, I would have happily traded places with you," Sylah snapped. "How is it you came here unscathed?"

Dew answered. *Not unscathed, there were some injuries between us. Though we learned the changes of the world quickly. We were fortunate to meet a family fleeing from the Shariha, so we learned from their struggles.* The sign for Shariha was the symbol for cage and binding combined—a swipe of their mouth and a tap on the upper part of their left wrist. It seemed pertinent to Sylah.

Dew continued. *They led us through the Mistforest, but parted ways when we reached the Academy. The floods were fierce, and we circled the citadel before entering it. We were spotted by a scout in the City of Rain, and they led us to them.*

"Where's the rest of the crew?" Sylah asked.

They are here, either helping or resting. Petal remains on the Baqarah*; with the acid rain we needed someone to stay back and maintain the ship.*

Sylah nodded; it made sense, though she'd miss Petal's multicolored attire brightening her day.

"The councillors told you everything? About the Zalaam, about the truth of the founding wardens?"

Ravenwing signed, *It is a truth we have long suspected through the words of our ancestors.*

Jond exhaled to himself. "It's all a little unbelievable."

But believable, Ravenwing signed.

"There's something they're not telling us, though," Sylah said and filled them in on the symbol they had found.

"They denied the Fifth Councillor existed, but we have proof. From the diary and the chamber," Jond added, chewing on a fruit they called a "banana." It was like a plantain but smaller and sweeter.

What diary do you speak of? Reed signed, her expression suspicious. Sylah relayed her question to Jond.

Jond sat up straight, guilt flashing across his features. "Well . . . the diary of your ancestor, Elder Petra."

Ravenwing stood up so fast the couscous platter spilled onto Ads's lap, who screeched.

"I was still eating that," Sylah grumbled.

You stole our ancestor's diary? Ravenwing thundered with black eyes. Sylah's translation was said with less anger.

"I . . . may have. Yes, I stole it." Jond rolled his shoulders back and lifted his eyes to Ravenwing's.

You dare defile what is not yours?

Where is it now? Dew interjected, and Sylah translated.

Jond looked sheepish. "With the Shariha."

There was a pained collective groan from the elders. Sylah winced to hear it.

"Does it matter anymore? We're all going to die anyway," she said sullenly. The Shariha had Anoor's sword too. The thought still stung.

Sylah's morose verdict dispersed some of the anger that fizzed around the table.

"So what could the Fifth Councillor do? I never finished reading the diary," Jond asked, once more retrieving Rascal, who was face-deep in the couscous. Her pink nose was speckled with food as he sat her down on his lap.

They could infuse beings with life, Dew signed. Sylah relayed the elder's words to Jond.

"What does that mean?"

When none of the elders answered, Ads shrugged and said, "Seemed like they could replicate life in inanimate objects. Like turn stone into spiders or something like that."

She's right, the law of creation allowed those who wielded the runes to bring life to objects that had no soul.

"Right, so this Fifth Councillor . . . is missing?" Sylah said.

The elders looked between them.

"We haven't had a Fifth Councillor for over four hundred years." Kara had appeared in the blink of an eye, answering Sylah's question as she came to stand at the head of the table.

"Why?"

"The last Fifth Councillor was the prophet of the Zalaam."

"What?"

"So you see, the Academy has never done 'nothing.'" Kara shot a sly smile Sylah's way before settling into a spare seat. "We housed and nurtured the very heart of the Zalaam.

"The fifth charter is the law of creation. To infuse life into the spiritless," Kara went on, reaching for some food. "It is the most complex of the five disciplines, for it takes more."

"What do you mean?" Jond asked before Sylah could jump in.

Kara took a breath before reaching over Sylah to spoon food

into her mouth. They all waited for her to swallow. Sylah ground her teeth.

"There is a reason why we say 'infuse' and not 'give,' because no one in this world can truly *create* life. Even the first charter can only grow it from a seed. Or a spore," she added, waving up at the mushroom ceiling.

"Don't you dare take another mouthful," Sylah warned. "We've come a long way for the truth and I'm not sitting here while more bits of couscous wedge between the gaps in your teeth."

Kara bared her gums at Sylah. But she laid down the spoon.

"When you infuse an object with life, say, this spoon, you give it a tiny bit of your soul."

"What?" Jond and Sylah said at the same time.

"Soul, life-force, energy, Anyme . . . whatever you want to call it. You must feed it to give it life."

Sylah shuddered and clutched her chest as if her soul was harbored there.

And the consequences of infusing too many things? Elder Dew had made the conclusion before anyone else.

"There was a strict quota on the number of objects students and teachers could infuse throughout their life. It didn't take the Academy long to learn that overusing the runes stripped the orb-users of their morality, their soul diminished, leaving them half-crazed."

". . . The Fifth Councillor . . . the prophet . . . went over his quota," Sylah concluded.

"He didn't just go over his quota, he started experimenting with bone marrow. He called it 'godpower,' and the beings he created 'godbeasts.' The consequences on his mind . . . were dire. Though I suspect one of the Zalaam would counter that point and say he was touched by the many hands of their God, Kabut." Kara laughed lightly.

There was a beat of silence. Rascal meowed, breaking it, and Jond scooped her back into his shirt.

"Could they . . . infuse dead bodies with life?" Jond asked. Sylah wondered if he was thinking about their dead family or Loot.

"No. Only the spiritless, inanimate objects and such."

Sylah struggled to contain all this new information in her mind.

Kara picked up her spoon again.

"And that is that. He was expelled from the Academy and the law of creation discipline was disbanded. They should have killed him then. They didn't realize how the religion would grow to become a cult, more dangerous than anything the world had ever seen."

Sylah opened her mouth to ask more questions, but someone ran into the room. They were panting, their words running together.

"There was a tsunami. The Shard Palace has fallen. The queen is missing, suspected dead."

Kara's spoon clattered onto the table. The hand that had been holding it was gone before Sylah breathed out.

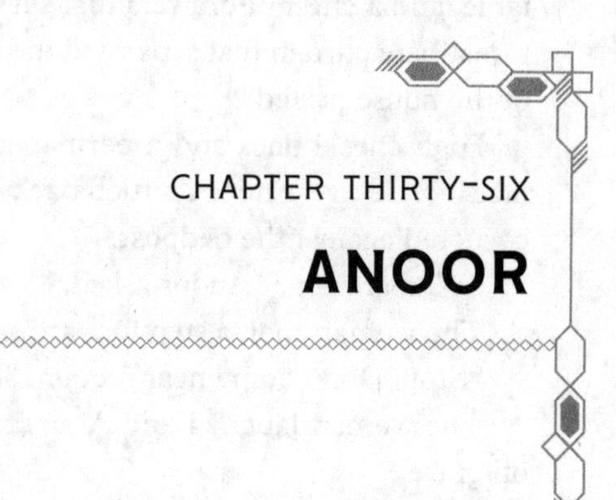

CHAPTER THIRTY-SIX

ANOOR

Inquisitor Abena looked at the child. She was small, with hazel eyes that yearned to be loved. She came from a home where her mother chose to sharpen her rather than love her. But how could Abena not?

She vowed revenge that day, revenge on the woman who chose to hurt the child so.

—"The Past Meets Present" from *The Tales of Inquisitor Abena*, featured in *The People's Gazette*

Anoor's eyes were sticky with sleep. She rubbed her hands across them, her arms feeling heavy. The room smelled musty, and she reminded herself to clean it at some point today. She moved onto her side and felt her mattress crunch beneath her. Had she fallen asleep on her books again? She slipped a tired arm under the sheet.

Strands of something dry and brittle broke off in her hand. She pulled one out and held it in front of her face.

Straw. She was on a straw mattress.

Anoor sat bolt upright.

"Where am I?" She attempted to scream, but it came out a whisper. The room was turning slightly to the left, and she tried to counterbalance it by pushing herself right.

"Stop it, stop it, stop it," she commanded the spinning room. There wasn't much by way of furniture. Just a straw bed, a bedside table, and a chest of drawers that sat crookedly on three legs. The threadbare curtain that separated the bedroom from the other side of the house parted.

High cheekbones and a permanent frown made the woman's face look severe. Anoor scuttled backward on the bed until she was cornered against the bedpost.

"Who are you?" Anoor asked.

The woman took a step forward.

"Stop. Don't come near me, or I'll have you taken to jail."

The woman laughed and Anoor winced; it was like eru claws on gravel.

"I won't hurt you. You are under my protection."

"Why do I need protection? What happened?"

Anoor tried to piece together her last few memories. Was she with Kwame? In the Dredge? No, that couldn't be.

Then she gasped.

"My trial. I need to get to my trial." Anoor pulled the covers off herself and realized she was in her undergarments. "I need my clothes, where are my clothes?"

"Anoor." The woman tried to be placating. "Your trial is over. You were rescued by your friends and brought here so you would avoid the sentence of jail."

Anoor's heart started to race and she felt fear heat the corners of her eyes. "Who brought me here?" she asked.

The woman cocked her head to the left and, if Anoor hadn't been so afraid, she'd have been struck by the similarity in this woman's jawline to her own.

"A man, Kwame, and Hassa. But I think they were also helped by your chief of staff."

"Gorn," Anoor choked out. "I need to get out of here. I'm not safe."

She needed to get to her grandmother, explain the whole thing. Maybe they'd grant her clemency if she offered the truth.

"Anoor, you can't, they'll capture you. You'll be in jail for the rest of your life."

"But it wasn't me. I didn't kill her." Anoor was sobbing now, half from anger, half from fear.

The woman's face grew softer, and she perched on the edge of the bed.

"Who are you? Why are you helping her?" Anoor asked. This must be the woman Gorn was meeting in the city. She might even be the assassin.

Pain flickered across the woman's face. Pain and then raw dread.

"My name is Lio," she said finally. "I haven't seen you since you were two years old."

Anoor knew that name. Sylah had scrawled it on a piece of paper along with an address. It was the last thing she left for Anoor before she ventured on her quest.

"You're . . . my mother?"

Anoor felt all expression ebb away from her features, leaving them blank. But emotions churned just under the surface.

"Leaving you in that cradle was the hardest thing I've ever done in my life." Lio spoke haltingly. "No day has passed, no sun has risen, without a thought for you."

"And yet, still, you left me to die."

"I did. And honestly, I'm not sure I wouldn't do it again." Lio lifted her chin, which reminded Anoor of Sylah. "I believed so completely in the cause, even knowing the pain your loss would bring, I wouldn't have been able to convince my past self. Azim . . . he had my heart and soul completely. More than that, he had my loyalty."

"You lay the blame at a dead man's feet?" Fury crept into Anoor's voice, and she tried to quash it.

"No," Lio said with a touch of frustration herself. "I do not speak of blame. Only purpose. And by swapping you, I had one."

Lio spread her hand absently against the sheet of the bed, and Anoor realized that this was Sylah's room. And lying in Sylah's bed, she'd never felt more alone.

"I do not ask you to forgive me, I do not deserve that. All I ask is that you let me know you. Not as a mother, I know I will never be that, but as someone that one day you may be able to trust."

Trust? This woman conspired with Gorn to murder Uka, to kidnap Anoor, and keep her imprisoned in her home.

I must be careful with my words. Feign ignorance, gather knowledge. Then escape back to Grandmother.

"And you ask for trust while keeping me prisoner?" Anoor said lightly.

"You are no prisoner, though I must ask that you remain indoors and away from the windows for your own safety. There are still very many patrols searching for you."

Anoor nodded.

"Would you like some tea? Your friends will be back soon; they will come under cover of darkness, they said."

Friends. She pondered on the word. Lio looked at her, waiting. Here was her mother, her true mother. Fate had truly a twisted sense of humor. First Uka dies, then Gorn betrays her, and now her blood mother appears, wanting her trust.

Three mothers, but still motherless.

"Yes, tea would be nice."

I hope I choke on it. The desolate thought struck her between the eyes. *No, I will not give up.* She would use her fear to build a fortress just like Sylah taught her. Block by block.

And in my castle, there'll be a jail, where they'll all rot. Until their flesh turns to ash.

"I NEED CLOTHES," Anoor said.

"They burned the ones you were wearing for the trial. Wear something from there."

Lio directed her toward the chest of drawers. It was filmed with dust and sand that burst into blue clouds as Anoor opened the top drawer.

Inside the clothes were worn, and some put away dirty. Anoor selected a tunic and string-waisted pair of pantaloons in a dark gray pattern.

Lio watched her as she dressed, her face a mask of concern. Anoor wondered what it must be like to see her true daughter wear her adoptive daughter's clothes. She dismissed the thought a second later. She didn't really care what Lio thought.

Anoor followed Lio through the curtain. The next room along must have been Lio's bedroom. It was bare but for the drawing of a whitestone farmhouse. Anoor realized with a start that it must have been the Sanctuary, where Sylah was raised.

Anoor felt a strange pang of guilt being in Sylah's home without her, wearing her clothes, and sleeping in her bed. It should have made her feel closer to her, but instead it reminded her of the differences of their upbringing and the home stolen from Sylah by Lio's actions.

"It's a humble villa," Lio said without apology. "But large by Duster standards. I'm sure it is not what you are used to."

Was there a barb there? Or was Lio's scorn just guilt, redressed? Anoor didn't answer.

They made their way down the wooden staircase to a space that consisted of a living room, a stove, and a small cupboard that hid the privy out the back.

"Sit, please." Lio pointed to the wicker sofa, and Anoor shook her head, instead choosing to watch Lio make the tea.

Lio frowned but didn't argue.

Anoor's eyes followed her mother as she moved around the small kitchen area. She filled the kettle with water and added the powdered tea leaves. Chamomile and mint, Anoor noted. She wondered if her mother was trying to soothe her with the choice of herbs. She peered closer as Lio withdrew a spoon from the utensil drawer and Anoor noted the sharp knives there.

The kettle didn't take long to boil. Soon an over-honeyed cup of tea was thrust into her hand, and she was herded to the sofa.

Lio and Anoor stared at each other over the rims of their mugs.

"You knew Sylah?" Lio asked.

Anoor nodded, not trusting herself to say her name.

"She helped you win the Aktibar?" Lio pressed.

"I don't want to talk about her."

Lio's lips drew into a thin line. She put the mug of tea down and stood.

"I'll be right back."

As soon as Lio closed the door to the privy, Anoor sprang up. She moved to the kitchen area with light steps and withdrew the sharp knife she had seen. She pushed the shaft down her waistband, careful not to cut her skin. The cold metal was soothing against her lower back. She was glad to have some form of protection at least.

When Lio returned, Anoor was sitting coolly on the sofa, her back only a little more upright than it had been before she left.

"You have been asleep for some strikes. Sunset approaches and your friends will be here soon. We will then make a plan." Lio was trying to be reassuring.

Let them come. The plan is set.

DARKNESS FILLED LIO's house with shadows. She only had the one runelamp and it flickered uncertainly in the center of the room. Anoor still had her inkwell, and she could have fixed the slight imperfection, but instead she left it, enjoying the shifting of the light.

They waited. Every so often Lio's eyes would slide to Anoor's, and she would hold her gaze, wondering what thoughts churned inside her mother's head.

Mother . . . the word didn't sit right.

"I was told you like zines. I went to get you the latest one while you slept."

Lio presented the bright pages to her. Anoor leafed through them without enthusiasm. She was living the life of a zine right now. She didn't need to read about it.

There was a small sound outside. At first Anoor thought it was the tinkling of the incessant trinkets in the joba tree next door, but then she heard the quiet whisper of a voice she recognized.

Lio was first to the door. She pulled it open, ushering Kwame and Gorn inside.

Anoor was nearly knocked flat by Kwame's hug.

"I'm so sorry. I gave you too much laudanum, I was so worried you weren't going to wake."

Anoor didn't relax into his embrace. She saw Gorn watching her warily over Kwame's shoulder. She had an arm in a sling and a graze on her chin. Anoor didn't ask how she got them.

"How did you get here without the Abosom following you?" Anoor asked stiffly. She wanted to know who else was involved in this mutiny.

Kwame pushed her away, and it was then that she saw his mustache. Despite everything, she laughed.

"That disguise couldn't have worked."

Gorn stepped forward. "No, though he refuses to take it off now. The Abosom are a little preoccupied following Zuhari around the Ember Quarter. We set them off on a false trail. It was Zuhari's idea to fill a basket with supplies, poorly hidden. They think she's taking you food."

Clever. Anoor didn't voice the thought.

She spun on her heel and took a seat on the sofa.

"I'll put on some coffee," Lio said stiffly.

Kwame and Gorn took their seats in the two wicker chairs opposite.

There was silence. Until there wasn't.

"I know you must be angry . . ." Gorn said, her large brow furrowed.

"And why would you think that?" Anoor said quietly, reaching a hand down her back. Biding her time.

Kwame leaned forward, spreading his hands wide in explanation.

"Because you wanted to sacrifice yourself, give yourself up. And we took that away from you."

Anoor laughed.

"You still think that's what I was going to do?" she asked him. Then she turned to Gorn. "So, you haven't told him the truth?"

"What truth?" Kwame's head swung from Gorn to Anoor.

"Why you've been slipping out to meet someone in the city? Why you disappeared the night of my mother's death? Why you researched how to kill someone?"

Gorn's face went blank. It was more frightening than her anger. More frightening than her fear.

Anoor was sick of feeling afraid. She withdrew the knife from her waist and leveled it at Gorn. Kwame squawked in disbelief.

"Who else was in your employ? If not Kwame, I assume this one"—Anoor tilted her head at Lio—"had something to do with it. Zuhari? Hassa?"

Kwame stood, coming between Anoor and Gorn.

"Anoor, what are you doing? Are you really accusing Gorn?"

"She hasn't denied it," Lio said from behind. "Though I'll correct one part of your theory: the first time I met this woman was five minutes ago."

"Shut up," Anoor said to her. Fine, Lio wasn't a part of it, but the rest, that was true. She knew it was true.

Gorn cleared her throat, her face still so smooth.

"Anoor, do you truly believe that I killed Uka?"

"Of course you did, I have the evidence in my satchel. Or did you burn that along with my clothes?"

Then something extraordinary happened. Gorn's face cracked, and she began to cry.

Here is the confession. At last.

Relief mingled with grief and Anoor felt her throat constrict.

"Up," she choked out. "You're going to walk ahead of me and we're going to find one of those patrols or an Abosom and turn you in."

Kwame's face had fallen slack.

"No, no, no," he murmured.

Gorn stood and Anoor guided her to the door, the kitchen knife leveled at her back.

In no world had Anoor imagined this scenario.

But as they reached the door, it opened ahead of them.

"Hassa?"

Hassa took in the scene before her, her gaze thunderous. She dropped Anoor's satchel at her feet, her notes spilling out.

How could you be so foolish?

Anoor frowned. Because Hassa wasn't talking to Gorn. She was talking to Anoor.

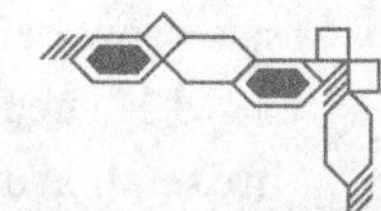

CHAPTER THIRTY-SEVEN

HASSA

In a world not far from ours, where animals speak, and the sky is full of stars, we find a kori bird tending the land.

"What are you doing?" the fox said to the kori.

"Why, I am sowing seeds because I need to eat. Why are you hunting, fox?"

"Because I am hungry, I need to eat."

Down came the jaws of the fox.

The next day a new kori came and worked on the land, only to die as well.

On the third day, the monkey, having watched from his tree, shouted down, "Why do you let the fox kill you each day? You know he is coming. Fly away. Fly away."

The kori birds laughed.

"We know the fox is coming. We know he hunts our kind. But look at our fields and what we leave behind."

The monkey looked at the seeds the kori birds had sown and saw the abundance of food.

"Even the tree you climb was once planted by our forebears, so understand the sacrifice we make. And why we do not fly away."

Are you the kori? Or are you the fox? I know who I would rather be, and who I would rather not. I could not be that monkey. Sitting high in the tree. Not knowing who planted the seed, who sacrificed for my need.

—"The Kori and the Fox," spoken by Griot Sheth

Hassa was unsure about leaving Anoor with Lio. The woman couldn't be trusted, but she was their only option. Anoor was asleep, the laudanum still taking effect, and in the end practicality won out over Hassa's unease. If Lio did turn in Anoor, she'd be jeopardizing herself.

Kwame went back to the Keep. He brushed a kiss across Hassa's brow before he went.

"I'll check on Gorn, make sure she's okay. It looks like she broke an arm. I'll meet you here later?"

Maybe, there's something I need to check in the Dredge. I realized that all the bodies surround the tidewind shelter.

Kwame's eyes widened. "You're right. How did we not realize that earlier?"

Hassa shrugged. *It might be nothing. I'll check it out.*

She turned to leave but he reached for her arm, spinning her back around. She fell against his chest, and he kissed her. Deeply and thoroughly.

"Are you laughing?"

She pushed herself away. *Your fake mustache, it's tickling me.*

Kwame laughed and kissed her brow one more time. "I'll see you soon."

She watched him leave. As he walked, he stuck to the shadows of the street, but he was too bright to be so disguised. His smile warmed anyone who looked at him.

When he moved out of sight, Hassa turned toward the Dredge. Instead of heading to the tunnels she stayed topside, listening and watching the stream of people move around in the late afternoon heat.

The Dredge was decaying at an alarming rate, the tidewind pulling down villas like matchstick houses. The number of homeless people must have increased hugely.

I hope the tidewind shelters are really protecting people, Hassa thought. She so rarely hoped. It was pointless in a world that thrived so readily on the suffering of its native citizens.

A cluster of healers crossed the street ahead of her. They were escorted closely by a platoon of officers. They walked with purpose toward the tidewind shelter.

Hassa kept to the shady edges of the ruined buildings as she followed the healers. She didn't really need to hide. She was a Ghosting, and this was her quarter. But as she turned onto the street toward the shelter, Hassa was shocked by the sight of the crowds lining up outside. It was strikes before nightfall.

Hassa listened in to their conversations.

". . . I hear they give you food and medicine, enough to feed you for three mooncycles . . ."

"My sister said that her friend knew someone who was given a bed to sleep in and a sack of slabs. He left and bought himself a little villa on the coast . . ."

". . . I got turned away yesterday, they only have ten spaces."

Ten spaces? That didn't make sense, the shelter was huge, as it was meant to house the homeless and those whose lives had been impacted severely by the tidewind.

"This is the third time I've queued up, and I've never got in."

The healers entered through a door on the side of the building and Hassa strained to see beyond the doorway, but she saw nothing but darkness.

A little later a delivery arrived by eru. This time Hassa was able to see the produce as it was unloaded from the carriage.

Blocks of ice? Why do they need ice?

Ice was an expensive commodity, shipped in from the highest hills in Jin-Gernomi. Even the Keep only had two ice boxes.

Hassa was more confused than before. She rocked back and forth on her heels and waited for any more clues.

The queue wasn't moving, though it grew bigger as night fell. The rumors seemed to bloat as darkness deepened, and Hassa heard people talk of the riches and dishes that lay beyond the shelter walls. But what was curious was that none of them had yet been inside.

HASSA MOVED THROUGH the tunnels toward the Nest pondering all she had learned, and all that she hadn't.

She thought back to the deliveries Gorn had been making. There had been no food there, just medical supplies: tubes, needles, medicine, and vials. Lots of vials. And now ice? It didn't make sense.

Maybe someone else delivered the food. Anoor had said that all the wardens were invested in the shelter so maybe Faro, the duty disciple, was in charge of the food.

She was so immersed in her thoughts it was a long while before she heard the voices.

"I think there's another path this way." Hassa recognized Maiden Turin.

"Are you sure?" the other responded.

"Yes, if Loot can navigate the tunnels, so can we."

"But I—"

"Jami." Hassa knew that name: Maiden Jami was a competitor across the way from Turin's. "If we're to take Loot's throne we must take his throne room."

Hassa breathed out slowly. Turin was making a play for Warden of Crime. The woman was brutal, ruthless, and perfectly suited to the role.

The wavering of their runelamp came into view. They were lost. The Belly was on the other side of town. If they went left at the fork up ahead, they'd stumble into tunnels afflicted by exploding gas; if they went right, they'd end up in the Ghostings' haven. As much as Hassa wanted to guide Maiden Turin left, if she sparked an explosion caused by natural gas it could cave in more tunnels than just this one. Hassa needed to get them to turn back.

First, she threw a rock.

"Did you hear that?" Jami whispered.

"Of course I heard that. Shut up and listen."

Hassa began to growl low in her throat. She rubbed her wrist on the wall, making a scratching sound with the edge of her dress. Then she stamped her feet.

"What is that?" Jami sounded terrified.

Hassa's growl increased in volume.

"Run!" Turin shouted.

Hassa's growl turned to silent laughter. She scuttled away, tears streaming down her face as she imagined the look in Turin's eyes.

She was still laughing by the time she got to the Nest.

Hassa brushed her wet cheeks and pulled out the map she had made with Kwame. She unraveled it on the table in the center. As she pushed down the edge of the map, Anoor's satchel fell from where Hassa had left it, the notes from her trial spilling to the floor.

Hassa began to gather them up. Most of the papers were jotted with facts: the time of the incident, the report from the healers, a sketch of the jambiya. Hassa collected them up, her hand catching on a heavy book. She pulled it out from underneath the scattered notes.

It was a journal, bound in red eru-leather, a little worn. Hassa opened it and pages fell to the ground.

Pages and page of notes, all accusing Gorn of Uka's murder.

Oh, Anoor. How wrong you are.

Hassa pulled the satchel over her head and ran.

She needed to save Gorn before Anoor did something really stupid.

HASSA DROPPED THE satchel of notes on the floor by Anoor's feet.

How could you be so foolish?

Anoor's eyes went wide at the accusation.

"Get out of the way, Hassa. I'm turning her in."

Rage thrummed through Hassa now.

Drop the knife, Anoor. You are doing something you will greatly regret.

"I don't think I will." Anoor set her shoulders.

Gorn didn't do this.

Gorn's eyes were red, her chin dipped in defeat. It hurt Hassa to see the fierce woman broken down this way.

"Then explain all that." Anoor pointed at the journal.

Hassa's eyes scanned the room until she saw what she was looking for: *The People's Gazette*, with the colored cover of a zine sticking out.

Kwame, pass me that zine.

Gorn's eyes flashed.

"Hassa, don't, it doesn't matter anymore. If she needs me to be the murderer, then I shall. Anoor will then be free."

Kwame gave Anoor and her knife a wide berth as he passed Hassa the zine.

Hassa threw it at Anoor's feet.

She's the author of the Inquisitor Abena series. Is that explanation enough for you?

The knife clattered to the ground first. Then fell Anoor.

Hassa had known for a long time that Gorn was the author of the series. She'd seen Gorn making the trip to the printing press over the years with her folder clasped to her chest containing the next installment in the story.

Gorn had never spoken of it, so neither did Hassa. But Anoor's foolish endeavors had put her freedom at stake.

Hassa knelt on the ground by the sobbing Anoor and touched her chin so she would face her.

You were going to send your friend to jail for life. That is a scar you will bear for the rest of your life. It is a scar you deserve.

Hassa let the rage guide her movements as she signed.

This woman has given you everything. Everything. Even the stories you read, the ones she created to bring you comfort.

Hassa scowled and stood up. She didn't want to be near Anoor. *You were supposed to be a leader. You were supposed to bring change. Instead, you conspired to bring down one of your family.*

With that Hassa ran back into the night.

She didn't go far. Hassa wanted Kwame to come for her, so she lingered by the end of the street. The clockmaster called tenth strike, but already the tidewind was picking up. Kwame and Gorn would have to leave soon.

"Hassa," Kwame called. The rose oil in his hair glittered in the moonlight. It was rare she wished to be more than she was, but in that moment, she longed for fingers to twirl his curls between.

"I've never seen you so angry." He came up behind her and wrapped his arms around her. She leaned into him, enjoying the solidity of him, the sureness of his affection. "I can't believe Anoor thought it was Gorn."

Hassa moved out of his embrace and signed, *She thought it was me once too, and Zuhari before that.*

"Yes."

I wonder if you're next.

Kwame hung his head.

Gorn was willing to sacrifice herself.

"Her love for Anoor is endless."

And yet Anoor will happily accuse her.

Kwame looked to the sky before answering. "Her term as disciple hasn't been easy. I'm not making excuses for her, but she feels like a failure every day. The weight of the truth is a hard burden to bear. Harder still when you know you can't share it."

Those sound like excuses.

"We can't give up on her."

Hassa considered his words.

She needs to get back to saving the empire instead of saving herself.

Kwame nodded. "That's true."

And I know where she can start. The tidewind shelters. We need to get inside.

WHEN HASSA RETURNED to Lio's, she was surprised to find both Anoor and Gorn sitting on the wicker sofa leafing through the zine. Both were red-eyed. Lio lingered from afar watching the exchange with unconcealed jealousy, but Hassa could sense what the others maybe could not. Something had broken between Gorn and Anoor and it would never be fixed. It wasn't quite trust, but something akin to it, loyalty perhaps.

Anoor had lost Gorn's loyalty.

Hassa knew this because she felt it too. It had settled on her shoulders the moment Anoor had accused Hassa of killing Uka.

Anoor looked up as Kwame and Hassa came in.

"I owe you all an apology." Her voice was hoarse. "I don't deserve your forgiveness. I know that. But I will say it anyway. I am sorry."

Hassa sat in the wicker chair opposite Anoor and Gorn.

"Apology accepted," Gorn said as she eyed both Kwame and Hassa, daring them to oppose her. "Let us put it behind us."

Oh, yes, something was broken between them indeed.

"Wait," Anoor said, "I also want to thank you. For saving me. If I had gone to that trial, Gorn would be in jail now."

Anoor met Hassa's eyes and she saw the pain there. Hassa's words were true: there was no greater punishment than the scar she would bear on her soul for this mistake.

Hassa nodded once, and some of the tension in the room released.

I think something is going on with the tidewind shelters, Hassa signed.

She brought Anoor up to speed with what she had learned. Coffee turned to firerum as they discussed the implications beneath the flickering runelamp.

Anoor drummed her fingers on her glass.

"I don't understand. Why would they only take ten people?"

"It doesn't make sense. The supplies I have been delivering are for hundreds of citizens," Gorn said.

But you never supply food, right? Hassa pointed out.

"I assume Yona has someone else helping on that," Gorn replied.

What of Zuhari?

"Zuhari has been overseeing the army's training regime, under Yona's instruction. Apparently, her skills with a jambiya are unmatched, so her time has been spent advising on the teaching standards. With Yona as acting warden, she couldn't refuse."

Hassa sighed. Who cared about the army right now? Yona, clearly.

Anoor jerked upright as a thought seemed to come to her.

"Tanu," Anoor said abruptly. "Didn't you get Tanu to help you with the inventory? Maybe ask her if any of the other disciples are organizing the food."

"Maybe." Gorn's eyes shifted away.

"You can trust Tanu, she tried to help me . . . with the trial."

The tension snuck back into the room, but Hassa had no time for it.

We need to get in there, figure out if the dead bodies are really coming from there.

Lio hadn't said much throughout the discussion. She occupied a leather pouf on the floor and still seemed as if she sat higher than them. Now she spoke. "The woman on the corner who sold fried plantain . . . she got into the shelter. I really liked her plantain."

"You didn't see her again?" Kwame pressed.

"No, someone said that she had got a job in another city. She had no family here."

They all stewed on their thoughts.

We should ask her, Hassa signed to the group, knowing that Lio couldn't understand her.

They looked at each other. Then Anoor nodded.

"Lio, will you try and get into the tidewind shelter for us?"

"You want me to go into somewhere you think is killing people?" Lio laughed.

"Yes. And monitor the process. We need to know what the wardens are doing," Gorn said.

"What if I'm the one who gets killed?" Lio muttered.

"It's unlikely, as the proportion of bodies doesn't add up to the number who go in. Besides, we'll be watching out for you."

"Why can't one of you do it?"

Kwame and Gorn exchanged a glance. "We're all Embers . . . and Anoor's . . . wanted."

"Oh." The truth seemed to waft an unpleasant smell under Lio's nose. "I suppose they're not taking Ghostings?" She jutted a chin at Hassa.

"We're not sending in a Ghosting. They've suffered enough," Kwame said, his voice sharp.

Lio raised an eyebrow as her gaze shifted between Kwame and Anoor. "And this will help you?"

"Yes," Anoor said.

"And you're *sure* they won't kill me?"

Hassa gave Kwame a dark look. No one could be sure of that.

"It's a risk," Gorn said, and Hassa saw the muscle in her jaw twitch.

"Will you do it?" Anoor pressed.

"I will, I have a lot to make up for in your life. This is one small way in which I can repay you." Lio held Anoor's gaze and smiled tightly. Anoor nodded once, then broke the stare, making Lio flinch.

"It's settled then," Anoor said, her expression lifeless. Hassa could only wonder what was going on under the surface.

One mother dead, one mother betrayed, and one mother the betrayer.

Let's hope Lio doesn't betray her again, Hassa thought.

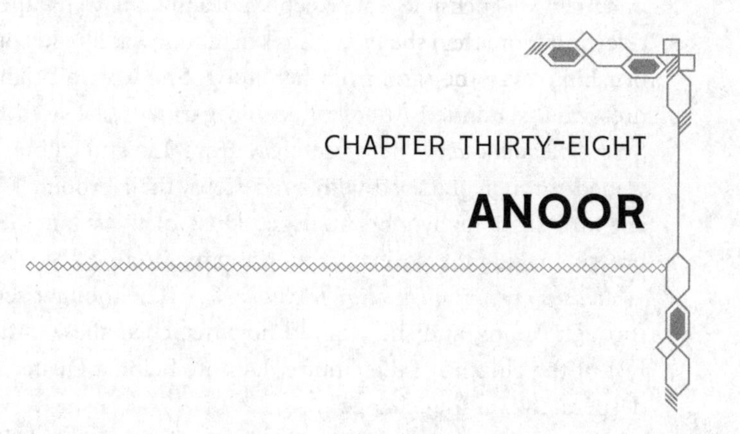

CHAPTER THIRTY-EIGHT

ANOOR

I've found a substance that will make our bloodwerk stronger.

—Message from Disciple Faro to Disciple Tanu

Anoor tried not to think about the day of her trial. Of Gorn's broken heart. Anoor would spend the rest of her life mending it if it was the last thing she did.

She slept restlessly, the straw mattress digging into her through the thin sheet. The sheet needed changing, but she didn't want to bother Lio.

The woman had gone out that night and tried to get into the tidewind shelter, only to return half a strike later.

"No space," she said and retired to her room.

Morning came, but Anoor wasn't sure she had slept. The tidewind had rattled against the wooden shutters of her window so violently she wondered how anyone got any sleep in the Duster Quarter.

She pulled up the manual shutters, revealing the morning light.

The world was covered in a blue film thicker than she had ever imagined was possible. The Keep's gates must have hampered the tidewind more than she knew. Lio's neighbor was already out there brushing away the sand from her stoop. She wore a bright green dress that reminded Anoor of an old garment she used to own. Street cleaners drew her gaze away from Lio's neighbor as they waded through the road with tired steps, their brooms sweeping left and right in hypnotic unison. Dust blew up on the gentle breeze, making the poverty around them glitter.

This is my first night away from the Keep. The thought sent a jolt through Anoor, and she realized how detached she was from the rest of the citizens of the empire. Despite being a Duster, despite desperately wanting change.

One of the street cleaners dropped their broom and the other went to help them.

"Brush the sand toward the breeze. Let the wind help you," one cleaner said to the other.

I could learn a lot from these people.

Anoor felt her resolve harden. She felt a flicker of the person she used to be, the one that walked the five hundred steps with hope in her heart.

She stood and moved into Nuba formation one. It had been a few weeks since she'd last exercised. Sylah would be disappointed in her. And not just because of that. Anoor was meant to revolutionize things. But she'd failed; instead she'd been consumed by her own problems and not the problems of the empire.

Sylah, you'd be so ashamed of me. The thought was desolate, but it didn't make her feel helpless. Rather, she felt a surge of affection.

She will love me, no matter what I do. The knowledge was freeing, and though it did not assuage her guilt, it drove her to keep trying. She wouldn't give up on the people of the empire. Not yet.

All Anoor needed to do was get back to helping people. If she was destined to be stuck in this villa for the rest of her life, then she wouldn't wallow. She would fight. But not for herself, for the

Dusters and Ghostings she'd vowed to help when she took up her mantle.

Anoor was in formation eight when she saw Lio watching her from the curtained doorway.

"Your form is good. I can tell she taught you." Lio didn't say Sylah's name, as if saying it would somehow make her absence more painful.

"Thank you."

"Breakfast is simple fare. But come, it is time to eat."

Anoor followed Lio down the stairs.

Breakfast was a porridge made of grains, topped with plantain chips. It was delicious, but Anoor didn't say it.

Lio cleared her throat.

"I . . . I want to tell you about the Sandstorm, and maybe you will see how, if not why, I left you."

Anoor's stomach sank. She didn't want to hear this, but she didn't have much choice. Leaving the villa wasn't an option.

Lio took Anoor's silence as permission to continue. Maybe not permission but acceptance. Anoor was sure the woman hadn't ever asked permission for anything.

"I was pregnant when I met Azim, though I didn't know it. I had a few suitors among the servants of the Keep and to this day I do not know who your father is."

Dusters working as servants in the Keep was a past that Anoor struggled to conjure in her mind. The blue-blooded had so long been banned. Ever since the Night of the Stolen, when Anoor had been swapped with a red-blooded.

Lio continued, "We met in the Maroon, a tavern in the Dredge."

"I know it." Sylah had taken her there.

Lio's eyebrows quirked just a little.

"Azim had just come from the fields. He had been whipped for not meeting his quota. He was a little drunk. But when he spoke, others listened." Lio's gaze went deep into her memory, and she smiled. It freed the muscles in her face and made her look almost pleasant. "He spoke of a world where Embers weren't our wardens. A world where Dusters weren't laborers, but leaders.

"There was a crowd around him, a lot of them Gummers, which makes sense now I know the Sandstorm was funded by the Warden of Crime. When the crowd dispersed, he saw me."

Lio let out a breath.

"Azim had a way of truly seeing people. And there in that moment I was seen. I don't know if he knew I was pregnant, maybe he did, and it was why he approached me. Either way I believed so completely in the world he wanted to build. And the world he wanted to burn.

"Nine mooncycles I carried you and slowly Azim's plan came together. I introduced him to other servants in the Keep. Some of them my friends. They joined the Sandstorm readily, for we were tired of the life we led. One day Azim called on all the parents of the group and sat us down. I will never forget the words he said to me then:

"'What I ask of you is the greatest sacrifice anyone should make. But sacrifice is a tool, and we must wield it like a scythe on the neck of the empire. And though the sacrifice wounds you, it won't be fatal, but fatal it must be for the world we know.'"

Anoor shivered, holding her elbows to her chest.

"He was a fanatic," she spat. "He wanted to kill all Embers, he wanted to destroy everything. How could you follow him?"

Lio's eyes flashed as she was brought back to the present with Anoor's words.

"One day someone will say something to you that will resound in your very marrow. It will be a truth so clear that you will do anything to make it *become* a truth. Then you will understand why I gave you up. Then you will know how it feels to truly believe in something greater than yourself."

Anoor frowned at the words that sounded so very like a prophecy. But she had that already; she believed in humanity and preserving the good before the tidewind took it.

Lio stood.

"I have to go out, I'm helping Abod the baker deliver stock in exchange for a few slabs. I'll be gone until the market closes. Do not go out. There is food under the counter."

Anoor nodded. "I'll be here, don't worry."

Lio scowled as if to say, "I do worry."

As soon as the door closed behind her Anoor rushed to the window. When Lio became a speck in the distance Anoor went to grab a headscarf from Sylah's belongings. She wrapped it tightly around her curls. Her hair was the most identifiable thing about her, and being so strangely dressed in drawstring pantaloons and a threadbare shirt, she was sure no one would recognize her.

She lifted the straw mattress to hide her inkwell while she was gone and caught sight of a slip of paper.

Roughly drawn bloodwerk runes in old blood had been scoured onto the surface. An attempt from long ago.

Anoor smiled. *Look how far your bloodwerk has come, Sylah.*

She dropped the mattress.

". . . and look how far I have fallen." The words brought her comfort.

Dust always rises in the tidewind.

THE DREDGE WAS busy. Dusters hurried to and from their destination with purpose, carrying Anoor along. Ruins of villas spread out into the street, debris and litter filled the gaps that weren't limestone brick. Sewage leaked from upturned septic tanks and children ran through the streets barefoot.

Anoor saw few Ghostings, and she was grateful. At least they were safe somewhere to the north. For now. She wasn't sure where she was going; she'd been too focused on her trial to read up on the notes of the tidewind shelter, but she knew it was near the plantation fields.

She felt a perceptible change when the crowds thinned to reveal more officers than she'd ever seen outside the Keep. They lingered in clusters around one street in particular, and though she knew it was risky, she went down it, keeping her head lowered.

". . . she's long gone, I don't know why they're bothering to search for her anymore."

"Good riddance, I'm glad Yona's back in charge."

"Warden Yona," the other chastised.

Anoor had known her fate was sealed now that she'd run away, but it was very different hearing it out loud. She kept her smarting eyes focused on the ground.

There was the unmistakable scratching of an eru's claws coming from behind her, and Anoor pressed herself into the ruins of a villa in time to see a carriage rattle down the street. For a moment she thought she saw the glitter of blue scales, but it was just the reflection of the sky across the cream hide of the eru. She had a surge of longing for Boey, her eru who had traveled with Sylah to the Chrysalis.

The carriage stopped in front of a building that couldn't have looked more out of place if it tried. It was boarded up with reinforced steel and spanned three or four villas across.

This must be the tidewind shelter.

Anoor watched as someone jumped down from the driver's seat. They locked eyes with her, and she jolted.

Tanu. Tanu was here.

Part of Anoor wanted to rush forward and hug her colleague and explain everything. But the risk was too great. Instead Anoor dropped her eyes.

Tanu didn't look like she'd recognized her and instead went to help the officers with unloading the goods. Anoor strained to see what they were unpacking, but the carriage was blocking it.

"What are you doing?"

Anoor jumped so high her sandals nearly came off.

An officer had come out of the side of the building and was watching her.

"Nothing," Anoor mumbled.

"Then get going." The officer unlatched their runegun and leveled it at Anoor.

This is the first time I've seen a runegun from this angle.

She should have been frightened, and the logical part of her brain was, but mostly she was enraged. This is what it's like to be a Duster. *Truly* a Duster.

She wanted to fight the officer and turn the gun on him. But instead, she cooled her anger and replied, "Sorry, I will be on my way."

The officer's bushy eyebrows went upward, whether it was from her smooth dialect or her fearless response, she wasn't sure. Either way she felt a prickle of uncertainty and practically ran all the way back to Lio's.

Once she was inside, she lay her beaded brow on the cool whitestone wall and laughed.

"Too close, too close."

There was a knock on the other side of the door that rattled her teeth.

Anoor opened it with a beating heart.

"Hello, Anoor."

There on the porch was Tanu.

"WHAT ARE YOU doing here?" Anoor's tongue was heavy, her mind blank.

"I think that's a question for you, no?" Tanu cocked her head like a crow, her black strip of curls flopping to the shaven side of her head.

Anoor looked down the street. There were no officers, and thankfully Lio's neighbor was out. If Tanu hadn't brought other officers, then maybe she wasn't here to turn her in.

Anoor pulled her into the living room.

"What happened to you?" Tanu said, looking around the room in disbelief.

Anoor hesitated.

"Are you going to turn me in?"

Tanu laughed. "I ask you again: did you kill Uka?"

"No."

"Then why would I give you up to the wardens?"

Anoor wasn't sure why she deserved such loyalty from Tanu, but she was grateful for it.

"Sit. I'll tell you everything."

When Anoor got to the part about Gorn being the author of the Inquisitor Abena series Tanu couldn't stop laughing. Her cackle grew in volume.

"An author? A blood-forsaken author of a trashy *zine*?"

Anoor bobbed her head. "Yes, and I nearly condemned her for life."

Tanu sobered at that. "That would have been a mistake and a half . . ."

"Tanu, I need to ask you about the tidewind shelter. I've been hearing . . . things."

"Things? Shouldn't you be trying to get yourself free?"

"No, I don't care about that anymore."

Tanu's brow creased, and she watched Anoor pensively. "Really? I'll be sure to tell Yona. She's out of her mind about losing you."

Anoor felt a shred of guilt. "She is?"

"Yes, it's a battle. The Abosom versus the army. Yona wants to find you so she can help you, the Abosom want to find you so they can jail you."

"Is she . . . mad?"

"Aho, madder than a desert fox protecting her young. She's still claiming you're innocent." Tanu shrugged. "That's good at least."

Anoor missed her grandmother. *I hope she can forgive me for giving up.*

But she wasn't giving up, not completely. She was just concentrating her efforts elsewhere.

"The tidewind shelter, Tanu. What's going on? I've heard that only ten people are let in a night . . . and only medical supplies are being delivered, no food, no blankets."

Tanu snorted.

"I just delivered fifteen crates of food, so that's not true."

"Oh."

"And Faro is in charge of all material goods, clothing, blankets and such. I know Faro made a delivery the day before yesterday, I think."

"Really?"

"Yes, and Qwa is helping with the logistics. All three of us meet with Yona once a week and she gives us jobs. I thought you'd be happy? It's all happening, even the curfew is coming into place tomorrow."

Anoor didn't know what to think. Maybe Hassa's assumption was wrong, and it wasn't the tidewind shelter but something else, a new crimelord maybe?

"Is there anything I can do to help, from here?"

Tanu looked around the room doubtfully. "You really want to stay here? Who even owns it?"

"A friend."

"I didn't think you had friends," Tanu teased but the insult hit home. "Except me of course."

Anoor felt her spirits lift. Here was a friend willing to help.

"Tanu, if there's anything I can do. Anything at all, I'll get bored out of my mind otherwise."

She shrugged. "I might have some paperwork you can help with. Shall I bring it tomorrow?"

"Yes, please. But be careful, I don't want anyone to know I'm here. Come after tenth strike and I should be alone. If someone else answers the door, feign ignorance."

Tanu chuckled as she walked to the door. "Isn't it funny? She writes zines and you're living one."

Anoor gave her a weak smile.

"I'll see you tomorrow?"

Tanu gave her a hug, and Anoor leaned into the physical contact.

"Yes, tomorrow. Maybe I'll beat you in a game of shantra," Tanu said over her shoulder.

Anoor turned and saw the shantra board tucked into the side of the wicker sofa. The diamond tiles looked worn out. The tokens too were broken with the paint peeling from being overused. She saw Sylah in her mind's eye playing with Lio until the early morning, her face pinching as she lost over and over.

Sylah was never any good at shantra.

"Whoa, you don't need to cry about it, it's only a game of shantra. We don't have to play if you don't want to," Tanu said, her expression alarmed.

"No, I'm fine." Anoor pressed at her eyes with the back of her hands. "We can play. But I'll win."

Tanu smirked.

"There's the Anoor I used to know."

Tanu was still laughing as she skipped out into the street and away.

Anoor didn't know what to do with herself for the rest of the day. She had tidied Sylah's room, done the dishes, and swept the house clean of sand. She'd burned her hands on lye trying to wash her sheets, an activity she had never done before and didn't look forward to doing again.

She tried playing shantra on her own, but there was no fun in battling oneself, so she put away the pieces after spending half a strike setting them up.

Hassa had left Anoor her satchel full of notes, and with a heavy heart Anoor began to sort through them.

What is the point in keeping any of this? It doesn't matter anymore, I will never know who killed my mother.

Anoor hustled the papers together and threw them in the stove. The relief she felt as the pages turned to ash was freeing. The only thing left in her satchel was Warden Biq's journal that had hidden her notes on Gorn.

With nothing else to do, Anoor began to read.

Today marks the fifteenth Aktibar of our great nation. The Wardens' Empire will honor its hundred-and-fifty-year dynasty with a test like no other. As Warden of Duty, I am in charge of the festivities and will ensure that every competitor is rightly celebrated.

This journal was nearly three hundred years old. Anoor looked at the seams of the binding and realized that the book had been rebound at some point in its past.

She remembered that Yona had said she might find answers here, so she kept reading.

Tonight, I have set a place next to me for the granddaughter of our late Warden of Duty, the first of my guild, one of the founding quartet to give us this great home.

Anoor skipped ahead.

The celebration was a success. The Ghostings are much more obedient following their penance. My honored guest delighted me with tales of the continent passed down from her grandfather. She spoke of the Spider God, Kabut, and how the Zalaam had honored him by sacrificing two ships on their journey. She believes that Kabut granted us the utopia of the empire as a result.

Few believe in the Spider God anymore. Anyme is the deity the natives follow and so our citizens have been swayed from what once was. I didn't have the heart to tell her, she is a hundred years old and her mind wanders. If she still believes, then I will allow her that grace. But the Zalaam are no more, we are the Wardens' Empire now. We are the Gods that walk this earth.

The founding wardens were Zalaam?

The question didn't answer anything because Anoor still didn't know who the Zalaam were. She missed Yona in that moment. Maybe her grandmother would be able to answer her questions about the Spider God and the Zalaam.

And about the tidewind shelters.

CHAPTER THIRTY-NINE

ANOOR

Anoor believes I keep my mother away from her out of spite. In truth, my mother's ways frighten me more than I care to admit.

—Journal of Uka Elsari

Lio didn't get into the tidewind shelter that night, or the five nights after. While they waited, Anoor's life took on an uneasy rhythm.

Nuba formation practice at dawn. Then breakfast in the morning in silence with Lio. Once Lio left on her day's errands, Tanu would stop by. Anoor hadn't seen Hassa, Gorn, or Kwame since that dreaded night. She expected it, they had things to do, lives to lead as well as researching what was going on in the tidewind shelter.

That day Tanu was with her. She had given Anoor administration tasks to alleviate her boredom, though at the moment the paperwork sat next to them untouched.

"Another round?" Anoor laughed.

Tanu was leaning over the shantra board with consternation.

"I don't know how you do it."

"Practice."

"Hmm." Tanu began to reset the board. "I really should go."

"To the tidewind shelter?" Anoor still didn't know what to think. Maybe Tanu didn't know what was really happening on the inside.

"I have a meeting with your grandmother, actually."

"Oh?"

"Yes."

Anoor thought back to all the questions she had for Yona. All the things she wished she could ask about the founding wardens.

"Tanu, do you know who the Zalaam are?"

Tanu's eyes narrowed.

"Didn't Warden Uka ever tell you?"

Anoor shook her head. She had spoken to her mother rarely. And now she wouldn't ever again. She dismissed the sudden wave of grief with a flick of her head.

"The Zalaam were the founding wardens."

"But who were they?"

Tanu shrugged. "Believers."

"In what?"

"A better world." Tanu was inspecting a shantra piece. The token was a smooth oblong made of cheap pine with a circular base. She ran her thumb over the grooves of it. Anoor wondered if Sylah had done the same thing with the exact same piece.

Tanu placed the piece on the board with a clatter. She laughed when she saw she'd startled Anoor with the sound.

Tanu wasn't Sylah.

"What do you mean by a 'better world'?" Anoor asked.

Tanu's eyes went distant. Her voice drew out the words as if pulling them from the corners of her memory. "A world we must fight for." She smiled in the throes of a recollection. "My father used to say that all the time . . . though it's no longer his fight." She grimaced and brushed a delicate hand over her forehead.

Tanu had never spoken of her parents. Anoor knew that they'd died before she'd moved to Nar-Ruta. She'd been raised by a couple out in Jin-Gernomi, who had moved to the capital when Tanu was eight. Her adoptive parents were tailors and worked for the wardens in the Keep, which was why she was housed and schooled alongside Anoor. Tanu, in defiance or genuine uninterest, never partook in the Keep's fashions. Even today she wore a loose-fitting dress that sagged low under her armpits.

"What was he like?" Anoor asked tentatively. It was rare to see the softer side of Tanu, and she relished these moments. It made her feel like a true friendship was building between them.

Tanu gave her a crooked grin.

"Harsh, hardworking, strict . . . but generous. So generous . . . I miss him all the time."

"He sounds like my father."

"General Ahmed?" Tanu asked, picking up another shantra piece and inspecting it. Anoor noted how she had filed her nails to a point. Like talons.

"Yes, he loved stories. I got that from him." Anoor was drawn back to the present with the reminder that the stories she had so loved were written by Gorn out of love for her. And Anoor had thrown that in her face by accusing her.

"So, the Zalaam? They wanted a better world?"

Tanu sighed. "Yes, but why does this matter? Who cares who the founding wardens were?"

"I think it's important to know the history of the empire, especially a history that erases the theft of an entire island." Anoor didn't mean to let slip that bit of information, but Tanu didn't even blink. She *knew*. She knew that the Embers and Dusters were just colonizers on the Ghostings' land.

What else did she know? Did she know any blood color could bloodwerk? Did she know that there was still a mainland?

Too many questions lodged in her throat. While she was silent, Tanu took the opportunity to stand.

"You still have that headscarf and cowl?" she said.

Anoor frowned. "Yes."

"Well, put on your disguise, we're heading out."

Anoor wanted to say no. But she'd been stuck in this bloodforsaken house for too long.

"Let's go."

Tanu walked a little bit ahead of Anoor. She stepped so lightly, her petite form slipping past the crowds of people on the Tongue. Anoor tried to keep her gaze down, but she worried that if she lost sight of Tanu for a second, she'd disappear like a leaf on the breeze.

The trotro rattled past, bursting with root vegetables for the Ember market. Dusters accompanied the train, their shoulders slumped, their eyes downcast, avoiding the numerous patrols that crawled through the city.

Anoor was pushed roughly out of the way.

"Move."

She opened her mouth to retort but closed it a second later as the person's purple uniform came into view. She dipped her chin and shuffled to the side. The officer smelled of radish-leaf smoke and cheap whiskey. The kind that Kwame brewed. Anoor flinched with every footfall of the officer's feet.

"Too close, too close," she whispered to herself.

Anoor reached the end of the Tongue, but Tanu had slipped somewhere through the streets of the Ember Quarter ahead of her. Panic burned the back of her throat.

There was a whistle, too shrill to be a kori. Anoor spun and saw Tanu's back disappear down the street to her left. Anoor quickened her pace to keep up.

They walked along the edge of the Ruta River, the churning sand more than a hundred handspans below them. The villas on the edge of the quarter were a lot smaller than those in the heart of the Ember Quarter, mainly because they were owned by Embers with less wealth. The properties were not as desirable for the higher-ranking nobility as the view from the windows was that of the Dredge and the Duster Quarter on the other side.

Tanu skipped down a small, cobbled street and disappeared into a glass-fronted villa.

The words "Sphinx Tavern" were embossed in gold across a metal hanging sign. Anoor pushed open the heavy wooden door.

The tavern was thankfully full, so few people looked up as she entered. Anoor scanned the room for Tanu. She noted more than a few Ember servant garbs and the occasional eru driver uniform. Though the establishment was well presented, with leather cushioned seats and gilded tankards, if you looked closely, you could see it wasn't as premium as it seemed. The wood paneling of the walls was pockmarked with a woodlouse infestation and the wines that lined the shelves weren't as expensive as those served in the Keep. It was the kind of tavern you'd expect to see officers drink in.

Thankfully there weren't any there that day.

Anoor moved slowly through the groups of drinkers. Her nondescript clothing gave her some anonymity.

Someone grabbed her elbow with sharpened nails. It was Tanu.

"By the blood." Anoor scanned her arm for any cuts. Bleeding blue among Embers, even those of the lower class, was never a good thing.

Tanu rolled her eyes at Anoor's overreaction. She had no idea what problems she might have caused.

"This way," Tanu urged.

Anoor followed her to the back of the room where a small staircase led them down into a cellar. The air was thick with damp from fermenting alcohol. Anoor tried not to gag.

"Where are we going?"

"We're nearly there."

Sunlight disappeared as they descended. Instead, it was replaced by the red flickering light of a single runelamp. The cellar was a small space, and the floorboards were sticky with spilled drink and a strange white substance that looked like chalk. Casks and barrels lined the walls, some leaking pungent liquids from between the wooden planks.

One of these barrels had been rolled to the center to be used as a table. The runelamp sat atop, with two people around it.

Anoor recognized them immediately. The sharp stab of betrayal was overcome by fear.

"You're late," Qwa said with a drawl.

"I was fetching our guest of honor," Tanu said and thrust Anoor into the warmth of the runelight.

Faro gasped, and their hand jerked forward in shock, knocking the runelamp to the ground.

It shattered into the silence.

"Well done, Faro, you are the clumsiest person I have ever met. You'd trip over sunlight." Tanu sighed. "I'll go fetch another."

As she pranced away in the darkness Anoor stood there tugging on the hem of her shirt.

"Trial didn't quite go as planned, did it?" Qwa said somewhere to her left.

"No. It wasn't Gorn."

Qwa drawled out a sigh. "All the evidence pointed to her."

"It wasn't her," Anoor repeated firmly.

"I bring light." Tanu turned on the runelamp with a flourish.

Qwa looked at Anoor with half-lidded eyes. Faro was picking at their nails with nervous energy.

"What's that face for?" Tanu said, noting Anoor's scowl.

Anoor swung her gaze to the person she thought was her friend. The friend who had just sold her out.

"What am I doing here?" Anoor hissed.

"I've already filled them in, they know Gorn didn't do it—" Tanu said as if Anoor hadn't just spoken.

"What do you mean, fill them in? Have you been sharing our *private* conversations?" Anoor's volume dropped to a near whisper.

"They weren't exactly personal. I needed to keep them filled in; we're your allies, remember? You don't need to keep anything from us."

Tanu sounded hurt. Somehow, she'd turned the blame back to Anoor. It was a habit that Anoor now recalled from their childhood. Clearly, she hadn't grown out of it.

"We're here to help you," Tanu continued. She reached out and touched Anoor's forearm. The contact soothed Anoor's anger, and she felt herself nodding.

"I'm sorry, it's hard to accept help sometimes."

"I know."

Qwa and Faro nodded too.

Anoor looked between the three of them and was grateful. Tanu winked as Anoor's gaze landed on her, and Anoor felt a smile grow.

"There we go," Tanu said, and all tension left the room. "Anoor has some questions about the Zalaam."

Faro's eyes snapped to Tanu's.

"The Zalaam?"

"Turns out Uka didn't tell her much."

Qwa barked out a laugh. "Did you tell her that we don't know much?"

Tanu frowned. "But we have theories. And I think she deserves to know them."

"Tanu, we have a meeting with Yona in one strike. This meeting, which I'd like to point out was a *covert* meeting, is for disciples only," Faro cut in.

"I'm a disciple," Anoor said with an edge to her voice. "I deserve to know the truth."

Qwa grunted.

"Oh, truth? That is a very slippery thing."

Tanu turned to Anoor.

"We were all told about the empire's origins when we became disciples. Although each warden recounted the history differently, the essence of the story was the same. The Zalaam found a land ripe for harvesting, and the empire was born."

"Too true," Faro said softly.

"The three of us weren't quite satisfied with the 'truth' our wardens chose to share, so we have been searching ourselves. Though the warden library doesn't really piece together much more than what our wardens say," Qwa added as if speaking were a chore.

"You've been meeting in secret to compare what you've each found in the library, in the wardens' journals?" Anoor asked.

"Not just the journals," Qwa said ominously.

Tanu reached around the barrel and pulled out some papers from a satchel.

"We found this."

Anoor leaned forward and read. The script was old, the cursive archaic.

A Child of Fire whose blood will blaze,
Will cleanse the world in eight nights, eight days,
Eight bloods lend strength to lead the charge
And eradicate the infidel, only Gods emerge,
Ready we will be, when the Ending Fire comes,
When the Child of Fire brings the Battle Drum,
The Battle Drum,
The Battle Drum,
Ready we will be, for war will come.

Chills ran down Anoor's back, the words searing into her mind with the feeling of a memory.

"What is it?" she whispered.

"The Zalaam had the ability to commune with their Spider God, Kabut. And they prophesied the coming of a war. They were powerful, truly powerful." There was something in Tanu's voice that Anoor recognized. Ambition.

Anoor leafed through the other notes.

"Prophet . . . communes . . . segregation . . . where did you get all this?" Barely any of it made sense to her, but it was clear that these scrawls hadn't come from the warden library. Some of the pages were too big to fit in the bound journals that filled the shelves there.

The three disciples didn't immediately answer, until Faro said with a small smile, "There are so many secrets in this empire that when you uncover one, you need only turn it over to see another."

Cryptic. Annoying.

"If the Zalaam were powerful, then surely so would we be, given we are their descendants."

"But we stopped believing, don't you see? We forgot the very name of our God, of our heritage, and now we are punished," Tanu said.

Anoor looked to Qwa, as the Disciple of Truth. This was blasphemy. He met her eyes.

"God is God whether their name is Anyme or Kabut."

Anoor looked to the ground. Chalk lines were scrawled into the floor, and she followed them, her eyes going wider. She understood now what it was.

"A shrine, you've made a shrine to the Spider God." Because that's what it was, a spider, with the barrel in the middle. Anoor pressed her eyes shut. *By the blood, these three have gone insane.*

"We have been . . . trying to commune with the God . . ." Faro admitted.

"What do you mean?" Anoor asked.

Faro looked defensive. "We've tried a few things, sacrifice being one."

Anoor recoiled. Sacrifice? She looked at the exit.

Tanu's expression turned fierce. "If you don't believe the power of the Zalaam then watch this."

Tanu pushed her stylus into her inkwell and drew a few runes Anoor didn't recognize onto a ribbon of paper. Anoor watched the red blood seep into the sheet.

She should leave now, go before she was sucked into their madness. But then the paper moved. Not like the push and pull of bloodwerk, but with the movement of a snake. It slipped off the barrel and scuttled along the floor. It was alive, sentient.

Anoor jumped back.

"By the blood, what is that?"

Tanu laughed and tore the paper snake to pieces, rendering the bloodwerk useless.

"Godpower, Anoor. That is godpower given to us by Kabut."

Anoor held her head in her hands. She'd wanted the truth, but not this truth. Not this truth *at all.*

A thought came to her.

"Will godpower save the empire from the tidewind?"

"Godpower will save the world," Qwa said, and he smiled, teeth gleaming red in the runelight.

ANOOR MADE IT back to Lio's in a daze. The disciples didn't have a lot of time to discuss their findings, as they had to rush to their meeting with Yona. Anoor left first.

"Come back tomorrow, same time. My cousin owns the tavern, and we can speak freely here," Faro said to Anoor.

She wasn't sure she was going back. What had started out as a mere question in a journal had become something much . . . darker.

Godpower and prophecies?

But the power, Anoor couldn't deny that. If worshipping Kabut allowed them to stop the tidewind, then she'd do it, she'd do anything.

The Battle Drum,
The Battle Drum,
Ready we will be, for war will come.

The words haunted her. If war was coming, they needed to be ready for it. And this Child of Fire, who and what were they?

Anoor paced up and down the small living room at Lio's. A headache blossomed at her temples. Strikes and strikes went by. Consumed in her thoughts, she was shocked when the tidewind rattled against the window. She rushed around the house pulling down the wooden shutters, lest the thin glass smash in the onslaught.

Lio didn't come home.

CHAPTER FORTY

HASSA

We burn our dead, so they are free. The smoke will carry their souls to the sky and Anyme will welcome them into their nation above. Those not burned will haunt the world forevermore, their souls trapped.

—Teachings by the Abosom

There she is. Hassa nodded toward Lio's shaven head as she made her way out of the shelter.

"I can see, I have eyes," Kwame said.

They'd been bickering all morning. Hassa liked it.

I see you have eyes, but sometimes I do wonder if you know I have eyes too.

Kwame half-smiled, half-scowled. "Shh, you." He offered a hand to Hassa's arm and helped her down the ladder to the street below. She didn't need the help, but she took it anyway.

"Lio." Kwame waved her down.

"Oh, it's you." Lio's lips puckered in a grimace, and she continued walking toward the Duster Quarter. She walked stiffly, like she'd slept on a hard bed. Her brown cardigan and blue pantaloons were creased worse than her frown lines. "I'm tired, can we talk later?"

No, you imbecile, people are dying, let's talk now.

"What is she flapping about?" Lio said, waving a limp hand toward Hassa.

Hassa ground her teeth and exhaled slowly.

"She's just saying how lovely you look in that patterned blouse," Kwame said sweetly.

Lio gave Hassa a perverse look. "Right."

"Please, we need to know what happened. We need to know what you saw."

Lio stopped in the middle of the street and looked around. "I hate it here. It's so rotten. I don't know why anyone would choose to live here."

No one chooses anything in this empire, except Embers.

Kwame read Hassa's signing and looked away, a sad frown on his face.

Ask her again, Hassa demanded.

Kwame pursed his lips. His kissable lips. But he didn't prompt Lio a third time; instead he chose to wait.

Lio eventually filled the silence.

"They gave me a cup of soup. The medical team checked me over. I was given a set of night clothes and a pallet to sleep in. I stayed up all night and saw nothing untoward."

Hassa's shoulders drooped.

"Nothing?"

"Nothing," Lio confirmed and continued her march as if the conversation had concluded.

There can't be nothing. The bodies. We've seen them. We saw one this morning.

"Are you sure?" Kwame pressed Lio.

Lio looked at Kwame as if she hadn't realized he was still there. "Yes, I'm sure."

Ask her if there were different rooms, if it was all in the open or not?

"Were there different rooms?"

"No, just one big one."

"And everyone who entered remained in that room at all times?"

"Except for the privy, yes."

I don't believe it. Make her remember each detail.

"And no one left the room?" Kwame stood in her path, stopping Lio from stomping away.

Lio was getting impatient, much to Hassa's delight.

"No one left." Lio's teeth ground together as she spoke. "I have had no sleep, my stomach hurts from the thin water they called soup, my back hurts from the hard pallet, and right now, all I want is to go home. So, good day to you."

Please, give her a medal.

Kwame held out placating hands, one toward Hassa and one toward Lio.

"I understand you had a hard night, and we're really very grateful to you. I know your daughter is as well."

Lio's eye twitched.

"But I need you to think really carefully about what happened last night. We have a reason to believe that some people didn't make it out alive. So we need to know if there was any opportunity for someone to be taken away. People are being killed, and every moment we waste doing nothing, another person is at risk. Why don't you talk us through the whole process?"

Lio stood still, breathing heavily. "I queued up like I had done every day for the last week. The queue moved quicker last night, and I found myself at the front of it for the first time. They asked my name and occupation. Both of which I made up as you suggested. They asked if I had any family. I said I had a daughter. They showed me in. I went through a medical review with a healer. I changed behind a screen and they—"

Hassa touched Kwame's arm and signed, *The screen, ask her about the screen.*

"The screen, what type of screen?"

"Opaque glass. Three walls, an opening to enter."

"How many screens were there?"

"Two, maybe three."

"And you only needed to use them to change?"

"Yes, for the medical. They checked me over when I was in my underthings."

Ask her if she saw anyone administer drugs.

"Were there any drugs given out?"

"Well, yes, there were a lot of decrepit types." Lio sniffed. "Though I tried to stay away from them, I saw a few injections given out by the healers. That was all some people got. Injections."

"What do you mean?"

"There were more people coming in than beds available."

And she didn't think that was an important piece of information? Hassa bared her teeth at the woman.

"Did you see people leave?"

Lio thought for a moment.

"No, I didn't."

Maybe there's another area behind one of the screens. Could they drug them before taking them through?

Kwame conveyed Hassa's theory.

"Possibly, I can only tell you what I know. And what I know is that the shelter does exactly what the name suggests. Now can I go?"

Ask her to go back tonight. Ask her to look behind the screens if she can.

"No," Lio said once Kwame translated.

"Please. For Anoor," Kwame added softly.

Neither of them had been to see Anoor in the week she'd been at Lio's. Though they were busy, they also needed time to process the damage she had done in accusing Gorn. They needed time to heal some of the trust that had fractured.

If they ever could.

Lio's chin dipped.

Only Kwame could charm the most stubborn woman in Nar-Ruta.

"Fine, I'll go back tonight." Lio marched off, her sandals kicking up dirt from the road.

HASSA SPENT THE next day with Kwame, so her patrol of the Dredge was a little later than usual.

"You're so beautiful, Hassa," he'd murmured against her bare skin as they lounged in his bed. She shivered with the memory, holding her elbows against her chest.

He'd loved her thoroughly, slowly, his lips traveling across her navel to the apex of her thighs.

Oh, he was very good. Very *good.*

She was still caught up in the haze of lust as she walked through the Dredge. Then she saw the corpse.

No, no, no, no.

The moon shone down on the body, illuminating their short hair, grown out in tufts from the stubble it used to be.

Lio.

Hassa's cry choked the back of her throat. Lio had been thrown against a dirty wall of a villa. She wore no clothes, the scars of her life bared proudly in the night.

Hassa had not liked Lio. Lio had not liked her. But this was no way to die.

I can't leave her here. I must give her the funeral Sylah would have wanted. Sylah—

Tears were flowing freely now as Hassa imagined telling her friend that her mother died at the hands of the very people she hated the most.

The wind pulled at Hassa's servant clothes. The curfew would be starting soon.

Hassa knew of a route to the tunnels beneath the city twenty handspans away, under an old eru stable. But twenty handspans was as long as twenty leagues with a body heavy with rigor mortis.

Without a backward glance, Hassa ran all the way back to the Keep, the wind at her back an aid and a warning.

NO TALKING, JUST come. She pulled on Kwame's arm, dragging him from his bed.

"Hassa? What's going on?"

No time.

She couldn't spend the few precious minutes they had explaining how Lio was dead.

"Wait, I need my shoes," he shrilled, but even pulling on his shoes as he ran he caught up with her in a few strides.

Hassa led the way through the Keep and out toward the Ember Quarter. There was a patrol of officers barring the way at the Tongue.

"Curfew in half a strike. Where do you think you're going?" The captain turned to Kwame, ignoring Hassa completely. She tapped her foot in impatience.

"Official business, Captain. On behalf of Acting Warden Yona Elsari." Kwame pulled out his Shadow Court token and Hassa resisted rolling her eyes.

Half a strike until curfew and the tidewind could strike at any time between then and now. They'd have to run fast through the Dredge.

"Official business . . . in your night clothes?" The captain eyed up Hassa with lifted brows.

Hassa made a small sound in her throat to speed things along.

"Yes. Please let me past or Warden Yona will hear of this."

The captain clearly didn't take too kindly to Kwame's brusque tone, but there was nothing they could do.

"Officers, let him and his servant through," the captain commanded.

As soon as their runeguns were out of sight Hassa began to sprint.

Hurry, she urged Kwame behind her.

"Okay, okay, I just wish you'd told me we'd be running. I wouldn't have worn my velvet loafers," Kwame grumbled.

As they reached Dredge Square the tidewind began to build.

No, I won't let her body be destroyed like this. I can't.

Hassa ran harder as the sand whipped up into her eyes and she had to run blindly, letting instinct lead her through.

"Hassa, we need to find shelter," Kwame was shouting.

Just a bit farther.

"Hassa!"

Kwame came up behind her and pulled her into his arms as a gust barrelled into him, sending them both reeling. She felt something wet on her face and realized it was blood. Kwame's blood. The tidewind had pulled the nightshirt off his back leaving his skin bare.

She accepted defeat. It was time to head to the tunnels.

In the brief respite from the tidewind's wrath, she led Kwame toward the nearest Ghosting villa, hoping that it had an access point to the tunnels below.

She claimed victory for the first time that night and found a small hatch in the rubble. Kwame was breathing heavily beside her, but he helped her lift the wooden opening that revealed a ladder into the darkness.

"You go first, quickly now," he said, his signature smile a ghost on his lips.

Hassa went down into the tunnels. Kwame hissed in pain as he came down behind her.

With no runelamp he had to cling onto Hassa's servant's dress in order to follow her.

"You have a lot of explaining to do, Hassa," he said without anger.

The sound of their footsteps filled the silence. Every now and again the tidewind's roar would shudder the walls and Hassa would feel Kwame flinch.

It wasn't far to the Nest. As reluctant as Hassa was to bring Kwame there without the elders' permission, he needed medical attention, and she had supplies there.

The scent in the air shifted from the dank smell of the tunnels to the fresh bread of a home as they entered the Nest.

Hassa lowered Kwame into Elder Zero's favorite chair before feeling her way to the hearth. In moments the fire set the room alight with an orange glow.

"There you are." His lips were pale, his skin shining with sweat.

Hassa sprang into action. She leaned him forward on the chair. His back was in ribbons, the skin torn to shreds by the lethal force of the tidewind. They were lucky it was just the start of the tidewind.

She wouldn't be able to stitch him up, but she had other ways to aid his healing.

"Is that tree gum?" he said weakly as he watched her paste the substance onto strips of cloth.

She nodded once.

"Okay. I trust you."

Hassa faltered.

He trusts me? she marveled. *Me, the empire's hassa beetle?*

She wanted to tell him not to, that bestowing trust on her wasn't wise. Her actions were always fueled by the will of her elders, of her community. And he was not one of them.

But she realized she trusted him too. And that trust was more powerful than love could ever be.

"What are you smiling at?"

She shook her head and brought over the strips of cloth. Slowly, carefully, she began to pull the edges of his skin together with the gum and material. He didn't complain once, though she could sense him holding his breath throughout.

A strike or so later she had made him more comfortable by propping him up on his side. She'd found a bottle of firerum to help dull his pain, and before he drank, he swirled the liquid with distaste. He preferred whiskey, like Embers.

He is an Ember, she reminded herself.

The reminder unsettled her, and she busied herself with making her hormone replacement tea with the herbs she had bought from Ren's apothecary. The drink was bitter, and she sweetened it with honey. She finished it before filling Kwame in on what had happened to Lio.

"So she's gone," Kwame said. His eyes had already turned glassy from the alcohol.

Hopefully her skeleton will be there in the morning. We should burn it.

"Yes. Smoke into the sky and all that." His fingers fluttered upward, and he spilled his drink.

Maybe that is enough firerum.

"Probably." He conceded his glass to her. "Hassa? What's that?"

He pointed to a lump of metal fashioned into a cuff that sat on a table. Hassa dropped her gaze.

"Is it an inkwell? Are you trying to make an inkwell, Hassa?"

She shrugged. She had been. But fashioning one for her limbs had proved harder than she thought. The lump on the table was the result.

It was just something I was trying.

"Hmm." Kwame's voice grew sleepy. "You should try using a quill, just strap it to your limb like you do with other things. Then dip the end in blood. It should be easier."

He was right. She was trying to re-create something that was made for Embers. She should just go back to basics: a quill and a pot of blood.

The thread of the conversation was pulled by Kwame's new lack of inhibition, thanks to the firerum.

"Did you have a good childhood?"

She thought about it.

No, I don't think I had a childhood at all.

He nodded deeply, so deeply she wondered if his head would make it back up.

"I didn't either." He said it like a secret. "My mother abandoned me when I was a child, left me at the Keep's steps. I was raised there by a handful of servants. One of them . . . used me . . . you know?"

Hassa's heart broke to see Kwame's smile fall so far from his face. She reached for it, trying to stroke it back on with her limb. He closed his eyes at her touch.

"They stopped when Papa found out." Kwame smiled. "I called him Papa, because he became so dear to me. He used to be the firelighter in the Keep, setting alight all the hearths on cold nights. Now illness plagues him, in his bones. He doesn't have long."

Hassa hadn't realized his father was so close to death.

"I'm not sure I can be sad for Lio. She abandoned Anoor." His lips wobbled.

Hassa leaned into his chest and began to hum. It was a haunting melody. It was the song of freedom sung by Ghostings. The tune had filled the halls of the Nest on many cold nights.

Soon they were both asleep.

When Hassa woke, Kwame wasn't sleeping next to her. She sat up quickly, the blood pumping to her head in a rush.

The fire still flickered, and it was in the wavering light of it that she saw Kwame's shadow.

He looked up as she joined him.

"It's morning, if that small slash in the ceiling is anything to go by." He turned to her with wide eyes. "I can't believe I didn't see this yesterday." His hands reached out to the carvings on the wall. The story of the Ember and Duster invasion.

Don't touch it.

"No, of course, no, I won't." His hand dropped as if burned by fire. "But, Hassa, it's beautiful and so sad. So very sad."

There were tears in his eyes, and she reached to wipe them away.

We will make it right again. We will reclaim our home.

". . . what happens to me when you do?" He whispered the question that Hassa didn't have an answer to.

I don't know, she answered honestly. *But the elders are not the Sandstorm.*

He nodded.

How is your back?

"Sore," he admitted. "But whatever you did has helped."

She inspected his wounds. The bleeding had stopped, and the bandages had adhered well to his skin.

Go see a healer when you go back to the Keep. I fear you may have some scars.

"Battle wounds."

What?

"Battle wounds, not scars."

She laughed and went to get one of Elder Ravenwing's loose shirts. She handed it to Kwame.

Come, let's go and retrieve Lio's remains. We should burn her where we light the pyres for the sleeping sickness. It'll be the first time a real body will be burned there.

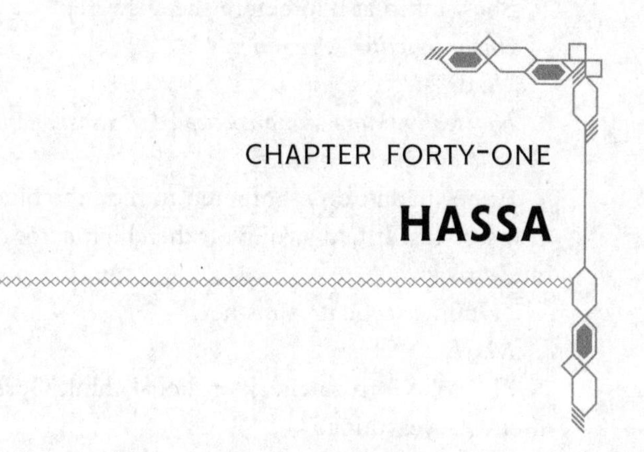

CHAPTER FORTY-ONE

HASSA

TUNNELS BENEATH CITY ARE UNSAFE

THE WARDENS ARE urging all citizens to refrain from using the tunnels beneath the city. An explosion, caused by gas pockets, resulted in four Nowerk deaths. Use them at your peril.

—*THE PEOPLE'S GAZETTE,* year 302

Anoor didn't cry when Hassa told her of Lio's death.

Another mother, lost.

There was something new in Anoor's eyes, something that worried Hassa. It was the same way an Abosom would look before slitting the throat of a goat at an Ardae celebration.

Hassa knew Anoor was sneaking out of the villa every day, even if she didn't know where she went. It was a risk Anoor was taking, and Anoor would reap the consequences if caught.

"How is Anoor?" Kwame asked Hassa. He was lying on his back for the first time in days. The tidewind wounds had healed well, aided by a poultice from the Keep's healers that would have cost a Ghosting three years' salary. Hassa watched his naked form with keen interest.

"Stop looking at me like that." He smiled in a way that made it sound as if he'd like her to continue doing just that.

She winked at him before she answered.

Anoor is acting . . . strange.

"Sad?"

Not really. More . . . preoccupied. I also noticed she was using her blood to do bloodwerk practice.

Anoor hadn't even bothered to hide the blue blood on the tip of her stylus. It had swung on the chain across her chest, leaving blue streaks.

"Hmm, maybe it calms her."

Maybe.

"I'll ask Gorn to check on her. I think Gorn's avoiding going after . . . everything."

Hassa understood.

"I've been thinking—"

Hassa wriggled her eyebrows. *About me?*

Kwame laughed. "Always. But on the rare occasion when I'm not thinking about you, I've been thinking about the shelter."

Hassa waited for him to elaborate.

"I looked into building deeds to see if there was any floorplan of the site that we could use to find a way in." Kwame frowned.

Did you find one?

"No, there wasn't much, just a deed of sale marked six mooncycles ago. Yona bought the shelter long before Anoor announced the Tidewind Relief Bill."

That would explain why I found some before the shelter was announced.

Kwame nodded.

"We need to find a way in there. Find out what they're really doing."

I agree, but I don't know how.

"What about the tunnels, is there a way under the shelter where we can get in?"

Hassa exhaled through her nose and sat up in bed beside him.

There are some tunnels even Ghostings don't go down.

"What do you mean?"

There are pockets of gas beneath the ground that have caused explosions in the past. The north of the Dredge lies in that district. No one's been in those tunnels for some time.

Kwame's brow furrowed with concentration.

"Could they now be safe?"

It's possible, she admitted. *But I've never wanted to test it.*

"Is there a way of detecting the gas?"

Fire, she signed. *It goes green when gas is present. It also explodes if gas is present.*

"Oh," Kwame said. Though she could still see his mind working painfully hard. "What if we used mirrors?" He sat up quickly and winced.

How?

"We douse balls of fabric in oil and set them alight, I could push them with bloodwerk—my skills are not the best, but I can definitely master *Kha* to push the balls along. Then we use mirrors to watch the fireball around any corners we can't see down. If it turns green, then we're not near enough for the explosion."

We'd need to be very, very far away.

"But it could work?"

It could.

Kwame had agreed to meet Hassa in the Dredge at sixth strike. She could see the beaming of his white teeth twenty handspans away. He was giddy with excitement. Next to him was a crate full of Hassa's reflection.

The two mirrors were ornate, and Hassa was surprised he hadn't been mugged brandishing such wealth where few had enough money to eat.

"I want to donate the mirrors when we're finished with them," he said, sensing her disapproval.

She gave him one of her genuine smiles.

Hopefully we'll still be alive.

He laughed. "We will, trust me, I've got a battle scar now."

She didn't laugh. Instead, she looked deep into his dark eyes as she signed, *I trust you.*

He swallowed, not fully understanding but sensing the importance of her words.

"Thank you."

She led him away down to the tunnels of her lair.

HASSA AND KWAME picked their way through the tunnels beneath the tidewind shelter. It had been a long time since anyone had been this far through the northern path. The recent onslaught of the tidewind had exacerbated the decay of the aging structures.

They followed the orange glow of the fireball, the mirrors proving helpful in navigating their way around corners. Sweat beaded on Hassa's forehead, clear like her blood. All she could hear was the sound of their breathing and the flickering of the flame up ahead.

Kwame touched her arm.

"Are you okay?"

She nodded. With her other arm strapped to the mirror, she couldn't sign to him.

They reached a crossroads, and Hassa indicated the direction Kwame needed to direct the bloodwerk fireball. He tinkered with his inkwell until the fireball moved off.

Hassa watched the orange waves of the flame in her mirror, and the sight soothed her beating heart even as the ceiling arched low above her head. They were close now, mere handspans away.

Hassa's heart sank as the tunnel was lit up by the fireball and she saw the way ahead of them blocked by a caved-in wall.

She pulled off the straps of the mirror, dropping it to the floor, and began to move rubble. Kwame helped until they had created a hole, just big enough for her body.

She touched Kwame's wrist.

Stop.

". . . Hassa, I can't fit through there."

We can't risk moving more of the whitestone, the walls may collapse, or we might release a pocket of gas. She waved to the blocked path. *I'm going to go alone. The fireball hasn't turned green, so we know there's no gas in the immediate vicinity. If my calculations are right, there should be a ladder on the other side leading to the shelter.*

"I'm not leaving you."

I know. She smiled and kissed him deeply. He sighed against her skin.

See you soon.

The collapsed tunnel turned out to be a blessing really, as Kwame had all the stealth of a desert monkey with a limp. Without him, Hassa could get in and out in no time.

She moved through the gap in the rubble and her clothing ripped, the beige fabric revealing beige skin. She sighed. Another uniform that needed repairing.

On the other side of the cave, she saw a circular opening in the arch of the tunnel. As she crouched and craned her neck, she could just make out the rungs of the ladder.

Made it. She was pleased. The tunnels were a maze few knew how to navigate, and though they were her home, she hadn't been sure she'd be able to find the tidewind shelter. The passages had always been a way of escape for the Ghostings. Once the natives had their land invaded, the underground provided a network of transport and a means to get out of the city undetected. But many tunnels ended in cellars or sewage drains, because of a long-abandoned scheme by a former Warden of Duty who had once aimed to "better" the Dredge.

Now that she'd found the shelter, she had to hope they hadn't blocked the exit from the tunnels with cement.

She pushed herself up through the opening and began to climb. The tunnels were all between a hundred and a hundred and fifty handspans underground. Her arms were burning as she reached the top. The hatch above was metal. Usually, metal meant a private cellar.

Hassa pushed at the metal door. It wouldn't budge. There were so many passageways under the city that it wasn't possible to reclaim them all. Especially if the exits were in people's homes.

Hassa tried again, and she heard something shift above. Ah, so it wasn't locked—something was on it. She gave the hatch one more forceful shove, and it swung open, flinging whatever had been on top of it to the other side of the room with a clatter.

"What was that?" The voice was distant, but still sounded close enough for Hassa to freeze.

"Something fell."

"I gathered that, but *what*?"

"I don't know."

The voices grew louder. Hassa could go back down, leaving the tunnel open and risk them finding the opening. But that would be it: they'd lock it up and she'd never get another chance to find out the truth. Or she could close the hatch and risk making more noise, which would result in the same outcome.

There was one other option: Hassa would have to make a dash for it. She hadn't realized her mind had been made up until she was halfway out of the opening. There were boxes to her left and she dived for them. As she landed she scrunched up her small form into a ball in a bid to hide from the shadows making their way through the room.

"Did you hear that?"

They were close, so very close now. If they found the opening, they'd look for her. Hassa looked around her, her breath coming out in short uneven puffs.

"It was probably a rat."

"It would have to be a real big one," the other commented. Hassa winced at the doubt in his tone. He wasn't convinced it was a rat.

Next to her foot was a jar of pale blue liquid, just smaller than her wrist. Hassa clutched the jar in her arms and launched it across the room, hoping the sound would draw them away from the opening.

As she'd predicted, they jogged toward the sound of broken glass and away from Hassa.

"A broken harvest. You better throw that out somewhere so the warden can't see it. You know how important each vial is."

"Me? Why is it my fault? I was the one who said it was a rat."

"Well, maybe it was, but even so, I'd hide the evidence if you don't want to be fired."

The two of them bickered into the distance, and Hassa released a breath. She surveyed the area. She was in a storage facility of some kind. Natural light streamed in from the direction the voices had gone in, illuminating the boxes piled high around her. She opened the closest one. Cold air fogged out. The box was full of ice, but under the frost, glinting like starlight, were more jars filled with the same blue liquid, frozen solid.

Hassa slipped one in her pocket to examine later. The weight of the jar dragged her dress down on one side and froze her thigh from the inside.

With careful steps she made her way through the boxes toward the door. She caught sight of the street beyond through a slit in a shuttered window. She was, without a doubt, in a warehouse connected to the tidewind shelter. She knew this, because across the road she could see the villa where she had watched Gorn unload the carriage.

The door to the warehouse opened, and Hassa was startled into the nearest shadow.

"How many more do you have?"

"Ten."

"No deaths last night?"

"None."

"The healers are getting better."

Hassa heard the clinking of glass being packaged away. She peered around the edge of her hiding place to see two uniformed officers carefully sealing a box.

"Where are you stationed tonight?" the taller of the two asked.

"Back at the Keep. The wardens are still on the lookout for Uka's killer—"

Hassa heard a scoff. "It was definitely the daughter."

"You think so? I'm not so sure. She was always nice to me. Once she brought me some kunafa while I was on shift."

"It's always food with you. I, for one, am glad to have a day off from this dump. I haven't spent so much time across the river since . . . well, never."

"Same. It really does smell. If it isn't the rubber from the plantations, then it's the stink from the people."

"True, either one or the other. Plus, the work is boring. I'm still not sure why they need us to guard the harvest . . ."

"You know how the wardens are—paranoid. Remember when Warden Wern thought she saw an intruder in her chambers, and it was just a desert fox? She made me escort her everywhere for a mooncycle? Even to the privy. I know more about that woman's bowel movements than my own husband's."

There was a snort of laughter.

"Come on, let's do another round of the ward. Some of the patients got loose from their restraints last night, best to tuck them in tight tonight."

Out they went. Hassa released a shallow breath and followed the way they had gone. She wasn't leaving until she got some answers.

THE DOOR IN the warehouse led Hassa down an empty corridor. She followed the sound of voices until she came to a doorway. If her calculations were right, to her left was the shelter as the outside world knew it, and to the right was an additional facility that must be where a few people were taken. Maybe next to the screens where Lio saw people being treated with injections.

Hassa knew she didn't have long before the guards made their way back. Being as careful as she was able, she edged the door ajar and pranced backward, just in case someone had spotted the movement. She counted to ten, her breathing coming faster. Nothing.

She crept forward and peered through the crack in the door. What she saw sent her stumbling backward again.

Patients were strapped to wooden pallets in rows, fifty at the least. They lay on their stomachs, their hands tied up above them as healers moved in and out administering water and thin soup through metal straws. Long tubes of pale blue liquid made their way into the patients' bodies through cannulas in their backs.

The holes in their bones.

The liquid wasn't going in. It was going out.

They're harvesting bone marrow.

Hassa felt her body begin to tremble. She had got her answers, and although they posed more questions, she found herself wishing she had never come here at all.

"Hey, you, what are you doing here?" It was the tall officer.

Hassa sprang down the corridor back the way she'd come. The officers followed her, shouting at her the whole way.

"That's a big rat, Ty, I knew we should have checked it out."

"Hurry up, they're getting away."

"I can't run any faster."

"How the hell you ever passed the training regime I will never know."

"Caught you. What the hell are you doing here?"

Hassa drowned them out as she skidded through the Warehouse. The metal of the hatch lid gleamed in the moonlight, and she dived down it.

Wait . . . "Caught you"? They hadn't caught her . . .

Dread ran through her veins like ice. She lifted herself up to peer over the edge of the hatch and what she saw nearly made her loosen her grip.

But she still felt like she was falling.

The two officers held Kwame down, his cheek pressed to the ground as they knelt on top of him. They'd spotted him, and not her.

Kwame's gaze found hers.

"Go," he mouthed. "Go, quickly."

She didn't want to leave Kwame. But she knew she had to. Someone had to tell the truth about what was happening in the shelter. Tears fell down her cheeks.

She slipped down the ladder and pulled down the hatch as quietly as she could. But the sound of the cover closing, and that of her cries, echoed through the tunnels.

When she reached the bottom of the ladder she began to run. She noted the gap Kwame had made for himself in the rubble and winced.

Why, Kwame? Why couldn't you have stayed put?

The fireball was resting in a nook of rubble that Kwame had moved. The green flames cast a flickering shadow against the white-stone. Without the bloodwerk she wouldn't be able to use the fire-ball, so she abandoned it where Kwame had left it.

Green flames.

Green flames.

Hassa ran, her throat burning with the effort. She had seconds. She had mere breaths.

Hassa began to laugh from the rush of fear, she laughed for the patients. She laughed because she had no idea what was going on. But most of all she laughed because if she didn't, she'd weep all the harder.

Hassa was still laughing when the tunnel caught fire. There was a *woosh* and a *bang*.

Then the walls collapsed in on her.

CHAPTER FORTY-TWO

NAYELI

I leave the care of the orb in your hands, leaders. But know that I will not return without the Child. Then war will come.

—Last words from the Wife to the commune leaders of the Zalaam

Nayeli looked out across the sea. The vessel she had commandeered was little bigger than a fishing boat, but if her brother told it right, she'd soon meet the sea creature that haunted the waves. After that it would be a straight route of seven or eight days to this new land.

The Wardens' Empire.

Nayeli laughed into the breeze.

"Wife? Are you well?" her companion asked. Robi. He had small eyes and an even smaller brain. But he had been the first one to offer up himself as a sacrifice for her to make it across the sea.

"I'm well, Robi." Nayeli exhaled and watched him pull on the mainsail. "Show me how you direct the sail in the wind." She'd have to learn how to do it herself in the end.

A messenger in her brother's employ had made it to the Volcane Isles to tell her his tale. Nayeli had called the commune leaders to hear his words, and they had sat in the open temple as light rain fell and merged with their tears.

Inansi's fishing vessel, as the messenger told it, had been caught in the aftershocks of an earthquake, pulling him and his husband into a harsh current that waylaid them in the middle of the ocean. The family had survived off raw fish, the two children growing weaker with each passing moment without water.

On their third day at sea, the water churned, and the wind picked up, bringing with it sharp particles of blue sand. They thought that was the worst of it.

But then something rose from the deep. A creature of stone and glass. It capsized the boat. With shuddering breaths, the messenger recalled the tale of how it swallowed Inansi's children whole and retreated back to the depths. The messenger broke down into quiet sobs at this part of the story.

At first Nayeli thought the messenger wept in grief for the children, her own grief sharp and painful.

But when asked he explained, "I too had to sacrifice a life in order to pass by the creature of the sea. My friend—" The messenger choked on his tears and said no more.

Sacrifice. Of course. It always came back to sacrifice. Whatever this sea creature was, it was an agent of Kabut, that she saw clearly.

Once the messenger recollected himself, he went on to tell the story of the Drylands, of the wardens that lived there and the "bloodwerk" they used to control those they had conquered. Nayeli had cast a glance to the commune leaders of Red and Blue. Were they ashamed that their brethren had forsaken the Zalaams' truth? The four ships that had been lost at sea, all this time believed to be gone, taken from this earth. But in fact, two ships were lost to the sea monster, the Tannin as they called it, while the other two conquered a new land.

Red-bloods were always so righteous. *Wardens.* The name was enough to make Nayeli laugh, though she didn't.

"Why has it taken so long for a messenger to arrive to share with us Inansi's story?"

He swallowed. "Nayeli—"

The commune leaders hissed, Andu more fiercely than the others. It had been a long time since her birth name had been spoken.

"Wife." The messenger corrected himself. "Inansi has been sending messengers every year. I am the first to make it across the sea. Some, I fear, couldn't bear to sacrifice a comrade." His expression grew haunted.

Nayeli was silent, all eyes on her.

"It was my husband's will to grant you passage." Nayeli turned to the commune leaders. "I will journey to this other land and bring back the Child of Fire. It is clear to me that this is the path I must take."

There was murmuring, concern, even a flash of relief from the Clear Commune leader—they had never truly committed to Nayeli's place next to Kabut's.

The preparations had only taken a few days. And so now she found herself slipping through the sea foam on a boat made for two with a man so dim-witted she had considered sacrificing him ahead of the Tannin's presence.

On the third night the wind began to swirl and, in the moonlight, Nayeli could see the glittering blue particles of sand dancing on the breeze.

"It's time." She stood, calling Robi to her. The wind whipped her silk saffron robe around her and for a moment she felt like she might take flight. On each side of her chest she had pinned one of the two brooches Inansi had made. They gave her strength.

She closed her eyes and called to the sea demon.

"Come, I am ready to give you the life you deserve. Come, creature of Kabut, and take this sacrifice."

The water parted unnaturally in the distance. Fins of glass cut through the water like slices of moonlight. The waves, repelled by the creature's speedy passage, rippled outward in a spray of froth.

Nayeli laughed as the Tannin propelled itself toward her, the crown of its head emerging from the depths of the ocean. Higher and higher its head rose, and Nayeli saw the stone that it was built from and the engravings that covered its flank like scales. The Tannin was godtouched, made from the runes Nayeli had spent decades perfecting.

She cried tears of joy. This was a godbeast to behold.

"Take my sacrifice, beast of my heart. Godbeast of the sacred runes." Nayeli held her hands outward, palms toward the sky, relishing the ocean water that poured down from the snout of the Tannin like holy water.

"Robi, now," Nayeli said, but the man had frozen to the bow of the boat. The Tannin's neck retracted, ready to pounce.

With a curse Nayeli grabbed Robi by the collar of his shirt and threw him overboard. There was a moment of silence as the Tannin considered Nayeli's lonely form on the boat, but then it lunged with the creaking sound of stones scraping together and plunged into the depths after Robi's flailing body.

NAYELI HAD BEEN sailing for more than two weeks when land eventually slipped onto the horizon. She knew she had gone wrong somewhere in her navigation, but she'd been through worse than dehydration.

She had the scars to prove it.

The nightly hurricane had been another matter. The storms threatened to destroy the boat with every gust. And even though the messenger had prepared her for the hardships she'd face, it never got easier cowering in the hull of the metal vessel as sand whipped up the waves around her.

Now the land came into view. A land of blue sand dunes and bloodwerk. Here she would find her Child of Fire. She knew it in her heart.

Nayeli had learned from her brother's messenger that she'd have to hide her blood color or it would cause a revolt. So when the hull of her boat scraped along the rocky shore of the empire she felt her body shift. Today she was someone entirely new.

"Aho, Traveler. Have you come from Jin-Gernomi across the waves?"

The stranger spoke the common tongue with the same guttural accent as the messenger.

"Yes," Nayeli agreed. "From Jin-Gernomi." The words were foreign on her lips.

"Nice to meet you, I'm Yona." The stranger waved a calloused hand at her.

"Yona." Nayeli rolled the name around her tongue.

The stranger gave her a perverse look that vanished into one of concern when she saw Nayeli's scarred skin.

"By the blood, are you all right?"

"I would like some water if you have some?"

"Of course, of course, I never go fishing without some. Here." The woman handed her a leather flask.

The water tasted sweeter than Nayeli was used to.

"Thank you, may my husband bless you."

"Huh, I'm sure." The elderly woman looked concerned for Nayeli's mental state.

"Do you know how far I am from Jin-Sahalia?"

"Jin-Sahalia? Why, one or two leagues away, my fellow traveler. If you follow the sun, it will lead you there. Unless it is setting, of course, then you'd be going in the wrong direction completely." She tipped her head back and cackled.

Nayeli took the opportunity to slash the woman's throat. Her laughs ended in gurgles.

"Husband, take this sacrifice of a blasphemer, and lead me to my brother."

Hot blue blood covered the sandy ground as Nayeli said her prayer. When she was sure the woman was dead, she took her waterskin and set off to the city of Jin-Sahalia.

JIN-SAHALIA SMELLED OF shit and rotten vegetables. Both were in abundance in the market square. Sellers peddled their wares filling the bustling center with a cacophony of shouts.

Giant cages lined one side of the dirty street filled with scaled creatures of all colors.

Nayeli had jumped to the side the first time she'd seen the giant lizards on the road, but once she realized they were docile beasts, domesticated for transport, her beating heart calmed.

Her sandaled feet were sore, but she knew she wasn't far now from her brother's home. The instructions were clear. Second villa along from the Grainstore Tavern near the Jin-Sahalia market.

"Could I trouble you for directions?" Nayeli approached a man in crisp clothing by the side of the crowd. His eyes went to the scars across her scalp, and he stepped back.

"What do you want? Filthy Nowerk."

Nayeli looked down at herself. She was cleaner than the majority of patrons in the market.

"I'm not sure what you mean by filthy, nor Nowerk. I am the Wife of Kabut and I am looking for the Grainstore Tavern."

"I don't care who your partner is. Get away from me. Go, go away." He shooed her as if she were a crab pecking at a carcass.

Nayeli moved away, perturbed by the man's lack of respect.

This country is rude. Its weather is rude. Its people are rude. And the smell . . . it is rude too.

But the thought of reuniting with her brother drove her on.

"Did I hear you were looking for the Grainstore Tavern?" The woman had the pointed features of a peacock.

"Yes," Nayeli said, relieved. "Can you tell me where it is?"

"I can for the sandals on your feet."

"You want my sandals?"

Nayeli was shocked. But there was nothing for it. She handed them over.

"The Grainstore Tavern is behind you." The woman laughed shrilly and dipped into the crowd.

Nayeli memorized her features.

You will make a good sacrifice for Kabut one day.

Nayeli turned and found the tavern's entrance painted in bright letters behind her. Maybe her slippers had been the sacrifice she needed to allow her to see.

The ground was hot on her feet as she approached the villa.

She knew it was Inansi's from the yellow painted spider on the door.

Tears welled in her eyes, and she knocked.

There was a curse behind the door and a scowling face appeared.

"Who are you?" The man was not Inansi.

"I must have the wrong house . . ." Nayeli looked down the street and counted.

"Wait, the spider brooch . . . that was his." The man stopped scowling, his face going blank. "You're his sister?" He whispered it, and Nayeli dreaded what was coming next, but she nodded, her words lost to the fear of the moment.

"You're too late. Inansi's dead."

NAYELI CRIED FOR precisely one strike. The grief was merely a recollection, revisiting an old wound that had long scabbed over.

Now it was time to plan.

The man, Ama, sat opposite her on a worn leather chair. He wore a dark purple suit that looked very tight across the shoulders. A bottle of a foul-tasting liquid he called "firerum" sat between them. Nayeli poured herself another glass, wondering if Inansi had enjoyed it.

"The wardens, they live in the capital? Nar-Ruta?"

"Yes," Ama responded. The man had been patient with Nayeli's probing, though Nayeli had offered little explanation for her own appearance. Ama's eyes kept flicking to her head.

"And to become a warden you must win the Aktibar? A set of trials?"

"Exactly."

"And all the best people in the empire go to those trials?"

"Yes, the best Embers."

Embers. Nayeli liked the sound of it, like a spark of the endless flame. She could pretend to be one of those, she supposed. The Aktibar, that's where the Child would be. Where they *must* be.

"When is the next Aktibar?"

"Two years."

That was a long time to wait. But something in her heart told her the Child of Fire would be there.

Ama drank down more firerum and Nayeli followed suit.

"Who were you to Inansi?" Nayeli asked him.

Ama smiled sadly.

"A friend mostly. I work for the imir of Jin-Sahalia as one of the family's personal guards. Inansi once saved my life, and in turn I kept his secrets. Helped him. Though I didn't always understand his ways."

"Will you help me? Or is your debt to my brother paid?"

Ama straightened, as his gaze dropped from her scalp to the slip of scarred leg under her dress.

"What do you need?" he asked her.

"Everything, and more."

He'd give his soul up in the end. For there is no prosperity without sacrifice.

PART FIVE

EMANCIPATE

Freedom is not free. It has a cost. But it cannot be bought or given.

Only taken.

And it is time to take ours.

—The Commander of the Chrysalis signing to the Ghosting army

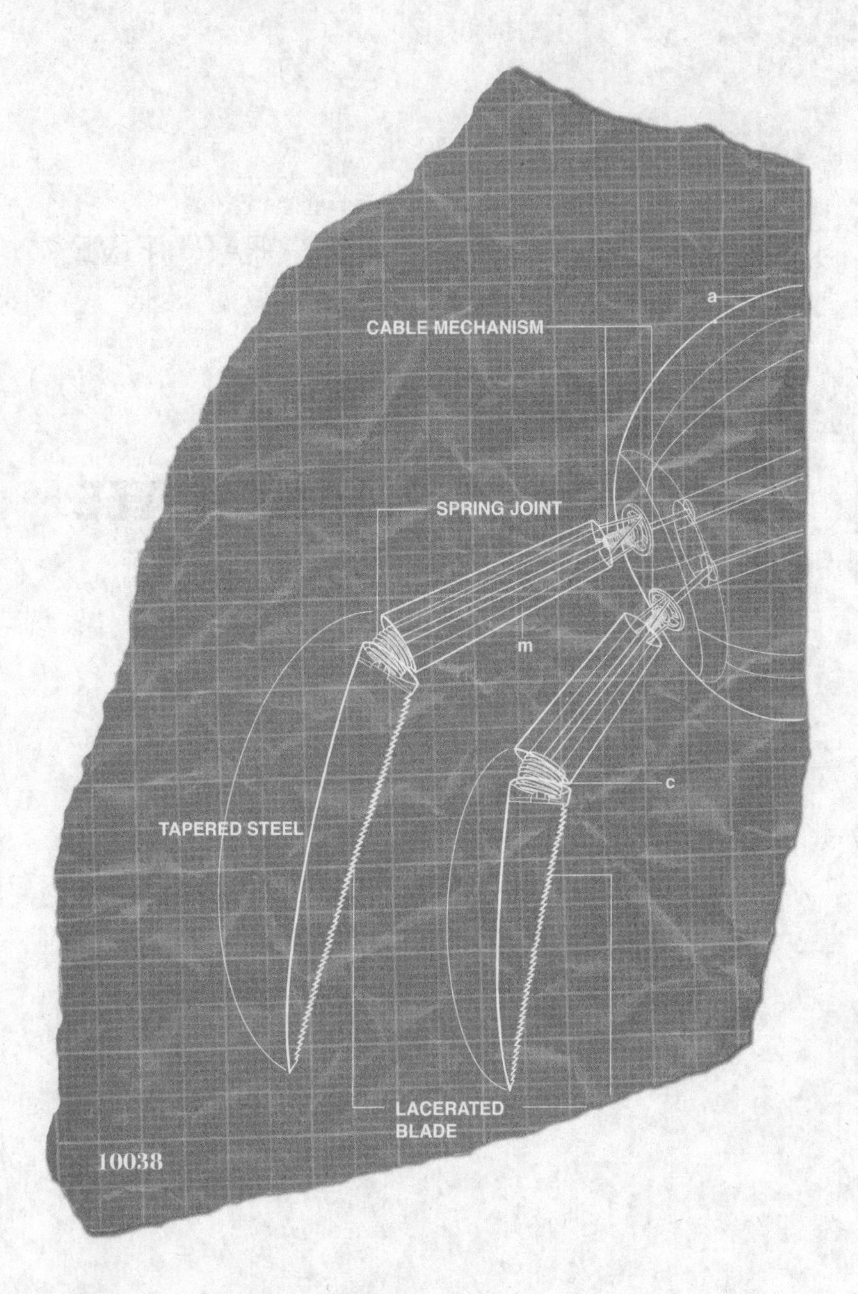

Torn part of a schema found on the Volcane Isles

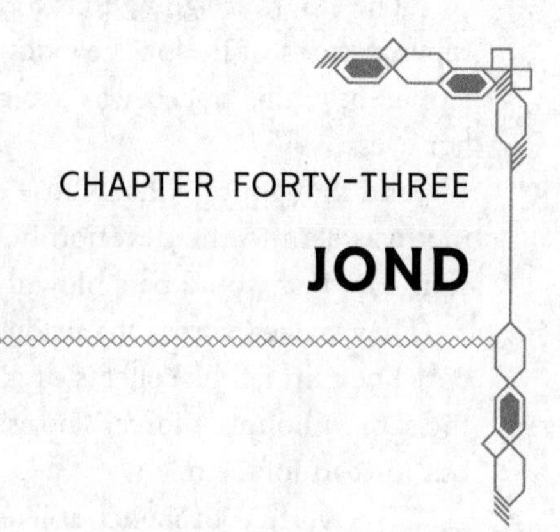

CHAPTER FORTY-THREE

JOND

The palace has fallen. We were struck in the night by a tsunami, the likes of which this world has never seen. The queen and her family are presumed dead. Our monarchy lost forever. I send this message with the last standing flighter in the queen's service. All surviving Sea Lords and Earth Lords must report to the Zwina Academy. Councillors, the power of the land of Tenio is now in your hands.

—The last missive from the hand of the queen

Jond watched Kara disappear faster than he could blink. He didn't even see her move her orb to imprint the runes. He understood then the skill required to master such power. Bloodwerk was a slow, primitive thing in comparison to the deathcraft they wielded.

For a few breaths, the only sound was the messenger's panting. Then Niha was running out of the room. The elders moved next, Ravenwing taking the lead as they headed out onto the next bridge.

"She's not our queen, why do you care?" Sylah was saying to Dew, who was signing quickly to her.

Jond didn't know what the elder said, but Sylah responded, "Fine, I'll come."

"Sylah." Jond reached for her, and she flinched. It hurt him more than he cared to admit.

"The elders are going to the central meeting hall to discuss the repercussions of the palace's downfall with the other councillors. Apparently, this queen was a big deal or something." She rolled her eyes.

Jond thought of Niha, whose devotion to the queen he'd never met was akin to the devotion he'd seen on the faces of the Abosom. Her loss would be a blow to him.

They walked across the bridge back toward the council chamber. The rain fell like sheets of glass and struck them with nearly the same amount of force. The assault made it hard not to despair, but instead Jond smiled.

"The world is broken, but like an eggshell, life can bloom from broken things." It was something Azim had once said, but now, in this context, it fell with a different meaning.

Jond was a survivor first and foremost. Growing up in the Sandstorm was itself a feat of survival. And then, when the officers came and the runebullets took him in the chest, he survived again. Even when Sylah's runebomb that had killed Inansi struck him, he had only dislocated his shoulder.

Maybe this new world had a place for him. Maybe he could earn it.

Rascal squirmed against his chest until her head peeked out of his collar. Couscous flecked her whiskers. She licked at the air, taking her fill of the rainwater before disappearing again.

If this tiny kitten could survive, then so could he.

They entered the central meeting hall to find the three other councillors in a heated debate. Discarded mugs of tea sat cooling on the table among scrolls of notes that shifted in the breeze of the councillors' gesticulating.

"We cannot just take control of the whole country." The small councillor of the first charter was shaking his fist in the air. Jond noted his hands were gloved.

"And yet, we must." Zenebe's dark face was serene.

The councillor with green veins was pacing.

"I wish Kara hadn't just left without speaking to us first. She forgets we rule the Academy by democracy."

"Exactly, the *Academy* . . . not the country."

Jond moved toward the edge of the room where Niha stood. The man's one eye was shining.

"The majority of the Earth Lords and Sea Lords were in the palace when it was crushed," Niha said to Jond in a low voice, careful to not interrupt the councillors. "They were seeking refuge from their own districts . . . now they're gone."

"What does it mean?"

"It means we're a country without a functioning government and the only advisers left from the royal cohort are in this room arguing."

"Kara? She went to the palace?" Jond wondered how far her deathcraft took her.

"What is left of it, I presume."

Jond watched Sylah commune quietly with the elders on the other side of the circular chamber. He knew she didn't care about the state of Tenio. All she wanted was a way to save the empire.

And to save Anoor.

He looked away bitterly. Niha noted Jond's grimace.

"Don't sell your fish from within the sea," Niha said.

"What?"

"Don't be overeager. Patience and a little tact will win her around."

"I don't know what you're talking about."

Niha gave Jond a knowing smile then turned back to the councillors.

But instead of three councillors there were now four.

Kara sank into a recessed seat. Her hood had fallen back, and Jond found himself following the contours of her cheekbones with an imaginary finger. Tears were drying there; her expression was bleak.

The whole room flocked around her.

"It's . . . gone. The tsunami . . . it used the palace towers like wrecking balls, dragging them through what was left. There are a few survivors . . ." She choked on her words.

"The queen?" Niha asked. Kara looked at him, and her violet eyes hardened.

It was enough to set Niha weeping.

"What next?" Sylah said, cutting across the next barrage of questions.

The councillors looked at one another.

Elder Dew signed into the silence.

"Exactly," Sylah agreed with them. "Elder Dew wants to know how we're planning on taking down the Zalaam?" Sylah walked over and perched on the edge of the table.

Kara's expression went from despair to disgust in moments. She did *not* like Sylah. Jond wondered if it was because they were so similar. Both so beautiful, both so brittle.

"A plan?" Tears were still falling into her red curls.

"Yes, it is time to fight back," Sylah said.

Kara laughed, and the elders bristled. "Who are you to demand terms of us? You have been hiding on your continent while the world has slowly been imploding. We have lost everything. Everyone. We owe you nothing."

"No, that's not right." Sylah pounded her fist on the table. "You owe us everything. We came to this Academy to find a solution, but what we ended up finding was the cause. The root of everything. So, tell me. How are you going to fix this?"

Zenebe sighed into his hands. "Survival has been our number one priority, the queen ordered—"

"She's dead, let's move on," Sylah said.

Zenebe winced.

Sylah exhaled, tried again. "Why should we care about survival if the world is going to explode anyway? We need to shift the priority. We need to fight."

The elders were nodding. Sylah translated Dew's words at their behest.

"There is enough experience in this room to build an army. Enough wisdom to create a new world."

"An army?" Kara guffawed. "A new world?"

"Yes." Jond stepped forward. He wasn't sure why, but he felt the pull of purpose on his soul, like a puppeteer's string. Sylah's eyes were on him. "We know a war is coming and we must be ready to meet them on the battlefield."

"The war has already come, and we've lost." Kara's voice was hoarse.

The air shifted and she was gone.

"Give her time to grieve," Zenebe said. "Give us all time to grieve. Night has fallen. We will discuss again in the morn."

Sylah looked like she wanted to argue, but Dew held her back.

Everyone started to disperse, and Jond was glad. Sleep tugged on the edges of his eyes.

"I'll stay with Lune tonight. Sylah can take my bed," Niha said beside him. He seemed to have recovered from the grief that had choked him.

"Thank you, Niha."

Jond waited for Sylah to stop talking to the elders.

"What is it?" She noticed him hovering on the outside of their circle.

"There's a bed for you in my room. Not *my* room, but *a* room. *Their* room."

Sylah tilted her head, listening to him stumble with unconcealed mirth. "Say room one more time."

Jond's eyes crinkled. "Room."

Sylah said her goodbyes and let Jond lead her away.

THE DIRTY WASHBOWLS had been cleared away and the food replenished with a bowl of fruit. Jond, Sylah, and Rascal spent some time sampling it.

"But what even is this? It's hairy on the outside and bright green in the middle. Are you sure it's a fruit?" Sylah waved the hairy egg-shaped thing in his direction.

"It must be. It was next to the grapes."

Sylah sniffed it. The green flesh was speckled with black dots with a creamy white center. Her tongue darted out as she tasted it.

"What . . . wait . . . ugh . . . oh . . . I like it?"

Jond laughed.

Sylah continued. "It's like tangy and fizzy, but sweet and a bit sour?"

She offered the fruit to Jond, who shook his head. Rascal was interested, though. It seemed there was nothing she wouldn't eat.

The sampling session ran its course, and they soon took to their pallets. Neither of them could sleep. Instead, they listened to the rain patter on the roof, both weighed down by the truth they had just learned.

"The prophet of the Zalaam was the councillor of the fifth charter." Sylah repeated the words Kara had spoken earlier.

"Yes," Jond said, though it wasn't a question. Rascal was purring on his chest, and he tried to let the sound soothe his churning mind.

Sylah burst his bubble of calm with a frustrated sigh. She threw the covers off her.

"These blankets are too soft," she grumbled.

"You should tell the First Councillor, he grew the cotton."

Sylah snorted.

Jond heard her feet touch the ground, and she padded over to his bed. Rascal, seeing the opportunity of a whole empty bed full of residual warmth, jumped down and settled on Sylah's pillow.

"That's her bed now," Jond said.

Sylah didn't respond. Her chin was tilted down, her mouth open and about to speak. She came over and sat on the edge of his bed. He watched her silhouette in the darkness, waiting.

"Jond . . . Thank you. Thank you for saving me." Her hand reached for his, and they connected in a lattice of fingers.

He inhaled sharply at her touch.

"You would have done the same for me."

They both knew she wouldn't have.

"So, Rascal's got my bed, huh?" she said.

Sylah fingered the edge of the bed cover, and he felt his heart rate quicken. He remembered what Niha had said, "Don't sell your fish from within the sea."

Sylah was a wraith of beautiful shadows. He wanted to reach

for her, to pull her against his bare chest and feel her warmth seep into his skin.

Instead, he moved over, offering her a slip of space to call her own.

She lay down and shivered, pressing her body backward against his. Jond felt desire prickle through him like the burning of fire-rum.

"Good night, Jond," Sylah said.

That was all she wanted. Companionship, not love. But his love for her was like a spool of cotton dragged in the tidewind, unraveling in the wildness of the breeze.

And he wasn't sure it would ever stop.

THE GAS LAMP had run dry at some point in the night. Jond woke to darkness and a stiff neck. Sylah had dragged the covers off him and was sleeping on her side, snoring softly. He slid out of his side of the bed, careful not to wake her.

There was a small mewl as Jond walked to the door.

"Shh now, go back to sleep, Rascal."

The kitten was sprawled over Sylah's pillow, her head lolling upside down. The one eye that watched him was half-closed. She purred softly and stretched before going back to sleep.

Jond pulled on the waterproof clothing as quietly as he could before heading out of their room.

The corridor still glowed with the light of gas lamps, and Jond squinted in the harshness of it.

Yellow light is so eerie. I'll exchange them all for runelamps someday.

He stroked his inkwell. It had a few dents in it, thanks to the Shariha. He thought of the orbs the councillors used and wondered what it would be like to have an open wound in the center of your palm. And the *precision* required by deathcraft, how restrictive it was. The skill required to master it far outweighed bloodwerk, resulting in many more barriers for the average person to overcome.

Maybe that wasn't a bad thing. Maybe bloodwerk *should* be less accessible. If the councillors were right about the perils of the world's energy, then the fewer people who used it, the better.

Jond reached the opening to the bridge and was pleased to see it wasn't raining. The sky was a vibrant blue, the color a precursor to the dawn. He paused partway across the bridge and looked out over the horizon.

Fog hung heavy on the Truna Hills, obscuring the land beyond. The air smelled of sweet moss and the breeze was light. A caress. It brought with it another smell: mint. He closed his eyes.

"Autumn used to be my favorite time of year," Kara said. Jond hadn't heard her footsteps, because she hadn't walked. Again he thought about precision and how a misused rune would have had Kara plunging to her death.

She continued, "During the harvest, students of the first charter would grow crowns of wheat and pumpkin flowers and hand them out to everyone in the Academy."

Jond turned to her. Her hood was down, her red hair free. It roamed like a pack of wild foxes behind her. In the morning light he noticed she was freckled, her brown skin dusted darker along her nose and cheekbones. Cheekbones that some would say were too hollow. Jond thought it made her look regal, and he imagined her with a crown of wheat and pumpkin flowers on her brow.

"But autumn is also a dying time. Even the first charter knew that to prosper the leaves must fall." She brushed a tear from her eye. "This is the world's dying time."

"But the trees don't die," Jond said. Kara turned to look at him with half-lidded eyes.

"No, they don't."

"They come back stronger, bigger, healthier."

Kara nodded but her shoulders had drooped, her chest concave as if she harbored a pain there.

An ant crawled along the rope bridge between them. They watched it.

"How did the law of creation work?" Jond asked.

Kara lifted her chin. "There are four primary runes, like in all the disciplines. The fifth charter could infuse life, diffuse life, mimic life, and take life."

"Four runes on which all the supplementary ones are based?"

"Yes."

"Just like bloodwerk."

She looked to his inkwell.

"Don't forget the deal we struck."

Jond would have agreed to do anything to help save Sylah's life, and offering them the knowledge of bloodwerk was a small price to pay.

"Maybe it could help us in this fight," Jond said.

"Why do you want to fight?"

Jond frowned.

"Don't you want to survive?" he asked her.

"I do, but I'm not asking myself the question. I'm asking you. Why are you so keen to launch into battle? Who are you but a lovesick boy following the whims and wiles of those more powerful than you?"

Jond balked, shifting the rope bridge beneath them. *How dare she?*

Kara smiled. "Locust plague, I've hit a nerve."

Jond exhaled, letting his thoughts settle. He wasn't one to speak in anger. He preferred to let anger mellow before choosing his words.

"I have been pulled and tugged and pushed into believing what is right and wrong my whole life. Choice was not something I have ever been granted. This fight, though, this battle, it feels like my choice." Jond's voice hardened in defense. It was as if his words were not for Kara but for Azim and Inansi. Even for Sylah.

Kara laughed. "You're doing it because you choose it? That's not a good enough reason."

"It's good enough for me. I've chosen what is right and what is wrong, because what are we without morality?"

Kara's violet eyes widened.

"I wonder if that's what the Zalaam tell their children. Who are we to tell them what they think is right, is wrong?"

"There are no villains in any battle. Only believers," Jond admitted. "But I tally the suffering and I pick my side. I choose to fight rather than let the Ending Fire take us. I choose life over death."

Kara's smile was sly, seductive. "You're wise, lovesick boy."

She blinked out of existence.

CHAPTER FORTY-FOUR

SYLAH

Creatures made do not live long. They are infused with a piece of life that the orb user has granted and so, the fragment they take does not sustain them.

Still, to create life is something to behold. But most of all, something to fear.

—Past teachings from the fifth charter

When Sylah woke, Jond wasn't in the bed. She wasn't sure of the time, despite the clock that hung on the gray wall. No one in the empire knew how to tell the time except clockmasters. Sylah reveled in the novelty of always knowing the time.

How strange it must be, how constricting.

Rascal was still asleep on her pillow, and she stooped to collect the kitten, who gave a disgruntled chatter.

"Let's go find your papa, little one."

She pulled on a raincoat robe and tucked Rascal into her pocket. It took her two or three tries to retrace her steps back to the kitchen.

Jond and the elders were inside sipping tea in silence, though the elders spoke between themselves. Ads was not yet awake.

Rascal jumped out onto the table and made her way to Jond. He fussed at her and scratched her chin.

It was such a strange sight to see, but she was glad Jond had found something to love.

Other than her. The thought was a little cruel, but true.

She had been so lonely last night. She couldn't bear to sleep alone. Partway through the night she had reached for Jond, thinking he was Anoor. Guilt gnawed at her empty stomach.

How she longed to cup Anoor's face and lower her lips to hers. To touch the softness of her curls and to hear the tinkling of her giggle.

Jond's laughter shattered her recollection as Rascal skidded across the table after a morsel of food he waved in her face. Sylah threw him a scowl.

She settled down next to Elder Dew and reached for some tea.

Sleep well? Elder Dew asked.

"Yes, as well as could be expected when everything I thought I knew has been turned inside out. You?" Sylah slurped on the bitter tea. It burned the top of her mouth, blistering the skin.

I too had a bad sleep.

Jond had turned to fiddling with his inkwell, a small crease in his brow.

"What is it?" Sylah asked him.

"Trying to figure out how this was made."

"Why?"

"I said I'd teach Kara how we bloodwerk in exchange for your healing."

The room churned in silent uproar as the elders clambered to sign. Sylah winced at the ferocity of their words.

How dare he sell our ancestor's secret? Ravenwing was standing, signing over and over again his anger.

Reed pushed herself back in her chair and signed. *The Zalaam blood runs strong in this one.* Her face twisted in disgust.

This was not his decision to make, Dew signed.

"I'm guessing the elders are not so happy that I made this deal . . ." Jond said, wide-eyed.

Sylah dropped her head in her hands and prodded the burnt flesh on the roof of her mouth with her tongue. Strands of skin pulled away from her probing.

"I'm not sure I see the problem here," Jond said. "In fact, I think this might help them win the war with the Zalaam. It's easier to work than the orbs they have, and the runes themselves are totally new to them. We can only hope the Zalaam on the Volcane Isles don't know of them."

"But bloodwerk, deathcraft, whatever you want to call it, is what causes the destruction," Sylah said.

"But think about it. If the world had lived in balance for so long without any problems, then using bone marrow must have been what tipped the scales. I think they're using excuses not to fight," Jond said.

The elders were conferring between themselves. Niha slipped in with Ads by his side.

"Aho, the tension in here is like syrup," Ads exclaimed and mimed walking slowly through a thick substance. No one laughed.

Niha took a seat next to Jond. "What's going on?"

"They found out I made a deal to share my knowledge of bloodwerk with the Academy in exchange for healing Sylah," Jond said.

"Oh."

"And they're not happy," Sylah added pointlessly. "But I agree with Jond, it could be the only thing we have against the Zalaam."

The Academy has already proven they are not capable of protecting knowledge. They abused it once and we believe they will abuse it again, Ravenwing signed, his brow puckered.

"What do you mean?"

The Tannin.

A creature made of stone and glass brought to life.

"The Tannin was made by the law of creation." As soon as Sylah said the words, she realized the truth behind them.

Reed's shrewd eyes watched Sylah. The elders had reached this conclusion before her. *It is what we believe*, she signed.

"Do you mind translating?" Jond said softly. Sylah relayed Reed's words.

He nodded then said, "Why would the prophet of the Zalaam create a monster that would destroy a quarter of their ranks?"

They all mulled over Jond's thoughts. Sylah's skin prickled as the air shifted and Kara appeared. She sneered at Sylah as their eyes met.

"The councillors are ready to discuss."

Kara didn't wait for a response, disappearing as quickly as she came.

"I guess we've been summoned." Sylah stood. "Which is good, because I've got a few questions for these councillors . . ."

SYLAH STRODE INTO the room to find the four councillors sitting at the recessed table.

"We've come to an agree—" Zenebe started.

"The Tannin. I want answers."

"I have never regretted saving someone's life more," Kara said quietly.

Sylah didn't acknowledge her presence.

The Tannin is the creature that separated us from this land. It has isolated us for over four hundred years. It is our right to know the history of it. Ravenwing growled softly as he signed. He towered over the councillors. Sylah translated with gusto.

It was the First Councillor who took up the explanation. The short man wore a thin circlet of vines around his throat, and touched them with a gloved hand. Elyzan was his name.

"History is full of mistakes, is it not?" he said and pulled off his gloves.

Sylah's eyes widened, a gasp of air escaping her mouth. His left hand, the one that didn't contain his orb, was entirely engulfed in leaves. No, his hand *was* the leaves: the fingers were branches, the skin barked wood.

"This was my mistake, long ago. The first charter is perhaps the simplest of all the laws. The four foundational runes replicate a plant's core needs: light, air, water, and nutrients. I was foolish once. I placed a seed in my flesh to see if it could grow. And grow it did. It took root in my hand, and it is only thanks to the quick nature of my colleague of the third charter that I did not die." Elyzan nodded to Zenebe.

Sylah wanted him to get to the point, but she also was fascinated by the way his hand moved as he spoke, the leaves curling and uncurling, the bark rippling.

Elyzan continued, "Those who come to the Zwina Academy have ambition. They need it in order to have the discipline, the drive, to learn. But ambition is a lonely feeling and often accompanies pride and honor in the lucky, and arrogance and megalomania in the unlucky. The prophet, as we have discussed, was the latter. But also touched by a madness none of us can ever know."

"Okay, so you're all a bunch of egotistical assholes. Tell me something I didn't know." Sylah was never good at filtering her thoughts. Elyzan's lip curled up, but he ignored her.

"Back then there were few students of the fifth charter. The runes were more intricate than the others, and the sacrifice required to wield them was great. In order to infuse life into inanimate objects it took a piece of your soul, but the creation of life is more complex than anyone truly knows. When the prophet betrayed everything the Academy stood for, the students of the fifth charter decided to seek revenge on the Zalaam."

Sylah watched the leaves on his hand quiver and sway as he spoke.

"They chose to create a monster out of the ruins of one of the temples. A beast so large that it required every student left studying the fifth charter to help complete it. Each of them infused a piece of their soul, though just a small piece, in order to retain their sanity.

"The students knew they were making a monster, but it wasn't a concern for them. Creations never lasted much longer than a mooncycle or two. But then again, no one had ever made a creation with so many pieces of soul.

"Because here is one other thing you should know. When a creation is made it takes on the semblance of its former occupation. We call it an echo. If you wanted to create a mining aid that worked really well, you would create it from mining tools. If you wanted to create a transport mite that could memorize the routes of the city, you infuse a map in its core."

"So . . . when the students built the creature out of the ruins of the Zalaam's temple . . ."

Sylah's mouth had gone dry.

Elyzan finished the story. "It took on the essence of the Zalaam's God. They created a creature of sacrifice. Of death. The fifth charter was disbanded."

The tidewind . . . ? Dew signed behind Ravenwing. Sylah thought she knew the answer.

"The weather phenomenon the Drylands experiences is a result of the Tannin stirring during the peak strikes of the moon when the Zalaam would worship their God. The deathcraft power drains the energy in your lands, and its very presence has unbalanced your home since the Zalaam invaded."

"But it's been getting worse?" Sylah asked.

"And that brings us back to the present moment. To what you see happening outside across the world. The Zalaam have been rising. They are draining the world of more energy than ever before. And perhaps their worship continues to fuel the creature."

Elyzan pulled his gloves back on and looked around the table carefully.

"The Tannin is an example of what the Law of Creation can do with just blood. Imagine what it could do with a substance much more powerful. Bone marrow. The Zalaam call it godpower and the creations they make godbeasts.

"The latest scout that made it onto the Volcane Isles reported that earthquakes were a daily occurrence. Though the Zalaam believe it is their God speaking to them, not the world breaking apart from the very power they wield with bone marrow."

Sylah felt like she was falling. Her hands slammed down on the table. Everyone looked at her.

"Why are we sitting around just talking?" Sylah was shouting. "We need a fucking plan."

There was silence as everyone waited. But no plan was forthcoming.

We came here for aid, and it seems like what instead we must do is aid ourselves. Dew frowned, their signing fatigued.

"You mean to go back? To the empire without a solution?" Sylah said.

There is no solution, Reed signed.

Jond looked like he had pulled together the threads of the conversation and interjected.

"We must fight."

Kara was watching Jond with an unreadable expression.

"Jond Alnua is right. You cannot go back to your homeland. And we cannot go back to cowering. It is why we invited you here. There are neighboring countries who may be willing to fight against the Zalaam. Your bloodwerk could be what wins us this battle. It is time to form an alliance, to pool together everything between us and start preparing for war."

The silence rippled outward as the elders signed to themselves.

Sylah let them discuss. Fighting back against the Zalaam was everyone's individual choice. Jond had clearly made his, and though she ached for Anoor, Sylah's only choice was to stay. Anoor wouldn't forgive her otherwise.

"I can be an ambassador, you know, from the Drylands . . ." Ads spoke up.

Ravenwing shot her a glowering look.

"It might be helpful . . . when you send missives to other countries," Ads added.

Kara gave Ads an indulgent nod.

"I can take charge of the scouts. My past with the hunters and my contacts within the Souk will give us a good range of informers," Niha said, and he grew in standing in Sylah's mind. "That is, if you are willing to rescind my exiled status."

"We have discussed it. It is time to set aside old grievances. Though your orb will never be returned to you, we will allow you to join this alliance," Zenebe said. As the councillor of Niha's charter—which practiced the third law of healing—he had the authority to grant this clemency.

"No," Sylah said, surprising herself. "You cannot deny him his orb. Reinstate him as a healer. We need everyone we can get."

"But there must be rules—" Zenebe insisted.

Kara interrupted him. "There are few rules in war but living and dying. She's right: healers are going to be important."

Kara, *agreeing* with her? Sylah hid her shock and looked at Zenebe. He looked troubled, his eyes downcast.

"Agreed," he said with a sigh. All the stiffness in his features bled away. It had been a mask for his true feelings of relief to see an old student. "Welcome back." He smiled.

Tears ran down Niha's face.

"I'll be in charge of the armies," Jond said quietly.

There was a breathy "'ha" and Sylah looked to Ravenwing, who had broken away from the elders' discussion.

The armies are mine, he signed.

"In our land we have a strategy commander who directs the troops and a major general who leads the units in battle," Kara said.

Ravenwing and Jond met each other's eyes.

I will be strategy commander.

Sylah conveyed the words and Jond nodded, happy with the title. He mouthed "major general" to himself when he thought no one was looking.

Sylah snorted. "I wonder how many major generals this world has seen with a kitten stuffed down their shirts."

He shot her a lopsided smile.

Each of them chose a role, Sylah at first offering to handle communications until Kara laughed, pulling a smile from everyone.

"Why don't you take care of soldier recruitment," Jond said kindly. Sylah smarted. She had much more to offer than recruitment.

Hope swelled in the room with each breath, and Sylah soon found herself smiling with the others.

The green-veined Second Councillor, Sui, spoke for the first time that day. "We must give life to this new government." Because a *government* was what they suddenly were.

"Give life?" Sylah wasn't so sure about the sound of that.

"It is a simple ritual. One we do to bind the loyalty of a new council."

"Bind?"

Sui smiled. "A phrase merely, but it is poignant to mark the beginning of this new . . . collective."

What do you need us to do? Dew asked.

"Bleed," Sui said.

A needle was produced. Every person in the room donated a single drop of blood to a shallow wooden dish.

Zenebe bled indigo, Kara violet, Sui green, and Elyzan red.

The air was full of power and iron. Sylah reveled in the possibility of it. They all waited, silently, watching Sui brandish her orb and roll it in the dish of blood.

Slowly she circled the group, rolling a pattern of runes on each of their forearms.

Sylah's mind itched.

"You can all project your thoughts within this circle. This is called a mindlink." Sui's voice reverberated between Sylah's ears. It was more a feeling of a thought than a full sentence. It certainly wasn't like listening to speech.

"Forever?" Sylah whispered in her mind.

"Not forever, just tonight. To bind the alliance together."

"We need a name." Ads's thoughts were just as annoying telepathically.

There was a flicker of an image of two knives circling a droplet of blood. It translated into three words: the Blood Forged.

Sui's thoughts accepted the name and claimed it with the words, "Together we will fight. Together we will lead. Together we will protect. Together we will bleed.

"The Blood Forged we will be."

CHAPTER FORTY-FIVE

SYLAH

Eight tribes once roamed, now there are none,
The land of Tenio now a queendom,
Some queens reigned high and some reigned low,
But none as loved as Karanomo.

—Nursery rhyme sung in the schools of Tenio

The City of Rain came alive with preparations. A room was set up as a war chamber, and a map of the world unraveled across it. Ravenwing and Sui sat together conferring in silence as they spoke in their minds. New Sea Lords and Earth Lords were appointed from the small population left in the city.

Sylah came to discover that the City of Rain was mainly occupied by the surviving students of the Academy and the lesser elite who hadn't been at the palace. The rest of Tenio's population had either moved inland or become refugees in the Hadir mountain range. The region had a harsh climate that threatened their food reserves but at least the floods didn't reach their settlements. The Earth Lords were organizing resource deliveries to these camps from the City of Rain.

Students were given back their orbs, completed or otherwise. The students' fear of deathcrafting was still hard to dispel. There were no scales to know how the world's imbalance was influenced, but the theory that blood drained less energy than bone marrow was the most likely logical explanation. And that theory was the one the Zwina Academy taught every student.

It took them a week to source a smith from the city's dwindling population. A flighter was sent to all shanty camps as a priority. The smith was needed to create inkwells for Jond's bloodwerk students.

Sylah had tried to teach the students. She had after all taught Jond boodwerk. But the students were too quiet, too attentive to Sylah's every move. These were *professional* students, people who had spent their lives studying a particular law just to achieve the status of completing a full orb. They frustrated her with their overeager smiles and nods of encouragement. After the second strike of teaching Sylah gave up, and Jond, a more patient tutor, took over.

Her job now was to inform Neera, the smith, how to build an inkwell.

"Do you have a schema?" Neera asked as she fed the fire with one hand. They were on the ground beneath the mushrooms as they couldn't risk the heat of the forge burning through the flesh of their homes. With every flood they had to pack up quickly and run to the lifts. Once it abated, they'd return and relight the forge with dry coal. The fire itself had been dug into the ground, the edges of the pit lined with planks of concrete brought in from the ruins of the Academy. The air flow was maintained by a foot pump that Neera was pumping now.

"No schema," Sylah said. She was cross-legged on the ground, the moist earth cold beneath her, but the fire warm on her skin.

"Okay, measurements?" Neera asked.

"No, every one is different."

"One I can copy?"

"No, Jond needs his to teach."

The smith turned to Sylah and pulled down her scarf. Braids fell like waves around her, ending in tips that had been dyed blue.

Her lids were lined with thick charcoal—well, she always had a supply—and they accentuated the cat-like shape of her eyes. Sylah found herself wanting to trace the lines of her fine orange veins that shone through her light brown skin. They made her skin glow.

"What can you tell me then?" Neera asked.

Sylah had forgotten her own name.

"Hello?" Neera waved a finely boned hand in front of Sylah's face.

"Oh, sorry. Here." Sylah reached out and grabbed the smith's hand. "You can measure it. Just imagine you're making a big metal cuff."

The smith gave Sylah a strange look. "Okay."

They worked together by the sweltering heat of the furnace for strikes. Sylah watched Neera, mesmerized by every droplet of sweat.

Sylah needed Anoor. She needed her now.

"What are you thinking?" Neera asked, dismembering her latest prototype that hadn't quite fit.

"I was thinking of someone back home."

"Your love?"

"Yes, I suppose you can call her that. I just call her Anoor." Sylah gave a smile, and Neera recognized the shape of it.

"Love indeed." She laughed.

Sylah probed the gap in her teeth with her tongue. A hot flash of joba seed cravings coursed through her, and she felt her hands begin to tremble in response. Though the physical symptoms had lessened, the mental strain that addiction had caused still burdened her. But it was a pain she welcomed.

Every day was a battleground. And every day she won.

She knew that victory wasn't a given. She had to fight for it, even without access to the drug. And maybe one day, when she got back to the empire, she'd lose. But she knew the next day she'd be ready to fight again.

She squeezed her trembling hands until they stopped.

"How's it hurting?" Jond appeared like he often did, uninvited.

"Not bad, think we're nearly there. How are the students coming along?"

"They're doing good, they're familiar with the precision—did you know they only get one chance to carve each rune on their orbs? They were taught one rune a year. A *year.* And that's just the foundational runes. If it doesn't work, then the sequence they might need just simply won't work."

"Let me guess, they'd get kicked out."

Jond shrugged. "Perfection or nothing. And the intricacies of rolling such a small object in the right direction for the sequence they want? It's baffling. Though of course, they think drawing a line of runes every time is difficult—which I suppose it is."

"Here, try this." Neera handed Sylah a warm inkwell made of copper. They had decided that it was the best material. Though hard to procure, copper would last in the rain and acid of the mainland much better than any other material.

Sylah slipped it on and turned it backward and forward. It was one clean sheet of metal that curved around the contour of her wrist and protruded over her hand with a cuff that looked like shimmering fabric.

"Is the placement of the vein all right?"

Sylah inserted the steel-tipped stylus and watched her blood bead to the top. "It's perfect." And she meant it.

"Now you can come back to teaching," Jond said with a lopsided smile.

"No, thank you," Sylah said and stood.

"Thank you for my inkwell," she said to Neera. "It's good to have one back."

"No problem, only five hundred left to go." Neera chuckled.

Sylah began to walk to the lift.

"Teaching's interesting," Jond continued as he fell into step with her. "They have the same principles as bloodwerk, four foundational runes and then a series of supplementary ones that indicate direction, triggers, or protection. For example the second charter, communication, has four foundational runes: talking to one person, talking to everyone, listening to one person, listening to everyone—"

"I still have nightmares about that experience." Sylah shuddered. After the pledge to the Blood Forged, they had been able to hear each other's thoughts as they made initial plans. But Sylah got so frustrated she wiped off the runes. She had a headache for a week.

"If we learn the runes, we can do them with bloodwerk too."

That had Sylah interested.

"You mean I can heal or flight and stuff?"

"Potentially, though I haven't actually asked the councillors if they'd teach us . . ."

Sylah laughed. Alliance or not, the councillors wouldn't share their knowledge easily. Part of Sylah was glad of it. If anyone could do what they could, the world would be a very different place.

Sylah had drawn bloodwerk runes on the lift earlier that week and so they zipped up to the top with speed. Rascal was waiting on the landing. Jond picked her up. She'd already gotten too big to nestle under his shirt.

"Jond, have you found where they've hidden the alcohol yet?"

Jond's mouth shut and split into a sly smile.

"Come with me."

A FEW STRIKES later and Sylah was well and truly inebriated. She dashed along one of the many bridges strung between the different mushrooms of the City of Rain.

"Sylah, wait."

Sylah's legs felt like two loose pieces of string that were being pulled along in the rain. Her arms flailed happily beside her, one bejeweled with a new inkwell, the other clutching an empty bottle of date wine.

Jond caught up with her and grabbed the bottle out of her hand.

"You finished it?" His form seemed to waver in the rainfall.

"I needed it more than you," Sylah grunted, then laughed as Jond's face twitched into petulance.

"What?" he said.

"You look stupid."

"*You* look stupid." He pushed her shoulder with the heel of his palm.

"Ouch, that hurt." She pushed him back.

"No, it didn't, don't lie."

"I don't lie." Sylah pushed him harder. He stumbled back, one hand reaching out to grab the rope railing, while the other spun backward trying to regain his balance. The empty bottle of date wine went flying off the edge.

"Maiden's tits," Sylah cried and ran to the edge to watch the bottle careen through the air.

"Oh, fuck." Jond was equally worried. "Wait, there's no one down there anyway. They're all dead."

Sylah laughed. "They're all dead."

"Gone." Jond was chuckling.

"No more tiny people down below."

They were bellowing now, their laughter rolling through them in uncontrollable fits. Their tears merged with the rain. Sylah laughed until her sides hurt, and she needed Jond to hold her steady.

"Sylah." He was there, so close. He wasn't Anoor, but he was there.

"When did your laughing stop?" Sylah asked and looked into his softened features. He loved her, after everything, he loved her.

"My Akoma—"

Sylah pressed her lips against Jond's and through the wrongness she knew she was satisfying a primal need that had been missing since she had last slept in Anoor's arms. His skin was always so hot, so scalding, and he grabbed the small of her back with urgency and pressed his body close to hers. Not a drop of rainwater could separate them.

He tasted of date wine and home.

"Sylah . . ." It came out as a groan and a warning sign. This was going to go too far.

Sylah broke away from him but didn't let go of his hand. She led him to their room knowing every step of the way that she could never give him what he wanted. But he, at least for tonight, could fulfill her.

He wasn't Anoor, he never could be. But maybe for tonight she could push Anoor from her thoughts, just a little.

What are you doing, Sylah? The thought had Anoor's voice, and for a moment she faltered.

But when she looked behind her, Jond was there, like he always was, looking back with love.

When they entered their room Sylah began to undress. Jond's eyes smoldered as she moved with deliberate slowness.

"Sylah, stop."

"You want me to stop?" Her fingers hovered above the buttons on her trousers that hung low on her hips. Jond's eyes were glued to the seam of her undergarments that were just visible.

"Yes." His voice was rough.

"I don't think you do . . ." She slipped her hand down.

"Stop, Sylah, I can't do this. I can't."

"What?" She heard it, the refusal.

"And I don't think you can either."

"You're rejecting me?" Sylah suddenly felt very sober.

"Yes." Jond looked away from her. "You know how I feel. And sometimes I think, if you let yourself, you could find your way back to me. But you're not mine. You never were."

Sylah felt her mouth twist bitterly, and she opened her mouth to speak.

Jond interrupted the insult she was sure to throw his way. "You're not hers either. You're not anyone's and I don't think you can ever be. We're all broken, in our small ways. Some of us try to get better, some of us prefer to be broken and will keep breaking ourselves until there is nothing left."

"You think I'm broken?" Sylah's voice cracked.

"I think you want to be. Look at yourself. Weeks after being healed you turn to drink. Mooncycles after choosing Anoor, you're here. With me. Trying to . . ."

"Well, I didn't realize this was going to turn into a fucking launderer's tea party. If I wanted to chat, I would have spent my evening with Ads."

"Sylah." Jond held out an open hand of peace. "I just want you to know, want you to understand. If, one day, you allow yourself happiness, and if that person you choose is me . . . I will be there. But you are not choosing anything but self-destruction. I look at you and I see a flame, the same fierce and loving woman I have known nearly all my life. But fire's nature is to burn those around it."

Sylah felt her stomach churn with the truth and two bottles of date wine. Okay, three.

"Can you love fire?" Sylah asked.

"Yes, you can."

Sylah felt herself break apart a little. She felt the trauma of the journey catch up with her, and she cracked and spilled forth her tears. Jond was there, holding her. Not in the way she had wanted, but in the way she needed.

"I'm sorry," Sylah whispered against his shoulder. "I'm sorry I wanted to kill you."

Jond's laugh was short and unexpected. "I'm sorry I wanted to kill you too."

They held each other like that for a moment, and Sylah drank in the warmth of his skin.

"Sylah . . ." The tone of his voice had changed, a minor key.

"What is it?" She pushed herself away and looked into his eyes. They were sorrowful.

"When you asked me what I knew . . . about the Sandstorm and Loot . . . I wasn't entirely truthful."

Sylah was standing, her heart racing. "What?" The word was a whip.

"I was angry at you, and I was angry at *her* . . . and remember, I still believed they were right . . . that Azim was right . . ."

"Jond."

"I thought I was protecting them, saving them from you—"

"Jond."

He took a sharp breath in and exhaled slowly. "I wasn't the only one of the Sandstorm that made it into the Aktibar. Those years I trained with Loot, I . . . I wasn't alone."

"Who else?" Sylah stepped forward, a look of murderous rage on her face.

"Tanu Alkhabbir, Qwa Hala, and Faro Ellen."

Sylah hissed low and steady.

"You're telling me that all the disciples of the Wardens' Empire are part of the fucking Sandstorm?"

Jond let his shoulders slump.

"Yes, I am."

"WHAT ARE YOU doing?" Jond took a step toward Sylah as she ran around the room stuffing a pack she had found with the spare clothing they had been given.

"Do not come anywhere near me, Jond, or I promise to any fucking God you want that I will gut you like I should have done mooncycles ago."

Jond winced and sat back down on his pallet. He watched her pack and then said, "You can't leave, Sylah, you have to let her go, what we're doing here is more important than what's happening in the Wardens' Empire. You don't know, they might not have tried anything."

"They might not have tried anything? They're agents of Loot's; if you were in their place would you just let Anoor live peacefully?"

Jond didn't answer. "We have more important things to do. Rally the armies, teach them bloodwerk."

"That's the only reason I'm not cutting you up right now." Sylah was glad he didn't point out that she didn't have a weapon.

"But the Tannin?"

Sylah paused. "I'll figure it out." It meant killing someone, but she'd do it. She'd do anything to save Anoor.

"I don't know the other disciples very well . . . there was another sanctuary, you see . . . other children drafted in . . . but it's unlikely she's still alive. She would have been assassinated within the first few days of her tenure."

Sylah sniffed; when had she started crying again? "I have to try, Jond, nothing, nothing is worth it if she doesn't survive."

"That's selfish."

"It is."

The door to their room shifted and someone pushed through

it. "Did you drink all of the date wine?" It was Ads, her mischievous face screwed up in annoyance. "I told you where that was in confidence, Jond."

"Ads, go away," Sylah barked at her.

"What are you doing?" Ads's eyes widened, and she looked from Sylah to Jond. "Are you leaving?" The question went up at the end like a squeak.

"Anoor's in danger," Sylah found herself explaining, then regretted telling Ads. "Go away, Ads, this doesn't concern you."

Ads's smile slipped.

"Ads," Jond said tiredly. "Go."

Ads took the dismissal harder from Jond, and Sylah thought she saw the girl's chin wobble. Sylah couldn't look at her any longer and pushed Ads out through the doorway.

"That was unnecessary."

"Don't worry, she won't have to deal with me for much longer."

"Where are you going?"

"I need to stop by the kitchens, stock up on food."

Jond nodded weakly.

"I'm going back to Anoor, and not you, the councillors, or the fucking Spider God can stop me."

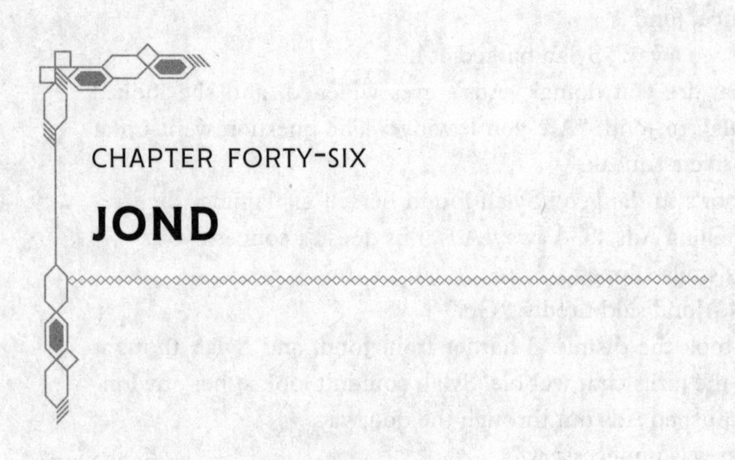

Prepare your armies. We go to war.

—Letters sent from the Blood Forged to the chief of the Winterlands, the clerics of the Entwined Harbor, the tsar of the Wetlands, and the emperor of Bushica

Sylah was leaving. Giving up on the Blood Forged before they had even begun. She told Jond not to follow her, so he didn't. But nor could he stay in this room.

For the first time, Jond enjoyed the rain as it cooled his skin.

Why did I tell her? Why didn't I tell her before? The two questions raged in his mind. He walked across a second bridge, his footsteps carrying him forward to familiar ground.

The study rooms. He turned on the gas lamp and looked out across the empty seats. He enjoyed teaching. While they still had no armies it was all he could do to spend his time.

Elyzan had grown the furniture out of an oak seed, building Jond a desk at the front. He sat down at it now.

A chest sat to Jond's right. It was full of the orbs of past students that had been confiscated when deathcraft had been banned. Most had found their owners again but some of those students had passed on, having died from the various problems wrought on the land. Now the chest lay locked and secure in this room.

Jond thought of what he had said to Sylah about learning other runes. He knelt by the chest and touched the seven padlocks that bound the lid shut. There were few locks that bloodwerk couldn't penetrate. He drew a combination of runes with his stylus and the locks broke apart, the metal shattering. A world without bloodwerk was an Ember thief's dream.

Nestled in the chest were a handful of unfinished orbs. Jond retrieved them with care. He inspected them, trying to discern which rune did what. He wasn't foolish enough to try drawing any of them. Elyzan's petrified hand was enough to warn him away from that.

Jond gave up his inspection and had begun to put the orbs back in the chest when he noticed its right side was thicker than the left. He pressed his fingers against it, finding a latch. He tugged, and a drawer slid upward revealing another orb, hidden.

Jond knew what it was straight away. An orb of the fifth charter. Perhaps the last completed one. Jond knew what he had to do.

JOND FOUND SYLAH at the lift, her pack full of stolen food and supplies. He wasn't sure if it was tears or rain on her face.

Jond hovered on the landing, the ironwork of the cage separating them.

"Are you really doing this?" he said.

"Yes."

"If she has survived, do you think she'll be grateful that you dropped everything to go back to her?"

"She'll understand." Jond wasn't sure she would, and from the look on Sylah's face, she wasn't so sure either.

"Skies above, we made a pact, to fight the Zalaam. To battle until the end."

"My fealty is to her first." Sylah pulled on a braid by her ear. A green shell glittered in the gaslight.

She was going, she was really going. Loss choked him as he imagined navigating the Blood Forged politics without her.

He fondled the orb in his pocket, hesitating to give it to her. But if she defeated the Tannin then maybe her leaving wouldn't be the worst thing.

She defeats the Tannin, or she dies.

"Sylah, here." The orb rolled from his palm to hers. A small thing full of such destruction.

"What is it?"

"An orb of the fifth law."

Sylah hissed. "How did you get this?"

"It doesn't matter. All that matters is that you destroy the Tannin."

"But I don't know how to use it."

"You'll have to figure it out. All I know is that the foundational runes must be those larger ones. They can infuse life, diffuse life, mimic life, and take life."

Sylah breathed deeply. The knowledge weighed heavily on both their chests.

"I'll have to practice," she murmured.

"Yes, but be careful."

Sylah nodded and reached for him. They had splintered this thing between them so many times. Azim's words came to him once again and he spoke them aloud to her now.

"Like an eggshell, life can bloom from broken things."

Sylah smiled and squeezed his hand. It wasn't forgiveness. Sylah and Jond were beyond that. But maybe it was a little bit of understanding.

"Bye, Jond."

"Bye."

The lift clattered down. He waited for it to return, empty, before he fell to the ground and sobbed.

RASCAL SLEPT ON his chest all night, clinging to him like she knew he needed the comfort more than she did. He was woken by Kara upturning a glass of water on his head. Rascal shrieked and scuttled under the covers.

"What did you do?"

One of them must have found the unlocked chest.

"Thank you for the shower," Jond said, flicking water out of his hair. Half of the twists had been pushed flat to his scalp.

"The orb, where is it?" Her nostrils flared.

"Sylah took it."

"I will retrieve it from her, then."

"She's gone. She's going to destroy the Tannin." Jond had decided to omit Sylah's true reasoning. He couldn't imagine the Blood Forged would forgive her if they knew the truth.

"What do you mean?"

Jond pulled open the covers and stood. His chest was bare, and he was pleased when he saw Kara's eyes linger on the contours of his hip bone.

"Sylah has taken the orb to destroy the Tannin. She thinks she can master the skills in order to kill it. If she fails, she will return."

Jond was thankful they weren't currently mindlinked.

"That wasn't her decision to make."

"But if she is successful, won't you be glad?"

Kara's lip curled. "Whatever the outcome I'll be glad."

Jond got her meaning.

"Sylah has given us time to focus on building the army. She'll destroy the Tannin. And we can destroy the Zalaam."

Kara huffed out a breath before disappearing, the explanation over.

Jond was washing when Kara appeared again.

"She stole the fucking war map," Kara seethed. She suddenly noticed Jond's naked body. She gave a small, soft laugh, her anger disappearing, followed by her presence as she blinked away.

Jond exhaled. "I don't think I'll ever get used to that, Rascal." The kitten wound herself between his legs, licking the water that had splashed onto his calves from the basin.

Jond had to go over the whole thing again with the elders in the war chamber.

Ads's translation was very clearly softened because Ravenwing looked curious rather than thunderous.

And she will be using the Baqarah*?*

"I presume so, but honestly she didn't tell me much of her plans." Jond had a throbbing headache from the date wine, and all he wanted to do was stop talking about Sylah.

"The *Baqarah*, that is your ship?" Zenebe asked.

Yes, it took us ten years to build. One of our own, Petal, has been maintaining it on the shoreline, Ravenwing signed and Ads translated.

Zenebe nodded and looked over the new map they had taped firmly to the table. "Maybe we should build our navy first?"

He posed the question to the room, then answered it himself.

"It would be the best option. We can't presume that the Zalaam will bring the fight to us. If anything, we should strike first, find the best territory. We'll need ships for that."

Ravenwing nodded. *And who will provide this fleet?*

The councillors looked among themselves.

"There's only one place with the number of ships we will need. The Entwined Harbor," Kara said. She had pushed her hood back over her head, and Jond couldn't read her expression.

"Too dangerous. The last Sea Lord to parle with them didn't return," Elyzan said. Jond was learning that he was the most risk-averse of the four. Likely his brush with death made him so. Elyzan tugged on the edge of his glove.

"They once sent an invitation to the queen. I think they have been hit harder than we think. They may be ready to ally with us. I could go, request an audience," Kara said.

"Or cut off our noses," Elyzan replied.

"They cut off noses?" Ads sounded both horrified and amused.

Kara clicked her tongue. "They haven't cut off noses for centuries, Elyzan."

"And what of the soldiers occupying these ships? Our legions are scattered, should we not consolidate our efforts here first?" Elyzan went on.

I will see to that, Ravenwing signed.

"I can go with Kara," Jond offered.

"I do not need a bodyguard, *major general.*" She dragged out his title with a sneer.

He should go with you. You can take one other, can you not? Is it not better to have a representative of the Drylands and of Tenio? Dew signed.

Dew was always the mediator; it was why they were lead diplomat of the Blood Forged.

"Shouldn't I go? I'm an ambassador?" Ads whined.

Kara's teeth flashed. "I'll take Jond Alnua."

Ads sagged in her seat.

You can accompany Ravenwing to the shanty towns, as we will find soldiers willing to fight there, I am sure. Dew patted Ads's arm.

"We will leave on the morrow," Kara said, brushing past him, muttering under her breath as she went, "lovesick boy."

"Make sure you feed her three times a day, maybe four. Just whenever you eat, give her some. And she likes banana crisps and chicken, but not with bones."

"Jond, may I remind you that *I* was the one who rescued her?" Niha said dryly.

"Yes, but you don't know her like I do."

Rascal was sleeping happily in Jond's arms, and he didn't want to disturb her. But he couldn't take her with him, as much as he wanted to. He brushed a kiss on her head, and she grumbled.

"Remember when you wanted her to die?" Niha laughed.

Jond flinched. He didn't like to be reminded of that fact.

Niha retrieved Rascal from Jond's arms.

"You've come a long way, boy, and not just in leagues."

Jond nodded. "And further yet to go."

He left Rascal asleep on Niha's lap. Kara was waiting for him in the war chamber. At her feet were three of the largest packs he'd ever seen.

"That's a lot of stuff. How long are we planning on staying?"

Kara pointed to one. "That's for you."

Jond opened the front pocket. It was full of patterned silks and flowing robes.

"Are those clothes?"

"We might have to do a bit of diplomacy, eat their food, drink their drink. Smile and make friends. You know, what your friend Sylah is really bad at."

Jond didn't want to hear her name from Kara's mouth.

"Why do you hate her so much?"

Kara laughed. "I don't hate her. I just recognize her type. She is someone who destroys those closest to her. I could see how much it hurt you to be near her and yet . . . back to the flame you went."

Jond swallowed. She had garnered the truth so easily.

"Shall we go?"

She laughed at his change of topic.

"Yes, we shall. But a warning, the trip might be a bit bumpy. I'll have to flight us a few times before I get us to the Ica Sea."

"The Ica Sea?" Jond said, alarmed.

"Yes, where did you think we were going?" She picked up her packs and indicated Jond should do the same.

"To the Entwined Harbor, you know . . . on land."

"The Entwined Harbor is a moving collection of ships all knotted together."

"What?"

Kara began to roll a combination of runes onto his skin.

"I hope you don't get seasick."

Jond felt a lurching in the very fragments of himself before he could respond.

And then they were gone, leaving the war chamber empty.

CHAPTER FORTY-SEVEN

SYLAH

No creature can be made from nothing.
Surrender your soul and it will form.

—Notes from the last councillor of the fifth charter,
also known as the prophet

Sylah rolled out the map she had pilfered from the war chamber. She followed the same route the elders had taken, which circumvented the flooded citadel completely, staying on higher ground across the Truna Hills. She traced the route she had traveled over the last week and looked around her.

I should be able to see the Gana River by now.

She had reached a valley some strikes ago, and though the map hadn't labeled it, she had continued north. Now she was convinced either the map was wrong, or she had somehow gone west without realizing.

"I could be on the Oarigha Plains, I suppose." She tapped the map with a frown. The valley she was in was shallow, dissimilar to the flat landscape drawn on the map. The ground beneath her feet had barely dried out from the rains.

But it hadn't rained for days.

Sylah bent down and pressed her hands into the dirt. The mud was thick, the product of a heavy rainfall or a flood. She tilted her head up, her stomach sinking. But there wasn't a single cloud in the sky. The air smelled earthy, almost fishy. She stood and wiped her hands on her clothing.

She continued on a few more paces until she saw something white protruding from the ground. She approached it, pushing it with her foot.

It was a bone.

She pushed her toe deeper into the mud, flicking up the remains of the skeleton. It was five handspans long and tapered with thinner bones along its rib cage. Without a doubt it was a fish of some kind, but what was a fish doing in the middle of this valley?

Then realization struck her. This wasn't a valley: it was a dried-up riverbed.

She had reached the Gana River after all.

"What happened here?" she whispered to the dirt and dead things.

But she knew the answer. It curdled with guilt in her stomach.

The Zalaam. This is their doing.

Hurricanes, floods, acid rain, and now drought. Sylah spat the taste of shame from her mouth. Anoor needed Sylah more than the Blood Forged did. They'd be fine without her.

"Destroy the Tannin," Jond had said to her. It was a plea and a request.

Her fingers curled around the orb in her pocket. She'd been too afraid to try the runes with blood. So far, she'd practiced the shapes of them in the dirt. The orb itself would be too dangerous to wield, she didn't have the delicate skills required to move it through a wound like the councillors. No, she'd have to draw the runes with her inkwell, and that meant getting them right.

Sylah looked down at the map again. Now she had reached the Gana River she could head west toward the Souk where she could trade supplies.

THE SOUK WASN'T at all what Sylah expected. She knew she'd been there before, but her memories of her journey to the City of Rain were thin, wispy things that her mind didn't want her to see. Like strands of a whip that, when they came together, laced her with pain.

Sylah coiled the pain away.

The stalls in the market were empty. But signs of their former owners clustered in forgotten corners. A silk scarf, a wooden doll, a mug half-filled. Some of the roofs had caved in and as Sylah drew nearer she saw they were dented with lumps as big as a fist.

Dread was a familiar friend now.

"Market's closed." The voice crackled, as if it moved through fire to reach her. Sylah turned to the sound. It had come from an elderly woman sweeping the floor a few stalls along. She didn't look up as Sylah approached.

"What happened?"

"Hail the size of duck's eggs."

Sylah could smell the cloves and cinnamon in the air but the tubs by the lady's hands were empty.

"Some of us stayed. Some of us have nowhere to go. So, some of us died." She drawled the words out, her tone matter-of-fact.

"Go to the Truna Hills, you'll find there the City of Rain, they'll take you in, feed you."

The woman stopped her sweeping.

"The City of Rain, you say? I heard talk of this. The Blood Forged."

Sylah was surprised. The student flighters had made fast work of communications.

The woman went back to sweeping. Sylah saw there was no dust.

"I'm too old for fighting, though. All I have is beneath this broken roof."

"You won't have to fight, there are other ways you can help."

The old woman looked up, and Sylah was shocked by the brightness of her eyes. Hazel, like Anoor's.

"Ain't you going the wrong way, then?"

"I'm on a different mission for the Blood Forged." She was, in a way. *Destroy the Tannin.*

Sylah began to shrug off her raincoat.

"Take this, the material will protect you from the rain, but stick to higher ground."

The old lady didn't reach for it at first.

"You going to the coast?" she asked Sylah.

"Yes, Nsuo."

The woman groaned as she bent to retrieve something from under the shelf behind her.

It was a copper wide-brimmed hat with a sheet of metal that fell to either side.

"I will not take your coat, but I will trade for it."

Sylah looked at the contraption doubtfully. The woman saw her scowl and laughed.

"It will protect you from the acid rain. You can wear it as you walk, but I recommend you stop and set it up like a tent around you and wait for the rains to pass."

The woman's advice might have just saved her life.

Sylah nodded gratefully. "Thank you."

They exchanged items.

"I think that might have been my last ever trade," the woman said. Her voice was now the dying hiss of cinders.

She looked up at the sky and murmured, "We'd both better move. The hail can come at any time. Move quickly now. Farewell, traveler. Farewell. May the queen bless your speed and safety."

Sylah opened her mouth to tell the woman that the queen was dead. But no, now was not the time to strip away her hope. So Sylah returned the sentiment.

"May the queen bless your speed and safety."

IT WAS AN arduous journey to the coast. When the rain turned acidic Sylah was almost glad, because it meant her travels were nearly at an end.

She was grateful for the copper canopy the woman had given her at the Souk, but Sylah wished she'd traded more for the coat than just that. She had run out of food two days ago and had resorted to eating plants she'd found. One of her culinary explorations had set her back a whole day. Food and water passed through her every five minutes until she was drained, and her ass burned.

She still had a canister of fresh water left, and it had to last her until she got to the *Baqarah*. Sylah had only experienced one acid rainfall. She'd been worried that her shoes wouldn't last on the acid soil. Though it was clear they were far more worn than they should have been for a three-week journey, they didn't break apart. Whatever the Academy had made them out of had lasted.

Sylah was wary of entering Nsuo and the roads around it. She'd slept little and scouted lots. The Shariha had been trading people to the Zalaam for years. Sylah couldn't let herself be captured, because capture meant being drained of bone marrow. Capture meant death.

It didn't matter that her ancestors were Zalaam. Sylah was just another opportunity to them. The true Zalaam were the believers: not a race, but a cult. Thankfully the Shariha didn't make an appearance. It didn't stop her from having nightmares of a toothless woman sucking marrow out of her bones.

When the *Baqarah* came into view Sylah nearly collapsed with relief. It was still there. She ran the last hundred handspans and assessed its condition. There was a little damage on the deck where the rain had eroded some of the thinner bits of metal like the railings, but it was mainly cosmetic.

Sylah jumped aboard and let out a long, exhausted sigh. She had made it. Her relief was short-lived as she spotted a shadow with a dagger ripple across the decking toward her.

Sylah recognized the Ghosting immediately. She wore the patchwork dress she had donned on their journey there, her fair hair tied up in a bun on her head. A kitchen knife was strapped to her forearm.

"Petal?"

The Ghosting let out a surprised cry and dropped the knife to the ground.

What are you doing here? I thought you were a scavenger.

Sylah was so glad to see her, she almost cried. Without Petal's ability to navigate the sea, she'd have no means to get back home.

"We're to go back to the empire."

What do you mean? The elders ordered me to stay here to maintain the ship. I have to oil it every day.

"New orders," Sylah said with as much sincerity as she could muster. "I've an important message for Anoor that must be received immediately."

What about the Tannin?

Sylah gave Petal a wolfish smile.

"We're to destroy it on the way."

It seems there is a lot to tell.

"Yes, but first, let's set sail."

Sylah thought Petal might refuse. Then the Ghosting nodded once and sprang into action.

Sylah followed Petal to the control room of the ship as she triggered the runes that set the boat west and went back to the top deck to watch the land of Tenio disappear behind them.

The brittle smell of acid went first. Then the shattered city of Nsuo. And lastly the coastline, a golden blade on the horizon that grew sharper before disappearing completely.

Petal looked toward the sea, her eyes haunted.

How will we destroy the Tannin, Sylah?

"Look, it's a long story, but I'm glad for your company, truthfully. I hope there's coffee still in the mess hall because I've been craving it like you wouldn't believe."

Petal nodded, and Sylah tilted her head back in relief.

"Come on then, I owe you a tale."

Petal was an ideal audience for Sylah's story. She cried with horror and stamped in anger at all the right moments. But it was Rascal that had her in honking hysterics, her silver tooth glinting.

Jond, with a kitten?

"Yes, indeed. A kitten. A white puffball with blue eyes."

Somehow that image made it funnier.

It was nighttime when Sylah got to explaining the orb. It sat between them now.

Petal reached for it, her wrist touching the runes.

To infuse life, to diffuse life, to mimic life, and to take life. What does it mean?

"I have only recently begun experimenting with blood. But I think I understand the four basic runes." Sylah went to retrieve a utensil from the drawer. "Say I want to bring this fork to life, I would use this one here: infuse. The fork would then do what is in its nature, so probably stab food. To stop it I would diffuse the life with this rune here. It would stop on its own after a few weeks, depending on the power of my blood. If I wanted the fork to act, say, like a spider, I would have to use the mimic rune and draw that on the spider I would want it to mimic."

Creepy.

"Very fucking creepy," Sylah agreed. "But in order to do any other of the prior three runes I have to mark myself with the final rune. I would have to take a piece of my soul."

It takes a piece of your soul?

Sylah shrugged. "So they say."

What if you diffuse the creation you've made, does the soul go back to you?

Sylah shrugged, unsure.

"There's so much they don't know about this power. There's so much *I* don't know about it."

Petal patted her arm.

So, the plan is to use the diffuse rune to take down the Tannin?

"Yes." Sylah breathed out. "I'll need to figure out the other supplementary runes on the orb to make sure I get the right sequence, though."

And then there'll be no more Tannin?

"There'll be no more Tannin."

Petal nodded and smiled a little sadly.

It was my job to keep the prisoners alive. The Embers, the ones we sacrificed. I don't think I'll ever forgive myself for that.

Sylah touched Petal's shoulder, and she recoiled.

I'm fine. It had to be done.

Petal stood up from the bench.

Good night, Sylah. I think I will sleep much better than I have for a long time.

Sylah picked up the orb. It was still warm from her body heat.

For her, sleep would have to wait.

SPIDERS ENDED UP being the best thing to practice on. A family of them had taken to living on the boat. Printing them with a rune was another matter, and Sylah spent the first few days squishing their bodies with the force of her stylus.

She tried to print using the orb, but it had been a disaster. It had slipped from her grasp and imprinted the table with a series of runes, bringing it to life. There was a mad second where the table bucked and squirmed against the bolts that bound it to the floor. She lurched forward, quickly drawing the rune for *diffuse* before it ripped through the decking.

Sylah decided on a new approach. If she merged her knowledge of bloodwerk runes, she could fashion a bomb made of glass jars, which, instead of spraying shards of glass made to destroy, burst with ribbons of rune sequences that pressed into the Tannin's body and diffused it. Bloodwerk runes taught in the empire didn't work on people, but the Tannin wasn't a person, it was stone.

Sylah practiced day and night, but she only had a limited supply of glass jars. Petal watched her work, her frown line growing deeper as they got closer to the Tannin's lair.

At first, Sylah was invigorated by the power the orb gave her. She delighted in making the forks in the kitchen chase Petal like a hoard of spiders or making the runelamp turn on and off whenever it wanted. But after weeks of practice Sylah began to feel the strain of creation.

You look tired, Petal signed, then tugged on the hem of her rainbow-colored dress. Like all her clothing, Petal had saved and traded for the material, creating a patchwork ensemble that put some of Anoor's garish outfits to shame. Sylah liked that Petal had discarded the beige of the Ghostings' uniform so thoroughly.

"You look tired too." Sylah had woken Petal up more than once from night terrors that left the halls of the ship echoing with screams. Sylah wondered how much the sacrifice of the Embers had really cost her. And if it had been worth it.

"I think I need a break. I'm beginning to understand why the Academy took twenty years to teach them the runes. One a year. I'm trying to pack it all into three weeks."

Here, have some tea. Petal began to pour from the kettle but jumped back as it moved on its own.

Sylah drew a rune on its side to stop it. Petal looked perturbed as she took over control of the handle, the life from the kettle now diffused. She handed Sylah the tea.

Go to sleep. I will stay up tonight to navigate. I think we'll be heading into the worst of the tidewind soon.

But as soon as Petal finished signing the boat swung to the left.

Their eyes locked, gray facing dark. Full of fear.

"It can't be the Tannin. It's too soon."

The currents, maybe they're faster on the way back, Petal signed.

Sylah scooped up the three jars she'd been working on with shaking hands.

Three chances.

It wasn't enough.

Sylah led the way to the top deck, the tidewind swirling in the moonlight. Specks of sand glittered on the wind, fragments of her home dragged on the breeze. They scoured her cheeks leaving bloody tears.

The Tannin plunged through the water toward them, its snout parting the sea like a quill through black ink. Sylah took aim and threw the jar just as the head broke the surface. The glass shattered into tiny pieces, the ribbons of runes fluttering away uselessly. She missed, the glass having broken on the edge of the railing.

"Fuck." Sylah ran closer to the edge and aimed for the Tannin again. It watched her with intelligent eyes, and Sylah felt the weight of all the students' souls looking back at her. She threw the second jar and the Tannin lunged backward, like it knew what she was trying to do.

Last chance.

The Tannin slipped down to the depths, and Sylah watched its shadow circle the *Baqarah*.

There was a sharp scream behind her as Sylah leaned forward on an eroded bit of railing. Sylah lost her balance. Petal caught her just before Sylah fell into the darkness of the ocean.

But the final jar had gone. Sylah had seen it sink, along with their chances of survival.

The two women knelt on the deck, their knees touching.

Sylah looked into Petal's eyes.

"I'm so sorry." Tears and sand and blood drew tracks down Sylah's face.

Petal smiled.

This is Anyme's way.

Sylah didn't know what she meant. Neither of them had ever discussed what they would do if the runes failed.

The Tannin was rising again. Sylah could feel it in the rumbling of the water, in the way the tidewind grew frenzied.

Petal stood up, her legs parted for stability in the churning gales.

Sylah reached for her, not letting Petal do what she intended, but wanting her to do it all the same. Because there was only one thought Sylah had in that moment.

Nothing will stop me from getting to you, Anoor. Not even the Tannin.

Sylah watched as Petal reached the broken railing, her brightly colored dress whipping around her. Sylah still had her arm outstretched.

A hand poised to push or pull.

Petal gave Sylah a knowing grin that broke her heart.

Then she jumped into the jaws of the Tannin and smiled no more.

WHEN SYLAH REACHED the shores of the Wardens' Empire she wept. She unbraided her hair as she cried, each plait slowly unraveling in her hands. She laid out her trinkets, her treasures, and cleaned them using sand and sea water.

A piece of bone from the Sanctuary, Loot's spider brooch with "Inansi" engraved on the inside, a green shell, the silver wire of Zero's belt, the orb of creation.

Then, she added another piece to her collection, a strip of patterned cloth.

Sylah sat there and braided them back in piece by piece. Slowly she dried her tears and put herself back together.

It was time to save Anoor.

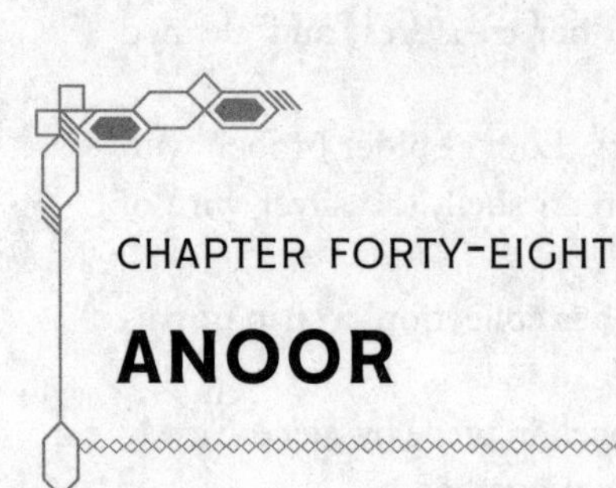

CHAPTER FORTY-EIGHT

ANOOR

My name is Nayeli, I am the new leader of the Sandstorm. Enclosed you will find notes on the origins of the empire, including the dynasty of the Zalaam. Study well.

—Letter found in Tanu Alkhabbir's chambers

Anoor had been meeting with the disciples every day for the last week. The gleam in their eyes, which had once scared her, now shone in hers.

"We have something we want to show you, Anoor," Tanu said.

They were standing around the barrel in the cellar of the Sphinx Tavern, the runelight making their skin glow a deep red.

"I hope you're not going to make the paper come to life again. That was scary enough." Anoor's laugh was nervous. Truthfully, she wanted to see that spectacle again. She couldn't stop thinking about it.

"No," Faro said. Their hand was enclosed in Qwa's as they grew more comfortable exposing their relationship to Anoor. She wondered how long they had been together. "It is something a little different," Faro continued. "We found a . . . a new substance that improves the power in our blood."

"What?"

Qwa was fiddling with his inkwell. Anoor hadn't noticed before, but there was a small hinge on his bracer. He flicked it open, revealing a catchment a lot like Anoor's. He pulled out the thin glass vial that was hidden there. Anoor gaped.

"You've been using someone else's blood?" She instinctively brought a hand to her own inkwell. Did they know about *her*?

"Not exactly," Qwa responded with a twist of his lips.

He placed the glass vial on the barrel with a clink.

Anoor could see now that it wasn't red. It was blue. Not like the deep twilight of her blood, but as pale and pastel as a noonday sky.

"What is it?" she breathed.

"We found the instructions in some teachings from the Zalaam." Tanu propped her elbows on the barrel, and the vial teetered. Qwa lunged for it before it could smash.

"Careful," he hissed. "I only have the one vial."

Tanu rolled her eyes.

"Show her what it can do then."

Qwa's answering smile was grim. He placed the vial back in the catchment and inserted his stylus into the hole. Now Anoor had spotted it, she could see the stylus wasn't as flush to his wrist as it would have been if connected to his vein.

Qwa withdrew a pebble from his pocket.

"I'd step back if I were you."

Anoor frowned but followed the others to the darker shades of the room.

She watched Qwa draw *Ru* on the pebble's surface. He dropped the pebble to the ground and stepped back. The rune should have pushed objects away from the bloodwerk, but Qwa had rolled the pebble so the rune was facing down, against the stone tiles. All that would happen was the stones might tremble or shift slightly.

Anoor felt the floor move, then the pebble disappeared.

"What just happened?"

Qwa grinned.

"Come look."

Anoor took tentative steps toward the space where the pebble should have been. A hole the size of her fist had been blasted through the stone. She couldn't see the bottom.

Tanu came up behind her. "It pushed the floor away from it. Our last experiments estimate the hole is about twenty handspans deep." Tanu tilted her head to the side and Anoor noticed the patched-up floor around them, the stones a different color from the originals.

"How is it so powerful?"

"Kabut," was all Tanu said.

Anoor nodded. Here was evidence that the Zalaam were special, that they had godpower.

Imagine what I could do with that kind of power. She thought of the wardens, and how they had sneered at her plan. And the tidewind, how with forces like this she could take it on, maybe destroy it completely.

Tanu reached for her hand and squeezed it. Her fingers were warm and dry.

"With this we can do whatever we want."

Anoor looked around the room, ambition a frightful thing between them.

"But what do you want?" Anoor asked them.

It was Faro who responded, their voice broken glass, sharp and thin.

"To rebuild the world."

Lio's words came back to her: "One day someone will say something to you that will resound in your very marrow. It will be a truth so clear that you will do anything to make it *become* a truth."

Was this it? Was this *the moment?*

But the disciples weren't Azim: they didn't want to destroy. All they had ever done was try and help her.

Anoor's smile was wide and freeing.

"What's your plan?"

Anoor didn't go straight back to the Duster Quarter. She made her way to the Dredge. It was early afternoon, and the summer heat was lessening into the cool days of early autumn. She pulled her shawl closer over her shoulders.

It was Lio's. Anoor had taken it from her chamber that morning. Well, Lio no longer needed it.

Anoor pressed her temples, banishing the feelings that tried to seep out. Anoor didn't even know the shape of them. Were they anger? Grief? She wasn't sure anymore. Too much had happened for her to confront them now. She pushed them back, sealing them within her mind fortress.

Her time with the disciples had reminded Anoor of the moments of discovery she'd had with Sylah. Uncovering the truth had been what brought them together. But it had also forced them apart.

Anoor reached the street where the tidewind shelter was. She came here sometimes, just to watch.

How did you die, Lio? She pushed the thought out toward the sealed doors of the building.

As if in answer two officers emerged. Anoor slouched against the villa like the Dredge-dwellers she'd walked past many times. She wished she'd thought to stain her teeth red.

". . . I heard that it's a disease, that they're extracting it from their blood."

"Really?"

"The wardens are keeping it quiet. With everything going on, they don't want to scare the citizens."

"They're barely citizens, just Nowerks."

"But we've still got to try and save them. By the blood, imagine if there were no Dusters? Who'd work the plantations?"

They both smirked and moved out of sight.

A disease? This was new. But it gave Anoor comfort. If Lio had died from a disease, then she hadn't been murdered.

Anoor would ask Tanu tomorrow. She set off back toward the Duster Quarter.

The next street along was a little busier, and Anoor had to raise her head in order to navigate her way through the crowd. Her eyes locked on to someone she knew, and her heart stopped.

She exhaled: it was only Zuhari. The woman didn't appear to have seen her yet, so Anoor moved to follow her. But just before Anoor reached an arm out to touch her, Zuhari slipped into a shop. The door sighed out a puff of herbs as it shut behind her.

The token at the front of the window was a broken blade. The handle was burnished, but Anoor could see the logo of the guild of strength. It was an old army weapon. Anoor peered through the window. The place was small, only big enough for three people to stand in at most. Dried herbs hung from the beams of the villa and vials of potions lined the walls.

Anoor remembered then that Zuhari's partner ran an apothecary. The glass of the window was dirty, but Anoor could see the woman move from behind the counter. She walked with a stick, wincing as she made her way to kiss Zuhari on the lips.

Anoor smiled, feeling guilty and privileged to see such an intimate moment.

"You going in?"

Anoor squawked at the man hovering next to her.

"Sorry, no, after you," Anoor said.

The man must have thought she was hesitating, unsure whether to enter or not.

"Ren's offers the best deals in the city, you know. Gives a discount to Nowerks."

"Oh yeah?"

"She shattered her leg in the revolt of the hundred. Lost her daughter too. Turned her hand to medicine. I think it's her hate of Embers that means she charges them double." The man winked and entered the shop.

Anoor stood frozen in place. Pieces of memory unraveled. Reformed. Rearranged.

Ren and Zuhari had a daughter. A daughter that died in the revolt of the hundred. Why did that feel so significant?

Then there was a rumble under her feet. A groaning in the very foundations of the city. Dust shifted and people screamed.

Then it stopped.

Anoor held a shaking hand to her heart. Whatever that was, she needed to get back to Lio's villa fast.

ANOOR HAD BEEN back at Lio's for less than half a strike when there was a knock at her door.

Anoor opened it, expecting Tanu.

"Hassa?" The Ghosting's skin was puckered on one side, the flesh oozing clear liquid. Her servant's clothes were singed as if they had been burned. The material was wet too. Anoor's eyes widened as she realized what it was.

Her blood.

"Skies above, Hassa." Anoor sprang into action, leading the girl into the center of the room. "What happened?"

Hassa shrugged her off, drawing Anoor's eyes to her signing.

They took him, they took Kwame. Her dark eyes were wide and fearful.

"What?"

We got into the tidewind shelter. But Kwame, the fool, he followed me. And he got caught. Her face crumpled, tears merging with her blood down her face.

"Caught by who?" Anoor pressed.

"Officers."

Some of the dread Anoor had been feeling ebbed in relief. "I'll talk to Tanu and get him freed."

Hassa's distraught face turned curiously blank.

Tanu?

Anoor waved a dismissive hand. "Yes, yes, I've been meeting with her, it's fine, you can trust her."

Hassa took a step back, her eyes wide.

"Let me clean your wounds, Hassa." Anoor reached for her gently.

Hassa took one breath before nodding once.

Anoor went to her sink and began to tear strips off the dress she wore. She wet them and rubbed them in soap, then she led Hassa to the edge of the sofa, moving the notes she had started to compile from that afternoon's revelation. Gently she dabbed at Hassa's wounds.

"There's some firerum that might help as an antiseptic, it might hurt some."

Do it.

Hassa leaned against Anoor's shoulder and let her apply the alcohol. She didn't wince once.

"You need to see a healer, Hassa, the burns, they look bad."

I can't afford a healer.

"Use mine, in the Keep."

Hassa frowned. *No healer in the Keep will treat a Ghosting.* She pulled the tattered shoulder of her uniform up from where it had drooped. She clutched the fabric with her two limbs before releasing them.

I'll be fine. I've suffered worse. Her gaze rested on the raised scars on her wrists where hands had once been.

Hassa had suffered much worse.

"Tell me what happened."

It was a few minutes before Hassa could rouse herself to sign. Her forearms were limp, tiredness clearly settling in.

Kwame and I, we decided to go into the tidewind shelter through the tunnels.

"But I thought you couldn't? Because that area was dangerous because of the gas . . ."

Realization dawned on Anoor. "It was you, wasn't it. The explosion under the city? The earthquake?"

Hassa nodded miserably.

Kwame shifted some of the rubble and released flammable gas. Anoor, do you really think you can free him? That Tanu can help let him go?

Anoor patted her arm. "Yes, remember he's an Ember. Even if he did get sentenced it will be a few lashes on the back or a few days in jail."

Hassa's face turned curiously blank again.

I remember, she signed.

Hassa took a shaking breath and signed again.

Anoor, they're harvesting . . .

"What? Sign that again."

Hassa slid her forearms together and made an inward motion. It was close to the sign for blood, but Anoor couldn't be sure.

"Sorry, I don't know that sign."

Hassa made a soft growl then, remembering, she withdrew something from her pocket. Whatever it was it had broken into shards of glass. Her shoulders slumped.

This was a jar I saved to show you. But it shattered in the explosion.

Anoor reached for the glass that Hassa had dropped to the floor. It looked like it might have once been a glass container.

Suddenly Hassa tensed.

"What is it?"

Anoor heard the person approach long after Hassa did. They both ran to the window peering sideways to see who it was.

Anoor's stomach sank. She knew that figure.

We can go out of the upstairs window. Hide the pieces of the jar.

Anoor nodded, numb. Then she remembered her notes, picked them up and clutched them to her chest.

But *Kwame*. If she ran now, she wouldn't be able to help him.

"Hassa, wait. Take this."

She pushed the notes into Hassa's arms. If she was going to jail she wanted someone to know the truth. Hassa's brow creased but she nodded and took the notes.

Rap-rap-rap.

"Promise me you won't turn her in," she said quietly.

Hassa frowned, not understanding.

"Promise me," Anoor pressed, time was running out. "There has been enough suffering."

Hassa nodded.

Rap-rap-rap.

They looked at each other.

Hassa's dark eyes were unreadable as she dipped her head

toward her friend. It wasn't a bow, or a salute, but a sign of respect. It made Anoor stand taller.

Anoor went to the door and opened it, her heart pounding with the euphoria of finally being caught. It was over now.

"Grandmother, please come in."

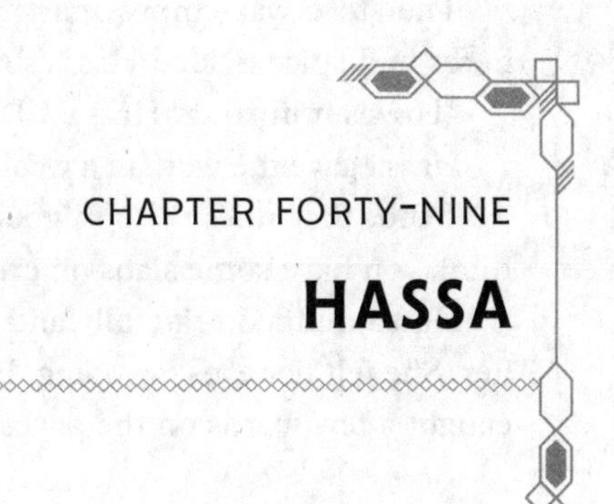

CHAPTER FORTY-NINE
HASSA

Brothers, sisters, siblings, this tale is one of truth. These last mooncycles I have been learning from the Ghostings, I have traveled to their settlement though they blindfolded me all the way.
A war is coming. But not from within.
From without.

—Missive from Griot Sheth to the griot network

It was easy for Hassa to climb out of Sylah's window. The catch was worn from being opened too many times, and she wondered how often Sylah had used it as a means of escape from Lio.

As she moved, Hassa's wounds stung, but Kwame's absence stung harder.

She thought of the look in Anoor's eyes as she'd gone to the door. Anoor was a woman with the fierceness of the tidewind. It was the first time since Sylah had left that Hassa had seen the flicker of the woman she used to know, the woman Sylah loved.

Save Kwame. That's all I ask, Anoor. The thought was a red-hot poker through her skin. It reminded Hassa that she needed to get some salve on her wounds before they grew infected.

The streets were emptier than usual, the explosion having

scared people into their homes. It didn't take Hassa long to reach Ren's apothecary in the Dredge.

The store was empty apart from Ren. The peppery smells of herbs and spice tickled Hassa's nose as she entered.

"How's it hurting, Hassa?" Ren greeted her.

Hassa gave the woman a weak smile and pointed to her wound.

"Aho, that doesn't look good. Let me get you some salve, I think you have some slabs on credit."

Hassa nodded gratefully and leaned on the rack of jars behind her. She felt her eyes drooping. But as her lids started to close, she caught a few words on the pages clutched to her chest.

Zuhari killed Uka.

It was written in Anoor's cursive script at the top of the page. Hassa felt a prickle of fear. Then of annoyance. Anoor was accusing her supporters yet again.

But then Hassa kept reading.

> *Uka led the charge against the revolt of the hundred. It was her decision to cave in the tunnels. Ren and Zuhari's daughter, Rola, was killed. Zuhari has a bloodink tattoo of her daughter's name across her arm, hidden by her sleeve. Gorn rightly pointed out that the murderer's clothes would have been soiled by blood—Zuhari was wearing her old officer's uniform that day, but the day after the murder she told me she had disposed of it. Zuhari has a number of skills that would enable her to carry out this attack. The broken weapon above Ren's apothecary was Zuhari's old tool, stamped with the token of the guild of strength. In addition, Zuhari was the only other person in my chambers that day who had access to my bedroom.*

The truth wrapped around Hassa's throat with talons. It tried to starve her of air, but she wouldn't let it. Hassa looked to the shop token at the front of the store. It had never occurred to her that it was anything special. But now she saw it, the way the blade curved at the edge where the metal had been shattered.

It was a jambiya.

Clack, clack, clack.

Ren's cane hit the ground as she came through the shop toward Hassa.

"Here you are." Ren offered Hassa the salve. "Do you want me to hold those while you put the salve in your pocket?" Ren tilted her head toward the notes.

Hassa's eyes went wild as she shook her head. She pressed the papers to her chest trying in vain to enfold them into her skin.

Ren frowned, only lightly, before offering, "Shall I put the salve on for you?"

Hassa had no other option. She nodded.

Ren propped herself up on the counter with her elbow. She rested her cane on the side and dipped her fingers into the paste. It was thick and creamy, with lumps that looked like oats.

Hassa held her breath as Ren gently applied the salve.

"Are you all right?" Ren asked. "Does it hurt?"

Hassa shook her head.

Ren didn't look convinced, but she moved away. "There, that should help the healing. You come back if you need anything else, okay? Don't worry about the cost, just come see me."

Hassa didn't respond. She spun on her heel and ran out into the street.

Air burst from her lungs and she gasped. The truth still burned her throat, and it hurt with every inhalation.

Zuhari killed Uka.

"Promise me you won't turn her in. Promise me," Anoor had said.

Hassa wasn't sure she could promise that. She hated the empire's penal system; it favored Embers.

At least it will favor Kwame. The thought lifted her spirits marginally.

She looked back at the storefront and saw the shadow of Ren as she moved across the store. Zuhari wouldn't be sentenced to a ripping, but she would likely be locked in jail for the rest of her life. She had killed a warden; they would punish her severely.

And Ren, she would lose the woman she loved.

Hassa had to talk to Gorn.

She collected herself and began to walk toward the Tongue.

HASSA NEEDED TO change before going to the Keep. The afternoon sun beat down on the torn areas of her dress, blistering her skin dark gray.

Maiden Turin's villa was quiet, the stables empty. There were only a handful of Ghostings left in her employ, the rest Hassa had helped leave.

Hassa thought of Kwame and wondered if it was time for her to leave too. Maybe they could leave together and go to the Chrysalis.

Even as she thought it, she knew it wouldn't happen. Kwame wouldn't leave Anoor, especially now she'd been caught by her grandmother. But Yona hadn't brought any officers with her, and she'd dressed like a Duster, covertly hiding her status. It was possible she wasn't there to capture Anoor, but the alternatives were worse. What if she took Anoor to the tidewind shelter?

The thought left her as the door opened and Turin greeted her with a wide smile.

"Hassa, my dear."

Dear? she thought.

"Where have you been? It has been a few days since you last came home." She pouted and Hassa was truly at a loss for words.

Turin let her pass as she stepped into the living quarters of the maiden house.

There was something different. The musk of sex no longer filled the air. It smelled fresh, like lemons. But of course, the radish-leaf smoke Turin puffed was still clinging to the fabrics.

"Come, sit with me a moment."

It was then that Hassa noticed the men, musawa, and women lining the walls of the room.

"Oh, don't mind them, they're just my Gummers." She winked as she lounged on the sofa. Her robe was thin as the smoke around her.

Gummers. Turin had claimed the title of Warden of Crime.

"Aho, yes, indeed, I am the new, and much improved, Warden of Crime." She grinned and Hassa was reminded of a desert fox.

This was not good. Not good at all.

"I have a proposition for you." Turin savored her words, drawing them out with a sly smile. "It has been made clear to me that Loot"—her mouth twisted—"had his own Ghosting servants. Come work for me."

Turin laid out a strip of kente cloth of purple and yellow. A sash for Hassa's servant dress that would mark Turin as her master.

Hassa's eyes flickered to the Gummers in the shadows. This was not a choice. She swallowed.

She knew what the elders would have wanted. She could hear their words in her mind: *take the opportunity and stay close to her. Hear her secrets.*

But part of her balked against learning more. Hassa was tired of secrets; they moved heavily through her bones.

Turin placed the sash on Hassa's knee and wrinkled her nose.

"You do have another uniform, though? Because that one looks a little singed."

Hassa nodded, and Turin clapped.

"Fantastic, it is settled. You will report to me in the morning. I will give you the night off, like the kind warden I am." She laughed.

Hassa's head dipped in submission. It hid the fire brimming in her eyes.

THE WARDENS' KEEP bubbled with a strange kind of energy. It reminded Hassa of the fevered excitement before a ripping, a sordid mix of horror and fascination. She thought of Kwame and hoped that the Ember jail was better furnished than the cells in the Old Nowerk Jail. The prison had collapsed years ago, leaving just a few spaces. Hassa had been there once. They were small, cramped cubes, haunted with the souls of Ghostings and Dusters. Rather than rebuilding it, the Warden of Strength at the time introduced rippings.

The jail would have been better.

Hassa touched her cheek and winced. The salve was still there, thick and clotted. It drew a few looks from other servants, but nobody else noticed her, they never did.

Hassa found Gorn sitting in the living room in Anoor's chambers looking out of the window. She turned when Hassa walked in.

"Hassa? What is it? What happened to your face?"

Hassa felt her legs go to jelly. She collapsed in the nearest chair and let Anoor's papers fall around her. She signed with tired arms.

There is much to tell and more besides.

Gorn collected the pages and read them. Hassa watched the same emotions she had experienced earlier reflected on Gorn's face. First disbelief, then annoyance . . . and finally rage.

Gorn stood on shaking legs.

"It was *her*. It was her all along?"

Hassa nodded. The first person Anoor had accused had been the murderer. And they had all scoffed.

"I'll call the guards. She's due here soon."

No, Anoor doesn't want her punished.

"What?" The words came out of too-tight lips.

Hassa signed slower to ensure the meaning was conveyed.

"That's not her decision to make; why let Zuhari go free when we can save Anoor?"

That's not all. Yona was there.

"Anoor's been caught?" Gorn's voice dropped to a whisper, her knees gave out, and she sat back in her chair.

And yet, I have not finished. Kwame and I went into the tidewind shelter. Kwame was captured.

Gorn's skin seemed to sag with the severity of Hassa's words.

"Tell me all."

Hassa obliged her, signing wearily. When it came to explaining the bone marrow they had to resort to a book in order to convey the meaning. Gorn sat in frustrated silence until Hassa found the word.

"Bone marrow?"

Yes.

"And you told Anoor this?"

She didn't understand. I tried.

Gorn tapped her knee with an errant finger. Hassa wondered if it was to stop her hands shaking.

"Let's hope Yona is not involved."

Hassa raised an eyebrow.

"I have to hope." Gorn scrubbed a hand over her face. "Yona is with her now. All we can do is wait. At least Anoor should be able to free Kwame."

Did you know she was seeing Tanu?

"No," Gorn admitted. "I haven't been to see her since . . ."

Hassa hated the guilt on Gorn's face. She wanted to push it smooth. Anoor had made her choices.

"I hardly know what to do first," Gorn said.

The living-room door opened, answering Gorn's query.

Zuhari stood on the threshold.

"Gorn, I have the notes you asked for." Zuhari's twists swung by her ears. She spoke too earnestly.

Hassa stood, her eyes blazing.

"By the blood, I didn't see you there, Hassa." Zuhari took a step back. It was a calculated move. The move of an officer. Of a killer.

Zuhari looked from Gorn to Hassa, and then to the papers on the table.

For the first time since knowing her, Hassa saw the woman's shoulders slump.

"You know, don't you," she whispered.

Hassa nodded, her lips curling in a soft growl.

Zuhari looked like she might fall, but she kept herself upright with sheer will. Tears fell down her cheeks.

"Uka, she killed them all. Crushed them beneath the stone. She killed my daughter." Her voice was rough like it had climbed through sand dunes to reach their ears. Dry and humorless.

Zuhari clasped her hands behind her back, her eyes distant. Hassa gave her a touch of begrudging respect for not running.

"Why?" Gorn's voice was all menace. Zuhari had not just betrayed Anoor, but Gorn too.

"Rola was her name. Ren and I raised her together, but she was a Duster. And when she turned ten, she was forced into the mines as well. She was hungry . . . because I had forgotten to pack her lunch . . . she stole a sandwich. Just a sandwich . . ."

Zuhari had a hand to her chest, gasping in air as she spoke.

"When the revolt happened, I helped the Dusters, I thought I was freeing them. Ren got out, her leg shattered."

Zuhari choked out a laugh.

"When you offered me the job, I couldn't imagine my luck. So many years had passed, and I was still so angry. I knew this was my chance. I didn't think it through, not really. I stole the jambiya when you showed me through the disciple's chambers. I slipped it up the back of my uniform and the coldness . . . I will remember the coldness for the rest of my life."

She looked into the eyes of Gorn and Hassa.

"I didn't mean for it to come back to her. All I knew was that Uka would be in her dining room at seven, and if I could just get there before Disciple Anoor, then I could kill her. Then I dropped the jambiya . . ." A shaking hand rubbed her shoulder. "I have not the skills I used to."

Hassa felt her anger toward Zuhari distilling into something more akin to pity.

"Disciple Anoor, I believed in her. I believe in her vision for the world. She showed me truths I could not comprehend. But Uka, she deserved to die. I regret how it happened, but I cannot and will not regret that it did happen."

Silence. Painful silence.

"Write out your confession." Gorn's voice was brittle, and Hassa inhaled sharply at the sound of it.

Zuhari nodded and withdrew a pen. The confession was short, stating motives and her approach. She signed it and stood.

"May I write a letter to Ren? Explaining where I am going?"

Gorn looked at her, then muttered under her breath.

"Damn you, Anoor."

Hassa nodded, agreeing with the sentiment.

"Go. You have four strikes before I hand this letter in. Pack up Ren's shop and leave. But remember this kindness. Remember it came from the woman you betrayed."

Zuhari took a tentative step backward.

"I don't understand."

"I'm telling you to run. And run. And run. For the wardens won't forgive you, and Anyme knows I never will."

Zuhari didn't smile, didn't cry. She turned on her heel and did as Gorn bade.

She ran.

Zuhari's confession sat between them. Gorn's face was grim. Hassa's itched. The salve had started to dry and crack.

Well, that's one thing done.

Gorn huffed out a laugh.

"Yes, I suppose. How else shall we set the world to rights today?"

Kwame.

"Kwame," Gorn agreed. The pinafore she was wearing had wrinkled from her slumped form; it looked strange to see Gorn laid low. She stood.

"Anoor is our best chance at getting him freed. We need to find out what Yona has done with her. If anything."

Gorn's eyes lingered on the biology book on the table. It was open on the page about bone marrow.

And that?

"I have no idea." Gorn admitted. "Why would the wardens want bone marrow?"

What if it's not the wardens? They were freezing it for transport. It could be someone else entirely. Someone on the ground who's taken over the running of the shelter.

Something occurred to Gorn, something that hadn't yet struck Hassa. She leaned in.

"The disciples," Gorn breathed. "The disciples are running the shelter. A few weeks ago Yona drafted them all in. They'd know for sure what was happening."

Tanu, Anoor has been talking to her.

They exchanged worried glances.

Why would the disciples want the bone marrow?

Gorn shrugged, an unnatural movement of her wide, stiff shoulders.

"This information won't unravel itself without tugging. Let us go to Anoor, see what befalls her. It might be she knows more about this than we do."

ALL HASSA WANTED to do was sleep. Instead, she found herself walking back to the Duster Quarter with Gorn in tow.

I need Anoor to help free Kwame, Hassa reminded herself. She missed his laughing presence already.

Gorn walked slightly ahead, leading the way to Lio's with firm steps. Every time an officer passed, she'd look up, her gaze roaming over them and anyone they had chained up. But it was never Anoor.

The streets were still empty, but Hassa noticed that the few Dusters who were about were being drawn to Dredge Square. She pushed the thought from her mind and wondered idly about Ren and Zuhari. Hassa would have to find a new apothecary now. It was annoying, but Hassa was lucky there were many on this side of the river.

There was a couple ahead of them as they turned down Lio's street. Hassa listened in.

"Haven't seen Mirad since she went into the shelter last week . . ."

"I heard some people are being sent to other cities . . ."

They're dead, Hassa wanted to shout. *Or they're being drained for their bone marrow and soon will be.*

Gorn looked behind her and gave Hassa a sad look. She had heard their conversation too.

When they reached Lio's door, Gorn hesitated. "I didn't see her with any officers. Anoor must be inside. Yona might still be with her."

Hassa straightened.

Good. It was time for answers.

"Excuse me?" The voice came from behind them. Gorn and Hassa turned.

It was Rata, Lio's neighbor. She held a dusting brush in her hand.

"If you see Lio, please can you remind her to dust her joba tree?"

Hassa failed to hide her laugh. Gorn threw her a scathing look.

"We'll inform her, yes," Gorn said.

"Excuse me?"

You shouldn't have engaged with her, it's your fault, Hassa signed with a toothy grin.

"Yes?"

"Lio's had an awful lot of visitors recently."

"Has she?"

"Yes."

"Is Sylah back?"

Hassa stiffened.

"I'm afraid not."

"Lio told me she's gone to work in Jin-Sahalia."

"Did she?"

Hassa let them talk and slipped into the villa.

The runelamp had been turned on in the center of the villa, but Anoor was nowhere to be seen.

Hassa ran up the stairs and checked the bedrooms. Nothing.

"Hassa? Why in Anyme's name did you leave me with that woman, that was a low trick." Gorn scowled at the bottom of the stairs.

Anoor's not here.

"What?"

Gorn did the same search as Hassa and reached the same conclusion.

"Where could she be?"

That was when Hassa heard it.

Bang-dera-bang-dera-bang.

Hassa got to the door first. She flung it open and ran down the street. She didn't care who she pushed out of the way. She wouldn't let Anoor get ripped. She couldn't.

Dredge Square was crowded, and Hassa flung her limbs as wide as possible to get through.

"In the name of the four wardens, blessed by Anyme, our God

in the Sky, we bring forth the accused," an officer shouted out into the crowd.

They cheered.

It was then that Hassa noticed the eru carriages on the far side of the square. It wasn't uncommon for Embers to attend rippings, but this many? The victim must have been accused of something particularly sordid.

Whispers rippled outwards until they reached a cacophony akin to a hornet's nest.

"An Ember . . ."

"An Ember . . ."

"An Ember . . ."

Hassa didn't want to turn around. She couldn't, her legs wouldn't move. She focused on each limb, turning them slowly until she faced the stage.

The accused's chin dropped low onto his chest, his shoulders slumped in defeat, the rack slowly ripping him apart, notch by notch.

Blood roared in Hassa's ears as her eyes locked with his.

Kwame.

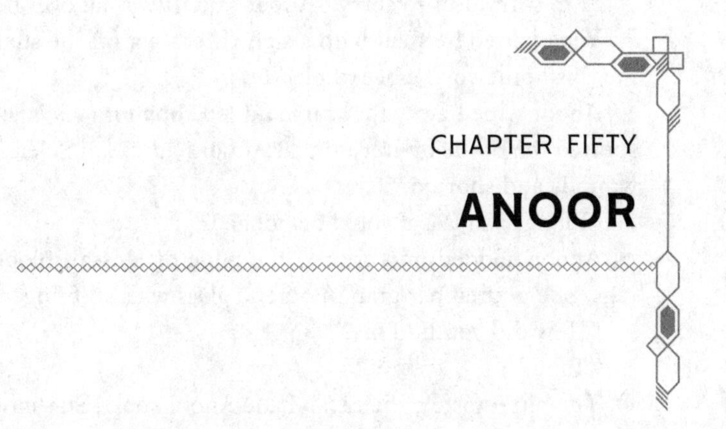

CHAPTER FIFTY

ANOOR

Hassa, I don't think I'm getting out of here alive. Know that I love you.

—Scratches drawn into the jail cell of Kwame Muklis

"Granddaughter." Yona greeted Anoor with a smile. It was both condescending and knowing. Like a spider assessing its prey.

Yona was wearing a deep blue floor-length gown and a brown leather coat. In place of a wig, she wore a hair wrap in a drab gray. Her clothes were unassuming. Plain.

It shocked Anoor to realize how easy it would have been for Yona to walk through the streets unnoticed. So few Dusters got close enough to the wardens to ever truly see them and know the folds of their face.

But Anoor knew her. Despite the lack of makeup and her hidden inkwell, she was her grandmother.

Yona made a small twitch of her arms, opening them slightly.

Anoor took the opportunity to launch into them, clutching her tight.

"I'm sorry, I'm so sorry," Anoor said. It was all over now.

Yona patted her hair with a sigh. "Let's get off the steps. Show me this home you've been holed up in."

Anoor wiped away the tears and led Yona into Lio's villa. Yona spotted the bottle of firerum that Anoor had used to clean Hassa's wounds and snorted.

"I'll have a glass if you'd be obliged?"

Anoor nodded and cleared the table of Hassa's bloodstained rags. She poured her grandmother a glass with stiff fingers.

"How did you find me?"

"Tanu."

The bitter taste of betrayal made Anoor sneer. She should have known.

Yona watched Anoor's reaction and added lightly, "I'm not here to arrest you, Anoor."

"What?"

Yona laughed a brittle, "Ha."

"Why are you here then?"

"Child, I don't think throwing you to the viper pit of wardens will help anyone. You didn't kill Uka, I know that."

"But how do you know that?" Like Tanu's, Yona's loyalty seemed unearned.

"For a leader, I find it strange how you struggle to accept your followers."

Anoor wasn't sure what her grandmother meant. She was about to ask when Yona spoke again.

"Perhaps"—she drummed her lacquered nails on her chin—"perhaps it is because of the secret you hold. You worry that those who don't know the secrets you harbor will reject you if they know the truth."

"I don't know what you are talking about." Anoor was surprised her voice was so cold.

"Why, your blue blood, of course."

Anoor choked on her firerum.

"I see you formulating a lie. I suggest you don't. I know the truth. I've known it for some time."

"How?"

"Loot," Yona said, a wistful smile around her face. "He and I had an arrangement since my tenure as warden. I allowed his smuggling ventures and he fed me information. I was sad to hear of his passing." Something fleeting, something like grief, crossed Yona's features.

If Anoor had been standing she would have staggered backward.

"Oh." It was all she could muster.

"Oh, indeed." Yona held out her empty glass to Anoor. The firerum felt heavy in her hands as she poured.

"But you haven't . . . told anyone?"

"I told you, I'm not throwing you to those vipers. Those fools." Yona's nose scrunched with scorn. "At first, I admit, you were a curiosity. I valued the truth of your existence, and though Uka wasn't aware I knew, she sensed it more than once. It proved useful to have that power over her." Yona swirled her firerum, growing nostalgic. "I remember when she noticed her journal was missing. Oh, the fuss she made. What a fool to write the words in the first place. But Uka was obedient to a fault. She had to write the truth because that was what the rules dictated. I often hoped that journal ended up in another warden's hands. Then I learned it had made its way to Loot."

"I stole it . . . before it was stolen from me." Sylah had taken it and given it to Jond.

Yona caught her breath. Then she laughed until tears streamed down her face.

"*You* stole it? Oh, that is just perfect."

Anoor wanted to laugh too but she didn't know what the joke was.

The room grew quiet.

There were so many questions Anoor wanted to ask. She chose one, formulated it, rolled the words around in her mind.

"Speak," Yona commanded.

"Who were the Zalaam?"

"Who *are* the Zalaam," Yona corrected. She took a swallow of her drink and hissed out the harsh fumes before continuing. "They are a powerful people who live north of the empire in a land called the Volcane Isles."

"How do you know this?"

"Because I've been there."

Anoor opened her mouth to speak but Yona held up a hand.

"Now I know that the wardens teach that there is no land beyond the Marion Sea, but that is a lie."

Anoor schooled her face into the appropriate amount of shock. Yona watched her curiously before continuing.

"The founding wardens were Zalaam, exiled from their country of origin. Eight ships left the mainland, two arrived at the empire, two were lost at sea. The Wardens' Empire wasn't called that back then, rather it was known as the Drylands. And it was populated by Ghostings."

Look shocked. Look shocked, Anoor chastised herself.

"The Ghostings had bloodwerk. A skill no one in the world had seen before. The mainland had blood power too but the knowledge was carefully policed, the skills difficult to master. And the runes the Ghostings used, no one had seen that before."

"They stole the land from the Ghostings." Anoor didn't have to fake the horror in her voice.

Yona narrowed her eyes. "Yes, I suppose you can say that."

"And the other four ships?"

"They thrived on the Volcane Isles, preparing for a war they knew would come."

Tanu and the disciples had been right. But there was something Anoor was not clear on, which she needed to hear her grandmother explain.

"How did the Embers hold power over the Dusters if they were both Zalaam?"

Now Yona's eyes glittered. They were green, flecked with yellow, and now the yellow shone gold.

"The Child of Fire. A person prophesied to be the catalyst for the final battle. The one that will lead the Zalaam to victory. The

Embers believed that the child would be red-blooded and convinced their brethren the same. Over time they forgot the truth of it, they forgot their beliefs, power corrupted them. And now the wardens are just a shadow of the Zalaam that used to be. They believe their lies so completely that even when a mainlander makes it to their shores, they suppress it."

When the Child of Fire brings the Battle Drum,
The Battle Drum,
The Battle Drum,
Ready we will be, for war will come.

The words had never left her, and they came to her now.

"Where did you hear that?" Yona had gone stiff straight, her dress taut against her chest.

Anoor hadn't realized she'd murmured the words.

"I . . . I . . . Tanu." After all, Tanu had been the one to lead Yona to her. But maybe Yona's visit wasn't going to have the dire outcome she had expected.

Yona leaned forward. "I've thought many years about the Child of Fire. I have explored every possible interpretation." Yona's expression was fevered; it scared her more than a little.

"And what conclusion have you come to?"

"That they are a leader. That they are someone who has lost everything, sacrificed and been broken so thoroughly that their very essence burns with the need for change. To rebuild the world."

To rebuild the world. The very same words Faro had said to her in the Sphinx Tavern.

Anoor felt the ghost of fingers creep up her spine and plunge deep into her rib cage. The fingers curled into a fist, squeezing her breath from her lungs.

Anoor choked on her next question. "So, you believe it? In Kabut, and the power of the Zalaam?"

There was a silence, and Anoor thought she heard the faint beat of drums.

"Do *you*?" her grandmother countered.

Bang-dera-bang-dera-bang.

Anoor's gaze went to the window. People had started to leave their homes, being drawn by the sound of the drum.

"A ripping?" Anoor murmured.

Yona tugged on the top of her collar that covered her to the chin. It was an oddly vulnerable movement, and Anoor wondered what she had to say.

"Anoor, one of my officers captured one of your advisers trying to steal medical supplies from the tidewind shelter."

Kwame.

"Stealing medical supplies?" Anoor frowned. Kwame and Hassa had gone in to spy, not steal.

"His father, adopted father, as I understand it, is very sick." Yona pressed on as gently as she was able. "We suspect it's a disease we've been tracking."

"I don't understand." Anoor knew Kwame's father was ill, it had plagued him for years. "What is the disease?"

"We don't know. It presents in different ways, a weakness in the limbs, sometimes ruptured skin. But we have limited treatments available. He was . . . trying to steal one of the tinctures from those seeking succor in the shelter."

Anoor's world seemed to tilt. The broken jar that Hassa had brought, the word Anoor hadn't been able to understand . . .

"But the shelters—I thought that you were harvesting something?"

Yona frowned. "We harvest a crop that helps in the making of the medicine."

"Medicine?"

"Yes," Yona said simply. "We're healing people. It has to be inserted through the bone, so some don't survive, but we've been trying."

Anoor couldn't pluck the truth from the lies any more than she could pluck dust from the wind.

"And . . . Kwame, he was stealing the medicine?"

Maybe he hadn't meant to. But his father . . . he *was* sick.

"It appears so," Yona said with a touch of finality that made Anoor shiver.

"What are you going to do with him?"

Yona's brow twitched. "The wardens voted for something quite drastic. Since he was part of your Shadow Court . . . they wanted a spectacle."

"A spectacle?" Anoor whispered.

Bang-dera-bang-dera-bang.

Dread coiled like radish-leaf smoke through her veins. Thick and cloying and red. The color of Kwame's blood.

"No," Anoor said firmly. "No, I don't care what he did, you cannot kill him. You cannot rip him."

"Anoor, it is our job as leaders to make sacrifices. Let his death fuel you. In the name of our one God, take this blessing." Yona was shouting because Anoor had begun to wail.

"I need to get out of here."

"Anoor!"

She ran out of the door and into the street below.

ANOOR WASN'T WEARING her scarf. But she didn't care.

She ran through the crowds of people going toward the square. The drumbeat getting louder and louder like the pounding of her heart.

Bang-dera-bang-dera-bang.

"No, please don't let me be too late."

She pushed her way through the throngs of Dusters and some Embers, not caring who saw her.

Then she saw the rack.

Kwame was bolted, star-shaped, onto the wooden device. The ripper, a poor Duster assigned to kill, pulled the lever that separated the jaw, spreading Kwame's limbs a little further.

Click.

He screamed and so did Anoor.

"No, stop!" They couldn't hear her. People pressed in all around her. She couldn't breathe, couldn't think.

Red blood blossomed under his shirt where the skin had already begun to tear.

Click.

She heard his joints popping as his arms were pulled from their sockets.

"Please stop, someone please stop this."

But the crowd was cheering, chanting for his death. He was an Ember finally getting the punishment Dusters had suffered from for years.

No one heard her pleas.

Click.

His screams grew hoarse. Anoor tried to push her way farther toward the platform.

"Kwame!" she shouted.

His head snapped up, panic searing through the pain in his gaze. But it wasn't Anoor he had seen. Hassa had launched herself onto the stage, her arms flailing as she pummeled the ripper who turned the lever.

The officer with the starting drum strapped to his chest was closest, and he grabbed her shoulders. Hassa's wrists pounded the instrument as she bucked against his grip.

Bang-bang-bang.

Her screams pierced Anoor's heart. They were shattered sounds. Haunted sounds.

Bang-bang-bang.

She hit the drum with all her strength. The beat pounded along with Anoor's heartbeat, a call, like the start of battle.

Click.

Kwame was watching Hassa. A smile, a soft smile on his lips. Blood was pouring from his midriff. It wouldn't be long now.

Anoor watched Hassa continue to fight the officer. She bit him with a snarl and he screeched.

"Watch out, Upa, looks like she's diseased, look at her skin."

Anoor gasped, seeing a strange growth covering Hassa's tear-streaked face. Had she caught the disease from the tidewind shelter? The officer hissed and flung Hassa away. The crowd parted for her crumpled form as if she were contagious. Hassa didn't get back up.

Click.

Kwame sighed, the smile still on his lips as his body ripped in two.

Anoor fell to the ground and retched. The tower she had been building in her mind fell down, each block obliterated by the corpse in front of her.

Kwame, her adviser. Her friend.

Gone.

"Anoor, get up." The voice was urgent and unmistakably angry.

Anoor looked up into Yona's shrouded face. She held out a dark cowl, the same as the one that covered her.

"Put this on. You're lucky no one spotted you. Thank the God for the crowds."

Anoor meekly covered herself in the wrap. She had nothing left. Yona steered her away from the rack by her elbow.

"Death has power," Yona said. "Use his sacrifice to fuel you."

Yona pressed something sharp into Anoor's clenched fist.

Anoor looked at the spider brooch glittering in the palm of her hand. The pin had stabbed her, drawing her blue blood, but she didn't hide it. She wouldn't hide it again.

She thought of Uka, Lio, and now Kwame, and something akin to madness snapped within her.

If death has power, then I'm very powerful indeed.

CHAPTER FIFTY-ONE

NAYELI

Sacrifice eight of the Shariha slaves to the Tannin and send me eight healers. I need their skills to harvest the marrow.

—Message from the Wife to the Volcane Isles

Nayeli pressed the spider brooch into her granddaughter's hand as she dragged her through the Dredge. She caught the look Anoor gave it, and it solidified Nayeli's resolve.

My Child of Fire, I have found you at last.

Decades of searching, decades of waiting.

The eru was packed and ready around the corner from the square. Anoor let Nayeli lead her into the shadowed cover of the carriage. The girl didn't even speak when she recognized the three people already in the back. Tanu tried to comfort Anoor. But the Child of Fire wasn't crying anymore.

She was burning.

It was there, in the tinder of her gaze.

Anoor still held the brooch in her hand; Nayeli could just see the edge of the engraving of her name. The other brooch, the one carved with the name "Inansi," she had given to her son.

Twins, she had, fathered by Ama. He had been the one to teach her the ways of this land; an old officer, he had trained her day and night for the Aktibar. He had been Inansi's friend, before disease had killed both Nayeli's brother and his husband.

Ama had been thrilled by the arrival of the twins. One female, one male. One red-blooded, the other yellow. One strong, one weak. Nayeli had given the weakest to her God under the cover of night, leaving the child to the tidewind's wrath in the Dredge, Inansi's brooch a parting gift for the son that wouldn't survive.

A sacrifice to ensure Uka was the Child of Fire.

The act had broken Ama's heart. He'd called her cruel, mad, a heartless heathen. And yet, he had sacrificed himself in the end, slitting his throat with her own knife. She had mourned but she knew Kabut would welcome Ama with open arms for the service he had provided his Wife.

For years Nayeli tried to light the spark in Uka. She tried to break her, build her, break her again. But there was nothing but devotion in her daughter's eyes. Devotion to the wrong God, to the wrong rules.

It was years later that Nayeli discovered the Warden of Crime was her true son. That the sacrifice she had offered Kabut had not actually been accepted. He had taken the name of Inansi from the brooch that had been tied to his swaddle. Loot was the nickname he rose to power with, but Inansi was the name he gave when it mattered most.

The carriage started moving, and Anoor's eyes snapped to Nayeli's.

"Where are we going?"

The other disciples followed Anoor's gaze. *Good, she already leads them.*

"The Volcane Isles."

Nayeli slipped her fingers under her wig and pulled it off. She ran her hands over the web of scars on her scalp, reminiscing about the pain. She unbuttoned her long-sleeved suit and dropped it to the ground. Scars covered her body, every handspan of flesh patterned with the cuts of the ceremonial knife.

The cheers of the Dusters from the street could still be heard. They had justly reveled in Kwame's sacrifice. Nayeli hoped Anoor would come to do the same.

"You all know me as Yona Elsari. But my true name is Nayeli Ilrase. I was born on the Volcane Isles as part of the Zalaam. You may all refer to me as Wife."

"You're the one who sent us the notes on the Zalaam, you're the one who's been leading the Sandst—"

Qwa coughed, cutting Tanu off.

Nayeli smiled softly, ignoring Tanu's revelation. She pulled off her inkwell and let it rest on the floor of the carriage. She reached into it, pulling out the thin glass cylinder that her blood ran through. She crushed it in her hands, revealing the red ink inside.

"Essence of hassa beetle, it stains my blood red." With a shard of the glass she added another scar on her skin. It bled yellow.

The disciples muttered. Faro leaned forward, with the interest of a scholar. But the Child of Fire, she just watched each *drip*, *drip*, *drip* of blood fall to the ground.

"Over forty years I have spent on this continent searching for the Child of Fire. Loot, the Warden of Crime, was my son. I aligned myself with him early on in my wardenship. Though he never knew me to be his mother."

"Loot?" Faro whispered.

Faro's mustache was a piece of string upon trembling lips.

"You know him as Master Inansi, the leader of the Sandstorm."

The disciples looked at each other, then at Anoor. She spoke for the first time.

"You three, you're part of the Sandstorm?"

It was Tanu who nodded first.

"And she, she's been leading it. But we didn't know it was *Yona*."

"Wife." Nayeli's voice was sharp, and Tanu flinched. The name she had borrowed from the first person she had sacrificed in the empire had never sat well on her skin.

Be gentle, this truth must soothe and not scare.

Nayeli closed her eyes and spoke again, softer.

"Inansi fed me with information in exchange for leniency for his guild members. His information led me to a fool, a man intent on bringing down the empire, Azim he was called. He intended to steal children—the most powerful children on the continent. So, I instructed Inansi to fund the rebellion. To monitor and to inform me of the children as they grew. Even my daughter's child they took to raise as I would see fit for a child of Kabut. I thought for sure the child foretold would be among them."

Nayeli's memories led her down the countless meetings with Loot. The reports and the details of each child as they matured. Even then, Nayeli's belief wavered; none of them seemed to call to her. One evening Nayeli had grown frustrated reviewing one of the sanctuaries in the north and had encouraged Uka to go to Ood-Zaynib in search of them. If they weren't going to be the Child of Fire, then at least they would be a worthy sacrifice in her search.

No, I cannot tell them that, though. Fear had entered the carriage and it wasn't abating.

"Uka was ignorant of my involvement, ignorant of my nature. For where Inansi was like me, golden-born with yellow blood, she was wedded to the empire as much as I am wedded to Kabut. An Ember. A warden. I would often remind her I had become a warden too. Though it took many years of training and many mooncycles of learning to bloodwerk. A simple red dye was all I needed."

She laughed, brandishing her red-dyed hands.

"Inansi didn't understand my task, he didn't believe in Kabut, or even understand the truth of the world. All he wanted was power. I often wondered if I had sacrificed the wrong child, if maybe Uka's death would have sealed Inansi's fate."

Her thoughts had slipped out; she hadn't meant for them to. And now fear turned to horror in the carriage.

Nayeli tapped the chest she was sitting on. The metal was cold from the ice freezing the tiles of bone marrow. It had been difficult to smuggle in the Zalaam to pose as healers, but they were the best at extraction, having done it for decades with the slaves from the

Shariha. And they needed all the bone marrow they could get if they were going to win.

Nayeli had been preparing the Nowerks to harvest for many moons now. Anoor's plan for the tidewind shelters had been serendipitous, allowing Nayeli to have a constant supply of bone marrow to send to the Volcane Isles.

Their sacrifices were worth more than their lives.

"Why did you let the Sandstorm continue? If you knew this empire was set to burn?"

Yona thought the question foolish, but Qwa was a little foolish.

"Loot's sanctuaries around the empire were the perfect test for the Child of Fire. The Aktibar was the ideal scenario for me to discover who had the means to lead us in the final battle."

The road had grown smoother underfoot. They must be nearing the main road out of Nar-Ruta.

"And," Yona added, "the chaos his intervention wrought would weaken the foundations of this country, making the last war ever easier."

The wind outside rattled the carriage doors and the disciples jumped.

Anoor did not.

"What do you want with us?"

Nayeli frowned. "That is not the question. The question is what do you want from me, Child of Fire?"

Anoor didn't hesitate, didn't acknowledge the title Nayeli had given her. It made Nayeli all the more sure of its place on her lips.

"I want to destroy them. I want to pull the Keep to the ground. I want each and every one of them to die."

Nayeli smiled.

"It is time to go to war."

EPILOGUE

HASSA

Hassa couldn't remember how she had spent the rest of the day. Grief had claimed it.

But now she found herself in the Maroon, a place where Sylah had often found her solace. She couldn't go to the Nest, the home of her elders where she had lain with Kwame.

She shivered, another tear running down her nose to her chin.

Bruises were spreading along one side of her body where she had been thrown down by the officer. Her gray-brown skin was puffy. She didn't feel the pain. Not that pain anyway.

Her head was bowed low to her chin, her eyelids closed.

Some of the tavern's patrons were celebrating Kwame's death, toasting his demise.

They didn't even know him. He was the most caring, selfless person she had ever met.

Though Hassa didn't hold a grudge against the Dusters cursing Kwame's memory. She could see their welts, gained from whips on the plantation, clinging to the cotton of their shirts. Scythes littered the floor by their feet.

Their anger against Embers was justified, but it stung no less to hear the man she loved talked of so.

He had trusted me, and I him.

Hassa could not hold herself together much longer. She felt as if she had been torn, just like Kwame. The pain burned like fire.

She touched her cheek with her wrist. The salve had been washed away by the tears she had shed. That wound would heal long before the other.

"Hello, little Ghosting."

A voice with the vibrations of a drum spoke beside her.

She turned to look at the griot. His locs had been twisted into an intricate knot on his head that added to his height. He smiled, his ears lifting upward as he did so.

"An interesting ripping? No?"

She knew then that he recognized her as the Ghosting on the stage. She shifted her feet.

"I'm sorry for your loss," he said with sincerity.

Hassa looked around her to make sure there wasn't anyone watching them. Her gaze snagged on two women on the other side of the bar. They held their drinks aloft.

"To resist and sow chaos."

Hassa stiffened. She hadn't heard the Warden of Crime's mantra for a long time.

"Ah yes, a new Warden of Crime has claimed the throne under the tunnels of the city," the griot said.

No one claims the underground but me, Hassa thought fiercely.

"The air is shifting in the empire, and not just from the tidewind. Do you feel it?"

Hassa nodded. More than he knew.

"The griots' network is diminishing. Though we continue to

stoke the fire of rebellion. Be sure to tell your friends that we are ready to fight when called upon."

Hassa wondered what the griot knew. The storytellers had their secrets and she had hers.

The griot made to stand, his hand disappearing into his tattered cloak.

He looked around him, fearful, before withdrawing an old book and pressing it into Hassa's arms. She took it.

"This is your people's. It was found by a griot in Jin-Laham. Her house collapsed in the tidewind, and they found a boarded-up cellar. Most of it was destroyed, but this. I think you'll find it helpful."

Hassa thanked the griot with a slow nod.

"The tidewind is near. Go home, little Ghosting. Tomorrow is not today."

Hassa thought of Maiden Turin, and the role Hassa had accepted with her, and wanted to cry all the harder. She left the Maroon before the tidewind struck, though the wind still plucked and pulled at the pages of the book she held.

It was time to go back to the Nest.

THE BLANKETS SMELLED of him. Rose oil and sweat. Hassa held them to her and rocked back and forth on her heels. She hummed the freedom song in defiance of her pain.

You will not be forgotten, Kwame. You will not be lost in the past.

Hassa cried until her throat was dry and muscles weak. She knew it was not the end of her tears, there would be no end, but in this respite, she would take care of herself.

There were few resources left in the Nest. But flour and water were all she needed to make flatbread. She kneaded the dough like she had pounded the starting drum. With anger and desperation.

When it was ready, she left it to rest and withdrew the book the griot had given her. Most of the pages had been torn, or damaged by damp.

Hassa flicked through it. It was a book of runes.

This must be one of the lost Books of Blood.

It would be helpful in teaching Hassa how to bloodwerk.

Anyme, my ancestors, thank you for guiding the griot to me with this treasure, she prayed silently.

The lump of metal she had tried to fashion into an inkwell sat on the table in the center of the room. Hassa knew the Chrysalis had been training the young ones with hands to bloodwerk with inkwells. Kwame had suggested Hassa try a quill.

"Go back to basics," he had said.

She rummaged through the elders' remaining belongings until she found what she needed. The feather of the quill was in tatters from being bound and unbound from an elder's wrist, but the nib was intact. Hassa strapped it to her limb. Without hesitation she dipped the nib into the open flesh of her wound. It sank with biting cold into her cheek, lacing the pen with blood.

She withdrew it with a sharp exhalation. The pain was familiar, and thus comforting.

Hassa bent over the table and drew.

She moved her wrist painstakingly slowly, following the pattern of the rune *Ru*.

It was impossible to know if the runes were precise enough. Her blood sank into the wood leaving little trace in the firelight.

She stepped away and held her breath.

There was a slight judder, then the table skidded across the floor with a screech.

Hassa laughed and skipped into the air, her arms pumping upward.

There was nothing an Ember could do that a Ghosting couldn't.

Nothing.

In her moment of joy, it took her a second to see the darkness swell and pulsate as something moved through the Nest. Hassa spun, her teeth bared, blood and tears on her lips. Then she saw who it was.

Sylah?

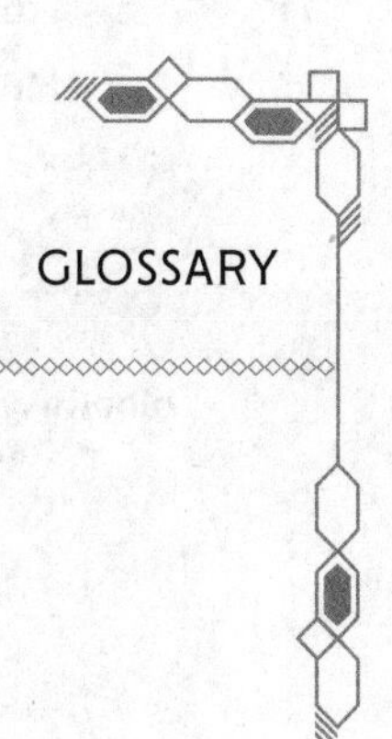

GLOSSARY

TERMS

Abosom	The devout followers of Anyme who serve under the Warden of Truth.
aerobatics	A type of gymnastics that incorporates aerial movements.
aerofield	Ranged combat, first trial of the Aktibar for strength.
aeroglider	Wind gliding sport, commonly practiced on the hills of Jin-Gernomi.
Akoma	The largest valve in the heart.
Aktibar, the	A set of trials held every ten years to determine the next disciples.
Anyme	The genderless deity worshipped in the empire. God of the Sky.
Ardae	A religious festival celebrating the anniversary of when Anyme first climbed into the sky. It involves a blessed meal, gifts, and offerings to the God.
Baqarah	Submarine ship made by the Ghostings.
battle wrath	A state of focus used in the martial art of Nuba.

blood scour Finger pinprick check points to test the color of your blood.

bloodink Tattoos, most commonly seen on Dusters.

bloodwerk The ability to use your blood to manipulate objects by drawing runes. There are four foundational runes. The rest are supplementary runes that guide in direction, activation, safety, and protection.

bloodwerk rune:

Ba Foundational rune: A positive pull drags the rune toward an object.

Gi Foundational rune: A negative pull drags an object toward the rune.

Kha Foundational rune: A positive push presses the rune away from an object.

Ru Foundational rune: A negative push presses an object away from the rune.

Book of Blood The sacred book of bloodwerk runes.

Charter The four different factions of the Zwina Academy that study:

The first charter: The law of growth.

The second charter: The law of connection.

The third charter: The law of healing.

The fourth charter: The law of presence.

Choice Day The day when twenty-year-old Embers are required to choose their guild.

clockmaster The role of timekeeping in the empire. The clockmaster projects the time every quarter strike through a chain of calls, starting with the First Clockmaster, based in the Keep where the only clock resides.

crimelord The leader of a criminal organization. Before Loot's reign there were four ruling in Nar-Ruta.

Dambe A form of boxing in which the opponents use their strong arm as if it were a spear.

Day of Ascent The day that the winners of the Aktibar ascend the five hundred steps to join their warden as the new disciple of their guild.

Day of Descent The day, once a decade, that the wardens of Nar-Ruta abdicate their places to their disciples by descending the five hundred steps.

deathcraft Rune magic, called bloodwerk in the Wardens' Empire.

disciples Seconds-in-command to the wardens. Leaders of the Shadow Court. They train under their specific warden for ten years before ascending to the title of warden themselves.

Dusters Citizens of the empire identified by their blue blood. The working-class tier of the caste system.

duty chute The postal tubes that run under main roads. The chutes carry messages through the twelve cities of the empire.

Embers The noble and ruling class of the empire. Only Embers are allowed to rule, receive a full education, or live in the Ember Quarter. Only Embers are taught to bloodwerk.

Ending Fire, the A phenomenon believed to have struck the world four hundred years ago, wiping out everything with lava, flame, and flooding. Nothing survived except what was on the wardens' ships.

eru Large lizard-like creatures that are trained as steeds. They can be ridden with saddles by the most experienced or driven with cart-drawn carriages.

flighter Someone with the ability to harness the law of presence.

Ghostings Citizens of the empire identified by their transparent blood, their hands and tongues are severed at birth. They are the lowest class of the empire.

Godpower Magic of the fifth charter, so named by the Zalaam.

griot Storyteller and truth-seeker.

guild of crime A counterfeit guild, originally led by Loot, that has no true jurisdiction in the empire. It is run in opposition to the true wardens. Vow: to resist and sow chaos.

guild of duty Manages the smooth running of the empire and domestic services. Vow: to nourish and maintain the land.

guild of knowledge Manages the educational system within the empire. Vow: to teach and discover all.

guild of strength Responsible for protecting and maintaining the peace. This includes the warden army. Vow: to protect and enforce the law.

guild of truth Rules the courthouse and upholds the law and religious rites. The Warden of Truth leads the Abosom. Vow: to preach and incite justice.

Gummers Members of the guild of crime, shortened from "guild members."

handspan A unit of measurement using the tip of your thumb to the tip of your little finger.

imir The twelve leaders of the cities of the Wardens' Empire. In inherited positions, the twelve imirs make up the Noble Court.

inkwell A device worn by Embers that allows them to bloodwerk. The metal cuff wraps around the wrist with a slot above a vein where a stylus is inserted. The blood then runs down a channel in the stylus to the tip of the stylus, allowing them to write with their blood.

jambiya Curved dagger.

joba fruit A red berry the size of a small plum with an extremely hard outer shell that requires a forge to crack. The flesh is often used to create dyes. The joba tree bears fruit only every sixth mooncycle.

joba seed The joba seed can be chewed, releasing a bitter juice that is a narcotic stimulant. Users of the joba seed often feel an initial rush of euphoria, followed by a dreamlike state. It is often coupled with a depressive comedown and is highly addictive. Withdrawals include seizures, sickness, and muscle cramps.

joba tree Joba trees are planted in the front garden of most Ember houses. The height of the tree indicates the status and generational wealth of the occupier. The trees are white with green leaves. They are believed to be a conduit to Anyme, as the God climbed a joba tree into the sky.

kori Small blue birds with iridescent wings.

Laambe A defensive martial art known for its open-palmed technique.

lava fish A deep-sea fish harvested for its pearlescent scales, which are used to adorn garments in glitter.

maiden The head of a brothel.

master crafter The leader of the Foundry on the Volcane Isles.

milk honey A white-leafed herb used in medicine to lessen nausea.

mooncycle A full rotation of the moon; a way to measure months.

Moonday The first day of the full moon.

musawa A third gender.

nameday The anniversary of the day you are born.

Night of the Stolen The night the Sandstorm stole twelve children from Ember houses.

nightworker Someone who works in a maiden house.

Noble Court Made up of the twelve imirs, they debate and propose changes to laws and legislation, then present them to the Upper Court.

Nowerks A slur used to refer to Ghostings and Dusters who can't bloodwerk.

Nuba A regimented code of physical formations that are implemented through strict mental codes, Nuba practice is difficult to master. The user has to reach a state of complete control and focus, known as battle wrath, in which anger fuels the Nuba artist to create precise movements that become deadly when paired with a weapon.

orb An obsidian sphere placed in an open wound in the center of the palm. It is used to print runes in blood. This technique is taught at the Zwina Academy.

peppashito A red, spicy pepper sauce.

rack, the A wooden contraption that slowly tears the condemned into two. It is operated by a ripper.

radish leaf Red leaves cultivated in the desert sand that give a rush of endorphins to those who smoke them. Expensive to procure. Slightly addictive. Smoked mostly by Embers.

rippers Executioners who operate the rack—always Dusters. The uniform is a blue jacket.

runegun Bloodwerk-operated firearm.

runelamp Bloodwerk-generated light.

sandsnail Small, white-shelled snails that live in the Farsai Desert.

Sandstorm A group of rebels founded by Loot Hisbar and Azim Ikila.

saphridiam A blue mineral found in the sand of the Farsai Desert, derived from volcanic matter.

Shadow Court The court-in-waiting assigned and led by the disciple of each guild.

shantra A game of strategy. A shantra board is made up of three different colors, patterned with diamonds. Each team has thirty-one counters, ten of each color and one black piece. The black piece is known as the egg. The aim of the game is to steal the egg from the opposing team, but each counter can only move onto its corresponding color. Only red counters can collect the egg.

Siege of the Silent The rebellion is taught in schools as the reason why the Ghostings are subjected to their penance. Four hundred years ago they rebelled against the wardens by laying siege to the Wardens' Keep for two months.

slab The currency of the Wardens' Empire, made out of carved whitestone with former wardens printed on the underside.

sleepglass Poison made with pepper flower and grass roots. Undetectable, it puts the victim to sleep for a short time.

starting drum The drum that indicates the start of a ripping.

Stolen, the The twelve children stolen from their cribs as babes and raised by the Sandstorm.

strike A unit of time measurement; one strike is one hour.

Tannin A fabled sea monster that lives in the depths of the Marion Sea.

tidewind A nightly phenomenon that blows and whips the sand of the Farsai Desert into a deadly frenzy.

tio root A dark wood that is worth more than gold. Short, stubby plant grown by the coast, hard to cultivate.

Trolley, the The bloodwerk-operated train that carts across the Tongue, also known as the trotro.

Upper Court Made up of wardens, disciples, and their key advisers, the Upper Court is where legislation is proposed.

verd leaf A leaf harvested for its painkiller attributes. High in caffeine.

wardens The four leaders of the Empire of Nar-Ruta, each charged with representing one of the four guilds: duty, truth, knowledge, and strength.

whitestone A hard-wearing substance that can withstand the tidewind, often used to build houses.

yambrini Poison extracted from shrimp.

Zalaam, the An unknown group.

zine Short stories featured in *The People's Gazette*.

PLACES

Arena, the Newly built amphitheater that houses the trials for the Aktibar.

Belly, the The headquarters of the Warden of Crime.

Blooming Towers, the The central buildings in the citadel of the Zwina Academy.

Bushica A country ruled by an empire in the northeast.

Chrysalis, the Ghosting settlement in the northeast of the empire.

City of Rain A new settlement next to the Academy.

Dredge, the Previously called the Ghostings Quarter, but after the Siege of the Silent, their numbers dwindled and it was taken over by businesses of ill repute.

Drylands, the Mainlanders' name for the Wardens' Empire.

Duster Quarter A district in the northwest side of Nar-Ruta, occupied by Dusters.

Ember Quarter A district in the south side of Nar-Ruta, between the Ruta River and the Wardens' Keep, occupied by Embers.

Entwined Harbor, the A cluster of ships off the mainland.

Farsai Desert Blue sand dunes that sprawl across the center of the empire.

Foundry, the A factory on the Volcane Isles where the Zalaam prepare for war.

Great Veranda The open-air center of the Wardens' Keep where functions are held. A roof automated by bloodwerk covers it during the tidewind.

Ica Sea, the East of Tenio.

Intestines, the The tunnels that run below the city of Nar-Ruta. There is a myth that one of the tunnels leads to treasure.

Jin-Crolah A city in the north, its main export is coffee beans.

Jin-Dinil A city that surrounds the central lakes of the empire.

Jin-Eynab A city in the west, known for its wine producing.

Jin-Gernomi A city in the center-east with lots of cultivated grass hills.

Jin-Hidal A city in the center of the island that produces the empire's coal supply.

Jin-Hubab A city in the northwest of the empire where grain and flour is milled.

Jin-Kutan A city in the southeast of the empire, one day's ride from Nar-Ruta.

Jin-Laham A city in the east that mainly exports cattle.

Jin-Noon A city in the west where the majority of cotton is grown on plantations.

Jin-Sahalia A city in the north known for the best eru breeding, and eru races that the imir hosts once a year.

Jin-Sukar A city in the northeast where sugar cane is farmed.

Jin-Wonta A city in the east that exports metal and mineral deposits.

Marion Sea The volatile and highly dangerous sea surrounding the Wardens' Empire. Superstitiously believed to be haunted by a sea monster called the Tannin.

Maroon Tavern in the Dredge where plantation workers drink.

Mistforest, the Area near the Academy.

Nar-Ruta The capital city of the Wardens' Empire, in the southeast of the island.

Nsuo A harbor town on the west of Tenio.

Ood-Lopah A village where salt flats are harvested.

Ood-Rahabe A fishing village in the north of the empire.

Ood-Zaynib A village in the north of the empire, close to the Sanctuary.

Ring, the A fighting ring operated by the guild of crime situated in the north of the Dredge.

Ruta River A quicksand river that separates the Duster Quarter from the Ember Quarter.

Sanctuary, the The farmstead where the Stolen were raised, situated outside of Ood-Zaynib.

Shard Palace, the Tenio's royal residence.

Souk, the Trading settlement near the Academy.

Souriland A country in the northwest.

Tenio The largest country on the mainland continent.

Tongue, the The black iron bridge that stands five hundred handspans above the Ruta River.

Truna Hills An area near the Zwina Academy.

Volcane Isles Area off the mainland settled by the Zalaam.

Wardens' Keep The governing center of Nar-Ruta and home to the wardens. The cobbled courtyard is adorned with the largest joba tree in the empire. Beyond that, the five hundred steps lead to a marble platform where the wardens ascend and descend. The western side of the keep houses the courtrooms, wardens' offices, wardens' chambers, library, and the schoolrooms. The eastern side houses the servant quarters, kitchens, and Anoor's chambers.

Wetlands, the A country in the south ruled by a tsar.

Zwina Academy A citadel of knowledge where people from all over the world come to study.

PEOPLE

Ads A Ghosting, unmaimed from birth. (She/Her)

Andu Yellow Commune leader situated on the Volcane Isles. (He/Him)

Anoor Elsari Daughter of Uka Elsari. Competitor in the Aktibar for the guild of strength. (She/Her)

Aveed Elreeno Warden of Duty. (They/Them)

Azim Ikila Former leader of the Sandstorm, deceased. (He/Him)

Bisma Oharam Librarian in the Wardens' Keep. (He/Him)

Boey Elsari Blue-scaled eru owned by Anoor. (She/Her)

Child of Fire Prophesied figure of the Zalaam, believed to be the catalyst of the Ending Fire.

Efie Montera Granddaughter of the imir of Jin-Gernomi. Competitor in the Aktibar for the guild of strength. (She/Her)

Elder Dew Ghosting elder. (They/Them)

Elder Petra Ghosting author of a pre-empire journal. (He/Him)

Elder Ravenwing Ghosting elder. (He/Him)

Elder Reed Ghosting elder. (She/Her)

Elder Zero Ghosting elder. (He/Him)

Elyzan Councillor of the first charter—the law of growth. (He/Him)

Fareen Ola One of the Stolen, deceased. Has a scar running down her cheek. (She/Her)

Fàyl Hisbar Watcher for the guild of crime and Loot's husband. (He/Him)

General Ahmed Uka's deceased partner, father of Anoor. (He/Him)

Gorn Rieya Anoor's chief of chambers. (She/Her)

Griot Sheth Storyteller who frequents the Maroon. (He/Him)

Griot Zibenwe Storyteller, killed on the rack for writing. (He/Him)

Hassa Ghosting servant and watcher for the elders. Friends with Sylah. (She/Her)

Ina A young Shariha slaver. (He/Him)

Inansi Ilrase Twin brother of Nayeli Ilrase of the Volcane Isles. (He/Him)

Inquisitor Abena Fictional main character of the zine "Tales of Inquisitor Abena." (She/Her)

Jond Alnua One of the Stolen who survived the massacre. Competitor in the Aktibar for the guild of strength. Member of the Sandstorm. (He/Him)

Kabut Also known as the Spider God, the deity of the Zalaam. (He/Him)

Kara Councillor of the fourth charter—the law of presence. (She/Her)

Karanomo Thalis Queen of Tenio. (She/Her)

Kwame Muklis Ember servant who works in the kitchens of the Keep. (He/Him)

Lio Alyana Sylah's adoptive mother. Member of the Sandstorm. (She/Her)

Loot Hisbar Former Warden of Crime, married to Fayl. (He/Him)

Maiden Turin Owner of a maiden house in the Dredge. (She/Her)

Marigold Hassa's adoptive parent, Ghosting. (They/Them)

Master Inansi Leader of the Sandstorm. (He/Him)

Master Nuhan Teacher of bloodwerk. (He/Him)

Memur A Ghosting based in the Chrysalis. (She/Her)

Nayeli Ilrase Master crafter of Volcane Isles. (She/Her)

Niha Oh-Hasan A traveler enslaved by the Shariha, previously of the Academy. (He/Him)

One-ear Lazo Competitor in the wrestling contest known as the Ring. (He/Him)

Petal A Ghosting solider and seafarer.(She/Her)

Pura Dumo Warden of Truth. (He/Him)

Rascal A sandcat. (She/Her)

Ren Keeper of an apothecary in the Dredge. (She/Her)

Rola Duster child killed in the revolt of the hundred. (She/Her)

Sui Councillor of the second charter—the law of connection. (She/They)

Sylah Alyana One of the Stolen who survived the massacre. Chambermaid to Anoor Elsari. (She/Her)

Tanu Alkhabbir Competitor in the Aktibar for the guild of knowledge. (She/Her)

Uka Elsari Warden of Strength, Anoor's mother. (She/Her)

Vona Esar Jond's guardian, deceased. Member of the Sandstorm. (She/Her)

Wern Aldina Warden of Knowledge. (She/Her)

Yanis Yahun Competitor in the Aktibar for the guild of strength. Captain in the warden army. (He/Him)

Yona Elsari Former Warden of Strength; Anoor's grandmother. (She/Her)

Zenebe Councillor of the third charter—the law of healing. (He/Him)

Zuhari Member of Anoor's Shadow Court, formerly in the army. (She/They)

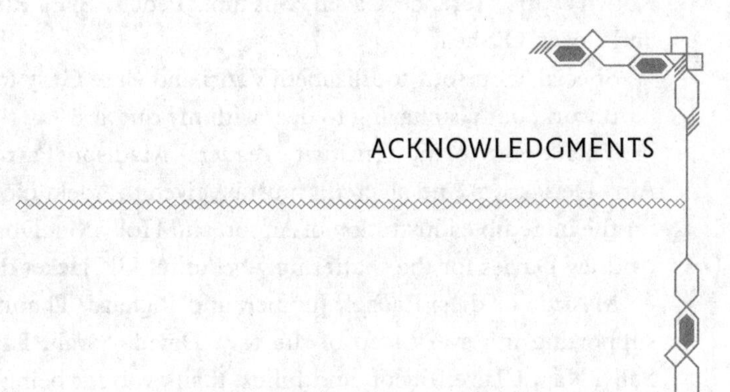

ACKNOWLEDGMENTS

It was with terror that I started writing *The Battle Drum.* I wasn't sure I could do it again; make it to the end of a novel. But then the words flowed quickly and freely. The untold story simply unraveling rather than needing to be written. And it is only because of the support of those around me that I was able to succumb to the tale.

To my incomparable editors: Natasha Bardon, your confidence in me has fueled me each and every day. Tricia Narwani, over the last two years you have taught me so much, and that is a gift I continue to treasure.

Juliet Mushens, my collaborator, my agent, my friend: you are simply a wonderful human. Thank you also to Liza, Kiya, Rachel, and Catriona at Mushens Entertainment. You continue to be the best agenting team in the world.

To my co-agent, Ginger Clark, whose hugs are worth flying across the ocean for, thank you for your unwavering faith in me. Gratitude also to Nicole Eisenbraun at Ginger Clark Literary for supporting me behind the scenes.

Of course, nothing would have been possible without the publishing teams who have turned my stories into novels:

From the Del Rey team: Ashleigh Heaton, Tori Henson, Sabrina Shen, Scott Shannon, Alex Larned, Keith Clayton, David Moench, Jordan Pace, Ada Maduka, Ella Laytham, Nancy Delia,

Alexis Capitini, Rob Guzman, Brittanie Black, and Abby Oladipo. And the VoyagerUK team: Vicky Leech Mateos, Millie Prestidge, Robyn Watts, Terence Caven, Susanna Peden, Sian Richefond, and Roisin O'Shea.

Special shout-out to Elizabeth Vaziri and Bree Gary for all the hard work, but also having to deal with my queries!

Thank you to my sensitivity readers, Madison Parrotta and Amy Derickson. And all credit must be given to Adekunle Adeleke for the incredible illustration of Anoor, and Holly MacDonald and Andrew Davies for the shatteringly beautiful UK jacket design.

My ride or dies: Rachel, Juniper, and Richard. Thank you for supporting me every step of the way. David, Sarah, Laura, Ali, Sally, Naji, Claire, Taylor, and Julius, thank you for being the biggest cheerleaders. You give me the courage to pick up my pen and keep writing.

To my very own Blood Forged: Kate, Tasha, Sam, Hannah, Lizzie, Amy, Cherae, Kat, Rebecca, and all the extended author community who have supported and welcomed me—you are the best colleagues and friends anyone could ask for.

Endless gratitude to my family: the Dinsdales and the El-Arifis as well as the extended family whose support has always been the foundation of my career.

Jim, your cheering for me has long grown hoarse—none of this would have been possible without you.

And finally, to the readers and dreamers. You bring Hassa, Sylah, and Anoor to life. My last words are always for you.

Thank you.

PHOTO: © MUSTAFA RAEE

Saara El-Arifi is the internationally bestselling author of *The Final Strife* and *The Battle Drum,* the first two installments of The Ending Fire Trilogy inspired by her Ghanaian and Sudanese heritage. She has lived in many countries, had many jobs, and owned many more cats. After a decade of working in marketing and communications, she returned to academia to complete a master's degree in African studies alongside her writing career. El-Arifi knew she was a storyteller from the moment she told her first lie. Over the years, she has perfected her tall tales into epic ones. She currently resides in London as a full-time procrastinator.

saaraelarifi.com
Twitter: @saaraelarifi
Instagram: @saaraelarifi
TikTok: @saaraelarifi